LETHAL CARGO

LETHAL CARGO

A CAULDRON OF STARS
BOOK 1

FELIX R. SAVAGE

Knights Hill Publishing

Cover design by Jamie Glover
Photography by Andrew Dobell
Published by Knights Hill Publishing

ISBN 978-1-937396-35-0

Typesetting services by BOOKOW.COM

1

MOMENTS after we touched down on Gvm Uye Sachttra, an antique floater bumped over the dirt field we'd been assigned as a landing pad. Several natives jumped out. They were about five foot high, furry, dressed in colorful diapers, with long muzzles crammed with teeth. "The *St. Clare?*" they said, through a ruggedized box hanging around the boss alien's neck, which translated their clicks and hisses. "Twenty standard tonnes of food aid and agricultural implements for the refugees?" They wore lanyards identifying them as employees of Help the Hungry.

"That's right," I said. "If I could just verify your IDs." They stretched out their forearms, and Kimmie, my admin, scanned the credit dots embedded in their blackish flesh. They checked out. It's always nice to meet honest aliens.

While we were unloading the crates, the boss alien said, "Travellers." He or she cast a dirty look in the direction of the vine-swaddled conifers that edged the pad.

"I know," I said.

The spaceport sprawled along the coast north of the refugee camp, and several rocky barrier islands. We were on one of the islands. The Travellers were on the next island over. One ship, a sow-bellied cruiser daubed with thermal paint pictures of the macabre Traveller pantheon. Two prizes, already hacked up and stripped of saleable parts.

"Lousy rotten demon-worshipping pirates," the alien's translation box said, while its toothy mouth hissed.

I'd have smiled if it wasn't so true. "Pretty much."

The alien nudged me. We were standing on the top deck of the *St. Clare*. I was wearing jeans and a parka, wishing I had brought a heavier coat, white-knuckling through a bad hangover. "This is a good ship," the alien said. "You could take 'em out. How about it?"

The alien wasn't wrong about my ship, anyway. I was justifiably proud of the *St. Clare*. She was military surplus, but not from the Fleet. She'd been the imperial flagship of a two-bit alien emperor who had been deposed shortly after commissioning her. I'd picked her up second-hand, and although she wasn't perfect, I steered my thoughts away from what we called our "mechanical failure." Not only was the *St. Clare* fantastically tough, she also boasted the armaments of the warship she had originally been. Forward of the superstructure, the elongated truss supported a flat top deck 50 meters long, which ended in a "head" whose serrated jaws concealed the mouth of a powerful railgun. We also had two turret-mounted large-caliber Gausses, plus a maser point defense system, and dual missile launchers on the belly for 360° coverage. Better have it and not need it than ... yeah. All too often, we did need it.

"How much?" I said.

The alien named a laughable sum.

I shook my head. When I was in the army, I had killed people for peanuts. But those days were long behind me. Nowadays, I wouldn't even consider it for less than seven figures. "If I hit them on the ground, it would depend on how accurate the strike was, but their antimatter containment ring might blow. Then you wouldn't have a spaceport anymore."

"Our chief-one-appointee made a deal with 'em," the alien said gloomily. "They get to sell their stolen goods at our spaceport. We get to live. *Probably.*"

And people wonder why aliens don't like us. As one of the two great powers in the Cluster, humanity poses as protector of all the little guys who got caught on the hop by our third colonization wave, and forever lost the chance to develop spaceflight capabilities in their own way and in their own time. To be fair, if it wasn't us it would have been the Eks, and we're nicer than they are. But space is *big*. Ungraspably, horribly big. The Fleet can't be everywhere at once. And unfortunately for our image, most of the predators out there are human, too.

Such as the Travellers, whom I had reasons of my own to detest. But I was trying not to think about that. Bitterness is ugly.

Dolph, my business partner and pilot, climbed down from the top of the bridge. He was tall and skinny as a rifle on legs, with a black ponytail straggling over the collar of his coat, and binos slung around his neck. "That ship has a HERF mast," he said.

"Charming," I said.

"Plus you have to figure they've got auto-nukes," Dolph said. "There are clamps on the ship, nothing there. They probably left 'em in orbit." He scowled up at the clouds.

Auto-nukes—autonomous nuclear missiles—are also illegal, for a very good reason. You can't tell 'em from regular sats, until they fall on your head. I crunched some vitamins and chased them with black coffee from one of those self-heating bulbs. My hangover receded some.

To be honest, any sane captain would have bailed at that point. But I was too experienced to back down … and too broke.

"God, it's cold," I said. Dust hazed the distance. This whole strip of coast had been deforested. Even in human form, I could smell woodsmoke blowing from the refugee camp, and the tang of the sea.

Martin, my engineer, lowered the final crate of food aid into the floater, and we got down to the best part of the process: collecting our fee. Kimmie, wearing two pairs of fingerless gloves, processed the balance of the aliens' payment. This far out from the Heartworlds, accepting payments is a dicey business. All transactions have to be physically cleared through the nearest node of the EkBank, which in the case of this planet was four light years away. Normally, we'd stick around until all our payments had time to clear, so we could chase up anyone who tried to stiff us. That could take days. I was not planning on sticking around here, but I knew that Help the Hungry was good for it.

Click, and I was 50 KGCs richer. That was payroll and operating expenses covered for the month, plus a few KGCs over that I could salt away for my daughter's education. What I told her was that I was in the aid business.

The boss alien sidled closer to me. "You are not really human, are you?" the translation box whispered.

I looked down at the odious little creature. "Sure I am." I was six foot one, with light brown hair that I kept short so it wouldn't flop in my eyes. My open, square-jawed face served me well in business negotiations. I looked more built than Dolph, but sadly, not all of it was muscle. That's what you get for spending too much time in freefall, and more time sitting on your keister.

"No, you are not." The alien seemed quite sure of it. "You do not smell like a human." It pointed a claw at Dolph. "Nor does he." Martin had gone off to fetch the refuelling stand from the edge of our pad. Irene, my weapons officer, had just come out of the ship with her second-best rifle slung over her shoulder. The alien pointed at her. "She is not human, either. All of you smell like ... *animals.*"

"Hot damn," Dolph whispered to me. "Sniffed out by an alien on Planet Back-Asswards."

"What about me?" Kimmie said. She was wearing a purple coat, to match her purple hair. She had a sweet, round face. A ruby sparkled in her nose.

"*You* are human," the alien said, and hissed at her. "Goodbye," it said to me. "Please give our regards to the team at head office." All the aliens went down the port ladder head-first, like squirrels, then got in their floater and drove away. The levitation field, now compressed down to a few inches, bumped over every little irregularity in the ground, making the cargo jump up and clatter. There's a reason floaters are not more widely used.

Dolph was laughing. "Good thing most people don't have that keen of a sense of smell."

"We are, too, human," I said. *"Homo sapiens versipellus."*

"Phooey," Kimmie said. "I'm just a boring mainstream human."

I smiled at her. "If all mainstream humans were like you, the Cluster would be a better place." She was the youngest of the crew, as well as the only normie. I had a soft spot for her.

Irene was climbing the ladder to the top of the bridge. That's what we called the three-storey armored superstructure, but most of it was the cargo hold. The actual essentials were safely tucked away below. While Dolph unloaded the remaining cargoes, I followed Irene up the ladder. The wind was like a wild thing, trying to rip me off the exposed rungs.

I knelt beside Irene behind the main radar dish, automatically falling into old habits of concealment from enemy spotters. From up here, we could see the Traveller ship over the untended hedges on the shores of the islands. This spaceport really was a dump. There were hardly any proper landing pads. Mostly you were just putting down on hardened dirt. In many places, rocks poked through like bones sticking up from a dessicated carcass. Most spaceships can cope with less than perfectly flat surfaces—the *St. Clare* certainly could—but all the same, it was an accident waiting to happen. Then there was the native greenery that had been allowed to grow up between the pads. A real mess.

There were two pads in between us and the shore of our island; one held an Ek landing shuttle, the other was empty. In fact, most of the pads nearby were unoccupied. Travellers can clear out a spaceport faster than rats in a kitchen. Despite what you may have heard about space piracy, the easiest place to steal spaceships is on the ground. The

Travellers' standard m.o. is to scream down out of a blue sky, land practically on top of their targets—they're good at flying, I'll give them that—and overwhelm them with high-speed ground assaults. Then they'll fly their prizes away, sell 'em or break 'em up for scrap, spend the proceeds, and repeat.

They were selling, not stealing, today ... *probably.* That margin of doubt was what had persuaded all the sane captains to leave.

"Looks like we missed all the fun," Irene said. She measured the distance to the Traveller ship with a professional look in her cool blue eyes. "I could make that shot."

"In this wind?"

"Sure," Irene said. She was a vet, as were Dolph and I. But whereas we had been in the special forces, Irene had been a sniper. She probably *could* make that shot. She was the best marksman I'd ever met, or rather markswoman—55 kilos dripping wet, with fine blonde hair pulled back in a severe ponytail, and a husband and two kids at home.

"Those ain't worth the antimatter in their containment," I said, eyeing the Travellers' prizes, a tramp freighter smaller than the *St. Clare* and a harp-backed scow. "Anyway, we still got a few more cargoes to deliver. The small-lot crap."

"You're the boss," Irene said, making a face. "I'll just stay up here and keep an eye on them."

Figures in black coats moved around outside the Traveller ships, mingling with aliens and humans who were probably dickering for the stolen ship parts. They were too far away to make out any of their faces. I thought about going back down to borrow Dolph's binoculars, then decided against it. I was better off not knowing.

I helped Martin hook up the water hoses to refill our reactant mass tanks, which involved dragging the refuelling stand across the pad on its rusty wheels, unkinking the hoses, attaching new sediment filters, and swearing like mad. At least it got us warm. While we were doing that, more customers arrived to pick up their stuff, and another floater delivered our return cargo—twenty tons of amateurishly packaged shipments for Ponce de Leon, mostly pre-processed rare earths, and some luxury items such as pelts and rare timber.

"Start loading," I yelled up to Dolph.

"Can't," he yelled back.

"Why the fuck not?"

We were all grumpy. We always looked forward to getting there, after days in the field: shopping, going out for a drink, mooching around and feeling the dirt under our feet. Even on a semi-civilized Fringeworld like Gvm Uye Sachttra, there's intel to be picked up and connections to be made, the lifeblood of the logistics business. Sometimes we'd make a side trip into the country and get in some hunting. All scrubbed off the agenda, because of the Travellers.

"Still got one shipment hasn't been collected," Dolph yelled.

"Oh, for—" I let loose with some curses that should have turned the air blue. "Which one?"

"The toy fairies."

I cursed some more. Some whimsical individual had ordered 9,000 electronic toy fairies from a Ponce de Leon supplier. Leaving aside the frivolity of shipping expensive toys to a refugee camp, it wasn't that unusual a shipment. Half of what we typically carried was aid and relief supplies. The other half was low-quality consumer electronics. Aliens love that junk.

I checked my phone. The customer's name was Rafael Ijiuto, and he owed me eight KGCs. That was the difference between buying Lucy a new holobook or not. I tried to call the guy. My phone wasn't working. No connectivity.

"I'll go look for him," I said resignedly. "Coming, Dolph?"

"Can I come, too?" Kimmie yelled.

"No, sweetheart," I said. "It ain't safe out there." Ignoring her look of outrage, I climbed the ladder to get one of the toy fairies out of the hold. It would help Rafael Ijiuto to identify us, since I didn't know what he looked like and vice versa.

The packaging was unusually heavy-duty: each fairy was encased in an airtight, opaque plastic bubble. I ripped one open with a knife and took the fairy out.

It had four wings, two for gliding and two that acted as a rotor. Basically, it was a fully functional drone masquerading as a toy. Lucy would love it. I decided to give her this one as a present. Rafael Ijiuto wouldn't miss it, and I would not have time to pick up anything better here.

I fastened the remote control bracelet on my wrist and pressed the up arrow. The fairy rose into the air, its wings and long tresses sparkling luminously in the dimness of the hold. Watching the thing circle above my head, I unaccountably shivered, like someone had walked across my grave.

The fairy turned its head down towards me. The violet eyes in its plastic face froze me with a malevolent stare. I took a careful step backwards, watching the thing without blinking. For an instant I was back on Tech Duinn, stalking through the undergrowth, scarcely breathing
…

I came back to myself when my right hand closed around the butt of my Midday Special. Flushing with embarrassment, I turned the toy off. It fluttered down placidly to my wrist. Tense, much, Starrunner? It was just a toy. Good thing no one had seen me overreacting like that.

There was a junky old electric buggy sitting under the trees. Dolph and I got it started, after some fiddling with the battery connections, and drove down the coast to the refugee camp.

2

WE spotted Travellers here and there on the main drag of the camp, browsing the stalls. They typically flew with huge crews, twenty or thirty people to a ship—their ground troops. The tattoos on their faces flickered and writhed, rendering them unrecognizable to facial recognition technology—not that there was any surveillance in a place like this, anyway. The skirts of their hideous black coats ballooned in the wind, permitting glimpses of the weapons strapped to their bodies.

The locals could have overwhelmed them at any time, a hundred to one. But whoever controls orbital space controls everything on the ground. That's just how it is, and that's why a few lunatics with auto-nukes can roll right over millions of dirtsiders, leaving a trail of pain behind them, like grass flattened by heavy tyres.

"At least it ain't Cole's clan," Dolph said.

"How do you know?" I said. "The attrition rate is something insane. We probably wouldn't recognize any of them by now."

Yuriops cut across our path, their horns making them fully eight feet tall, while the sensing cilia of stargends nodded to avoid the cat's cradle of power lines overhead. Eks fingered the local wares with their four hands. They knew the Travellers wouldn't mess with *them*. Humans were their preferred prey, and sure enough Dolph and I were almost the only humans left ... apart from the refugees manning the stalls. Cheap, flickery holo greeters in front of the stalls touted deep discounts, and desperation tinged the patter of the salesfolk.

"I need one of those," Dolph said through the bandanna covering his nose and mouth. I followed his gaze to a stall selling knives. Big, little, electrified, poison-tipped, auto-barbed, with grips made for hands that had five fingers, four, eight, or none. This place really did have everything. You wouldn't take it for a refugee camp, but that's what it was. The people manning the knife stall were as human as we were, probably more so. The eldest looked about sixteen. The youngest was no bigger than my own daughter. Some years ago, a human colony had fled a war on the far side of the Cluster, wound up here—and here they had stayed, and multiplied. The natives were signatories of the Sapient Refugee Convention, jointly formulated by humanity and the Eks, and co-signed by all other biologicals, whether they liked it or not. They may not have appreciated being told to turn over a piece of their planet to several thousand homeless humans, but it had paid off for them. With typical human ingenuity, the refugees had transformed this barren coast into a shopping mall.

"Yo, big guy," the teenager at the knife stall called out. "Wanna put some steel in your holster?"

"She's talking to you, Mike," Dolph said with an amused snort.

I gave the girl a second look. Dirty blonde hair hacked off at her shoulders, dust-colored skin, charity trousers and sweatshirt retooled into something more punk than refugee. A knife the size of a machete rode at her hip. But it was her eyes that caught me—gray, smoky, smouldering with the same desperation that gripped everyone in camp.

"Or you need a place to stash your blade? Got something just the right size." She pumped her hips, lifted her machete an inch clear of her scabbard, and laughed. She was a child, but she had the voice of a forty-year-old smoker, and a line in cheap innuendo to rival any streetwalker.

I practically had to put Dolph in a headlock to stop him from heading over to the stall.

"That's a genuine messer," he said in anguish.

For Dolph, it was all about the knives, not the girl.

"Gotta find this guy first," I said.

"Yeah, keep on walking," the girl shouted after us. "Whaddaya expect from a man with a toy fairy?" Her little friends giggled shrilly.

I glanced ruefully up at the fairy whirring above my head. I'd turned it back on to keep it visible above the alien crowds. The dust had soiled its costume and long tresses. It didn't look spooky at all now.

We reached a crossroads in the maze of the camp. Humans and aliens queued at the eateries. A crowd surrounded a chained Kimberstine haulasaur that was doing tricks. I even saw a couple of the Travellers in the crowd. Dolph muttered obscenities at their backs. I shook my head.

Suddenly, the toy fairy rose up to a height of twenty feet. I hadn't touched any buttons on purpose, but maybe I triggered something by accident. The thing let out a sinister peal of mechanical laughter, and began to swoop around, scattering fairy dust. Dolph and I watched open-mouthed as the stuff blew over the crowds and stuck to faces, cilia, horns, and tentacles. It was just glitter. We were standing upwind. Nevertheless, Dolph got some sparkles on his hair, and my watch cap would probably never be the same. The crowd let out that soft unguarded 'oooh' you hear when people have witnessed something unexpected and magical. Even the Travellers blinked in surprise. The Kimberstine haulasaur let out a melancholy roar.

The wind caught a last voluminous cloud of glitter and carried it away over the tent roofs.

"Did you mean to do that?" Dolph said.

"Nope," I said. "I don't think it's working right. I'm gonna find something different for Lucy."

The fairy descended towards us. I reached up and grabbed it. It struggled, its rotor trying to whirr in my hands. I found the power switch and turned it off. "Let's eat."

We were in the middle of a surprisingly good meal of ugali and stewed chicken—food aid remixed into something bordering on cuisine—when Rafael Ijiuto finally showed up.

"Hi," he said. "I'm Rafe. You must be Mike."

I swallowed my mouthful of food and half-stood to shake his hand. Dolph hooked a free crate with his foot. Ijiuto lowered himself onto it.

He looked to be in his twenties, hair buzzed to a quarter-inch all over, biscuit-colored scalp showing through. The hair was biscuit-colored, too, with a coating of dust. Making no concessions to the fact that he was sitting in a fast food joint in a refugee camp, he wore a suit and tie, the business-formal template that has stood the test of so many centuries it's practically encoded in male human DNA. I have a suit myself somewhere. At the moment, however, Dolph and I were both in jeans and heavy coats. Ijiuto's sartorial style helped to mask any anxiety he may have felt. He didn't look scared, he just looked cold. He ordered a cup of tea. The wind snapped the awning over our heads. Aliens and humans alike shouted at each other to be heard.

I had to lean in close to Ijiuto to catch his words. "OK to pick up the cargo directly from your ship?"

"Sure," I said. "We're on pad one-sixty-five, out on one of the islands. You got a vehicle? We're talking four large crates, one hundred kilos each."

Ijiuto nodded. "I'm going to hire a truck."

"I'll need the balance of your payment at that time."

"No problem." He was looking at the toy fairy. I'd set it in the middle of the table, where it had been drawing admiring stares from aliens who'd seen the fairy dust display. Dolph had spilled beer on its wings. "I love this product," Ijiuto said. "Only humans would think of something like this."

"To humanity," Dolph said, knocking his beer stein against Ijiuto's tea cup. "The only species in the Cluster with the gall to charge 300 GCs apiece for a mass market drone with a frilly costume."

"To human audacity," I said, wryly.

"Huh," Ijiuto said. "See those tattooed freaks walking around? They're human, too."

"We're a versatile species," I agreed.

We finished eating, paid the bill, and walked back towards the parking lot. Ijiuto was swiping at the screen of his phone. "I can't get through to the truck rental people. Can't even get a dang signal. I'm going to have to go over there. Catch you up at the ship. Pad one-six-five, right?" As he spoke, he was already angling away from us.

"Yeah," Dolph said to his back. "What kind of refugee camp doesn't even have decent phone service?" He snickered. Dolph had a strong sense of justice, in his own way.

His face changed. The almond eyes above his bandanna widened. He threw an elbow into my side.

I spun around and saw someone I had hoped never to see again, and yet had dreamt of meeting again, pretty much nightly for a while. Those were bad dreams. Bloody dreams.

The reality was worse.

A few meters away stood a blond, heavily tattooed man in a black leather greatcoat, glowering at us.

It *was*.

Zane Cole.

The man my wife left me for, seven years ago.

3

ZANE might've walked away. Or I might've.

Then he decided to recognize us, after all. He walked up to me and Dolph. We stood face to face.

The wind gusted over us, making Zane squint. I saw the white in the frown lines he'd acquired on Tech Duinn.

He mustered a normal voice. "Well, hey! I wasn't expecting to see you two chunks of space debris this side of Ragnarok."

My palms were damp. Heat surged through my veins. Intellectually, I knew I was angry at the wrong person. Zane had not forced Sophia to leave me, after all. She had walked away of her own free will. But I still felt like punching him to a bloody pulp.

Dolph stepped in. "Where'd you jack those ships?" He let Zane know that we weren't buying his 'hey ol' war buddies' bullshit.

"No law against selling hulks," Zane smirked.

"There is if you made them into hulks."

"We're contributing to the local economy," Zane said. "You here on business?"

Dolph ignored the question. Stepping in closer to Zane, he growled, "How many bank accounts you had yanked so far? How many postulants you burned?"

Zane had odd scraps of leather and hair hanging off the lapels of his coat, decorated with beads and such. I could smell them from here. "You haven't tanned those properly," I said. "Remember how we did the deer hides on Tech Duinn? We built smoke pits out back of the FOB."

"It ain't easy on board a spaceship," Zane said with a smile that made me want to claw his eyeballs out of his skull. "How's the shipping business these days?"

The weird thing was how *little* the black coat had changed him. He always had been an aggravating lightweight, even when we served together during the war. *Our* war, the one that liberated Tech Duinn and killed my youthful illusions about humanity. It should not have been a surprise to me that one of our own would become a Traveller.

It had surprised me—totally blindsided me, in fact—when my wife left me for this selfsame renegade.

Black spots danced in front of my vision. I realized I needed to breathe. I inhaled a lungful of dust, and felt something solid in my right hand. I was gripping the butt of my Midday Special.

Zane had to be armed, too. But Dolph was distracting him for me. He wouldn't have time to draw his own weapon before I could drop him. I could practically taste the blood that would gush from his wounds ...

Snapping out of my violent fantasy, I reminded myself that I was forty-four years old, responsible for the livelihoods of a dozen people. Furthermore, we were being watched by assorted beady-eyed natives, refugees, and aliens. I pictured Lucy's face.

I said, "So how's Sophia?"

Sophia. Never Sophie or Sophs. My ex-wife's name suited her perfectly, conjuring the dark-haired elegance and pensive gaze that I had fallen in love with. I'd managed to forget the world-weary sneer more often seen on her face towards the end of our marriage.

"Sophia!" Zane said. "Man, I haven't seen her in ages."

"*What?*"

"Yeah, man. She left the life."

I was speechless. All these years I'd been picturing them together.

"She washed out?" Dolph said. "Or you burned her?"

"Her? No way," Zane said. "She just decided it wasn't for her. It happens. I guess we'd all like to get in touch with her, but ..."

"Why?" I said.

"Why'd she leave? Search me. You can't make this kind of money in the Temple." This was how the Travellers referred to civilization: the Temple, with them on the outside, going their own way. Having insulted us, Zane pushed back the left sleeve of his ghastly coat. We both twitched. But there was no weapon sheathed on his forearm. Instead, a chunky silver watch glittered amidst his arm hair. "Check it out. Genuine Urush fortunometer."

"That the kind that tells your fortune as well as the time?" Dolph said.

"Yeah. Got it for 60 KGCs." Zane was simultaneously boasting about what a good price he got, and bragging on his spending power. I wouldn't net 60 KGCs in profit this whole trip.

Dolph flicked the watch contemptuously with a fingernail. "Don't need a fancy timepiece to tell *your* fortune," he said.

"How not?"

"I can read the future," Dolph said. "It holds a severe ass-kicking for you if you don't get outta our faces right now."

Zane drew back. His face reddened. "Shifter assholes," he said. "Shouldn't be allowed off the leash." He walked away, the bits of dead people on the back of his coat bouncing.

"You got ripped off," I yelled after him. He kept walking, but I thought his ears turned redder. "That's a fake for sure," I said to Dolph, forcing myself to speak in a regular tone of voice. The Urush—the extinct alien race who are thought to have been the first intelligent species to conquer the Messier 4 Cluster—left behind odd bits of tech that still work after all these years. I had heard of their fortunometers, but no way had Zane scored a genuine one in a refugee camp for a mere 60 KGCs.

"Yeah," Dolph said. He glanced at me.

"I thought they were still together," I said.

"Maybe she wised up," Dolph said.

We got in our buggy and drove back through the residential part of the refugee camp. Ragged tents surrounded open fires where people were cooking their messes, reminding me that the smell of woodsmoke was not only the smell of home but also of extreme poverty. It was terrible to see humans living like this. But I'd seen similar scenes, and worse, in a dozen different parts of the Cluster. Space colonization ain't easy, even without Travellers preying on the weak.

A few klicks brought us back to the spaceport. As we drove onto the causeway that connected the mainland to our island, the Ek shuttle that had been parked next to us took off, drenching the world in noise and filling the air with dust. We bumped through the racket onto our island.

I stopped the buggy.

"I don't believe it," I said, over the fading thunder.

"What?"

"Zane. I think he was lying."

"He lies every time he opens his mouth," Dolph said, "but why would he lie about that?"

"Because he didn't want me to know she's here."

"He said she left the life."

"Yeah, and as we've already established, he's a liar. I'm gonna go see if she's here." I opened my door.

Dolph reached across me and held it shut. "That's about the most boneheaded thing you could do."

I didn't wrestle him. We weren't kids anymore. I stared out the windshield at the alien foliage pressing in on the road. "She left me without a word of explanation, Dolph. I deserve some kind of a fucking explanation. And so does Lucy. I haven't told her anything. But she's eight. She already wonders why she doesn't have a mommy like other kids. Pretty soon she's gonna start asking me questions, and what the hell am I supposed to tell her? I tell her enough goddamn lies as it is." The words nearly choked me. "About what it's like, what we do out here."

"We don't do anything bad," Dolph said uncomfortably.

"Oh, not *that* bad, no. We deliver our cargoes. No contraband within five light years of the Heartworlds. We occasionally kill people, but only if we're paid a lot of money for it, and no one will ever find out. I agree, nothing *that* bad."

"You left something out," Dolph said. "We try to help other human beings. In some ways, that's the worst job of all." He popped his own door and stretched into the back seat for his backpack. "Those motherfuckers bring the whole species down. *I'll* go."

"Jesus, no! *You* can't—"

"I'll just go and see if she's there."

"If she is—"

"Then I'll pop her," Dolph said, "for having the bad taste to leave you for that fucking faggot." He grinned. "Just kidding."

"Douche," I said, with feeling. We had known each other since we were five, playing with stick guns in the forests of San Damiano.

"You're the captain," he said, "and that's why you get to go back and make nice with the customers, while I have all the fun."

He melted into the thickets.

I drove on, cursing violently.

4

My guts knotted with worry as I parked beside the *St. Clare*. It looked like we were dishearteningly far from ready to go. Power lines still trailed from the ship's belly across the dirt field, feeding ship's power into the grid. Places like this, you pay your landing fee with electricity. At least the refuelling stand had been rolled away. Kimmie sat on a bale of pelts beside the ship, writing up our manifest.

As I swung my legs out of the buggy, a ragged, undersized female accosted me. I had to struggle for a minute to place her.

"Mister, can you help me?"

That voice. Throaty, husky. It was the teenager from the knife stall. She was still clutching her cruddy plastic case of knives.

"Sorry, kid," I said. "I'm kinda busy."

"They got my cousins, mister. Please."

"What happened?"

"They did a sweep along the main drag. I hid. They took Jan and Leaf." Her eyes were huge with desperation. Her brash patter and precocious attitude had melted away. Now she was just a girl—scarcely more than a child—in mortal panic. *"Please!"*

"Oh, Jesus," I said tiredly. "They took them to their ship?"

"Yes. It's over there," she said, gesturing, as if I might not know where it was.

"Irene," I yelled.

Kimmie trotted over to us, leaving her holobook on the bale of pelts. "Mike, she says they came through and took all the children. It's the most heinous thing I ever heard of."

"You are young," I said. I walked towards the port ladder.

Kimmie walked fast to keep up with me. Her face set in the expression of flinty judgement that was the flip side of her sweetness. "We're really asking for it," she said.

I slowed my pace, making a show of patience. "Asking for what, Kimmie?"

"When the shit hits the fan, you know who'll be to blame? Us. Humanity. For what we do to each other. For what we do to ourselves."

"People are horrible to each other, Kimmie," I said. "We were horrible to each other with stone knives and catapults. We were horrible to each other with revolvers and cannons. And now, we're horrible to each other with spaceships and nanotechnology. The more things change, the more they stay the same."

The girl understood humanity better than Kimmie did, She yelped, "I can pay you, mister!" She fished in the neck of her charity sweatshirt and lifted out a pendant. It looked like a three-inch, slightly curved dagger in a sheath studded with diamonds. "These are genuine diamonds!"

"Sweetheart, I got bigger diamonds than that in my ship's bearings." I started up the ladder.

As I climbed, I scoped out the next-door island. The coast was rocky and choked with thickets. I had to figure Dolph had got at least that far by now. The channel between the islands was only about ten meters wide, choppy, laced with foam. I could tell it was shallow, 'cause waves broke on a ridge of rock in the middle of the channel. At low tide, you could probably walk out to these islands from the beach.

Irene came to meet me on the top deck, wearing a surgical mask, holding the business end of a high-pressure air hose. She must have been cleaning the dust out of the barrels of the Gausses. She believed in being prepared. "Where's Dolph?"

"Over there," I said, pointing.

"Oh, for the love of God, why'd you let him do that?"

I hesitated. Irene was blissfully ignorant about the whole Sophia saga—I hired her long after that all went down, so all she knew was that I had a daughter I was raising on my own. Matter of fact, her daughter and mine were best friends. Stripping away all egotistical pretense, I was plain scared Irene might think twice about letting her Mia play with Lucy if she knew that Lucy's mother was a Traveller. Or had been one. Which was it?

"That kid says they got her friends," I said at last. "Where's Dolph's binos?"

"I left them up top."

I climbed up the second ladder to the top of the bridge. The binos were lying behind the radar dish, next to Irene's second-best rifle. I fitted them to my eyes. More people were now milling around the Travellers' pad. Yuriops, stargends, several of the furry natives ... and a whole lot of human children. The binos brought their little faces right up to my eyes in heartbreaking clarity. As I watched, another duo of Travellers marched up the road, herding several more kids.

I went back down to the top deck. "I'm going over there," I said, not quite meeting Irene's eyes.

"And do what, Mike?"

"I'm not sure yet," I said. "Tell Marty to go ahead and load the cargo. I don't think that joker Ijiuto is ever going to turn up."

"I'll cover you," she said, heading for the airlock. "I'll just go get my other scope."

"Thanks."

"Should I tell Marty to unload Ijiuto's crates?"

"Hell, no. He hasn't paid me. We got enough mass allowance to take 'em home. At least that way we get a kill fee."

I climbed down to the ground on the starboard side of the *St. Clare*. Glancing underneath the ship, I saw Kimmie sitting with her arm around the refugee girl, consoling her. She had even given the girl her purple coat. The sight of them together made me feel strangely alone, and less than human.

Carrying my tactical backpack, the twin of Dolph's, I walked across the dirt field to the trees lining the back of our pad. I pushed the vines aside like a curtain, letting them fall back into place behind me.

In the dim greenish shadow under the vines, I stripped off my clothes. Stuffed them into my backpack.

Took a deep breath, hunched my shoulders, and Shifted into a wolf.

5

I'M a Shifter. Hundreds of years ago, extreme genetic modification was all the rage. The fad passed, but it left behind pockets of alt-humans with significant differences from mainstream humanity. We Shifters are the largest alt-human community, and if you listen to some people, we're the most dangerous. In my opinion, the reason people say that is because unlike other alt-humans, we're indistinguishable from normies.

Until we Shift.

Most Shifters have one, or at most two animal forms committed to muscle memory. Me, I have a bunch. But for the past couple of years I'd been favoring my gray wolf. I liked this beast's power, speed, and sheer scary factor.

The wolf also excelled at stealth. I flowed through the curtains of vines, carrying my backpack in my teeth. Ecosystem contamination is always a risk when you hang out your shingle as a trading post. These invasive vines, which I recognized from Ponce de Leon, had killed most of the conifers stone dead. Bone-dry needles and twigs littered the ground. My wolf did not crack a single one of them underfoot.

With a map in my head, I turned west at the corner of our pad and followed the next hedge to the south coast of our island. That Ek shuttle was long gone, so I did not have to worry about someone spotting a predator that belonged on a planet 7,200 light years away. Scrubby native bushes grew right down to the coast of our island. Staying under cover, I peered out of the brush at the mainland and the next island over.

No one was driving along the coast road. I was too low down now to see anything of the Traveller ship except its tail antennas, meaning they couldn't see me.

All clear.

I jumped into the channel.

Hell, that was cold.

For an awful minute I couldn't find the bottom.

I can't swim a stroke. Not as a human, nor as a wolf. Jumping into the water had been an act of faith and calculation. I had assumed the channel was walkable, based on how much of that rock in the middle was sticking out of the water. Was it deeper than I had thought?

My claws scrabbled on the sandy bottom. I raised my head and gulped air—and the *next* swell lifted me off my feet again.

I kind of hopped across the channel, timing my lunges to the swells that surged through the channel to break on the distant beach. It was terrifying. The swells also dragged me inshore, so I ended up crossing the channel at a diagonal angle.

I didn't lose my backpack.

I scrambled up a low crag and crawled into the bushes, soaked and shivering, with the taste of salt water in my mouth. I shook myself like a dog, then slunk uphill. The bushes got thicker. The leading tendrils of the invading vines entwined their tops. Now I was stalking under a roof of green leaves, which grew higher and denser as I got in among the dead trees on the edge of the Travellers' northern pad.

All the way, I sniffed the air. A wolf has a much more sensitive nose than a human being. This is one of the biggest advantages of tracking in animal form. Unfortunately, the smoke and dust that saturated the wind covered any scent of human beings, except for the occasional punch of latrine odor where someone had snuck into the bushes to do a number two.

I doubted the Travellers had anyone posted in these woods, anyway. What would be the point? They wouldn't be able to see out.

Chinks of daylight showed through the green roof ahead.

A sudden impact knocked me sideways.

I danced my feet under me and dropped my backpack in a silent snarl. Even before I felt the impact, I'd smelled a familiar scent: jackal.

The jackal now standing nose to nose with me was much bigger than a real jackal would be—almost as big as my wolf, and my wolf was bigger than a real wolf, tipping the scales at 82 kilos, same as me. Nothing is gained or lost in Shifting.

"Gotcha," Dolph said, around the strap of the backpack he held in his teeth. Our animal forms were exact replicas of the Earth originals on the outside, but not on the inside. Shifting wouldn't be much use if you lost your ability to talk.

"Well?" I said.

Dolph's ears went back. "She's not there. I've been watching them for the last forty minutes. I scouted all around the pads where they parked their prizes ... she's not there."

"Maybe she's inside the ship," I said.

"Mike, she's not there."

"Goddamn," I said. "I guess that asshole was telling the truth for once in his life." I felt strangely empty. Only now did I realize how much I'd built up the possibility of seeing Sophia in my mind. I had even begun to plan out what I'd say to her. I read a book on deprogramming once. It said that you should try to produce an emotional connection to their former life by showing them the faces of loved ones.

"Never mind," I said, emptily. "What's going on?"

"It's weird as hell," Dolph said. "All these *kids.*"

I pulled myself together. "That girl from the knife stall showed up at our pad, asking for help. She said they took her cousins."

We dropped our backpacks under a tree and flowed through the last few meters of the woods. The smell of the Travellers now reached us. Poorly cured leather, cigarettes, unwashed funk, and ... hot chocolate?

Crouched flat, we parted the vines with our noses, a millimeter at a time.

Aliens milled, buying shit from the Travellers. In addition to ship parts, they also sell pirated software, that kind of thing. Kids were running around everywhere. There must have been two hundred of them. Some sat on the ground, eating candy and drinking hot chocolate. The Travellers were handing it out in paper cups. It came from a hospitality tent where the Travellers were showing off their digital wares on display screens.

Over this bizarrely festal scene loomed the Travellers' ship. It was a monster. As high as a three-storey building, it measured a good 200 meters long from head to tail. A trio of tubular auxiliary engines supported it off the ground. Intricate thermal ceramic inlays decorated its fuselage and flaring engine bell, depicting figures from the Travellers' mixed-up mythology. All of us try to keep some part of old Earth alive in ourselves—wolf; jackal ... but the Travellers have cherrypicked the worst of our ancestral traditions to create their own pantheon of outcasts, spanning from Loki to Cthulhu. Whether they actually believe in these grisly gods is up for grabs. I suppose it depends what you mean by belief.

I picked out the kids from the knife stall without much difficulty. All the humans here looked kind of samey. Our ethnicities are muddled these days; the distinctions between normies and alt-humans have taken their place as our primary way of sorting ourselves out into categories. But you do still get similarities among people who all come from the same place. These refugees tended to unruly blond or brown hair, dark eyes, muddy beige skin. So did the kids I was searching for.

But something else distinguished them from the others. They were the only ones who looked scared.

Terrified out of their wits, in fact.

The little girl I'd noticed before, who was about Lucy's age, held a cup of chocolate without drinking it. A boy of twelve or so gripped her shoulders as if he thought they were about to be pulled apart.

A Traveller was talking to them, gesticulating impatiently.

Spaced out around the edges of the pad, more Travellers stood guard with battered old assault rifles. They were facing in, not out. I watched the one closest to us for a few minutes. His eyes had an unblinking, glassy lustre. His coat flapped in the wind.

Dolph and I retired into the woods again.

"Where are their parents?" I growled.

"Maybe they don't have any parents."

I made myself calm down some. "They couldn't fit all those kids on that ship."

"Nope," Dolph said, "and they're too young to be burners."

This business of "burning" people was how the Travellers maintained their access to the financial system. They played an endless cat and mouse game with the EkBank. As fast as the Eks identified them and closed down their accounts, they recruited new postulants to open burner accounts. Tragically, the Cluster's many failed and suffering colonies offered them a near-limitless supply of potential recruits. They left nine out of ten burned in their wake, dumped far from home, or sold off for body parts ... but you have to be eighteen to open an EkBank account.

"This must be their new thing," I said. "Recruit them young. Brainwash 'em hard. Make them repair the outsides of ships in the Core. They're probably going to take the ten smartest ones, and leave the rest wishing *they'd* been chosen. Hearts and minds."

Dolph's neck fur hackled. His ears were all the way back. "Well, what are we waiting for?"

I glanced up at the chinks of sky visible through the roof of vines. The light had not changed since we touched down. This planet had a long day.

"They screwed up," I said. "They're too close to us. They can't nuke the *St. Clare* without nuking themselves. So I think we can get away with it, if we move fast enough."

We talked it over for a few minutes. Then I held my backpack down with my teeth while I used a claw to activate the radio clamped to its strap. We had these little FM radios—they only worked over short distances, but they *did* work, even in places with no connectivity. "Irene," I whispered. "Come in."

"Reading you."

"You in position?"

"Yeah," she said. "Where are you? What's the plan?"

I told her.

"There's a .50 cal turret on top of that ship," she said.

"I saw. But they can't lower the elevation of that thing far enough to shoot up their own pad, even if they wanted to. It's for area clearance."

"You should've at least taken that alien's money."

"Point," I said, laughing. I cut the connection. I thought about how maybe I was about to die. "Well," I said to Dolph, "let's do this."

We split up.

Dolph went west around the pad, to the other side of the ship.

I went back to the location of that doped-up postulant and crouched directly behind him.

I gave Dolph a count of twenty to get into position.

Then I gathered myself and leapt out of the vines, pouncing onto the postulant's back.

6

I knocked the postulant flat on the dirt. He smelled like prey, and I couldn't resist clawing him up a bit. I ripped his trophy coat with my teeth and tore the skin of his back to ribbons. When he stopped fighting me, I left him lying. I kicked his rifle into the woods with a hindpaw, and dashed towards the two kids from the knife stall.

Some of the guards loosed off rounds, but we were fast-moving targets, and they couldn't get a clear line of fire. The aliens, and all the kids, were screaming (or hooting, or lowing) and fleeing. A thought shot like a meteor across my mind: the Travellers were the worst predators in the Cluster, yet these folks were running from a wolf? That's fucked up.

Before I could reach the kids, a Traveller the size of a yuriops plunged towards me with an axe cocked high behind his shoulder. An amateur with the weapon, he telegraphed his blow by shifting his weight. I anticipated the downwards sweep of the blade, danced outside his guard, and sank my teeth into his right forearm. His sleeve tasted like old cheese. I broke his elbow by twisting the arm the wrong way, and jumped over him as he crumpled.

Another Traveller charged in from my left, swinging at me with a katana. His two-handed grip suggested he had a clue about swordsmanship, but I was ready to bet he'd only ever practised on a human opponent. I leapt off the ground, all four feet together. His swing went under me, and his own momentum carried him into the collision.

I was already panting, tiring from the intense exertion. But in a head-on collision between a human being and a four-legged predator, the predator wins. Katana dropped his sword and jerked both arms up to protect his throat. I knocked him to the ground—I was bigger and heavier than he was—and mauled his forearms. The taste of blood filled my mouth, bringing a hit of exhilaration. I left him leaking and sprang clear.

A black-and-brown blur wove through the fleeing crowds: Dolph. I almost laughed as I realized the Traveller guards were no longer attacking us. They were trying to reach their ship. Dolph took his pick of targets and leapt on a postulant's back. His pointy, almost dainty-looking jaws closed on the man's neck.

In the same instant, my peripheral vision caught movement behind the tent. A rifle muzzle peeked out from behind it, pointing in Dolph's direction.

I hurled myself at the tent. It collapsed under me—on top of the rifleman. Human forms struggled inside the folds of grubby nylon. I stepped on them to reach the rifleman. His hand emerged, groping for his weapon. I was about to bite the hand off when I saw the knock-off Urush fortunometer on the hairy wrist.

Heaven forgive me.

I bit it off anyway.

Well, not quite. The wolfish joy I took in savaging my enemies did not quite blind me to practical considerations. The little voice of caution in the back of my head, that had saved my life many times on Tech Duinn, warned me not to go *too* far.

So I didn't literally bite his hand off. But I made sure he would be looking at an amputation or a long and painful reconstruction. I sank my fangs into his palm. His blood gushed into my mouth. His screams filled my ears. His bones cracked between my incisors. I wrenched my neck sideways, ripping muscle and sinew, tearing his hand into two floppy prongs, one of which was only attached by a bit of skin. The pinky was also hanging by a flap. I bit it off—

—and a bullet carved a furrow through the fur on my back, close enough to sting.

I spat out Zane's pinky, dropped him, put my head down and sprang at the Traveller standing on the steps of the ship. He was a big blond with all the tattoos and the raised worm-casts of clan scars on his neck and face. He had come halfway down the steps to make sure of his shot. I could see the black circle of his rifle barrel, a hole through to eternity. I was dead for sure—

Blood gouted from the Traveller's throat. He stood stock still for a moment, making a whistling noise as he tried to breathe through a windpipe that wasn't there anymore. Then he dropped his rifle and toppled headfirst down the steps. His head hit the steps with a *clonk* like when you slap a steak on a cutting board.

I landed on his back. Panting, I kicked his body the rest of the way down the steps. Although I didn't know for sure what had happened, I could guess: Irene had saved my ass.

She'd hit him in the throat from a distance of what we later calculated, using a sat map of the spaceport, to be 952 meters.

With an 11 kph wind gusting unpredictably.

There's a reason her old unit, the Ghost Gators, was known as the best sniper outfit on Tech Duinn.

She kept shooting, leading her targets as they scattered. Faint, distant *cracks* reached us on the wind.

Carried away by violence, I had almost forgotten what we were here for. Now I remembered. From this higher vantage point, I spotted Dolph near the trees. He was dancing around a group of children, snapping at them. The boy from the knife stall swung at him with a stick.

I leapt off the steps and hit the ground running. I bowled into the group of children, knocking them over, and got my teeth into the little girl's sleeve. Dragging her half off her feet, I sprinted towards the woods.

The boy followed. I thought highly of him for that.

The minute we got into cover, I let go of the girl and gasped, "Don't be scared. We're human."

She stuffed the tail of her shirt in her mouth. Her face glistened with tears and snot.

We had not fled a moment too soon. The *ta-ta-ta-ta-ta* of automatic fire erupted behind us. Leaves fluttered down and pale gashes appeared in the woody stems of the vines.

"Run!" I snarled.

We didn't have time to go back for our backpacks. We ran flat out. I wasn't sure if the kids knew they were being rescued, or if they were running away from us. I didn't care, as long as they went in the right direction: away from the Travellers, towards the shore of the island.

Stumbling through the coastal brush, we cut the corner and caught up with the Travellers' fleeing customers on the causeway. They provided cover for our escape. At the mainland end of the causeway, Dolph and I chivvied the children down to the beach. The tide had come almost all the way in. There was only a taupe thread of beach left. We dashed along it, with the waves licking our paws and the kids' sandals, and scrambled up onto the causeway of our own island.

The kids were done in, Dolph was limping badly, and we were exposed out here. I was wondering if we could make it back before the Travellers spotted us, when an electric buggy bounced out to meet us. I had never been gladder to see Martin. He said severely, "I feel very left out."

"Sorry," I said. "It was kind of impromptu. Hop in, kids."

Reassured by the sight of a human, the children squashed into the passenger seat of the buggy. Martin opened the back door for me and Dolph to jump in, then floored it.

We jolted across the causeway, between the hedges, and turned the corner onto our pad. The bales and crates were gone from around the *St. Clare*. Martin confirmed that he had loaded the cargo. Another vehicle stood next to the ship—one of the spaceport's rental pickups.

Rafael Ijiuto stood beside it, arguing with Kimmie.

"He showed up after I finished loading," Martin said. "Wants his stuff."

"Uh huh," I said.

Martin parked the electric buggy next to the airlock. I clawed the door open and jumped out. I noticed that Ijiuto had a rifle in his pickup, the type known as a dino gun. Maybe he was planning to get in some hunting.

"Hey, Ijiuto," I said.

He turned to me, registering shock that a wolf was talking. "You guys are Shifters?"

"No, I just happen to be a wolf right now," I said.

"Ha, ha. Hey, I got nothing against Shifters. I was just surprised."

"I understand that you want your cargo," I said. "Well, too fucking bad. If you had showed up in a timely fashion, I'd have delivered it with my compliments. But now it's at the back of the hold, behind twenty tonnes of rare earths and pelts strapped down in the precise distribution that won't mess up the center of mass of my ship. So you're not getting it. Sorry. Feel free to contact our complaints hotline."

Ijiuto's mouth opened and shut. "But," he said lamely.

The kids spilled out of the buggy, shouting. "Pippa! *Pippa!*" The older girl was climbing down from the port airlock, in such a hurry she nearly fell off the ladder. The three children hugged. Their joy brought a tear even to my hardened eye.

Kimmie marched up. "Excuse me," she said to Ijiuto, and bent down to speak to me. "Mike, I've been talking to her. I think we should take them with us. You wouldn't believe what their lives are like here. They've got no future. No hope—"

An engine thrummed. Dust spurted up from the wheels of Rafael Ijiuto's pickup. He had jumped back into the driver's seat and reversed away from the ship. The pickup bounced away across the pad as fast as it could go, and vanished around the hedge.

"Well, that was easier than I expected," I said.

Dolph held up his right forepaw. "I stepped on something," he said. Blood oozed from a nasty cut on his pad. "Think it was a sword."

He melted into a quaking mass of flesh, hard to look at, which resolved twenty seconds later into a naked man.

Shifting often has a revivifying effect. I can't quite quantify it, and no one has ever proved it scientifically, but it feels like it kind of "resets" your neural system, so you get a respite from whatever was troubling you. That's why I was able to bite a man's hand off in wolf form, and that's why Dolph stopped fainting from blood loss as soon as he became a man, and staggered upright, cradling his cut hand. Back in human form, he looked pretty shocking; stark naked, his straggly black hair loose, his mouth and chin smeared with Traveller blood.

I mentally shrugged, and Shifted back into human form, as well.

Kimmie was pushing the two younger children towards the ladder. Naked and shivering in the icy wind, I grabbed her arm. While the little girl and the boy climbed up to the airlock, Pippa hovered anxiously, her eyes popping at my nudity.

Kimmie had seen it before. She folded her arms. "Under the terms of the Refugee Convention, if they land on Ponce de Leon, the government's required to help them. Anyway, we can't leave them here."

I could still taste Zane's blood in my mouth. Now that I was in human form again, it was no longer a good taste. I spat on the dust. I had no time for this argument. We had to get gone. If enough of the Travellers had survived to launch their ship, we would be in trouble. "All right, all right," I said. "Whatever you want."

Kimmie broke into a smile as pretty as spring flowers. "You're the best," she said, and then a spaceship took off from the other side of our island. The noise drowned out her voice. It drowned out everything.

I made a move to get around her to the ladder. She sidestepped. And then her head exploded.

7

There's shooting someone in the head. Then there's shooting someone's head *off.*

I closed my eyes reflexively. Warm globs spattered my face, neck, and hands. Pain stabbed my cheek, and I knew I had just been jabbed by bone shrapnel from Kimmie's skull.

I hit the dirt. So did Dolph and Martin.

Of all the goddamn things. Of all the *damn* luck. We'd been so close to gone. So close to getting away with it.

Popping my head up, I saw Pippa staring down at Kimmie's headless body through her fingers. Most of the spatter had hit me, 'cause I was closer, but blood also tinted the girl's hair like red spray paint.

A foot to Pippa's left, a bright crater popped out on the ship's hull. They were still shooting.

I pushed up on my knees. "Get *down,*" I howled, my voice inaudible amidst the noise. I grabbed Pippa's ankle and jerked. She fell to her hands and knees. I slapped her on her rump to make her crawl under the ship.

Dolph and Martin crawled after us.

The thunder of the ship launch faded into the sky.

"Did the other kids reach the airlock?" I said.

Pippa nodded. Silent tears spilled from her eyes.

"Motherfucker," Dolph was saying, over and over. "Motherfucker."

"Help me with her," Martin said. he was dragging Kimmie's body by one ankle. Her head was gone. Correction: I was wearing it.

I took Kimmie's other ankle. Her neck left a bloody trail in the dust as we crawled underneath the *St. Clare*. A robust lattice of metal trusses at head height supported the auxiliary engine pods. The underslung missile launchers blocked my view forward, but that didn't matter. The shots had come from the other direction. From the Travellers' island. Thus, the aft port engine pod should now shield us from their gunner.

I already knew their weapon did not have facial recognition targeting or smart ammo that could recalibrate in flight. Because if it did, I'd be dead.

Zane. It had to have been him. He'd been aiming at me, but Kimmie had stepped in front of me while he was in the act of pulling the trigger, during that long instant after you commit your body to a course of action, when it's too late to take it back.

Why had I let him live?

We crawled to the other side of the ship. A ladder reached down to the ground on the starboard side of the fuselage, identical to the one on the port side. "Up you go," I said. Pippa climbed the ladder with Dolph behind her, while Martin and I struggled with Kimmie's body, cursing. There was no way we could get her up the ladder. It was dumb to even try, and I knew that on some level, but I was in shock.

The cargo crane bumped my shoulder. Its claws enclosed Kimmie and lifted her up.

We climbed up to the top deck, where Dolph sat naked in the operator's seat of the cargo crane, maneuvering Kimmie into a foot-high gap at the bottom of the hold door.

The sniper was on the Travellers' island, and now we had a three-storey armored superstructure in between us and them. I slapped the plate of the starboard airlock hatch, unlocking it for the others. Then I continued up to the top of the bridge.

Irene was still at her post, lying prone behind the main radar dish. She was toying with the Travellers, firing a shot every time any of them poked their nose out of cover.

"Kimmie's dead," I said.

"Saw," she said.

"Did you see the shooter?"

"No," she snapped.

"Or hear it," I said, "because they timed it to when a ship was taking off."

"The shooter was not on that island," she said, her eyes glued to the binocular sights of her Dayforce scope. "I would have seen them."

I understood her defensive reaction. But everyone makes mistakes. I was already beating myself up for Kimmie's death. For bringing her to a place like this. For hiring her at all.

"Did you find your wife?" Irene said.

In the act of belly-crawling up beside her—not a pleasant way to move when naked—I checked. "You know?"

"Course I know," she said. "Dolph told me over a beer at Snakey's, oh, a year back. You have no secrets, Cap'n."

After a moment, I said, "Ex-wife."

"Ain't no such thing," Irene said in a half-joking tone, referencing our shared faith. Most all Shifters are Catholics. Yeah, I got divorced, anyway.

"Well, I didn't find her," I said. "Turned out she left the life years ago."

"Good for her." Irene squeezed off a shot, in response to some movement I could not see from here. In the same tone as before, she continued, "The minute I let up on the pressure, they're gonna get up in that turret and hit us with the .50."

"Let 'em," I said.

"For real?"

"What's the worst they can do? Take out a couple of the dishes." I gestured to the radar dish and radio and laser comms receivers behind us. "So, we replace 'em. Get below."

"Aye aye," she said. Blindingly fast, she snatched her rifle off its tripod and vamoosed with the weapon in her hand. I followed her down the port ladder. I had reached the airlock before the Travellers opened up with the .50. They were slow off the mark this time.

I slammed the airlock behind me, sealed it, and half-slid, half-fell down to the crew deck. The first people I met were Pippa and her friends. The little girl squeaked, "Mister, where're your clothes?"

You'll note that Irene had said nothing about my unconventional nudity. That's because she was a Shifter, too. She knew that it happens.

"Looks like you're getting a ride to the PdL," I said. "I hope that's acceptable to you."

"Thank you," Pippa said, her eyes luminous with joy. "Thank you, thank you!"

"Thank me later." I squeezed past them. The corridors of my ship are considerably narrower than average, and so low that a guy my size can just barely walk upright.

On my way to the bridge—the actual bridge, deep in the bowels of the ship—I looked into Dolph's berth. Mechanical Failure was with him, tweezing splinters out of his cut and quacking about possible infections. Dolph said, "Make it stop."

I grinned and passed on. Irene met me on the bridge with some clothes.

With Dolph temporarily off the roster, I was short a pilot. But I could fly the *St. Clare* myself. I dropped into the center couch in front of the long, U-shaped console, leaving Dolph's couch on my right empty. The center seat had its own set of flight controls. I put on the AR headset that provided me with telemetry curated by the ship's computer. My hands flew over the banks of toggles and screens, making sure every indicator—virtual and physical—read green. I punched the intercom. "Everyone strap in for launch." But what about the kids? I didn't have enough couches … Oh, but, I did. "Go in the lounge, kids," I said. "You'll see a door opening off of there." That had been Kimmie's berth. She had begged me to take the kids along. I would get them safe and sound to Ponce de Leon if it killed me. "Lie down on the crash couch in there. It's meant for one person, but y'all are small enough you can squeeze up."

Irene strapped herself into the left seat and put on her AR headset. "Weapons systems nominal."

"Roger. Starting auxiliaries." The four auxiliary engines spun up with a whine that vibrated my teeth in my head. "Launching on my mark … and *mark.*"

I opened the throttle.

The *St. Clare* leapt vertically off the ground on four slender pillars of incandescent plasma. 100 meters up, I throttled back the rear pair of auxiliaries—or rather the computer did. The ship's ass dropped, and the main engine kicked in, adding a bass rumble to the rattling, roaring din that enveloped us. The *St. Clare* punched skywards on a curving trajectory that shoved us back into our couches. The refugee camp shrank to a brown scab on the coast of a blackly forested continent, and then the continent shrank to a black splotch on a mostly icebound globe.

Seven minutes into our burn, we achieved orbital velocity. I announced engine cutoff, and killed the throttle.

The roaring and rattling abated. Gravity packed up.

I stayed in my seat for another few minutes, programming our acceleration burn to go FTL. It was just a question of entering parameters and getting the computer to validate my calculations. I typed as fast and carefully as I could. Then I popped my harness and floated out of my seat.

No one's ever invented artificial gravity.

I know, it seems strange. We have skip fields that can multiply a ship's velocity to thousands of times the speed of light. We can field-strip our own DNA and put it back together (at least we used to be able to). We can create realistic artifical intelligences. We can juggle quantum probabilities to turn a man into a wolf. We can process a payment on one planet and have it show up 50 light years away within a few days.

Yet no one has ever figured out how to make your feet stick to the deck of a spaceship. They say it's legitimately impossible: the laws of physics, beaten back so far in other areas, drew their line in the sand when it comes to gravitation, and they're not budging.

Sure, you could just rotate your whole ship to simulate gravity, but the *St. Clare* isn't that big. And frankly, who cares? A little floating isn't a bad thing.

So I pushed off from the ceiling and went to grab a sorely needed drink. I'd conditioned my body to only accept bourbon after lunch, or beer in an emergency. Today called for vodka.

I was dispensing a shot into my micro-gravity mug when my headset flashed up a warning.

A ship had just launched on a trajectory expected to intersect with our orbit.

"Well, well," I said. "That was fast."

8

"GUESS they're pissed off," Irene said dryly.

The computer depicted the Traveller ship as a red blip rising towards our orbital altitude. Its trajectory was similar to the one we'd just taken, but longer and shallower. It would "cut the corner" and overtake us in a slightly lower, faster orbit.

I finished filling my mug with vodka and settled back into my couch. "Prepare to evade auto-nukes." I had assumed the Travellers would be too busy collecting their dead and patching up their wounded to sic their AI-guided orbital missiles on the *St. Clare.* I should have known better. *I should have killed Zane.*

"Nothing so far," Irene said. Through her AR headset, she was scanning our volume with computer-assisted IR and optical vision. "A few sats, but they check out."

"Keep your eyes peeled."

Dolph came weaving onto the bridge with his right hand encased in a bandage. "Let me at these scumbags," he said.

"I'd rather not fight them," I said. Kimmie's death had quenched my appetite for blood. I'd have taken Zane, but killing *all* the surviving Travellers, and any passengers they may have picked up, was a bit much. Also, if we blew the Traveller ship to pieces in orbit, the debris would foul the low orbital altitudes and make landing on Gvm Uye Sachttra a hazardous adventure for years to home. The little furry guys didn't deserve that. We humans had done them enough damage already.

I bent over the FTL computer. It was still processing my burn parameters. Instead of the notification I yearned to see, my headset delivered another warning.

Another ship.

This one had just curved around the planet. Travelling in a low retrograde orbit, it was approaching us head-on. It was still thousands of kilometers away, but every second brought it closer.

I looked up at Dolph, who didn't have his headset on and didn't understand why Irene was cursing. "The good news is they didn't have auto-nukes in orbit. The bad news is they had another ship."

Dolph rubbed his hands. "Two's company, three's target practice." He maneuvered himself into the right seat and grabbed his AR headset.

"How many painkillers did you take?" I swigged vodka. It burned on my empty stomach. "Never mind. Take the stick." I punched the button that reassigned the flight controls to the right seat.

Dolph played around with the sensor suite, making agile gestures with his left hand and clumsy ones with his bandaged right hand. "What happened to the radar? It's glitching out."

"Travellers," I said. "If it was the receiver, we'd have no radar at all. It's probably the data conduit."

Thanks to the radar glitching out, we could only see the ships with our optical and infrared sensors. At this distance, the ship rising from the ground was a small dot on our shared AR visualization. The one already in orbit was an even smaller one, being further away, but it was the bigger danger. I didn't have to worry about Zane's ship until it reached orbit. I had to worry about the other one right now.

My headset popped up a notification. The computer had validated my flight plan. I gave thanks to God, and then saw that I was required to circle halfway around the planet before starting my acceleration burn. Correct initial orientation is everything if you don't want to run out of power and end up drifting several light years from your destination, crossing your fingers that someone friendly comes along before you use up all your air.

"Power up the railgun," I snapped at Irene. "And prepare anti-HERF measures."

Her mouth set, Irene swept her hand over the sequence of switches that diverted shipboard electrical power to the railgun. A high-pitched hum filled the bridge. On the outside of the St. Clare's hull, our chaff ports valved open.

I drank off the rest of my vodka, sip by sip, waiting for the moment when we would be close enough to not miss. Without the radar, it was tough to judge how much separation remained. I was going on what the computer put together. All I could see was the IR blur of the oncoming ship's plume, at a slight angle to us due to the planet's curvature. Three thousand klicks. Two. One point seven— *"Fire!"*

At that moment, we orbited into night, and lost even our optics, as the shadow of Gvm Uye Sachttra blocked out the light from its star.

"Motherfucker," Irene said, banging one palm on her armrest in a rare flash of temper.

"Try targeting them with the comms laser," Dolph said.

"OK. Yeah. That's better." Irene's voice faded into a soft monotone. "C'mere, baby … Target acquired. And … firing."

The whine of the railgun wound rapidly up to a screech. A 15-kilogram steel slug rocketed out of the St. Clare's grinning mouth.

At the same time, the Traveller ship released a missile swarm. These things launch in hundreds. They are AI-guided, illegal, and incredibly dangerous. They lit up our IR like fireworks.

My headset popped up an alert. We had finally orbited far enough around the planet during the one-sided "fight" to achieve an optimal FTL orientation.

"Dolph, orient for exhaust burn," I barked. "Irene, hold those missiles off as long as you can."

My hands raced over the FTL console, powering up the skip field generator. I blitzed through the pre-skip checklist, trusting the computer to do its job. Dolph finessed the nose of the ship around to point in the direction of far-away Ponce de Leon, while Irene worked the point defenses. Maser beams stabbed out at the approaching missiles, and detonated some of them in the vacuum. Others kept coming.

"Initiating exhaust field," I said. The skip field generator kicked in with a loud ticking noise that was music to my ears.

"Initiating acceleration burn," Dolph grunted. He opened the throttle.

The main drive grumbled and then roared. Faster than any missile could follow, the *St. Clare* shot away from Gvm Uye Sachttra, into the black.

Moments later, our slug impacted the second Traveller ship squarely in its nose shield. It penetrated the shield and the hull thickness behind it. Then, deformed, stressed, superheated, and bereft of much of its energy—I'm going on how our computer reconstructed the impact—it tumbled in a destructive dance through the ship, pulverizing the interior bulkheads, before slamming into the antimatter containment ring.

Antimatter in greater than milligram amounts equals a nuclear bomb core. A ship like the *St. Clare* carries a few grams of the stuff. The Traveller ship had more. It is the best drive technology anyone's ever come up with … but safe, it ain't.

Containment rings are built to stand up to crashes and electrical failures. Not railgun slugs.

The explosion was kind of pretty.

9

GᴠM Uye Sachttra shrank to a dot behind us as the *St. Clare's* velocity multiplied logarithmically, from tens of kilometers per second to hundreds of kps, then thousands. Our military-spec drive could do up to half a gee of continuous acceleration for days, depending on how much mass we were pushing. Red-lining the ship's mass allowance like we were now, we only had a few hours of thrust remaining. But that was enough, thanks to the skip field.

Invented by humans. Rah, rah.

Of course, the Eks invented it too, independently of us and a millennium or so earlier. It's kind of obvious once you know how it works.

Still amazing, though.

The speed of light is one photon per Planck length. So, to go faster than light, you just skip 'em.

At present, we were only applying the skip field to our plasma exhaust, accelerating the speed of those particles, so they pushed away from the engine bell harder. The *St. Clare* vibrated and rattled loudly as the engine tried to punch through the fuselage. It sounded scary, but the noises didn't signify anything except the stresses the exhaust field imposed on the hull, which were well within tolerances. The loudest noises came when some infinitesimal piece of space gravel hit the force field shielding the *St. Clare's* nose, and that was because each hit triggered an alarm. There weren't very many hits. It was an empty system.

The three of us on the bridge sat in silence. I drank my vodka in small sips, seeing Kimmie's blood pooling on the chemically hardened dirt. I would have to write to her family. Explain to them that it was all my fault. She had been under my protection. I had failed her. Thank God my insurance covered crew death …

"Raising multiplier," Dolph said, every fifty seconds or so. "Ten. Twenty. Thirty. Forty."

He was taking it in big jumps, so we could get gone faster. Each notch sent a hard jolt through the *St. Clare,* a well-worn reminder that the universe is lumpy, not smooth, at the tiniest scale as well as the largest ones. Down there, you got Planck lengths; up here, you have almost unimaginably vast expanses of nothing with things moving through it, such as spaceships.

After a while, I checked our acceleration. Every captain tries to accelerate as little as possible, and raise the multiplier as high as possible, to save wear and tear and conserve reactant mass. With our mass fraction where it was right now, it was especially important not to burn too much of our water on the acceleration phase. We had to have enough to slow down again at the other end.

0.3 G. Good enough.

I swept my hands over the boards. "Deactivating exhaust field. Dolph, throttle down."

"Throttle down," Dolph echoed. The roaring and rattling stopped. Thrust gravity lost its hold on our bodies.

"External field up," I said.

"External field up."

The skip field generator quit for an instant, then started up again, ticking faster. Another jolt shook the ship, this one violent enough to throw us back against our seats.

The no-name star to port appeared to sparkle. Simultaneously it seemed to dim like we'd hit a switch on it.

In the instant before we roared out of the system, I saw a dot on the infrared, directly behind us. But I was so tired I immediately forgot about it again.

*

I slept, ate. Slept, ate. When I was feeling up to it, I wrote up an EVA plan and put my spacesuit on. As soon as I got out of the airlock, I felt a sense of greater peace.

The Cluster seen from a ship travelling at FTL speed is one of the most awesome spectacles I know. All around me, the stars seemed to blur and stretch out like streaks of rain on the side window of a car —but this "window" was the skip field surrounding the *St. Clare*. We were encased in a bubble of vacuum skipping through space, touching only every $1,339^{th}$ Planck length by this time. The faster you go, the fewer photons hit your eyes. So instead of appearing as spheres or dots, the stars stretched out into a hazy meteor shower of light.

I have never felt very secure in my humanity. That's my big secret. Even now, I still have nightmares where I Shift into something grotesque—a snake with feet, a lion with scales—and can't Shift back. But out here, paradoxically, I felt wholly human. Maybe it was the contrast between me—an organism encased in a scratchy, hot EVA suit—and the vast panorama of the universe.

My very first FTL flight, twenty-seven years ago, leaving San Damiano for the first time on a troop transport, the NCOs herded us all out on a spacewalk. Ostensibly it was to do a fingertip inspection of the hull. Truthfully, it was to show us the reality of where we lived. *In space.* I was hooked for life. It doesn't have the same effect on everyone, but for me, and also for Dolph in a slightly different sense, that day ensured that our army careers would be a mere detour on the road back to space.

And here I was. While Kimmie lay frozen and headless in the cargo hold, a few feet away from me. She'd been a space nut, too. She would never see the Cluster again. I would have to see it for her. I floated up to the top of the bridge and just hung there for a while, taking in the view.

The Messier 4 Cluster has an unusual history. It apparently originated in some other galaxy, got detached, and fell into our galaxy, picking up vast amounts of hot gas and dust along the way. This triggered a second spring of star formation in those clouds of gas. Now, millions and millions of years later, the Cluster has two distinct populations of stars: hundreds of old white dwarfs in the Core, and hundreds more nice, healthy stars in the Fringe.

I changed my handhold and turned to gaze at the Core. On that side of the ship, the waterfall of light looked thicker and brighter, because the stars in there are so close together, waltzing around our very own black hole. The Core is well known to be a no-go zone for biologicals. The few planets in there are lifeless. Too many X-rays. Of course, that doesn't stop the Travellers from hanging out there, in their heavily-shielded ships, sometimes hiding literally in the coronas of those cool old stars.

I sighed to myself. Space is *big*. Human beings are grains of sand. Deal with it. Move on.

I took out my tools and started to work on the radar. I repaired the conduit, stripping the shielding to replace the data cable that the Travellers' bullet had clipped. Then I spackled over some damage on the bridge's hull, where more of those .50 cal bullets had pocked the thermal shields, leaving nasty sharp edges that you could tear a glove on. When I got done with all that, I was good and tired. My suit liner was drenched with sweat, and I looked forward to peeling it off. A drink or three, and I'd be able to sleep without dreaming.

I went hand over hand back towards the airlock, transferring my grip from one handhold to the next. I had a tether, of course, and my suit incorporated mobility thrusters in my life-support backpack. Still, this was no time to take unnecessary risks. The skip field extended for no more than three meters around the ship in all directions. If any part of me stuck out of the field, I could kiss it goodbye.

As I descended to the top deck, I noticed that the view forward was getting hazy. On any FTL journey, the skip field picks up interstellar dust. It stops dead when it enters the field, so you end up travelling in an increasingly thick cloud of primordial dust-bunnies.

Although the dust spoiled my forward view of the Fringe, its density confirmed that we were almost there. This had been a relatively short trip—*just* three days to cover 18 light years, plus or minus a few hundred million kilometers.

On the top deck, I found Dolph. His faceplate reflected the shower of stars. He was kicking a football around. In freefall, that takes skill.

Ahead of the cargo crane, the Gausses, and the maser point defense system, all of which we had installed ourselves, the top deck stretched as flat as a pool table to the "head" of the *St. Clare*. When I bought her, the top deck had been a runway for small airplanes, which would have been stored in what was now our cargo hold. Dolph and I had no use for alien-sized fighter jets, so in a fit of exuberance, we'd repainted the top deck and marked it out as a football pitch.

Dolph had his left boot hooked into the top of the starboard ladder. The ball bounced off the housing of the point defense maser, and his right foot drew back and kicked it again. He swayed from side to side to catch the ball on each return, anchored by only one point. My hair would've stood on end inside my helmet if we weren't in freefall anyway.

"Want a game?" he said.

"We'd just end up losing the ball," I said.

"I have a theory," he said. "But first, I have a question."

My heart sank. I thought he was going to ask me why I had locked the pharma cabinet. If he did ask, I was going to say it was on account of the refugee children. Just to be clear, Dolph did not have a problem —at least, he hadn't had one for a very long time. But he did have a tendency to pop too many pills, given an excuse such as his injured hand, and then who knows, we might end up right back where we started. I was going to tell him to tough it out; generations of Shifters had made do without painkillers.

But I underestimated him. "Did you delete the external camera footage of the day Kimmie got shot?" he said, a touch awkwardly.

"Huh?" I said. "No. I haven't even looked at it."

"Whew," he said. I realized that was why he had come to speak to me outside. He had thought I might have gone into the system and deleted the footage for reasons of my own. "Just had to ask. I thought it might be an insurance thing."

"For once, no," I said flatly. "Actually, it's the opposite. I need to submit any footage we have to the insurance company. Is it really gone?"

"Yup." Dolph caught the ball and held it under one arm. "I searched all the aft external camera repositories. The whole day is missing."

"That's ... weird. You mean it got overwritten?"

"No, I mean the actual files for that day are gone. Guess it could be a system glitch."

"Why were you trying to look at it?"

"Aha," Dolph said. "Well, I was talking to Irene. She swears the rounds that killed Kimmie did not come from the Travellers' island."

"Yeah, she said the same thing to me."

"So I said let's have a look at the footage. Maybe we'll be able to tell from that. But it's gone."

Dolph had a bad habit of trying to fight Irene's battles for her. I said, "In all honesty, don't you think it's more likely that she just didn't see the shooter? Mistakes happen."

"Yup," he said, "they sure do." Reflections of the Core slid over his faceplate like rain as he glanced aft at the cargo hold behind me, where Kimmie's body lay. Of all the mistakes I'd made in my life—and there were many—this had to count as one of the biggest. I wished with sudden ferocity that Dolph would stop picking at it. But that's the way he was. He picked at things, endlessly. He could not let go.

"I didn't delete the damn footage," I said, "but—"

"Then who did?"

"I don't know, but there have to be backups. I'll ask MF. We need it for the insurance, anyway."

"Do that," Dolph said. He let the ball fall and kicked it again. It touched the edge of the maser turret housing and arced away from him. Freefall football doesn't have that much in common with the planetside game. It's more like 3D pool. Our ball was made of solid polymer and massed as much as a light dumbbell. It sailed past Dolph's outstretched leg.

He came off the ladder, grabbed the ball in both hands, and simultaneously fired his mobility thrusters. He was maybe twenty centimeters from the edge of the skip field at that point. He crashed into the ladder with the ball safely trapped under him.

"Handball," I said, when my pulse stopped galloping.

"Ha, ha. Douche." Dolph caught his breath. Then he kicked the football at me.

I caught it on the toe of my EVA boot. We kicked it back and forth a few times, and then went inside.

10

I didn't go to talk to MF immediately. I got good and drunk, and then I cleaned out Kimmie's berth, a miserable task I had been postponing. I folded her clothes and packed them into her kitbag with her toiletries and her kitschy Earth-shaped nightlight. Lastly I took down her inspirational poster of Mt. Everest. Yes, *that* Mt. Everest, the one on Earth, where none of us had ever been. 7,200 light years away ... you'd better have a damn good reason for making *that* trip. It would eat years out of your life, and that's if you ever got there, it being far from certain that the decaying colonies between Earth and here would let you land to replenish your consumables. Basically, we're on our own out here. But Kimmie had still romanticized Earth, which stands for the ideal of human solidarity. I got moisture in my eyes as I peeled the poster off the wall and rolled it up.

"Mister?"

I startled, and pushed off from the crash couch that took up most of the tiny berth. Turning in the air, I saw the littlest refugee child peeking in at the door. She had the tail of her t-shirt in her mouth, as usual.

"Sorry, mister ..."

It is always noisy on board. Fans, plumbing, and the vastly powerful antimatter containment ring on the aft engineering deck produce a throbbing, gurgling, humming melange of decibels equivalent to standing on the shoulder of a busy highway. The skip field generator's high-pitched ticking added to the ambient noise. The kid had sneaked up on me unheard. I took a deep breath to calm my racing heart. I really was on a hair trigger these days.

"How's it going …" What was her name, again? "… Leaf?"

"OK," Leaf said.

"Did you want to speak to me?" We floated out of the berth into the lounge. This was the largest room on the ship, measuring a whole four meters by two. At one end were clamps for long-distance life-support and exercise equipment, which we had left behind on this run to save mass. At this end, a big screen on one wall displayed an animated Ponce de Leon calendar as a screen saver. The fold-out sofa and table were folded away. You don't need furniture in freefall. That was pretty much it, apart from some plants rooted in plastic bulbs, whose tendrils grew towards the strip lights in the ceiling. I noticed that their bulbs were full of water, and bright globules clung to their bottom leaves.

"I finished cleaning the toilet." Leaf took her t-shirt out of her mouth long enough to speak, and then plugged it back in.

"You cleaned the toilet? Who told you to do that?"

"No one," Leaf mumbled. "Pippa said we should do something to help, since you wouldn't take her necklace. Jan cleaned the CO_2 exchanger …"

My esteem for the kids, already high, went up another notch. "Well, that's great," I said "I appreciate it, although those are supposed to be MF's jobs."

"Pippa watered the plants and scrubbed all the walls and floors."

Now that I looked at the walls of the lounge, they *were* unusually free of grubby handprints and paw-prints, although nothing could get rid of the rips where claws had torn the crash-resistant padding. Well, well.

"What should we do now?" Leaf said.

I smiled at her. "Relax," I said. "Get something to eat. You know where the galley is. We'll be on Ponce de Leon in another twelve hours, so …" I gestured at the big screen. "Maybe look at some videos, get a feel for the place. Do you know how to work the screen?"

"Pippa does."

"Good. Call one of us if you need help."

I drifted out into the trunk corridor. Time to tackle MF. I climbed through the child-sized pressure door at the aft end of the trunk corridor, into the dark, noisy universe of the engineering deck.

The Kroolth—the aliens who commissioned the *St. Clare* for their ill-fated emperor—were no more than waist high on an adult human. It was the ship's biggest drawback. We could not replace the airlocks. We'd raised the ceilings of the trunk corridor and the berths as far as possible, which involved tearing out all the wiring and plumbing in the interdeck spaces and redoing it, a huge job that had kept me and Dolph in construction overalls for one whole summer. Raising the ceilings on the *engineering deck?* With every bulkhead concealing vital conduits, and gigavolt electrical equipment built into the decks themselves? Not gonna happen.

Which was one of the reasons I'd hired an engineer whose preferred animal form was a snake.

"Marty," I yelled, floating in a hunched-over fetal position, peering into the dimness. Readouts flashed on the wall consoles and the hulking torus of the antimatter containment ring. Otherwise the engineering deck was dark … apart from the flickering light of a screen in the far corner, near the thermoelectric converter that generated the ship's housekeeping power.

The screen's light reflected dully on scales, and slit-pupiled golden eyes. A jet-black python slithered towards me, flexing his coils against the bramble-like knots of coolant pipes to propel himself through the air. "What's up?" It was strange to see the snake's lipless mouth form

English words. There's a reason there are not many reptilian Shifters. That's pro-level Shifting.

"MF here?"

"He's here," Martin said. "We're watching a movie."

"I figured." I flew after Martin to his cozy den behind the thermo-electric converter. He had stuck a foldable screen to the housing of one of the giant electromagnets which stood out from the AM ring. On it, a white tiger was doing something to a human woman that looked anatomically improbable.

"Oh yeah, give it to her, baby," Mechanical Failure cawed at the screen.

"Hate to interrupt," I said, "but if you could get your microprocessors out of the gutter for a moment ..."

"C'mon Mike, this is a good one. It ain't just the usual bestiality shtick."

"I'll leave that up to those who have watched enough of this crap to know the difference," I said, keeping my eyes averted from the screen.

"Meh," Martin said. "It's all fake anyway. Guaranteed natural don't mean a thing these days." He turned the screen off.

"Oh man," Mechanical Failure complained. "Let's just watch the bit where he, you know, on her tits." His googly, lamp-like optical sensors glowed in the near-darkness; the LEDs on the thermoconverter reflected off his boxy metal housing and long bendy neck.

You may be wondering how I got stuck with a hopelessly randy maintenance bot. I often wondered, too. The answer is that he came with the *St. Clare*. I was in a tight spot at the time I bought her, and didn't look too closely at what I was getting. The ship's eminently satisfactory specs and majestically tough build blinded me to the reason she had sat in that scrapyard for months: Mechanical Failure.

Our name for him reflected his unfitness for purpose. He was supposed to perform janitorial tasks, as well as assisting Martin, but he never did anything without being explicitly ordered to, which was why the ship's living quarters were so dirty that the refugee kids had taken it on themselves to clean the toilets and scrub the bulkheads. The pornography thing, we believed, was the flip side of his disinterest in his actual job. Bots—especially those not made by humans—can occasionally "transgress" their hardwired skill sets, developing quirky obsessions and fetishes. It could have been worse. At least MF mostly favored professional porn made by consenting adults. We kept him around because he was kinda likable, in his eccentric way ... and because he *did* occasionally come in handy.

"I was just wondering," I said, "if you keep backups of the external camera feeds."

"There's backups in the system," MF said. "Hey Mike, why isn't there much reverse bestiality porn? Y'know, where *he's* in human form and *she's* in animal form."

Bestiality is the awkwardly blunt Shifter term for sex where one partner is in their animal form, and the other isn't. I cringed. "Ask Martin, he's the expert. The files I'm looking for are missing out of the system. Don't you have a complete mirror in there?" I tapped the brushed steel housing that concealed MF's inner parts. It was like bot clothes. Once or twice I'd seen him open himself up to replace a component or something—he was like a coral reef in there, a motley, bulgy mass of components accreted around a hidden spine.

"Yes," MF said. "But it'll cost ya. Five gigs of guaranteed natural threesomes, preferably featuring big cats, with full-surround zoomable camera angles and high-fidelity audio."

"Jesus, now I have to bribe you for my own goddamn files?"

MF laughed—a creaky haw-hawing—and rocked in the air. Martin the python laughed too, his lipless mouth gaping wide. "The bot's just kidding. Lighten up."

"It's so cute the way you get all hot under the collar," MF cackled.

I tried to take it in good part, realizing that they aimed to cheer me up. "Fine, give me the files, and if what I'm looking for is there, I'll buy you something for your collection." It was only fair really, since MF did not require a wage. A thought struck me. "After you do that, I have another job for you."

"Nooo," MF said. "Not unless Irene's doing it, too. Is she?"

He had a total crush on Irene. It was tough for her. She had duct-taped over all the cameras in her berth to ensure MF couldn't spy on her naked, and she'd encouraged Kimmie to do the same. The thought of Kimmie made me frown at the bot. He had had a crush on her, too ... but now she was gone, he showed no grief. It destroyed the anthropomorphic illusion. "Sorry, suitcase," I said. "I want you to give those three kids literacy tests. I don't know if they know *anything*. Can they even read and write? Can they use a computer? Find out if they have any skills I could put on their asylum applications."

"Oooh!" MF said, perking up. "Pippa! She's such a cutie! Can I give her a physical examination, too?"

I took a secure handhold and swatted him with my other hand, sending him sailing across the engineering deck towards the exit. "Don't you fucking dare," I yelled after him. After the pressure door closed behind him, I sighed. "That bot is the goddamn limit."

"You take him too seriously," Martin said. He wound his coils loosely around me. It was cramped back here. "He'd never actually lay a finger, I mean a gripper, on any of our girls."

"I certainly hope not."

"What are you looking for in those files?"

"Maybe nothing. I'd rather not say until I find it."

"Fair enough." The AM ring hummed like a distant river. The skip field generator ticked at a panicky rate like a mouse's heartbeat. For a moment I wished I could stay back here forever, cocooned in the dark and the reassuring noise.

"I have to go reduce the multiplier again," I said, and pushed on the python's smooth, muscular coils to free myself. "No one's done the bills of lading or the customs paperwork, either. It's all just sitting there. Jesus."

Martin tightened his upper coil, trapping me. "Not to add to your worries, but we're also low on water. Pushing too much mass."

"Sorry about that," I said dryly.

"Nothing to do about it except dump the cargo or the kids."

"Very funny."

"But just so you're aware, we're not going to have much room to maneuver once we come out of the field."

"Got it," I said. "Straight down to the PdL, no messing around." I wearily headed back to the bridge.

11

WE dropped out of the skip field 100,000 klicks from Ponce de Leon. You can't travel at a significant fraction of light speed any closer to an inhabited planet. Mid-space collisions, however statistically unlikely, do happen, and the PdL has a *lot* of stuff in orbit around it. Satellites and space stations and on-orbit manufacturing facilities cluster in tightly managed bands out to 20,000 klicks, where the furthest observation sats roam. Another cluster of stuff, including fuel depots, FTL drone relay nodes, and the Fleet garrison's space dock, hangs out at the Lagrange point between the PdL and its larger, closer moon, 320,000 klicks away. Then there's *more* stuff in cislunar orbit, mostly related to antimatter production and defense. You get the picture. Ponce de Leon is one of humanity's three Heartworlds in the Cluster. It's busy.

I would never be entirely at home on Ponce de Leon. I came from San Damiano, the Shifter homeworld, outside the Cluster. So did Dolph. Martin came from some kind of screwed-up orbital habitat in the Cloudworlds. Irene, however, was PdL born and bred, and her eyes shone with anticipation and relief as we acquired our first images of "the Puddle," its oceans mostly obscured by the characteristic brownish haze of cloud.

My expression probably mirrored hers. While Ponce de Leon may not be the home of my dreams, it was where Lucy was. And wherever she was, was home to me.

Dolph flipped the ship, opened the throttle, and switched on the exhaust field, in the reverse of the acceleration burn that had begun our voyage. The *St. Clare* rattled and howled as we decelerated towards Ponce de Leon. I reached for the comms and reported our arrival.

"Welcome back, *St. Clare,*" said a warm female voice. Mainstream humans are so *nice,* when they aren't provoked. "Y'all are cleared to land at Mag-Ingat Spaceport at 14:37 local time. You can go ahead and transmit your customs declaration, a copy of your landing license, and your port fee. Have a great day."

"Thanks, and you have a great day, too," I started to say. Then Irene interrupted me.

"What do you want to bet that's them?" she drawled in weary disbelief.

*

I let out a string of curses that would have made my old commanding officer in the 15th Recon proud.

The image on our now-repaired radar clearly showed a Traveller ship. *Zane's ship.* It was about 10,000 klicks away, but overhauling us steadily as we decelerated.

"Holy crap," Dolph said. "They chased us all the way from Gvm Uye Sachttra?!"

Now I remembered that I'd seen a dot behind us just as we entered the skip field. Goddammit. The Travellers must have burned straight after us. Their ship had been invisible to our optics and IR because it had been plumb on our six, hidden by our own exhaust plume.

I broke out in a cold sweat.

We were trapped.

"They've got a HERF mast," Irene said urgently.

"If they get caught with that in PdL space, they're screwed," Dolph said.

"Yeah, but here's the thing," I said. *"We're* screwed."

Now that we were in Ponce de Leon space, every move we made would be observed by the authorities. And they had my transponder tag and my voiceprint. They knew exactly who I was.

"It won't do us much good," I said, "to disable or destroy them, and then get charged with a felony." I had hesitated to fight the Travellers in Gvm Uye Sachttra's orbital space, and the same considerations applied here to the power of ten. There was far more stuff around Ponce de Leon for a dead ship to collide with. Space debris is a massive problem that gets worse every time a satellite fails, never mind a 200-tonne spaceship. Orbital wrecking is a misdemeanor; ship killing is a felony. "We *can't* fight them," I said through clenched teeth, staring at the Traveller ship.

"You're breaking my heart here," Dolph said. "In that case, we'll just have to outrun them." Without waiting for my OK, he bent to the controls. "Pausing our deceleration burn." The ship jolted. When we switched off the external field, we had been moving at 0.25% of light speed, having steadily dialed down our multiplier since the midpoint of our voyage. But to decelerate outside of the field, you have to *increase* your exhaust field multiplier, blasting against your direction of travel. Now we were no longer decelerating. The Traveller ship began to shrink again.

But this, too, was a risky move. As Martin had warned me, we were low on water. If we were going too fast when we reached PdL orbital space, we wouldn't have enough thrust left to get into orbit. We'd slingshot away from the planet again, and end up drifting in space, a sitting duck for the Travellers.

"Can't fight them, can't outrun them," I muttered. "One option left." Without glancing at the others, I punched the comms. "Mayday," I snapped. "Independent freighter *St. Clare* to PdL garrison. This ship is under attack." The Travellers hadn't actually attacked us yet, but we all knew they were going to. "Request assistance, over."

"Oh boy," Irene said.

"Are you crazy?" Dolph yelped.

"Probably," I said.

"If the Fleet catches them," Dolph said patiently, through gritted teeth, "they'll sing. Then what?"

I was all too aware of the risk. If the Travellers were taken into custody, they'd tell the authorities what we did on Gvm Uye Sachttra. An explosion in orbit, dead Travellers on the ground—*how* many? I didn't even know. We might have left as many as a dozen corpses bleeding out on the alien dirt. All of them pirates, to be sure, but all of them men and women. Lives with as much value as anyone else's. The Sophia saga would come to light, as well. I saw a nightmare vision of myself paraded through a courtroom, electronic restraints on my wrists and ankles, Lucy watching.

"Naw," I said, with a confidence I did not feel. "They won't catch 'em. You know what the Fleet's like. They live for this shit. They'll blow 'em into a thousand pieces." Irene and Dolph did not look convinced. "Anyway, it would look worse not to call for assistance!" I said.

At long last my Mayday call was answered. "Reading you, *St. Clare,*" came a relaxed male voice. "This is the *Garibaldi.* We see that ship. Travellers, huh?"

"That's what it looks like to me," I said.

"Breaking the speed limit some, ain't they?" It was a warning to me, as well. I was also breaking the speed limit. "We are orbiting at 200 klicks, but will be with you shortly."

"Appreciate it, *Garibaldi.*" I located the Fleet orbital patrol ship's transponder tag on the radar, and cursed. It was 40,000 goddamn kilometers away, albeit closer all the time. "I may be compelled to take defensive action."

"Do what you gotta do, *St. Clare.* Out."

That wasn't much of a permission slip, but it was good enough for me. "Irene, get their range and put a warning shot into their armor."

"Just a warning shot?"

"Yes."

"OK," she said. "I'll put a couple of missiles in their nose shield. Scare the stinky black pants off them."

We carried active-guided missiles with conventional warheads, skirting around the civilian ban on AI guidance and nukes. Irene loosed two of our Raptor missiles from the launchers on PAIM's belly. They curved gracefully across the void. It was a complete waste of munitions. Twin explosions guttered out in the void.

"They've got point defenses as good as ours," Irene said angrily. "I could sit here doing this all day and it wouldn't make any difference."

All this time we were screaming towards Ponce de Leon. I checked our reactant mass reserves again. The news was not good. On cue, Martin rang up from the engineering deck. "You planning to crash right into the PdL, Mike? Or just do a fly-by?"

I gritted my teeth. "Copy." I thought of the refugee kids, all crammed into Kimmie's berth. They were counting on me to save them. "Dolph, we're gonna decelerate into orbit."

"You sure about that?"

"Yes." We didn't have water to burn on circularizing an irregular orbit, which was what we'd end up in if we didn't slow down now. "Initiating thrust." I opened the throttle.

"OK, here we go," Dolph said. He started dialing the exhaust field multipler up. *Jolt.* Seventy. *Jolt.* Ninety. *Jolt.* One hundred and twenty. The jolts were heavy as hell now. They felt like car crashes, each one delivering up to 40 Gs for a split second, punching us back hard against our couches. *Jolt.* One hundred and forty. *Jolt.* This was where the *St. Clare* really shone. No ordinary ship could decelerate this hard. In an FTL-capable ship, hull strength determines maneuverability, and my lovely ship could withstand stresses that would have crippled anything short of a Fleet fighter. Dizzied by the gees, I watched the radar altimeter spinning down. 3,000 ... 2,000. "That's it," I shouted.

Dolph was already on it, killing the field. Our velocity had dropped right down to 20 kps, and we were on course for orbital insertion, albeit with not much of a margin for error.

The Travellers had not decelerated anything like as hard, so now they were practically on top of us. They must've been cheering as I seemed to drop the *St. Clare* right into their jaws. They'd be singing a different tune when the *Garibaldi* slugged them—

"Do you read me, *St. Clare?*" the *Garibaldi's* captain yelled over the radio.

"I read you," I shouted, scanning the radar for the patrol ship.

"What the heck was that maneuver? Why didn't your ship just fall apart?"

"She's a good 'un. Where are you?"

"Where you *should* be!"

My heart sank. I found the *Garibaldi's* transponder tag. It was attached to an arrowhead screaming through a tight turn, 10,000 klicks beyond Ponce de Leon in the direction we had been travelling,

"Oh, great," I groaned.

The *Garibaldi's* captain had not expected that a mere freighter could do what we just did. My fast braking maneuver had left him where he had thought the fight was going to be ... too far away to get back before the Travellers closed with us.

12

"Jesus, what a clown!" Dolph yelled. "Where's his wingman, anyway?"

"Making a traffic stop?" I said, running calculations. No, we weren't going to be able to slip past the Travellers to the ground.

"This is what they call defending the Heartworlds? Seriously, Mike. Look at that punk. I've seen GPS sats fly faster. These are the guys who dropped us on Tech D in the middle of triple-A fire? These are the guys who taught us to fly spaceships on a moon with more craters than surface?"

"Guess the Fleet ain't what it used to be, after all," I said, watching the Travellers.

"They're catching up," Irene said. "Better do something."

I had a metallic taste in my mouth, like blood. I hit the ship-to-ship frequency. "Zane?"

I didn't recognize the voice that responded. I was never going to recognize it. Its owner was using a voiceprint scrambler which transformed his / her voice into an eerie robotic quaver—a Traveller trademark. "Stand by to be boarded," it said.

"Identify yourself," I shouted.

"Stand by to be boarded," the Traveller repeated, "or we blow your asses away in three ... two ..."

"Incoming," Irene said. "Firing point defenses."

A swarm of missiles streaked towards us. Our maser turrets swivelled and stabbed destructive beams at them. Where the masers made contact, they set off the explosive warheads, causing the missiles to expend themselves before they could do any harm. We left behind a fading ring of fireworks. But a few missiles got through. They always do. That's what AI guidance is for. The impacts shuddered through the hull.

"Aft port aux radiator's damaged," Dolph said. "Efficacy down to seventy percent."

I cursed. But we could still land on 70%. Ponce de Leon was getting bigger, closer. We were down to 1000 klicks, well into restricted-maneuvering space. Now Dolph had to focus on not hitting any PdL assets. Even orbital space is plenty big, and the computer had plotted a path that should keep us out of harm's way, but the missile impacts had punched us off-trajectory by millimeters that could rapidly yawn into kilometer-scale errors. Rigid with concentration, Dolph tapped the auxiliaries to keep us on course.

The *Garibaldi* was nowhere in sight. But the Travellers kept right on coming. As we and they curved around Ponce de Leon, they shot past us and slipped into orbit ahead and below us. It now looked as if we were chasing the Traveller ship, not the other way round. But it was facing us, and it continued to burn, closing the gap further while gaining altitude.

"Incoming," Irene said again. The radar broke out in missile-measles. Irene deployed our point defenses judiciously. More impacts rocked the ship. "Maser power reserves down to forty percent. For crap's sake, Mike!"

Desperate, I looked down at Ponce de Leon. We were scudding over the cloud-dotted expanse of the Orozco Ocean, just 140 klicks up, so low that I could have counted the islands in the Millions. The continent of Tunja would come over the horizon in about two minutes. We were so close to home.

Irene fired again. This time she scored a hit on the other ship's nose shield. Dolph and I cheered, but Irene's voice was harsh. "That's it, no more missiles."

The radio crackled. "This is your last chance," the Traveller on the comms said in his or her spooky scrambled voice. The ship's tail began to curve over its body, radar flagging the change in attitude. I saw their plan. They were going to HERF us in low orbit, killing our electronics. That would paralyze us, as they thought. Then they would be able to board us at their leisure.

My head rang, empty. I punched our chaff launchers. Clouds of silver billowed from the *St. Clare's* chaff ports. As I retracted our main antennas, I said tersely to Irene, "Railgun. Blow them out of the fucking sky."

"Roger that," she said.

The next milliseconds seemed to drag. Irene bent over the targeting console, her blonde ponytail spreading out like the petals of a daisy above her head.

And then a new voice broke into our comms. "Hold it right there! Hold your fire!"

A ship with a blade-thin, arrowhead profile screamed up past us, braking so hard that its exhaust plume caught the Traveller ship's HERF mast. Lurid sparks arced out of the mast and sizzled on the Traveller ship's own hull. Confused shouts and screams crackled over the ship-to-ship frequency.

"The Fleet!" Dolph yelled jubilantly. "Better late than never."

As he spoke, the Travellers' HERF hit us.

The comms cut out.

The lights on the bridge died.

So did the fans.

We floated in a sudden, sickening silence.

On our composite feed, the Fleet patrol ship parked itself right on top of the Traveller ship, at an angle to it, as if the arrowhead had precariously lodged in the cruiser's hide.

Then the displays went dark.

My AR headset was now a blindfold. I ripped it off and found myself staring at the others in the sickly glow of the emergency lighting.

"That was way too close," Irene said.

Dolph shrugged. "We're still breathing," he pointed out.

I ran my fingers through my hair. It was wet with sweat. "Everyone pray to St. Martin," I said.

Two seconds later, the lights came back on. "Well, that was interesting," Martin said. "Any more surprises I should be ready for?"

We all burst out laughing in relief. My tough-as-nails *St. Clare* had weathered the Travellers' HERF pulse with flying colors. As a former warship, she not only had chaff launchers but retractable antennas and redundant backup circuitry. Where an ordinary civilian ship would have been paralyzed, we'd just suffered a power cut. The AM containment ring had never been in danger, of course—it was air-gapped, not connected to anything else.

"Get me power to the comms and sensors," I entreated.

"Coming imminently," Martin said. "I just have to finish resetting the circuit breakers."

Seconds later, I had my displays back. The Traveller ship and the Fleet ship, still docked, were shrinking away from us towards the planetscape below. The comms carried incoherent bursts of static and shouting. The Travellers had left their channel open when they were rudely interrupted by the patrol ship. "Uh oh," I said. "They're boarding them. Shit, shit, shit."

No one else had anything to say. We watched for long minutes in silence. The two ships were falling out of orbit. You can fall for a long time from these altitudes.

"Whoa," Irene said abruptly. "Look at that!"

The two ships had separated. The Traveller ship was going down with its drive burning. Or else *it* was burning. A plasma plume is awfully hard to tell at a distance from a fireball ... the kind of long-lived fireball you get in-atmosphere, where there's oxygen to feed the flames ripping through decks and bulkheads and electrical circuits. The spark showed up brightly against the clouds over northern Tunja.

The Fleet ship soared away from it, burning back up out of the atmosphere.

"What happened?" I breathed.

"At a guess," Dolph said, "they scuttled their own ship. I hear they do that."

"Oh my goodness," Irene said. "I hope all the Marines got clear."

The jetstream drew a veil of cloud over the burning ship, and we saw no more, save a few glimpses of the lurid Tunjanese jungle.

The comms squawked. "Yo, *St. Clare. Garibaldi* here. Did you take any damage?"

I cleared my throat. "Nothing critical," I said. "What happened there?"

"Their ship was on fire when we boarded it. Your missiles musta hit something crucial. We had to withdraw our men and cut 'em loose." The *Garibaldi's* captain spoke accusingly, obviously getting ready to write a report that made it out to be all my fault.

Dolph snatched the comms mic from me. "Listen up, hotshot," he said, contemptuously. "I was on Tech Duinn. 15th Recon. If our close air support ever screwed up a call like that, theater command would've fed their asses to the Necros."

"Tech what?"

I grabbed the mic back. "Never mind," I said. "Before your time."

"I am required to report this incident to the planetary police," the *Garibaldi's* captain said stiffly. "You'll be hearing from them shortly. Do not attempt a landing until that time, or I'll dust your ass." *Click.*

Tunja passed beneath us and away. We circled the planet again. As we orbited back around to the dayside of Ponce de Leon, the radio blared, "Come in! Independent freighter *St. Clare,* respond immediately!"

"Right here," I said, thumbing on the video connection. Forcing a friendly smile took everything I had left, and then some. Looked like we were screwed, after all.

13

THEY let us land. Small mercies. We didn't even miss our landing slot. Following instructions from the police, I put the ship down squarely on the crosshairs of Freight Terminal 1028 at Mag-Ingat Spaceport.

Freight Terminal 1028 was mine. That is, I rented it. It was a square of reinforced concrete, 200 meters a side, with a hangar at one end. Landing on that thing was like throwing a dart into the right space on a chessboard with a thousand squares per side, from orbit. I had done this hundreds of times, which didn't make it any more fun with the knowledge that I had zero margin for a splashdown abort, and an unknown amount of electrical damage from the Travellers' HERF. Everyone on board clapped when the *St. Clare* came to rest on the ground.

I sat for a moment, stroking the familiar metal surfaces of the consoles, and the toggles and switches my hands knew so well. I felt completely wrung out. All I wanted to do was crawl inside of a bottle of bourbon. But that was not to be. I now had to give the performance of my life ... or we'd all be ending the day in jail.

As instructed by the police, we exited the ship. The sweltering heat of a PdL summer slapped us in the face. Ponce de Leon has two seasons: hot and hotter. We were now well into July, the hottest month of all. Sweat immediately prickled my skin under the Uni-Ex polo I'd pulled on in an attempt to present a professional image.

Leaving everyone else sitting and standing in the shade of the *St. Clare*, I walked towards the trio of police officers lounging in the entrance of my hangar.

The sea breeze carried rich odors of jet fuel and dead fish, and the sun beat down like a steel drummer's palms. I self-consciously kept my hands open and visible at my sides, feeling sick with guilt.

The officers were standing in the edge of the shade of the hangar, which forced me to stop in the sunlight in front of them. I saw myself in the mirror shades of the nearest police officer. My hair hung in lank, sweat-caked spikes over my forehead. Pits of shadow hid my eyes. My cheekbones stuck out like doorknobs. My shirt obviously came from one of those print-your-own places. I looked like a hungry, shady no-hoper.

I forced out my threadbare professional grin. "Jose-Maria! Long time no see."

"You crazy mofo," the police officer returned, and pulled me into a hug. He may have regretted it when he got a whiff of me, as he let go rather quickly. But his grin, framed in the fat of his stubbly cheeks, looked genuine. "You still hunting for trouble, Tiger?"

The police officer was Jose-Maria d'Alencon, formerly known to the men and women of 15th Recon as "Bones." Back in the day, Bones had been the sergeant in charge of intel at Red Hill, our forward operating base on Tech Duinn. Now he was a captain at the Cape Agreste precinct of the Ponce de Leon police department.

When I had badgered the police officer on the radio to give me the name of his captain, and that name turned out to be Jose-Maria d'Alencon, I had started to hope this would work out OK. Now my hopes rose tenuously higher.

"I ain't hunting for trouble, Bones," I said. "Seems like trouble has a hard-on for me. I never saw those guys before they started shooting at me in orbit on ... shit, I can get you the name of the planet."

"I don't need to know the name of the planet," d'Alencon said. "One of those alien mudballs y'all indies fly to. Natives don't even try and act civilized. Insurance companies won't touch it, even the EkBank holds its nose—right? Some washed-up buncha vets and rejects providing security, if you can even call it that? I know the kind of place."

He clearly did. After all, we'd fought together in that kind of place, back in the day. I spread my hands. "I didn't even catch sight of whatever security they got. There were Travellers selling stolen ships on the ground. I had words with them." I was treading carefully here. "We got into a quarrel, and they ended up shooting one of my crew members."

"Sorry to hear that," d'Alencon said. "I assume you're going to report it to the appropriate authorities."

"Already done." I had reported Kimmie's death from orbit while we were waiting to learn our fate.

"And then they chased you back here, Tiger? That's unusual. They don't normally come within twenty light years of the Heartworlds. Did you do something to provoke them?"

I started sweating again. I remembered the Traveller's spooky scrambled voice. *Stand by for boarding...* They hadn't just wanted to destroy me. There had to be something on my ship they wanted. *What?*

"Nothing that I can recall," I said, doing my level best to project sincerity. "Shit, Bones, they're *Travellers*. They don't have to be provoked. They're nuts, anyway."

"That's what everyone says," d'Alencon said in a neutral tone.

"I attempted to evade them," I said. "The rest you saw."

One of the other officers said, "Sure did. Was rooting for you."

"Next time you do something like that, give the Fleet more time to respond," d'Alencon said, with a rueful half-smile that said he was aware of the Fleet's shortcomings. I was, too, but our adventures today had really brought it home to me. The simple, brutal fact of the matter is that spaceflight makes planetary protection next door to impossible. Not all civilian ships are armed, but every one carries the equivalent of a city-flattening bomb: its antimatter drive. With that kind of power in the hands of everyman, the Fleet has no real firepower advantage, and their hands are tied by responsibility for millions of innocent hostages on the ground. So their usual m.o. is to sit in orbit, watch the traffic, and report incidents to the police. Who then file charges leading to life-destroying lawsuits against the unfortunate few.

That's real power. If d'Alencon chose to file charges against me, even if I didn't go to jail, my business would trickle away like a handful of sand into the pockets of the lawyers.

But I knew that, if he hadn't changed, he was a good man who gave his all to punishing the guilty, not the innocent.

And *he* knew that I had only done what I had to do. He didn't know what had happened on Gvm Uye Sachttra. With any luck, he never would.

"Didja see where the dickwads came down?" I said, mentally crossing my fingers.

D'Alencon shrugged. "Somewhere up north. We dispatched a search and rescue crew, but you know as well as I do they ain't gonna find anything."

I spat sideways and watched my spittle sizzle on the concrete, disguising my desire to shout hallelujah. D'Alencon was right, of course. Even supposing the Traveller ship had not burned up, there was nowhere for it to land in northern Tunja. The thickest, cruelest jungle any human being ever saw covered the continent. There was nowhere for a chopper to put down, let alone a spaceship. The only chance would be if the Travellers had bailed out before their ship crashed. Even then, their parachutes would get hung up on the trees, and they'd be hundreds of klicks from civilization, surrounded by the natural wonders of Ponce de Leon. And when did you last hear of a Traveller having an emergency radio beacon, much less activating it?

No. If Zane had been on that ship, he was dead. And dead men don't sing. I was in the clear.

"Bones!" Dolph arrived at my side. He had known d'Alencon in the old days, too. They hugged and back-slapped.

"Psycho!" d'Alencon said. That had been Dolph's nickname in the forces. No comment.

Dolph stuck out one thin, sweaty palm. "Where's our reward? That's one bunch of Travellers that won't be preying on the innocent again. All thanks to Uni-Ex Shipping. *We* should be collecting a paycheck from the government, not y'all."

D'Alencon laughed. "Might be able to get ya medals."

"Only if they got a 100 on one side and a KGC on the other," Dolph said.

The other police officers laughed sourly. Their annual pay probably amounted to less than 100 KGCs.

"Don't worry about it, guys," I smiled. "All in a day's work." I wanted to get Dolph away from the officers before he managed to insult them again.

"But for real, Mike," D'Alencon said, and my heart sank. "I keep thinking about the fact that they followed you back here. They may be nuts; they ain't suicidal. What the actual fuck?"

"It's like they're recklessly stupid criminals or something," Dolph said. He was trying to minimize the whole thing. I understood the impulse, but I could also see that d'Alencon wasn't buying it.

Our old friend took his sunglasses off. He twirled them by one earpiece. His eyes were baggy and tired. He looked shockingly old. I wondered if I looked that old to him. "You underestimate the enemy, you're hurting yourself," he said, echoing a slogan from our army days. "Are you aware of the Travellers' history?"

"Sure," Dolph said. "Monkeys see spaceships. Monkeys take spaceships. Dirtsiders cry boo-hoo. The Fleet sits on its collective ass."

I winced. D'Alencon did not react to Dolph's flippancy. "The Travellers are the biggest criminal organization in the Cluster," he said portentously. "In fact, they're the most serious threat facing humanity today."

Dolph shifted his weight. I knew he was about to scoff at the notion that the Travellers could be *that* big of a threat. After all, they bled and died like everyone else. I accidentally-on-purpose stepped on his foot.

"But it's interesting how they got their start," d'Alencon said, his eyes boring into Dolph. "They were mercenaries in the human-Ek war, working to protect the very same planets that they now rape. There's a fine line between protection and predation. Sometimes, those are just two sides of the same coin. What happened with the Travellers is they got ideological. When you start to think that the law interferes with your freedom, trouble ain't far off. Throw massive firepower into the mix, and the problem is out of control."

"I've always thought of the Travellers as more of a cult," I said quietly.

"They're that, too. A cult *and* a criminal organization. Both sides reinforce each other." D'Alencon shook his head. "What were they doing when you encountered them? Anything unusual? Even if it don't seem that significant to you, it might be a crucial piece of information for us."

14

I blinked, hiding surprise and a certain amount of alarm. D'Alencon had just implied that the Travellers were up to something nefarious. More nefarious than usual? That was a pretty high bar.

"We didn't see anything unusual," I said, remembering two hundred children running around the Traveller ship. A bearded, scarred Traveller interrogating the kids from the knife stall. If that was normal, I was an Ek. "Nothing apart from the Travellers themselves, that is. And sadly, that ain't very unusual at all."

Beside me, Dolph wiped stray bits of sweaty hair out of his face, adding nothing.

"That's too bad," d'Alencon said. "For a man in your position, it pays to keep your eyes open."

"How do you mean?"

D'Alencon shrugged. "You've been knocking around the Fringe for a while, Tiger. Ain't that many people with your kind of experience. You know how things are supposed to be, and how they're not. So when you head out there from now on, keep your eyes open. That's all I'm saying."

But that wasn't *all* he was saying. I got the subtext, and confirmed, "If we see anything interesting, you'll be the first to know about it."

D'Alencon crushed my hand in his pudgy one. "Good man, Mike. We'll file today's incident in the Shit Happens folder."

"See ya 'round," his officers echoed. They trooped away towards the cop car parked on the shady side of my hangar.

Dolph waited until they were out of earshot before saying, "Nice move, Tiger."

"At least I didn't insult their manhood, their earning power, and their intelligence inside of three minutes," I said.

He shrugged. "They're cops. If they get their panties in a twist over that, they're in the wrong job." He waved to the police car as it purred away. He was mad.

Not as mad as I was. I had basically just agreed to become an informant for the PdL PD, in exchange for their overlooking the whole ship kill in low orbit thing.

I sighed. "You know what, actually, it'll be good to have better contacts within the force. We don't have to actually tell them anything. And we'll make Bones buy the beer."

"I'd kill for a beer right now," Dolph said. He glanced around the hangar. "Mother of God, this place is a mess."

"Crap, they saw my calendar," I said, trying to lighten the mood. The calendar hanging over the workbench, a gift from Lucy, featured the cuddly, sparkly aliens of Gemworld Families, her latest craze. I remembered that I didn't have a present for her. "*What* am I going to give her?" I groaned.

Dolph shrugged. We walked back towards the *St. Clare*. The refugee kids peeked out from under the ship. They had hidden while the police were here.

"Poor kids," I said. MF had delivered the results of his literacy tests to me earlier. "Get this: Jan, that's the boy, and Leaf are functionally illiterate. They know nothing about anything outside of that refugee camp, except a few fairy tales from wherever all those people come from. Pippa can read and write and use a computer. But that's it. Their lives aren't gonna be easy here."

"No shit," Dolph said. "You better get them over to asylum processing before someone accuses us of people-trafficking. Good thing Bones didn't see them."

I sighed, giving up. He'd just have to stay mad. "Yeah, I'm going to take them over there now."

"Who's taking Kimmie to the morgue?"

"I am," Martin shouted down from the crane operator's seat. He was wearing a ball cap to protect his bald dome from the sun. "Get your scrawny ass up here and open the hold door."

Dolph climbed the ladder. I went to talk to Irene.

She was sitting behind the ladder, almost under the ship, where you couldn't see her very well. There was a reason for that—the same reason I had not taken her with me to speak to the police officers. She had a sketchy past. In between leaving the army and signing on with me, she'd worked with people I would cross the Cluster to avoid. All I knew about that part of her life was that I did not want to know any more about it. She swore the police had nothing on her, and that she would never go back to mixing in those circles, and I believed her. All the same, she preferred to stay out of sight, out of mind, where d'Alencon and his upstanding brothers in blue were concerned.

"Irene," I said, "I need to get the kids over to processing. Can you do the post-flight with Dolph?"

She stood up, her eyes darkening. I felt sorry to have to ask it of her. Instead of going home to her family, she'd be spending the rest of the day rolling the ship into the hangar, depressurizing the LOX tanks, sleeping the AM ring, dumping the sewage, and so on and on. With Dolph, what's more. They were not each other's favorite people, although they were grown-ups and worked professionally together.

But all she said was, "Fine, I'll do it, but I want tomorrow off."

"You got it," I said.

"I want tomorrow off, too," Martin hollered.

"And I want to win the lottery," I yelled back at him. I circled an arm in a go-ahead gesture. The crane arm snaked into the hold and emerged, gripping the body-bag that held what was left of Kimmie's mortal shell.

In silence, we watched it descend to the tarmac. No drums and fifes. No folded flag. Kimmie had not died for humanity. She'd died because she had stepped in front of me. Standing there with the sun hammering on my head, and one hand awkwardly placed on my heart, I silently swore to God that I would stick to the straight and narrow from now on. I would not risk something like this happening ever again.

Martin stowed the crane and came down the ladder. Standing over Kimmie's body, we double-checked the paperwork I had transferred to Martin's phone. The rental van I had rung for arrived—utilitarian, with a freezer compartment. We loaded Kimmie in. Martin led the truck away on his motorbike.

A wave of tiredness washed over me. I fetched my truck out of the hangar and told the kids to get in the back.

*

It was a long drive to the passenger terminal, along the intraport roads marked out between the pads, between big ships and little, old ships and new, the 200-meter steel dunce-hats of Ek ships and the infinitely quirky variety of human-designed spacecraft. With my adrenaline at a low ebb, I put my feet up on the dash and dozed, letting the truck drive itself. I woke up with a start when the truck stopped in front of the immigration building.

We queued for two and a half hours in the Others channel, amidst a stunning cross-section of sapient life, ranging from sleek huspathids to insect-like aiora, from various worlds that did not issue ID compatible with human computer systems. The kids stared and stared and stared. Leaf's eyes got as big as wishing wells. Pippa smacked the tail of Leaf's t-shirt out of her mouth once, but then she pulled the younger girl close and cuddled her. Jan gave the aliens his jaundiced refugee-camp glare for a while, but then he too edged up to Pippa and leaned against her.

They were entwined like that when we finally reached the front of the line.

"Hi," I said to the hatchet-faced gent behind the window. "These three minors are from Gvm Uye Sachttra. It's my understanding that they can apply for asylum as refugees. If they need a sponsor, I'll do it."

I felt really awful about abandoning them at this point. They were so far out of their element, and so plainly terrified. They may have dreamed of coming to Ponce de Leon, but they had had no idea what it would be like. I pinged their asylum application forms to the clerk.

"All right," he said.

I leaned on the counter, forcing him to actually look at me through his blast-proof, disease-proof glass wall. "I also would like to inquire about the possibility of Pippa—the oldest girl here—applying for immigrant status, based on her skills—"

Pippa interrupted me by tugging on my elbow. "Mike—" I'd finally gotten them to stop calling me *mister*— "we wanted to give you something." She poked Jan.

The quiet, dark-haired boy took a doll out from under his shirt. It was 20 centimeters high, hand-sewn from what I recognized as the fabric of Pippa's charity sweatshirt—and only now did I notice she wasn't wearing it. With a head as big as its body, and cunning little flippers for hands and feet, it looked oddly familiar.

Pippa said, "It's Blobby from Gemworld Families. At least it's meant to be." She stuck out her lower lip. "You were saying how you didn't have time to buy a present for your little girl, so we thought maybe you could give her this? We made it."

I took the doll, but did not speak for a moment. I was deeply touched. I said, for want of something better to say, "You know Gemworld Families?"

Jan said, "We lived in a refugee camp, not under a freaking rock." He shrugged, distancing himself from girly things such as sparkling aliens.

I smiled. Maybe they'd be OK.

Pippa smiled too, tremulously. She was still clutching her case of knives, the only "luggage" the kids had brought with them. I guessed those would be taken away from her in due course.

"Gotta ask you to step aside, sir," the immigration clerk said. "Kids that way."

I said, "Is that all? I mean, that's *it*?"

"That's it," he confirmed. "Have a nice day."

So I stepped aside, holding the handmade doll, and watched the kids trail away on the other side of the barrier. Pippa turned and looked back at me with a flash of desperation in her eyes. Then they vanished through a door marked *Processing*.

I shook myself and pushed back the way I'd come. I strode between humanoid and non-humanoid intelligent life-forms, and their equally various and weirdly scented luggage, while holo ads flashed and pulsated in every unoccupied bit of floorspace, but the sensory onslaught that had so shocked the kids was just wallpaper to me. This was my world … where bureaucrats treated little kids like numbers on a screen, and a dead girl went to her rest in a rented freezer van. Maybe civilization wasn't so great, after all.

Or maybe I just needed a drink.

15

By the time we finished putting the ship to bed, Dolph, Irene, Martin, and I *all* needed a drink, despite—or because of—how tired we were. We claimed a corner booth in one of the bars lining the road on the boundary of the spaceport's commercial cargo zone. These places cater to freighter crews, which is probably why they serve alcohol. It was a far cry from Snakey's, our regular haunt in the city, but the bourbon was just about drinkable. I ordered a double on the rocks. Irene had a single. Dolph had a beer. Martin had something fizzy with edible flowers floating on it.

Country music thumped from the sound system. Drunk aliens knocked into the tables. Humans staggered around clutching the backs of booths for support, weak from long journeys in freefall. Cigarette smoke hazed the air. No one noticed the four Shifters in the corner. It's *good* to be able to pass for normies. The bourbon loosened the knot of tension in my stomach. After a while I felt sufficiently revived to take my holobook out of my kitbag and place it on the table, wiping off chip crumbs and cigarette ash with my sleeve.

"Remember the footage that mysteriously vanished off the ship's computer?" I said. "MF recovered it for me."

Dolph made an uninterested "huh" noise. He was chain-smoking, a sign that he was still mad at me for the thing with d'Alencon.

But Irene sat bolt upright. "Really? I *know* I'm right. Let's have a look at it."

I turned the holobook away from the bar and played the footage in 2D on the screen, so that no one apart from ourselves would be able to see it. It was a tough watch. The *St. Clare's* aft port camera had captured everything in high-definition detail, albeit without sound. Again, Rafael Ijiuto drove away. "Like he saw a ghost," Martin commented. On the screen, I shrugged. Dolph Shifted back, and then I Shifted back. It was always unpleasant to see a Shift on video—it looked like a patch of the screen was malfunctioning. Back in human form, I grabbed Kimmie's arm while the little kids climbed the ladder. We argued. Pippa looked on nervously. Kimmie's head exploded. *Boom.*

I was dismayed by the ugly expression on my own face while I was talking to Kimmie. I really hadn't wanted to take the kids, had I? I'd grudgingly been doing Kimmie a favor; that was all. It was awful to know that that was the last thing she had seen.

Irene narrowed her eyes. "Rewind," she said.

"The whole thing?"

"No, just the last bit. And slow it down."

Irene was sitting next to me. Dolph and Martin were on the other side of the table. As I played the footage again, at an excruciatingly slow speed, Dolph suddenly tensed and leaned towards the screen like an animal spotting prey.

All right, all right, Kimmie. Whatever you want.

You're the best—

BOOM.

"Oh no," Dolph groaned. "No freaking way."

"There," Irene said, as blood sprayed over my face. *"There!"*

"What?" Martin said.

"One more time," Irene said. Before she could reach for the holobook again, Dolph dragged it away. He rewound the footage to the exact moment of the shooting. Kimmie's blood splattered as slowly as water falling in micro-gravity.

As Dolph froze it on a single frame, doubt hardened into grim certainty. I slouched lower on the hard bench and sank my face into my hands. "Go on and kill me," I said.

"It wasn't just you," Irene said. "It was all of us."

"I'm just a humble engineer, and I have no idea what y'all are talking about," Martin said. "Enlighten me."

I reached out and tapped the screen. "The secondary debris puff," I said.

"Look at the hull, behind her," Irene said. "It backstopped the bullet."

"The secondary puff gives us another point for where the bullet was," Dolph said. "First point being her head. Two points gives you a trajectory."

"Yup," I said. "And that trajectory doesn't point to the Travellers' ship. Not even close. The round was most likely fired from the thickets on the landward side of our pad."

"*Rounds,*" Irene said. "There were two shots."

"Smart ammo doesn't need to travel in a straight line," Martin pointed out.

"Except if they had smart ammo," I ground out, "they wouldn't have fucking *missed,* would they?"

There was a short silence.

"I knew it," Irene said. "I *knew* it."

"You were right," I said. "I was wrong."

"It doesn't actually make any difference," Dolph said.

"Oh yes, it does," I said. The country music was plenty loud. Plucked strings, analog percussion, a hoarse human voice soaked in the anguish of Ponce de Leon's early colonial period. I figured it was safe to speak, but I lowered my voice to a near whisper, anyway. "We had already killed a lot of them at that point. But If I had known they didn't shoot Kimmie, I think I would've held off on destroying their other ship in orbit. We didn't *need* to fire the damn railgun at them."

The explosion played out again in my mind's eye. *Pretty.* "And if we hadn't done that, Zane's lot wouldn't have come after us for revenge."

But was that really why they'd come after us? *Stand by to be boarded* ... Again, I felt a nervous twinge, knowing it didn't hang together. Even Jose-Maria d'Alencon had seen that.

"Then the Fleet wouldn't have got involved," I said, "and neither would the police. So. Yeah."

"Ultimately, whether it was them or not, it's the same damn crooks pulling the trigger," Dolph said, doing a 180 degree about-face to defend me. I appreciated that he had my back, but it didn't really help.

Martin picked one of the edible flowers out of his drink and placed it on his tongue, which was very long and red, even in human form. "I'm still not seeing it," he said.

"How not?" I said grumpily.

He tapped the screen. "Look at that pink mist. It has to have been a .50 cal. Nothing else does that kind of damage."

Dolph and Irene got into the weeds with him on calibers, distances, and bullet speeds. I did not join in the argument. It was beside the point. I drained my bourbon and stacked an ashtray on the empty glass. Another glass on top of that. A coaster. The menu gizmo to order more drinks. I topped the tower with the last of Martin's edible flowers, and stared at it blearily. This is your life, Starrunner. A shaky tower waiting to fall.

"It could have been a large-caliber rifle at close range," Irene was saying.

I sat up so suddenly that my tower toppled. A glass rolled off the table, and a yuriops trod on it. "Say that again."

"It could have been a large-caliber rifle ..."

"Like a dino gun." All at once, it clicked. *"Rafael Ijiuto."*

Three blank faces confronted me.

"He had a dino gun in his pickup."

I reached for the holobook, clicked on the *St. Clare's* footage, and frantically rewound to the moment when Ijiuto jumped into his pickup and drove off.

"Look," I said to Irene, "you can actually see it sticking up behind the seats."

I counted the seconds until the first shot.

"Two and a half minutes. That's long enough for him to get into position. The road to the mainland ran behind that hedge. He stops his truck, sneaks into the trees ... *Boom.*"

"That shady little creep," Dolph said softly. "Do we even know where he came from?"

"No." Out in the Fringeworlds, hardly anyone comes from where they're at, and I had long since formulated an executive policy that it did not matter to me where people came from, as long as they paid their fees. "I don't know a damn thing about him." I tapped around on my holobook, connecting to my customer database. "Rafael Ijiuto, wholesaler. No further details given, no links."

"I don't know, Mike," Martin said. "Maybe he coulda done it, but *did* he? Look at his face, here. He saw something that scared him. My guess is it was Travellers hanging out in the thickets."

I grimaced, my elation fading. Martin was right: it was by no means open and shut.

"Anyway, he's probably on the far side of the Cluster by now," Martin added, realistically.

"He is, but his cargo ain't." Dolph stubbed his cigarette out with a violent twisting motion. "Those toy fairies."

"Yeah," I said. "Those toy fairies." I remembered the weird gut reflex of wariness I had had when I took one of the fairies out of its packaging. I started to mention it. Then changed my mind. What did I know about anything? I had misidentified Kimmie's killer.

"The supplier might be able to give us a lead on Ijiuto's whereabouts, or his identity," Dolph said. "We have to return them to sender, anyway. I'll see what I can find out."

"Be careful," I said. "Don't let Bones catch you making enquiries. They'll probably be watching our data logs for a while."

Irene was sitting next to me. She did a shimmying thing with her upper body, which made her bosom move interestingly under her t-shirt. She rubbed her head against my shoulder like the big cat she was in animal form, and exclaimed in a voice that was not quite a plaintive meow: "All I want to do is support my family! Is that too much to ask?!?"

I freed the arm trapped behind her and patted her shoulder. "It'll blow over," I said, with a confidence I did not feel.

Dolph gave me a complicated look. He slid out of the booth. "Well, I'm gonna go see if Nevaeh is home," he said, referring to one of his on-again, off-again girlfriends. "Heaven is big tits spelled backwards."

"Does she know you talk about her like that?" Irene said.

"Not only do I talk *about* her like that, I talk *to* her like that," Dolph said, grinning toothily. He put his leather jacket on. "Wanna come?" he said to me. "We'll get her to call one of her friends."

"I gotta give Irene a ride home," I said.

"I'm going home, too," Martin said. He lived in a swish downtown apartment, where we suspected that he indulged in depraved binges with his reptilian friends. It's a common pattern among people who work in space: you're one person off-world, another at home.

We went out to the parking lot, still hot an hour after sundown. Dolph swung a leg over his bike. In the eternal debate between air and ground, Dolph—oddly, for a spaceship pilot—was a rubber-to-the-road man all the way. His bike was similar to Martin's, but lower-slung and lighter. They could talk bikes for hours. "See you tomorrow," I yelled after them, and followed the now-impatient Irene to my truck.

It wasn't that the idea of Nevaeh's friend did not appeal. Believe it or not, ladies don't line up to date single fathers with money worries. I had been single for so long that any female with a pulse had a certain appeal at this point.

But Lucy would be waiting up for me.

16

I live on 90th, between Shoreside and Creek. It's Shiftertown. At night, you can see the lights of the Strip bleeding into the sky, and the hollow roar of traffic rises and falls like the sea. Folks often sit out on their front porches until late at night, catching sea breezes to save on their A/C bills. I used to live in a fancier place uptown, but that didn't work out.

I set my kitbag down on my front porch, stepped out of my clothes, and Shifted.

"Really?" Irene said in amusement.

"Sssh," I said, when I could speak again.

"A tiger?"

"Lucy likes it. Sssh."

Irene shook her head and opened my front door for me, as I had no hands at the moment. Then she carried on up to her own apartment. The Seagraves lived upstairs from us. I could hear the holovision from upstairs, but from my apartment came not a sound.

I slid through the front door and crept stealthily down the hall. My tiger's pads made no sound on the grotty cork tiles.

Nanny B, however, had superhuman hearing. She looked out of the kitchen at the end of the hall.

I raised one paw to my mouth, telling her to be silent, and peeked into Lucy's room.

Bedcovers on the floor. Schoolbooks and toys piled in a corner, inartfully hidden by a towel. Lucy had "tidied up" in anticipation of my return. Her Gemworld Families took up most of the bed, a drift of sparkling, cuddly hailstones.

I prowled another step and peeked around the door of the living-room.

There she sat, cross-legged on the carpet, with her back to me. Gratifyingly, it looked like she was doing homework.

I silently drank in the sight of her—the thick, oak-brown braids, fuzzy after a day's play, falling on either side of her neck; the studiously lowered head; the sweetly pudgy knees sticking out of her shorts. She had turned eight in January, and I'd convinced myself she looked nothing at all like her mother.

I gathered myself to pounce.

"Hi, Daddy," she said.

Guess I hadn't been as quiet as I thought.

She turned around, grinning.

I pounced, anyway. As gently as a tiger can, I knocked her sideways onto the carpet, rolled on my back, picked her up in my paws, and bounced her in the air, flying her back and forth like an airplane. She laughed and laughed. I'd been playing airplane with her since she was a baby, and I could still see the baby in her when she laughed like this. Eventually I dropped her onto my belly and folded my paws over her back. "Missed you, Lulu."

"Missed you too, Daddy." She snuggled into my belly fur. Her thumb crept towards her mouth.

Before it could get there, I dumped her lightly into a sitting position on the carpet. "Homework?"

"I already finished my homework," she said, starting to sweep her hand across her crappy old holobook. The cover was held on with duct tape.

I caught her hand—tenderly—in my jaws before she could erase what she'd been doing. The whole virtual sheet of paper was covered with childish drawings of dolphins, grouped around a photograph of a real dolphin that she must have downloaded to copy.

"Great drawings," I said.

"I *like* dolphins," she said.

Despite my reluctance to be a controlling parent, I said, "Sweetie, you don't even like swimming."

"I *do*. I love swimming. Will you take me to the beach? Tomorrow? Please?"

"Well …"

"Rex said he's going to take Mia to the beach after school. Can I go with them? Can you come? Please?"

I knew that this onslaught of demands was a reaction to her feelings of neglect. I was away far too much of the time. Whenever I was here, Lucy displayed an almost frenzied eagerness to squeeze every possible minute of dad-and-daughter time out of me. But I couldn't take her to the beach, even if I wanted to. I had to work.

I deflected the issue by standing up and Shifting back. Lucy trotted out of the room to fetch me some clothes. Nudity is obviously not a big deal in Shifter families, and it was hot enough that I would have been just as comfortable naked, but Nanny B would have complained.

Lying on the carpet, panting, I heard the front door click.

I leapt up and bounded into the hall. Lucy was dragging my kitbag, which I'd left on the porch, into the apartment. "What?" she said in alarm when I shoved past her and shouldered the front door closed. It autolocked.

I managed a smile. "Just don't want you going outside by yourself after dark."

"I'm not a baby," she said. "You worry too much."

"Maybe," I acknowledged. "All the same, better safe than sorry."

"What are you worried about?"

"There might be bad guys around," I said, a warning which Lucy had heard from me so many times that she ignored it.

She started to open my kitbag. "Did you bring me anything? What's my present?"

I pulled the kitbag away and tossed it into my bedroom. I didn't want her to find that toy fairy, which I'd stuffed in there with my dirty laundry. I unsnapped the cargo pocket of the pants I'd just taken off, and presented Lucy with the doll that Pippa, Jan, and Leaf had made.

"What is it?"

"It's meant to be Blobby from Gemworld Families. It's pretty cool, isn't it?"

"It's ugly," she said with the clinical judgement of a child. "It doesn't look like my other ones."

"That's because it's handmade."

"You mean, someone printed it?"

"Sewed it."

"Oh." She set the doll on the living-room table. "So ... I'm not getting a new holobook?"

I grimaced. Goddamn Rafael Ijiuto hadn't paid me, and the kill fee for the toy fairies would only be in the region of 2 KGCs. "Not yet, sweetie. You can still use that one, can't you?"

Lucy's shoulders sagged. Disappointment settled around her like a black cloud. "Yeah. It doesn't play holos anymore. But I don't really like watching holos, anyway. It's OK, Daddy, I don't mind."

I knew I had let her down. "Well," I said. "Let's have some ice cream, anyway."

"Nanny B will say no," Lucy predicted.

"We'll see about that. Nanny B," I called out, "how about some ice cream?"

"Lucy has already had her dessert," Nanny B said, trundling in on her short legs.

Nanny B was a bot. I'd bought her after Sophia left. She had cost a fortune, in installments that took me years to pay off, but she was worth it. Four feet nothing, royal blue, she had a blandly smiling, rather simian face, a screen on her rounded tummy, and antennas bobbing on her head. Every aspect of her design was appealing and non-threatening. Yet, thanks to my copious and detailed orders, her teddy-bearish exterior hid a caregiver as strict as any drill sergeant.

"You have had enough added sugar for one day, Lucy," she said. "If you are still hungry, you may have a banana or an apple."

"See," Lucy said to me. "I told you." Sadly, she sat down with her beat-up old holobook.

I grabbed her around the middle. "Heck," I said, "Once in a while won't hurt. Nanny, override that. A scoop of chocolate ice cream for Lulu, and I'll have some, too."

As we cuddled on the sofa, licking our ice cream from big silver spoons, I felt a sense of peace that no amount of bourbon could deliver. No matter what I may have done out there, I was still a pretty good father. Lucy's love for me proved it.

And to think that I could've ended the day in jail! It didn't bear thinking about. And yet I couldn't help thinking about it. I privately renewed my vow to keep my nose clean from now on. If it hurt my business, so be it. Lucy could do without nice stuff. She couldn't do without her father.

"What's wrong?" she said.

"What do you mean what?"

"You're shivering."

She was right. I was trembling. It was a bad old sign that my humanity was wobbling, no doubt a reaction to everything I'd been through today. I felt a pang of pure panic. Waiting for it to pass, I said in a silly voice, "I need more ice cream. I ain't frosty enough yet."

The next morning, when I went into Lucy's room to wake her for school, I saw the handmade Blobby doll lying on her pillow. She had given it pride of place over all her other Gemworld Families dolls. One small hand pinned it possessively to the pillow.

I smiled, and made an impulsive decision. "Rise and shine," I said. "We're going to the beach today."

I needed to talk to Rex, anyhow.

17

IRENE'S husband was a lion. By this, I mean not only that his pre-ferred animal form was a lion, but that he was a lazy bastard who was quite happy to let his wife bring home the bacon. The scientists—yes, there are Shifter scientists, on San Damiano, not here—say that our animal forms have no relation to our personalities. A tiger, they say, is just as likely to be risk-averse as a snake; a dog can be just as independent as a cheetah. To that, I say bullcrap. We pick our animal forms ourselves, so obviously we pick ones that suit our personalities, based on preconceived ideas going back to the Stone Age. We can transform our own bodies in half a minute, but cultural assumptions aren't shifted so easily.

Of course, I'm the exception that proves the rule. But as far as I know, there's only one of me.

Anyway, Rex was lazy by predilection, not so much in reality. I was the last person to minimize the difficulties of being a house-husband to two young kids. By the time I met him outside the girls' school at home time, he already looked fed up. He was wrangling Kit, their five-year-old, in a pair of toddler reins that drew stares.

"Slow day at the office, Mike?" he rumbled from his 6'5" height. His shoulders, the width of an upright piano, strained a rugby shirt.

I shrugged. "Figured I'd take the afternoon off." In reality, Dolph and I had spent the morning surreptitiously searching for information about the crashed Traveller ship, to make sure there had really been no survivors. But I figured Rex had already had the whole story from Irene, and I didn't want to get into it now.

Waiting for the kids to come out, I shifted my weight from foot to foot and whistled through my teeth. Mentally, I was still not all the way home yet, and could not fully appreciate the bright pastel mosaic of Shiftertown row houses on either side of the school, or the tinkling bell of a candy seller, or the smell of the gravelnut trees lining the street. In the case of the gravelnuts, that was a good thing. They smell like dog poop. Rex grumbled about the heat, and I envied his effortless way of belonging here. He was as rooted in Shiftertown as a gravelnut tree.

"I don't like this," I said, gesturing at the school gates. Beyond them, a gravelled yard fronted the decrepit school building.

"Neither do I," Rex said. "Mia's teacher told them the other day that genetic modification is dangerous. So then she starts having nightmares that she's turning into an alien."

I cursed. "How about a bit of historical context?"

Given that this is Shiftertown, nearly all the kids at Shoreside Elementary are Shifters. However, their teachers mostly are not. And even the ones that are, have to follow the mainstream human curriculum, which contains a fair bit of propaganda against genetic modification. Sure, it's dangerous. Thousands of lives were sacrificed in the Big Shift. But that was centuries ago. It's a done deal, and now we are what we are, so what's the point of making kids feel bad about themselves?

Actually, though, that hadn't been what I was talking about. I pointed to the white-painted wrought iron gates and the low wall in front of the schoolyard, which was set back between closely packed buildings. "I was thinking about security," I said. "That's not gonna keep a dog out."

"This is Shiftertown," Rex said, meaning that we were among our own here, so who would want to break into the local elementary school, anyway?

"They could at least put a force field on top of that wall." I shook my head. "I'm gonna send her to St. Anne's next year."

"Sure," Rex said. "Let me know when they start offering scholarships to impoverished Shifters."

St. Anne's was one of the most exclusive schools on Ponce de Leon. It had a Catholic ethos, which appealed to my cultural preferences. I also liked the sound of the ultra-secure campus in the hills, with force-field fences that could keep out everything from mosquitoes to spaceships. I was in two minds about sending Lucy to a normie school. She'd have to live in a normie world when she grew up, anyway ... but in reality, it was a moot question. I could no more afford St. Anne's fees than I could afford to *live* in the hills.

"Next run," I said automatically, "is gonna be huge."

Rex was still mocking my pretensions when the kids poured out of school. Their voices echoed off the sides of the narrow street in an exuberant cacophony. Lucy and Mia ran up to us. We headed for the beach.

Nowhere in Mag-Ingat is far from the beach. It's a coastal city, cupped in the hills around Mag-Ingat Harbor, protected from storms by the high ridges of headlands that run out into the sea. However, we in Shiftertown are blessed to live within five minutes' actual walking distance of the sand. It makes up somewhat for the flooding (in winter), the sweltering humidity (in summer), and the bugs (all year round).

We crossed Shoreside Avenue, amidst traffic wobbling in heat mirages. The sea breeze flapped our clothes and threatened to carry the girls' school hats off. They had barely stepped foot on the baking sand before they were stripping to their bathing suits and dashing towards the water.

I rolled up my slacks and went in up to my knees to keep an eye on them. When the sun got too much for me, I told them to stay in their depth, and retreated to where Rex had parked himself in the shade of

St. Andrew's Pier. The fairground rides rattled and jingled above us. The wet sand smelled of seaweed. Waves slopped and sucked around the pier's massive, seashell-encrusted supports. Kit was building a sand fort.

"Beer?" Rex said. He had brought folding sun loungers as well as a cooler of beer and fizzy drinks.

"I was wondering," I said.

"What?"

I accepted a beer with a nod of thanks and popped the tab. It was cheap lager, now warm. "I'm gonna need a new admin officer. I guess Irene told you what happened."

Rex nodded heavily. "Sounds like it was a bad run."

"Bad don't even cover it," I said with feeling. "I never, ever want to get into that kind of mess again."

"If that's how you feel, maybe you should quit flying." Rex was only half-joking.

I sipped my beer. "I've thought about it, but what else would I do?"

"Get a regular job?"

"Sure. It's always been my dream to work security on the Strip, or sell insurance."

"You could find something uptown."

"Until they find out that I turn into a wolf from time to time."

"Goddamn normies," Rex said. I half-shrugged, not wholly agreeing but understanding why he felt that way.

It's not that the normies hate us. One on one, they're great. But they expect us, in general, to behave like animals, and unfortunately the statistics back them up. Hiring algos are based on statistics, so that shuts Shifters out of most occupations right there. That's why I started my own company. And having clawed out a niche for myself in the industry, I knew that I could never bring myself to sell the business I had built up with my blood, sweat, and tears. One day, sure, I planned to step back from off-planet operations ... but right now, I just wanted to manage my risks downwards.

I tried to explain all this to Rex, but I didn't get far before he cut me off. "Sure, sure. Fact is, you love flying. Irene's the same. If I had a GC for every time she told me she would be happy to quit *but,* we'd be rich."

I snorted beer out of my nose. "Damn you, Seagrave."

Rex chuckled. "If she wasn't flying with you, she'd be flying with someone else that ain't so concerned about the lives of his crew. So you can't quit, anyway."

I fet honored by his confidence in me, although it came at an awkward time, considering that I had just lost a crew member. "Well, that brings me to what I wanted to talk about. I lost my admin out there. She was young, idealistic. A real sweet girl. And she was a normie."

"Why did you even hire a normie in the first place?"

This question made me uncomfortable. "To prove that *we* don't discriminate? Or just 'cause I liked her."

"Oh yeah," Rex said.

"Not in *that* way."

"Sure."

"I never laid a finger on her. Swear to God. Ask Irene."

"Oh, I believe you," Rex said. "I know you wouldn't. I'm just messing with you." Grinning, he drained his lager and crumpled the can. "So you're looking for a replacement."

"That's right," I said in relief. "I wondered if you knew anyone."

"A Shifter, this time."

"Yup," I confirmed, even as I wondered if it was the right call. I may have hired Kimmie because I liked her, but at the bottom of that was my dislike of Shifter-only environments. It can get a bit ... intense. Kimmie had played an understated role of peacemaker on board, averting explosions just by being there. All the claw marks on the walls of the *St. Clare's* lounge came from before her time.

"You want someone who can handle themselves," Rex said.

"Exactly. That's why I figured I'd ask you." Rex knew the kind of people who could handle themselves. You can't get that from an algorithm.

"Guy or girl?"

"Don't matter." This wasn't quite the truth, either. I knew that Irene didn't want to be the only woman on board, with MF hovering around and ogling her. But I didn't want to express a preference for a woman in case Rex started ragging on me again.

"Well, let me think." Rex got out his phone and started scrolling and muttering to it. I lay back on my lounger and sipped my lager. Lucy and Mia body-surfed on the tiny, curling waves. Groups of alien tourists wandered along the sand. Parents watched over frolicking children. Out in the bay, Shifter sea-lions and dolphins gave tourists rides. Flying cars streamed along the skyway that crossed the bay, looking like jewel-colored beetles in the sky. Right now, I felt like I'd be happy to just stay on Ponce de Leon forever ... and then a cop car darted through the skyway in pursuit of some speeder, reminding me that my safety here was an illusion.

"OK, here's a few possibles for you," Rex said. He sent them to my phone. "The best candidate might be this guy, Robbie. He's on my rugby team. He doesn't have any experience in space, but he's smarter than your average Shifter. He'd be a quick study."

"I'll call him right now," I said. But then the girls dashed out of the sea, goosefleshed, with sand on their legs and inside their bathing-suits. We got them towelled off and into their clothes. Rex produced fizzy drinks. Then Kit needed his diaper changed. Yes, he still wore diapers at the age of five.

All four of us were wrestling with his powerful little arms and legs when footsteps crunched on the sand.

"Something stinks to high heck," said a deep and unpleasantly familiar voice. "Oh, it's the kid. Heh, heh, Starrunner, thought it was you."

I looked up into the face of my worst enemy.

18

Buzz Parsec was a fellow independent freighter captain. Naturally, we hated each other's guts.

I'm pretty sure Parsec wasn't his real name. Heck, Starrunner isn't my real name, either. It suited him, though. He had a bullet-shaped head on a body so bulked-out, he made Rex look positively slender. A layer of fat covered the muscle, and a pelt of dark hair covered his chest and back. His wifebeater and football shorts didn't hide enough of him for polite company.

Parsec seldom went anywhere alone, and I recognized the equally sizable gent loitering a few meters away as one of the Kodiak twins, either Larry or Gary. I could never tell them apart. Both of them were bears, as was Parsec himself. See what I mean about people selecting their animal forms for psychological reasons? Fat, bad-tempered, territorial—even if you didn't know that folks called this crew the Bad-News Bears, you'd be able to guess.

Squinting up at Parsec, I said, "Ever thought about going on a diet? Your personal mass allowance has got to be eating into your profit margins."

He scowled—well, he was already scowling, but he scowled more —and plied the electric fan he held in one fat fist. He was sweating heavily from walking his bulk around in the heat. "Worry about your own profit margins, Starrunner. Mine are just fine."

Unfortunately, I figured that was true. His ship was twice the size of mine, and he took more risks than I was comfortable with, principally in the area of customs avoidance. Not to put too fine a point on it, Parsec was a smuggler. *He* should have been in jail. He had come close to it a couple of times, but it hadn't made him change his ways. It just made him more sickeningly smug.

"Well, hey there," he added, to Rex. "If it ain't the King of the Beasts." He made the sobriquet into a taunt. A low, leonine growl crept out of Rex's throat, and I tensed.

But Rex had more sense than I did in some ways. He slapped Kit on his now clean-diapered rump. "Go play." Kit trotted off towards the water, and Rex followed him.

I rose to my feet, putting myself between the bears and the girls. As I stood up, I saw a black sub-limo illegally idling on Shoreside, its tinted windows seeming to stare across the beach at me. That would be Parsec's ride. He must have spotted us and stopped on purpose to say hello. How sweet.

"What can I do for you today, Parsec?" I had a tricky line to walk. I wanted to get rid of him without scaring the girls. "Wanna borrow a bathing-suit?" I gestured to the ones Lucy and Mia had just taken off, which were hanging over Rex's lounger. "Might not fit …"

The girls giggled at the thought of this enormous man squeezing into a little girl's bathing-suit. Parsec surprised me by reminding me that he had a human side. He played along: he picked up Mia's bathing-suit and held it in front of his chest, lumbering from foot to foot like a performing bear. The girls laughed louder than ever. "Try it on, try it on!"

"Naw," Parsec said. "I ain't in the mood for a swim today. Too hot. Matter of fact, I wanted to talk to your dad." It wasn't too hard to tell which child was mine. Parsec focused on brown-haired, sturdy Lucy, not blonde, sprite-like Mia. "Is Mike your dad?"

"Yes!" she said, smiling openly, under the mistaken impression that Parsec was nice. Maybe I had bent over backwards too far to avoid unpleasantness.

"What's your name?"

I intervened. "Well, it's good to see you around, Parsec." I gestured towards his car. "Wouldn't want you to get a ticket."

"Never got a ticket in S-Town yet." Parsec fanned himself and looked out to sea. We could see the blue hump of Space Island at the mouth of the harbor. A ship was taking off on a pillar of fire, pale against the afternoon sky. The rumble carried faintly across the water. "Heard you had some trouble on your way home yesterday."

"It was nothing." Of course, that's why he was here. He was fishing for any information he might be able to use against me. There were only two Shifter captains flying out of Ponce de Leon: me and him. We were in competition with the normie captains, too, and there was enough business to go around. But Parsec didn't see it that way, and I, too, had often fantasized about the longed-for day when he wound up in jail and I inherited the less distasteful portion of his customer base.

Now the balance of probabilities seemed to be tilting the other way: I was closer to the edge than he was. I had to find out how much he knew about my troubles. "How'd you hear about that?"

"Got sources," Parsec said.

"Yeah?"

"Heck, it was on the news," Kodiak made his first contribution to the conversation. "Spaceship crashes in the Tunjle? It was on all the feeds."

"I missed it," I said. "What did they say?"

"That it crashed," Parsec said.

"I coulda told you that," I said.

Parsec glanced around, an unnecessary move as there was no one else nearby. He did it on purpose to telegraph the information value of what he was about to say. "Is it true they were Travellers?"

"Now that I couldn't tell you," I said, too quickly. Parsec smirked. Inwardly, I kicked myself. My verbal flinch had confirmed his guess. But it couldn't have been a guess. No one would guess *Travellers*, not in the Ponce de Leon system. He really did have sources. Maybe even in the police. It had crossed my mind in the past that that might be one reason he displayed such agility at staying out of jail.

Well, so he knew I had tangled with Travellers; so what? D'Alencon had already given me his blessing. If anything, it made me look good to have struck a blow for the defense of our planet. It was more than Parsec had ever done. Recalling d'Alencon's words, I said, "If you have any information about the Travellers, don't keep it to yourself. "

Parsec's eyes went little and bearish. "Why would I know anything about those scumbags? Unlike you, I never been married to one."

I inhaled sharply. Of course, he had been acquainted with Sophia, in bygone days when he and I were friendlier than we were now. He had witnessed my anguish when she went over to the Travellers. But he wouldn't dare to talk about that in front of Lucy ... *would* he?

I turned to the girls. "Let's pack up." I didn't care if Parsec took offense at me for cutting our friendly chat short.

As I tossed stuff into Rex's beach bag, Parsec moved around me. He bent down and smiled at Lucy. "You're a cutie," he said.

She shrank towards me, having picked up by now on my ill will towards Parsec.

"What's your name?"

"Lucy," she whispered, speaking when she was spoken to, like Nanny B and I had taught her.

Parsec did not really know how to talk to children. He said, "Good, good," and straightened up. "She's gonna be a heartbreaker," he said to me. "You look after her, Starrunner."

I gritted my teeth and fantasized about Shifting into my wolf and clawing Parsec's back to bloody ribbons as he and the Kodiak twin finally shambled away.

Although Lucy was dragging on my arm, I did not take my eyes off the bears until they reached their car.

"Daddy! What does that mean?"

"What does what mean?" I said, watching the sub-limo disappear into the Shoreside traffic.

"What's a heartbreaker?"

I smiled in relief. She had not picked up on Parsec's reference to her mother. "When you grow up, lots of boys will want to date you, and your daddy will break their legs."

"So it should be leg-breaker!" said Mia. She was a year younger than Lucy. No one had called her a heartbreaker, but she took for granted that it applied to her, too. She had her mother's confidence, and a bubbliness that was all her own. She twirled around. "I'm a leg-breaker, a leg-breaker!" She rushed up to her father as he returned, hauling Kit, and karate-kicked his legs.

"Sorry about that," Rex said to me. "If I had to look at his ugly face one more minute, I'd've …" He trailed off, shaking his head.

"You would've broken his legs!" Mia said. "Daddy's a leg-breaker, a leg-breaker!"

Rex and I looked at each other and roared. The funny part was that "leg-breaker" was in fact a fairly apt description of Rex's former line of work. He and Irene had even worked with Parsec a time or two. Of course, that was ancient history now. Rex's reaction to Parsec proved it.

We picked up pizza on the way home. Irene was not best pleased to have us all pile into their apartment, bringing pungent odors of garlic and pepperoncini, in the middle of her me time. My weapons officer had a thing for meditation with scented candles. She would draw the curtains and put cloudwhale chants on the sound system. Me, I preferred three fingers of cask-aged bourbon. To each their own.

19

I was still mulling uneasily over the conversation with Parsec when I went into work the next morning. The office of Uni-Ex Shipping was on the eighth floor of an old building near Mag-Ingat Harbor. This side of the city, straggling out along the eastern headland, feels like a whole different world. It's industrial, lightly populated, tuned into the relentless rhythm of Cluster-scale commercial logistics. Road and rail and sea and space connections all meet where the East Causeway to Space Island vaults over the deep-sea harbor. There *are* other continents on Ponce de Leon, and other cities in Tunja, although I can think of no reason to bother visiting them. Dirtside freight mostly moves by sea, owing to the near-total lack of overland networks. Notice I said *near*-total. There are some roads in the interior, serving remote colony towns. The truckers who drive those routes had my respect. Their job made mine look like a walk in the park.

Our office overlooked the main freight railyard, where cargoes are loaded on and off the mag-lev that shuttles back and forth across East Causeway. It was noisy if we opened the windows, and stifling if we closed them. I preferred the noise. Mary, our receptionist, preferred the heat. She, being a mainstream human and worth her weight in gold, usually won. She had pictures of her teenage children on her desk, and a phone manner that made us sound like a much bigger company.

I spent the morning in a self-imposed bubble of normality, speaking on the phone and v-mailing with customers, juggling shipments for our next run, and in between times checking in with Dolph. He was out at the spaceport, dispatching our cargoes from Gvm Uye Sachtra on the final stages of their interstellar journey. Some of the stuff went by rail across the causeway to the very same freight yard outside my window, where it would be sent onwards by truck, plane, or ship. Other cargoes were picked up by their owners at Freight Terminal 1028. We carried a lot of small shipments. It wasn't worth putting them on the mag-lev, so customers often chose to pick them up and clear customs themselves.

Dolph said, "So, about the toy fairies."

"Did you find out anything?"

"Yep. Hang on."

The picture tilted as Dolph moved over to the mountain of cargo which had now migrated out of the *St. Clare's* hold and onto the floor of the hangar. The mountain was smaller now, but still considerable. Dolph would have spent all yesterday afternoon and this morning shifting it. He was stripped to the waist, his sixpack gleaming with sweat. I ruefully considered that I spent all too many days sitting on my rear, making phone calls. I was in decent shape, but that was due to Shifting, not exercise.

Dolph had placed the crates of toy fairies nearest the entrance of the hangar. He vaulted onto the nearest one and sat on it. "The supplier is a company called Mujin Inc. They're located at 12100 Bonsucesso Tower."

"That's a nice building," Martin's voice shouted from out of shot. "There's a patisserie on the mall level that does the best croissants on the planet."

"Maybe so, but guess who owns Mujin Inc," Dolph said. "I had to do some digging for this."

"Don't keep me in suspense," I said.

"Tomas Feirweather."

"Who's that?"

"Better known as Canuck."

"Whoa. OK, *that's* interesting."

Canuck was a skinny ginger bastard whose animal form looked like an oversized fox, although he insisted it was a cinnamon bear. He was known to be one of Buzz Parsec's less savory groupies. In fact he'd gotten banned from Grizzly's for fighting. That takes some doing.

"Since when does he own a toy company?" I said.

"It's not a manufacturer, as far as I can tell. In fact, their internet portal says it's a taxi company."

"A *taxi* company?"

"Yeah, and I had to look up their articles of incorporation to even find that. It's not on the portal. It's like they don't want anyone to find out what they do. But I do know one thing about that company ..."

"Canuck ain't the real owner," I said.

"That's how I figure it."

"He's fronting for a certain someone who, as a matter of fact, I ran into yesterday."

I told Dolph about my little chat with Parsec on the beach.

"That motherfucking crook," Dolph murmured, in an almost prayerful tone, but the intensity in his voice was loathing, not love. However much I hated Parsec, Dolph hated him worse. He had had a chance to put him in the ground once, but I had talked him out of it on principle. Thou shalt not kill, y'know? What a hypocrite I was. Dolph was not a hypocrite, at least when it came to killing. I had had to listen many times since then to what he shoulda, coulda, woulda done—with the implication, unintended by Dolph, but palpable to me, that I was to blame for arguing him out of it. "You shoulda decked him," he said now.

"Unfortunately, being on the beach isn't a punchable offense," I said.

"What did it seem like he wanted?"

"I thought he was just digging for dirt. But … I did the robocall thing yesterday morning, so if he's involved in this company's operations, he could've found out that the toy fairies were undeliverable."

"Right, and then he went looking for you to find out why."

I shook my head, still puzzled. "He didn't even mention it."

"Of course he didn't, because he didn't want us to know about his connection with Mujin Inc."

"OK, but why? What's the problem with them?"

"That's what we've got to find out." Dolph propped his phone up so that the whole front of the hangar, the dangerously grinning head of the *St. Clare*, and Dolph himself came into view. He lit a cigarette. "Wild guess, it's something very, very illegal," he said softly, breathing out smoke. "I really don't like the look of that company. Everything on their portal is vague, no substance. Looks like it was written by a computer. They're hiding something."

"Dolph …" I had a feeling we were better off not knowing what they were hiding. But at the same time, I hated the idea that Parsec may have arranged for … *something* illegal … to be transported on my ship. And if it was a risk he didn't want to take himself, it had to be a pretty big one. "Don't open any of those crates."

"Wasn't planning on it."

"Are they being shipped, or picked up?"

"Company's sending someone to pick them up later."

"Let me know when they arrive."

"Will do." Dolph's voice returned to its normal pitch. "By the way, they recovered some wreckage."

"What kind of wreckage?"

"Didn't you see the news last night?"

"I was watching Gemworld Families and getting drunk."

Irene's voice shouted from out of shot, "He passed out on my living-room floor."

"Gemworld Whatsits would do that to me as well," Dolph cackled. "No, but it was *totaled*. The search and rescue guy holds up a scrap of something about this big and goes, 'This may have been a piece of the engine.' So, I guess that's that."

"Did they say anything else on the news?"

"Nope. They didn't even admit it was Travellers."

All the same, I had to check for myself, of course. The news links plunged me into the rabbit hole I'd been trying to stay out of. There was very little information, but a whole lot of speculation, and by the time I got to the end of that, my lunch hour had come and gone.

I was eating a hasty sandwich at my desk when Rex's friend, Robbie Wolfe, turned up. I had called him earlier and asked him to come in for an interview.

"Sorry about this," I said, brushing crumbs off my desk. I leaned across to shake his hand. Mary withdrew, radiating disapproval. I could see why. Robbie was about twenty, with a baby-face that made him look even younger. Rex hadn't mentioned that he was so young. But the rugby-player build that Rex had extolled was on full display. His upper body was shrink-wrapped in a holo t-shirt with an embedded scene of two wolves fighting. The whole package screamed *thug*. That could be a plus, depending on what was inside.

"So did Rex tell you what the job is?" I said. "Nice shirt, by the way."

"Yessir," he mumbled, and then something I couldn't catch.

I got up and shut the window, cutting off the background whoosh and clatter from the railyard. "Sorry, it gets a bit noisy in here. What was that?"

"Rex said you was looking for an admin officer? I always wanted to go to space. Man, I can't tell you how cool that would be."

I still had to strain to make out his words. No, I wasn't going deaf. His English was so oddly accented, it almost sounded like an off-world dialect. I recognized the patois that Shifter youth adopt in order to sound cool, but I'd never tried to actually hold a conversation in it before. Was Lucy going to start talking like this when she got older? I resolved to double my monthly deposits into my St. Anne's fund.

However, once I got used to Robbie's verbal tics, he came off as a well-meaning young man. He was still living with his parents in Shiftertown, down in Smith's End—the bad end of S-Town, but I couldn't hold that against him. Heck, Dolph lived down there, as well. I interrogated Robbie about his life. He currently worked as a security guard at a skull shop on the Strip, but he was taking an online accounting course. He responded warily to my questions, but he loosened up when I got him talking about rugby. "You don't play yourself, sir?"

"Naw. Football," I said, leaving out that the only football I'd played in recent years was with a solid ball, kicking it around with Dolph in deep space.

"Too bad, sir, you look like you could have the form for it," Robbie said, smiling.

Then came the inevitable question when one Shifter interviews another. "So what's your animal form, Robbie?"

He proudly thumbed his chest. "Wolf."

I wasn't surprised, given his last name. Shiftertown is full of Wolfes, and most of them are what it says on the tin. "Whaddaya know? Me, too."

He wasn't to know I could say that to half of everyone.

"Really?! That's so cool. This is me, on the left here." He pressed the button built into the neck of his t-shirt, which restarted the gory holo of one wolf—Robbie himself?—rolling another onto its back and setting teeth into its throat. I assumed the blood spray was shopped in.

"Nice selfie," I said, "but if you decide to take the job, can I ask you to wear something different? That kind of thing wouldn't make a good impression on the customers."

"I got the job?!?" Robbie practically leapt out of his chair.

"I'd like to give you a trial," I said. The fact was, I had no time to devote to the search. I wanted to get it over and done with.

"Thanks. I mean it. Thank you so much, sir. I wasn't going to say anything, but my mom lost her job a while back, and we're struggling …"

He poured forth the story of his family's financial travails. I wasn't sure how much of it to believe, but privately decided to tack another ten percent onto the wage I had been going to offer him, bringing it up to what I had been paying Kimmie. "When are you going to complete that accounting course?" I asked him.

"Well, that's the thing, sir. I can't get nothing done at home. There's six of us, plus my sister's boyfriend and their kid …"

Mary put her head in. "Telephone, Mr. Starrunner," she said with the look that meant *you need to take this call.*

I winced. "Sorry, Robbie, if you wouldn't mind."

Robbie glanced at the clock and leapt up. "I'm gonna be late for work! Sorry, sir, thank you, I'll call you—" He vanished with all the speed of a rugby forward chasing the ball. Mary wrinkled her nose.

My brain flooded with nightmare scenarios involving the police, or alternatively Lucy's school. I thumbed my call waiting. "Uni-Ex Shipping," I said tersely.

"Michael Starrunner?"

"Yes?"

It was none of the things I feared. It never is, is it? Whatever you're afraid of, the universe is cooking up something worse.

"This is Ponce de Leon Immigration and Asylum Processing. You co-signed asylum applications for three human minors, Pippa, Jan, and Leaf?"

20

WITH a jolt, I remembered the three refugee kids. Shamefully, I had hardly thought about them since I deposited them in asylum processing two days ago. Too much on my plate.

"Yes," I said.

"If I could just confirm the details. They are refugees from Gvm Uye Sachttra, and they reached Ponce de Leon on July 28th, 3419, is that correct?"

"Yes."

"We have reached a decision in this case, and I'm calling to notify you of that decision." The caller was a human, but she was doing a good job of sounding like a robot. Maybe working in asylum processing does that to you. "Jan and Leaf have been offered asylum on Ponce de Leon. Pippa has been refused asylum. She will be deported to—"

"What?!" I interrupted. "Her application's been *turned down??*"

"Yes, sir, that is correct. She will be—"

Outrage boiled up. "I think you need to take another look at the applicable sections of the law," I said, leaning forward and stabbing a finger on the desk, as if she could see me. "The Refugee Convention clearly states that human refugees, if they reach Ponce de Leon or any other signatory Heartworld, *will* be given asylum on the principles of human solidarity and subsidiarity." I heard the words in Kimmie's voice as I said them. "Those kids clearly qualify as refugees."

"Yes, sir, however, the law makes an exception in the case of applicants with communicable diseases. Such applicants cannot be given asylum, as they would endanger the local population. Therefore, your applicants are currently being held in quarantine—"

"Wait. They have diseases? What disease?"

"No, sir, only one of them. The older female applicant, Pippa. However, the other two have expressed that they would prefer to be deported with her, and we are prepared to honor their preference, dependent on—"

I interrupted again. I couldn't believe this. "What's she got? Are you sure?"

"Yes, I am sure," the voice said with a touch of asperity. "A lot hangs on these tests, so we make sure we get them right. There is no doubt, I'm afraid. She's infected with interstellar variant kuru."

*

I could have left it there.

Could have put down the phone, said a little prayer for the kids, and gone on with my day.

I came damn close. I looked out of the window at the industrial skyline, and then at the framed original of Uni-Ex's Ponce de Leon landing license on the wall, thinking that I didn't need this.

The hesitation only lasted a moment or two. I got up, tossed the uneaten part of my sandwich, and told Mary I would be out for the rest of the day.

*

The detention center turned out to be unbearably grim. I had lived on Ponce de Leon half my life, and driven past the immigrations building hundreds of times, without ever visiting the walled compound behind it. Grudgingly admitted after another round of phone calls, I parked my truck in the employee lot and roamed from one admin building to the next, getting grumpier and grumpier, until I located the detention center. It was a concrete people-hutch. Bars covered the windows. Faint alien voices, and whiffs of alien smells, wafted out—a body-check of otherworldliness in that all-too-human place.

The quarantine wing had no windows.

No sounds, smells, or germs could escape from there, let alone any people.

I had to speak to the kids by intercom through a thick glass window, as if they were in jail.

Their asylum agent, the woman I'd spoken to on the phone, sat by my shoulder the whole time.

On the other side of the glass, Pippa, Jan, and Leaf sat in a row on a couch, wearing identical peppermint-colored tunics and shorts.

Their expressions tied my heartstrings into a knot.

Pippa's face streamed with tears. She leaned into the intercom mic, clutching it in both hands. "I *can't* have kuru!" she sobbed. "Tell them, Mike! Tell them I'm fine!"

I said to the asylum agent, "This is ridiculous. She doesn't have any symptoms."

"It's got a long incubation period," the agent said. She was a heavy-set woman with permanent makeup that made her look like a clown. A *sad* clown. In person, she clearly felt for the kids. "We wouldn't necessarily expect her to present any symptoms yet."

Interstellar variant kuru is among the nastiest infectious disease agents humanity has yet encountered on our haphazard tour of the Orion Spur. I had looked it all up on my way to the spaceport, my horror growing as I read the details. Kuru was an old Earth disease that damaged brain tissues, leading to the familiar catalog of tremors, dementia, and death. So far, so similar to other prion diseases. But at some point along the way, kuru got weaponized. The interstellar variant now prevalent in the Hurtworlds, and a few other unfortunate planets, is more virulent ... and incurable. IVK prions just shrug their ugly little misshapen protein shoulders at the treatments that work on spongiform encephalopathies, for instance. No doubt, more research would crack the problem, but it's a relatively new disease, affecting a relatively tiny number of people. On top of that, humans seem to be the only species affected by it. So the research hasn't been done yet. In this day and age, it seems impossible that there are still any truly incurable diseases—but there are, and interstellar variant kuru is one of them.

Incurable.

Terminal.

What an awful thing to lay on a sixteen-year-old.

Even sitting safely on my side of the glass, I felt the cold edge of Pippa's shock and terror washing over my skin.

"This is ridiculous," I said aggressively. "She can't have anything like that. She was on my spaceship, and I'm fine. *They're* fine," I added, gesturing to Jan and Leaf.

The agent said, "Sir, not all communicable diseases are equally communicable. To catch kuru from an infected person, you would have to consume their ..." She hesitated, and a moue of disgust crimped her perma-red lips. "Their infected tissues."

I nodded. I had read that on the internet.

"So there's very little risk of transmission, although we would advise you and your crew members to get tested to be on the safe side."

"In that case, why's she behind that glass? If there's no risk of transmission, why can they be in there with her, but I've got to stay out here?"

"You are a permanent resident of Ponce de Leon, and they aren't," the agent said shortly. Poor woman—I was giving her hell. "Interstellar variant kuru is a scheduled disease, and for that reason they can't leave this facility. As I said on the phone, the younger children have chosen deportation, so—"

"So how'd she get it?" I broke in.

Pippa, listening, joined her crackly intercom voice to mine. "I *can't* have it! If I did, they would, too!" She hugged her two younger charges. "They don't, so I can't! We've lived together since we were little! We share *everything!*"

"As I said," the agent repeated reluctantly, "the only transmission vector is ..."

"I'm *not* a *cannibal!*" Pippa screamed.

Her voice carried around the visitor room. Heads turned. Eyebrows went up. I smiled weakly at my fellow offended humans and aliens of civilized upbringing.

The unpleasant fact was, some people *are* cannibals. Always have been, always will be, I guess. From the primitive inhabitants of Earth's vanished wildernesses, to remote colony worlds where things have gone badly wrong with the food supply or with people's minds, human beings are capable of eating other human beings. And a few of them do.

But that wasn't to say Pippa had, or ever would. I believed her. I said, "And there are no other transmission vectors, right? So you see —"

It was the agent's turn to interrupt me. "In a place like the camp they came from, people tend to eat whatever they can get, I'm afraid."

Jan took the intercom mic from Pippa's hands. "We were poor," he said heatedly, "but not *starving.*"

Leaf spoke up. "We only ever ate food aid! Just in case—" Jan glowered at her. She stuffed the hem of her tunic into her mouth.

Into the silence, the agent said, "Another possibility, unfortunately, is that she was deliberately poisoned. So the relevant question to ask, Mr. Starrunner, is where does she come from?" The agent turned on me with a glare that said I should have asked this question *before* I decided to bring the children to Ponce de Leon on my ship.

And I should have. I admit it.

But I hadn't.

I said feebly, "They're from Gvm Uye Sachttra …"

The agent nodded, correctly taking this as a measure of my ignorance. The fact was, I made a point of staying informed … but there's *so much* information. It was a full-time job just to stay up-to-date on the hundred-odd planets I visited on a semi-regular basis. I knew next to nothing about *other* planets—the hundreds, or it could be thousands for all I knew, of planets where humanity was thriving, or struggling, or had never gotten a foothold, or had gotten a foothold and was now losing it, sinking into the wretched death spiral of colony failure, with no one even watching except maybe some Travellers waiting for them to get weak enough to take.

I assumed that was the sort of place the humans on Gvm Uye Sachttra came from. I had assumed they were lucky to even be where they were. Most of them had acted like it.

Hesitantly, I leaned forward to the intercom and said to Pippa: "Where *do* you come from?"

She didn't answer. She had buried her face in her hands. She was sobbing wildly.

"Weren't you born in that camp?"

She went on crying. Jan awkwardly patted her back. Leaf lay across Pippa's knees with her head wedged in between Pippa's lap and her upper body, her dark hair mingling with the curtain of Pippa's fair locks, sucking on the hem of her tunic.

"They won't tell us, either," the asylum agent said.

I went on staring through the glass at the kids, wondering what horrors lay locked in their past.

"It's unfortunate. However …" The agent's voice shifted abruptly into her impersonal phone register. "We do have to discuss the issue of deportation costs for the two younger children. The older girl will be deported at government expense …"

"To where?"

"Yesanyase Skont."

"Heard of it," I said grimly.

"The other two children, however, are not eligible for government-sponsored deportation. If you wish to assume the cost ..."

Still lost in horrified speculation about what kind of cannibalistic dystopia the children might have been born into, I stared blankly at the asylum agent as she continued to spout her bureaucratese. Eventually it clicked. She was saying that I was responsible for Jan and Leaf. If I didn't pay for them to be deported, they would be given asylum willy-nilly. They would receive care, shelter, and schooling—ironically, just what the three kids had yearned for.

"But we don't want to stay here if Pippa can't," Jan shouted, grabbing the mic on their side of the glass. "We want to go with her."

"How much is it?" I said dazedly.

The agent named a figure I would blush to charge my most credulous client for a full load.

"You gotta be kidding," I said.

It was all too much to take in, and I was almost grateful when my phone rang. It was Dolph.

"Yo," I said, turning away from the asylum agent. "You're not gonna believe what just happened."

"Whatever," he cut across my voice. "Where are you?"

I glanced around the bleak visiting room. "In hell."

"Phone says you're in the, what's this, detention center—"

"That's what I said."

"Whatever," Dolph said again. He was worked up, talking fast. "How quick can you get here?"

21

HOWEVER quick I could get there wouldn't have been quick enough for Dolph, so I told him to tell me what had happened as I drove.

"It was Kaspar Silverback."

"Who's he?"

"He came to pick up the toy fairies."

I slammed my palm on the horn. I was queueing at customs to get off Space Island. Twenty lanes, and my queue seemed to be the only one that wasn't moving. "Yeah, but who *is* he?"

"Kaspar *Silverback,*" Dolph crackled. He was somewhere ahead of me, on Space Highway, following this Silverback character back towards Mag-Ingat. He would be using the wireless headset built into his bike helmet, which always had poor sound quality, although you couldn't tell Dolph that. He had built it himself. Had to, as it's illegal to use a phone while operating a motorcycle.

It is not illegal to use a phone while driving a truck, since even a janky old truck like mine can drive itself. I knelt up on the seat and stuck my head and shoulders out of the window to see if someone ahead of me had got nabbed by customs, which would explain the delay. "Silverback sounds like a gorilla."

"He's a gorilla like Seagrave is a walrus," Dolph said. Fair point. Neither Irene nor Rex were marine Shifters; it was just that someone in Rex's ancestral line at some point had been, and their descendants kept the name. If you don't like your family name, you have the option of renaming yourself something like Starrunner.

"So this Silverback is a what?"

"He's a fucking idiot," Dolph cackled. "He's driving at five miles under the speed limit. Cars are *screaming* at him. He's probably the reason you're stuck in traffic." At that moment my queue finally got rolling. I cruised towards customs, a gigantic building spanning the outbound lanes of the highway before you get to Space Bridge. Twenty green arches and ten red ones, all of them as black as the pit of hell in the blazing sunlight. "He's a bear, of course," Dolph said. "None of that gang can drive for shit."

"He works for Mujin Inc?"

"He had corporate ID. It checked out on Bizlinks and everything. He was plenty pissed that I made him wait."

"Did he notice that one of the crates had been opened?"

"If he did, he didn't say anything about it."

"I assume he went through customs with them?"

"Green lane. I was right behind him."

"Hang on," I said. "I'm going through now."

The pit of hell swallowed my truck. All outgoing traffic must pass through customs, no exceptions. Weak light revealed a short tunnel with a metal floor and ceiling. The customs AI took over the controls of my truck and edged it forward into scanning position. "Please wait," a voice announced from the truck's speakers, and then I heard two heavy, clanking booms as automated portcullises slammed down in front of the truck and behind it, trapping me in place. A high thin whining noise filled the cab. I knew that scanners were non-invasively inspecting me and my truck down to the atomic level.

"Thank you," the AI's voice droned. The portcullis in front of me rose into the ceiling. I got control of the truck back, and drove out onto Space Bridge.

"OK, I'm through," I said to Dolph. "What were you saying?"

"Silverback cleared customs with no issues. But that don't necessarily mean anything."

"Yeah." The customs system is very high-tech, but for every high-tech system there is an equal and opposite hack. Everyone knew that Parsec occasionally, or frequently, managed to sneak contraband through customs. We suspected he had a contact in there who would turn off the scanners for him in exchange for a kickback. Amateurs hack systems; pros hack the humans operating them.

"There could be anything in those crates," Dolph said. "Data is my guess. We know Parsec has pulled that kind of heist before."

"Yeah." Data is the most valuable kind of contraband, and the easiest to conceal. For that, they wouldn't have even needed to hack the customs.

"Split the IP into nine thousand pieces. Hide it in the toy fairies' operating systems ..."

I remembered that moment in the cargo hold when I had been illogically convinced that *something* was looking back at me from that toy fairy's plastic eyes. I had almost pulled my gun on the damn thing. I pushed the memory away. No doubt Dolph was right. *All* that the fairies contained was portions of some insanely valuable, illegally obtained IP that Parsec had been planning to sell, through his front company, to Rafael Ijiuto, who'd then have sold it on to some damn gang of aliens.

I merged off the bridge onto Space Highway and picked up speed. The thrill of the chase kicked in. The wind from the open window whipped my hair.

"OK," I said, thinking aloud. "So we'll pay a little visit to Mujin Inc. Let Parsec know we're onto them."

"And give his minions a scare," Dolph crackled. "Those bears have had it coming for a long time."

"Where you at now?"

"Gillietown. Gonna take all freaking day to get back to the city. This guy thinks he's driving a schoolbus."

"I'll catch up with you." On my left, the jungly heights of Cape Agreste raked back from the road, steep and verdant. On my right, the bay sparkled. Mag-Ingat reared at the distant head of the bay, the tallest buildings of uptown seeming to spear the sky, coming in and out of view as the highway curved around the natural irregularities of the headland. Overhead, a stream of flying cars zipped along the air corridor that tracked the highway. I would normally consider myself an air person, not a ground person, and I was jealous of anyone who could afford a flying car. But sometimes a drive was just what the doctor ordered. The deathly gloom of the detention center faded behind me as I gunned the truck faster.

Back in Mag-Ingat, Kaspar Silverback exited onto Upperway. By this time I'd caught up with him and Dolph. I stayed way back—my truck was as generic as they came, a dirty white bullet like a million others, but Parsec would probably recognize it, which meant Silverback might, too. Dolph, anonymous on his bike, kept Silverback's truck in sight.

"He's turning onto Bonsucesso," Dolph crackled.

"Roger." I took manual control and spun my truck around an arched claw of reinforced concrete dug deep into the bedrock. Most of the uptown skyscrapers stand on legs, like old-fashioned rockets. This permits more buildings to stand *under* them. The four-legged base of this building, Bonsucesso Tower, sheltered a drab cluster of three- and four-storey office blocks. People wandered in and out of mom 'n' pop ramen joints and dry-cleaning places at street level.

"He's indicating," Dolph said as I emerged out of Bonsucesso Tower's shadow into the sunlight. "He's going into the tower." As he spoke, I saw the small shape of Dolph's bike zoom up a curving ramp, like the opening of a nautilus shell, into the bowels of Bonsucesso Tower. One of the trucks ahead of him would be Silverback's.

I turned onto the ramp and drove up into the parking lot. Dolph guided me to the third level.

We hid behind my truck and watched Kaspar Silverback, at the other end of the floor, unload the familiar crates of toy fairies onto a dolly. He had no robotic help. Nor human help, come to that. If Silverback was a Parsec minion, he had to be the most peripheral and poorly-equipped of all the Bad-News Bears ... "or the most *dispensable* one," Dolph hissed. "I'll Shift. You stay human. That way we got all the angles covered."

I glanced uneasily around the parking lot. "Too many normies. Wait until we get upstairs. Then we'll Shift and kick their asses until they talk."

We got into the elevator and rose up, up, up. Some people got on and off at the mall levels. After that we rose alone, first through blackness and then through air. The Bonsucesso Tower elevators travelled on the outside of the building's core, so we had a dizzying view of the other spires of uptown, and beyond that, the hills speckled with suburban communities like the one where I used to live. I felt a pang of wistfulness. The sunlight on the hills had turned red-gold. It was getting on for evening, and in Shiftertown Lucy was waiting for me to come home. I'd promised her a table-top barbecue for supper, just the two of us.

The elevator stopped at the 121st floor.

We stepped into a dim, mirror-walled hall.

Touch-sensitive flooring tiles changed color when we trod on them, so we left a trail of rainbow squares.

There was no sign of Kaspar Silverback, or anyone else, in the hall, or behind the black sweep of reception desk we could see through doors at the far end of it.

"I don't like this," Dolph muttered. His voice echoed so loudly, through some trick of the acoustics, that we both jumped.

"Crappy corporate décor is a matter of personal choice," I said. *Choice ... choice ... choice ...* the echo repeated.

We walked into the lobby. On the reception desk sat a large civic award trophy in the shape of a frosted glass Ponce de Leon. There was also a bell to summon a receptionist. I shrugged, and rang it. Echoes travelled through the lobby and bounced back from the hall.

A door behind the end of the long desk opened, revealing a glimpse of brightly-lit office activity. A woman in immaculate business attire came out. "Can I help you?" she said.

The inside of my head went blank.

It was Sophia.

22

Sophia. She didn't seem to recognize me. I doubted my own sanity for an instant. "Can I help you?" she said again. Then I knew for sure. That low, musical voice, now tinged with impatience ... it was her.

Her hair—that fascinating shade of dark brown that's *almost* black —curled around her white neck. It was cut shorter than it used to be. A rose tattoo curled up the side of her neck to her jaw. The ink was new; perhaps it was a legacy of her time with the Travellers. Her wrap dress, made of some stiff fabric that looked like dull green paper, accentuated her cleavage with a deep V-neck. Her waist was so tiny, you'd be forgiven for assuming she'd never given birth. She was as stunning as ever.

And she didn't recognize me.

I clutched the edge of the reception desk, desperately trying to get a handle on my emotions so I could *think,* instead of just feeling all the pain and anger she had left in my heart.

Dolph shot a worried glance at me, and then smiled at Sophia. If you knew him, that smile would make you run. But she never had known him that well. "Long time no see," he said. "Why's a nice girl like you working for a sketchy outfit like this?"

Sophia looked irritated. "I knew you'd track me down sooner or later," she said. "Mike, I guess this was your idea?"

So she hadn't forgotten me. She just … didn't care. To her, I was no more than an annoying former acquaintance.

"You owe him an explanation," Dolph said, making it worse.

"I don't owe him anything," Sophia said. "And if you're going to go all Shifter on me, I'll have to ask you to leave."

The threat jarred words out of me. "I heard you left the life." As soon as the words were out, I could have kicked myself. There was no need for her to know I'd been talking to Zane.

But instead of asking where I heard that, she glanced back at the door she'd come through. "Yeah, it wasn't for me," she said, using the exact same words Zane had. Her expression betrayed a hint of discomfort. My brain started working again, and I realized that her coworkers didn't know about her fling with the Travellers. And she would not want them to. I had something I could hold over her head. "But discussing ancient history probably isn't something you want to do," she said, in a classic Sophia move: attack to defend. She was referring to the early days of Uni-Ex Shipping. Believe it or not, I used to do *really* dirty shit. That was before I got married. Before Lucy. Sophia knew about a lot of that stuff.

"So now you're working as an uptown receptionist?" Dolph said, with a glance around the sparsely decorated lobby. "Guess money isn't everything, after all."

Sophia laughed. "Office manager, actually," she said. "We're light-staffed. Just getting off the ground. But you're right. Money *isn't* everything. I know you understand that, Dolph. You never cared about the money. You're only in it to punish … yourself." Jesus. Maybe she knew him better than I had thought she did. She stuck that knife in with a little smile, and turned to me, leaving Dolph spluttering. "But *you* still don't get it, do you, Mike? Newsflash, honey." She had never called me *honey* while we were married. It had a distancing effect. "Money can't buy you what you really want."

I cleared my throat. "Money's nothing to me," I said. "Nothing. Lucy is my everything."

"Who?" Sophia said.

I couldn't believe it. *"Lucy.* Your daughter."

"Oh. Of course. I always think of her as Elspeth." Sophia's jaw tightened in irritation at her slip.

Elspeth had been Lucy's middle name, chosen by Sophia. I'd had it deleted from Lucy's ID after the divorce. That was a matter of public record.

Sophia had never even bothered to look it up.

My anger came out in a soft, wondering tone. "How could you abandon your own child? It's not about me. Jeez. I don't matter. How could you do that to her?"

Sophia's mask of forgetting clicked back into place. "If you don't get it, I can't explain it to you. There are more important things in life, OK? Being a mother was not my—my destiny."

"Well, *whoopsies,*" I said. I was getting really angry now. I leaned over the desk. "Maybe you should have thought about that before you said yes." There were no rings on her fingers now. Not even a tan line where my ring had been.

"People are allowed to make mistakes, Mike! Jesus!" For a minute, I saw the old Sophia fire that had fueled endless arguments between us. Passionate arguments, that ended in bed … at least to begin with. Mostly about money, and what was permissible to do to get it. But we had both moved on from that now. She was right about that, anyway. She switched back into professional mode and took a step sideways. "Are you going to leave, or do I have to call the police?"

Dolph flinched. "C'mon, Mike."

But I had seen something else. I was leaning on the desk, my whole body angled towards Sophia, otherwise I wouldn't have seen it. Her hand stole towards a shelf under the desk. On that shelf, a dull glint of metal.

She was reaching for a gun.

I straightened up and took a step back. "You know what, I almost forgot why we came up here in the first place," I said.

Sophia froze. "Why?"

"We were trying to get a taxi," I said, breaking out my professional-grade smile. "This is a taxi company, right, Dolph? My truck broke down, and we need a ride back to Shiftertown."

"You still have that old truck?" Sophia said.

"Yup, still holding it together with elastic bands and spit. But I feel like taking a ride in a flying car today."

"You can't afford our cars," she said. But she moved away from the desk. From the place where the gun was.

"Maybe I'm doing better than you think I am," I bullshitted. "How about it? We're customers; you gonna turn us down? That ain't the start-up spirit." I wanted to know what they were *really* doing here. I didn't believe there was a single taxi in the place.

But I was wrong about that. "All right," Sophia said. "If that's what it takes to get rid of you." She marched to a door at the far end of the reception desk and flung it open.

Daylight flooded in from a garage. And what a garage. Taking up half of the whole 121st floor, it had three huge bays open to a stunning view of downtown Mag-Ingat and the bay. People pay millions for uptown condos with this kind of view, and Mujin Inc was wasting it on taxis.

Six taxis, to be precise. The gleaming SUV-sized vehicles stood here and there on the concrete floor. The garage was practically empty.

Except for our—that is, Mujin Inc's—crates of toy fairies, which were stacked to the right of the door, still on the dolly which we had seen Kaspar Silverback load them onto.

Of Silverback himself there was no sign.

"Take your pick," Sophia said. "And if you come around here again, I really will call the police."

Dolph shrugged. He told me later that he just wanted to get out of there before Sophia followed through on her threat to call the cops. He had not seen the gun under the reception desk, which proved that she was never going to call the cops—she was just bluffing. He walked into the garage, and I followed slowly, looking all around. Sophia stood behind us in the door to reception with her arms folded.

The taxis were all different makes and colors. Dolph, of course, gravitated to the best of the bunch, a sporty white Skyliner.

Charging stands, cleaning hoses, drains to let the water run away. It all looked normal …

Dolph opened the Skyliner's driver side door. "Come on," he said, shrugging.

At that moment a distant toilet flushed.

A door in the back wall clunked, and Kaspar Silverback walked out, drying his hands on his jeans.

I knew it was Silverback by the way he reacted to the sight of us, although I'd never met him before. He was smaller than your average bear, with a paunch and a bald spot.

He growled at Dolph, "What the heck are *you* doing here?"

"That's what I was going to ask you, asshole," Dolph said.

Silverback turned to Sophia. "Why'd you let these guys in?"

"It's complicated," Sophia said. She looked thrown. She must not have been aware that the toy fairies had been shipped on the *St. Clare*. Then again, I hadn't had the *St. Clare* when we were together, so she could have seen the ship's name without realizing it was me. "Do you know them?"

"They're dogs!" Silverback spat. That was all he knew. Dolph's jackal isn't even his primary form. He strutted towards us. He was outnumbered, but I soon saw why he acted so confident. He had a gun. It was in his waistband, but I could tell it was there by the squared-off bulge in his plaid shirt, which he wore untucked, a giveaway in itself.

What the hell was Parsec into here?

"Back off," Dolph warned him.

Silverback did not back off. "You followed me from the spaceport, didn't you? What gives?"

I said soothingly, "Just making sure the cargo was successfully returned to sender. Satisfaction guaranteed, that's my motto. I know Mr. Parsec is personally concerned about this particular shipment."

This was a pure shot in the dark. But it had a surprising effect. Silverback stopped approaching us. He glanced at the crates of fairies, and then scowled in confusion. "The boss brought *you* in?" Emphasis on *you,* like I was the last person Parsec would ever bring in on anything. Which was probably correct.

"Sure did," I said. "You weren't aware?"

"I gotta call him," Silverback said, taking out his phone. His other hand hovered near the gun in his waistband.

"Mike," Dolph said. "Let's go."

"In a minute," I said.

"Let's *go,*" Dolph repeated. He plopped into the Skyliner. The passenger side door sprang open, almost clipping my nose. I jumped back —and it was just as well I did, because the next second I heard a gunshot, and a bullet crunched into the open passenger door, making it bounce on its hinges.

Dolph told me later that while I was talking to Silverback, he'd been watching Sophia. That's how he saw another bear coming through the door behind her.

It was Canuck.

On paper, at least, Canuck was the owner of Mujin Inc, and it had given him a confidence never before displayed in his furtive, violent doings around Shiftertown. He wore an open-collared shirt under a blazer, with diamond stick-pins in the lapels, like he was some big shot now. When he saw me and Dolph, he checked, edged sideways, and propped his shoulders against the wall. He folded his arms and smirked at Dolph across the garage.

Then Dolph saw Canuck's gun hand sneaking inside his blazer. As Dolph said, "Let's go" for the first time, Canuck's hand was closing on the grip of his shoulder-holstered rig. As he said "Let's go" again, Canuck drew and fired.

With the report still ringing in my ears, I leapt into the Skyliner's passenger seat. A second bullet snatched the door out of my hand as I tried to close it.

Canuck crab-walked across the garage, shooting at the taxi. We had our heads down, but I glimpsed something in the rearview that made me feel sick. All the time this was going down, Sophia just stood there, frowning slightly, her head swivelling to follow the action, like a person watching animals fight. Or insects. Yeah, she watched us like we were insects.

My door finally managed to close. "Where to?" the taxi asked pleasantly.

"St. Andrew's Pier, and step on it," Dolph yelled.

"Certainly, sir."

The Skyliner accelerated forward.

Canuck broke into a sprint, with slow-reacting Silverback a few feet behind him. Now both of them were shooting at the taxi. Rounds thudded into the bodywork.

The force field in the nearest bay popped open automatically for just as long as it took the Skyliner to squirt through.

We plunged into the air, 400 meters above uptown.

23

THE taxi's shocks muffled the jolt as our levitation field expanded. A split second into our fall, it was no longer a fall but the characteristic rollercoaster swoop of a flying-car launch from a high point. Leaving our stomachs behind, the taxi quickly levelled out and rose towards the nearest skyway.

"I can't believe it," I said. "I can't believe it. What's she doing here?"

"Working for Parsec," Dolph said. "Obviously."

"It's so stupid. She comes from Montemayor." Montemayor is one of humanity's other Heartworlds in the Cluster, a wealthy and sophisticated planet. Sophia had wanted for nothing as a child. "She could do anything she likes."

Dolph gave me a brief glance of pity. "Such as working a good job in a glitzy office, a little bit gray-zone to keep it exciting?"

I rubbed my hands over my face. Then I looked up at the sky above and all around us. I've ridden in flying cars plenty of times, but it always freaked me out to be flying without the rattle and roar of a spaceship drive. The fan ducting airflow over the aerofoils beneath the car made only a soft whooshing noise. I leaned across to make sure the Stirling engine powering our forward motion was actually on.

"Get off," Dolph said, blocking me with one arm.

"You can't *drive* this thing. It's self-driving."

"Yes, I can. It's manual mode enabled." Dolph gunned the engine to prove it. We merged into the southbound skyway faster than was wise.

Of course, the reason even self-driving cars have controls is because some people like to, well, control their ride. But the AI is always there, waiting to step in and take over if you do anything dangerous. I glanced back at Bonsucesso Tower, reflecting that our taxi was still under Sophia's control. She could turn us around and bring us back to face the bears if she wanted to.

But apparently the bears had other ideas.

A glittery object tumbled out of an upper window.

It rapidly levelled out and flew straight towards us.

"Don't look now," I said, "but we're about to have company."

Dolph swore filthily. Then he said, "If Silverback drives that taxi like he drives his truck, I should slow down just to give them a fair chance."

"They're punching it," I said. "It's probably Canuck. He's not even in the goddamn skyway."

"I hate that guy," Dolph said. "He crashed Marie's birthday party. Remember?" Marie was a girl Dolph dated off again, on again, when he wasn't playing away with big-bosomed showgirls. "He pissed in her sister's closet. He was so drunk he thought it was the toilet."

"Classy."

"He even got thrown out of St. Patrick's one time."

"I didn't hear about that."

"They were filming snuff videos in the graveyard."

"You're kidding."

"Word to God. I heard he's into the ripper scene."

"I don't even want to know what that is," I said wearily.

Dolph rolled down the window. That wasn't as reckless a move as it sounds like. We were half a kilometer up, but flying cars don't actually go that fast—50 klicks an hour, tops, even if you're really punching it like Dolph was. Air rushed into the car, but the Skyliner barely wobbled as the AI angled the aerofoils to compensate. "Hey," Dolph yelled out of the window. "That the fastest you can go? Eat my exhaust!"

"Dolph …" I trailed off. I had known him long enough to know there was no reasoning with him in this mood. We had been expecting a teeth-and-claws fight. The bears had turned it into a gunfight. We might have got away, but Dolph was not going to forgive them for having made him feel stupid.

He closed the window and juiced a few more rpms out of the Stirling engine. I looked back again. Canuck and Silverback were catching up with us, because they were cutting across the curve of the skyway. That was illegal. The AI is supposed to make sure you stay in your corridor. Their taxi, too, was clearly on manual. It might even be jailbroken— the term means disabling the AI's drive controls, so it can't tell you no.

By now we'd left uptown behind. The streets and buildings shrank below us as the skyway passed high over downtown at the north end of the beach. From here the westbound stream of flying cars split into two: one half followed Space Highway out along Cape Agreste, and the other crossed the bay towards Mag-Ingat Harbor. A small number of vehicles peeled off onto a third route that tracked the beach a couple of hundred meters offshore.

That was supposed to be our route, but the bears had timed it perfectly to cut us off.

"Let's see how big their balls are," Dolph said. He yanked the wheel over hard, turning us onto a collision course with the bears' taxi.

"Jesus, Dolph!" I leaned over and wrestled him for the wheel.

"Fasten your seatbelt," he howled. "I got this—"

I had just time to check my seatbelt before the jolt hit.

There's a reason midair collisions never happen.

The technology makes it impossible.

Not AI control, but something more fundamental: the actual levitation fields that keep flying cars in the air.

These fields are the same force fields you use to keep bugs and burglars out of your yard—if you're rich—or to deflect space gravel from the nose of your spaceship. Expand a force field into a bubble 30 meters in diameter. Hey presto, you've got 14,000 m3 of vacuum lifting your car straight up. Shrink or expand the bubble to go lower or higher. And that bubble is also an invisible buffer keeping your car 30 meters away from everyone else's.

So when we were 30 meters from the other taxi, our force field hit theirs with a spongy kind of jolt. It threw us back in our seats. My teeth clicked together.

The two taxis started to slide past one another, 30 meters apart, the force fields repelling one another while the engines drove them forward.

Our levitation field had T-boned theirs. If they wanted to escape the collision, they could've just accelerated to let us slip past their tail.

Instead they turned into the collision, bringing us head to head.

"Oh, you wanna play chicken?" Dolph grunted. He fought the wheel as the auto-steering sought to bend us out of the collision. Our engine fans whined, revving but going nowhere.

I could see Canuck glaring at us through the windshield of their taxi. Silverback was rolling down his window, the one nearest us, on my side.

Suddenly, our levitation field pushed past theirs. Our taxi shot forward.

Silverback leaned out of his window, gun in his hands.

I automatically ducked to put my head below the level of my window.

I was now looking at the underside of my own seat. There was a gun velcroed to it.

Without thinking, I snatched it up. It was a small conventional automatic, the kind of piece we used to prize on Tech Duinn for concealed carry. I racked the slide one-handed, while hitting the window-open button with my other hand. I straightened up and twisted in my seatbelt. The window began to open. We were drawing level with the other taxi. I poked the snub nose of my own weapon out of the window as soon as there was room for it, and sighted down the barrel on Silverback's face. I fired. The muzzle of Silverback's gun flashed. I hardly registered it. My breathing was steady. So was my weapon. I fired twice more. Silverback's weapon flew up and he slumped forwards, half in and half out of his taxi. It all seemed to take ages but it could only have been a matter of seconds before we shot past the other taxi, and I no longer had a target.

I fell back in my seat. Wind buffetted my face from the open window. Dolph yelled, "Got him, got him," and thumped the wheel in exultation. "Where'd that come from?" He grabbed the gun off my lap and looked at it. It was a Blackbird, no markings.

"It was under the seat," I said. "Oh God, I think I killed him." I took the gun back from Dolph. My window was still open. We were in the beach skyway, cruising a kilometer up. I dropped the Blackbird out of the window. It fell invisibly into the sparkling sea.

"That was a good gun," Dolph said, but he made no further comment. He knew as well as I did that you don't hang onto a gun you just shot someone with.

I looked back. The bears' taxi was swooping towards downtown in what looked like an emergency descent. "They're going down." I wondered if I had hit Canuck, as well. I didn't think so.

"What was their goddamn game?" Dolph said. "They coulda killed us." He touched my knee. "Mike, they were going to kill us."

"Yeah," I said. "And what's gonna happen when Parsec finds out I killed him?"

A few seconds later, that was the least of my worries.

"I am effecting an immediate landing," our taxi suddenly said. Its voice was still mellifluous, but the words coming from its speakers were no longer customer-cosseting verbiage. We started to lose altitude. Dolph cursed, and pulled the wheel back, to no effect. "I have been placed under the control of the Ponce de Leon Police Department.

Remain in your seats with your hands visible until I come to a complete stop."

I glanced in the rearview. Behind and above us, two sleek black-and-white cop cars dived out of the sun.

"Well, who knew?" I said with heavy sarcasm. "You *can't* shoot someone, in heavy traffic, in broad freaking daylight, and get away with it."

"God*damn!*" Dolph said. *"Goddamn* Parsec! I'm going to chew his fucking nuts off ... I'm gonna ..."

"Hush," I said leadenly, as the cop cars swooped close enough for us to see the glaring officers at their gun turrets.

24

THE cop cars tailed us closely as our taxi sought somewhere to land. Both the beach and the Strip were equally crowded, no place to put down, so we ended up landing at our original destination: St. Andrew's Pier. There was a pick-up and drop-off point for flying cars between the funfair and the cluster of restaurants at the end of the pier.

Our taxi set itself down with AI-guided precision in one of the marked-out squares, near the Ferris wheel.

The cop cars landed in the nearest two available places.

Dolph and I sat unmoving.

Neither of us spoke a word. Dolph's jaw was knotted, his eyes cloudy with anger and frustration.

Self-disgust boiled in my gut. I'd shot at Kaspar Silverback without a second thought, hell, without a *first* one—just pure reflex. That was the Tech Duinn veteran in me. He was me, but I couldn't accept that he was the *real* me, the businessman and father who just wanted to make a decent living. And sometimes, like now, it felt like he was out to destroy me.

The cops sauntered over and told us to get out. We assumed the position. They searched us. People stared. They didn't find anything apart from our phones, which they took.

Then they handcuffed us.

I swallowed back the indignity and forced myself to speak. I knew I had only one card to play. "Call Captain d'Alencon," I said. "Give him my name. I ain't talking to anyone else." Slouched, defiant posture: check. Witless yet cunning expresion, with a glimpse of teeth: check. I was showing them what they already expected to see—a Shifter.

The cops went back to their cars and talked amongst themselves. The biggest and youngest officer stayed to guard us. His eyes glared pure poison.

"You try and Shift," he said, patting his gun, "ain't gonna be enough left of y'all to make a fur rug."

What did he think we were, idiots?

Don't answer that.

Time passed, and I needed to take a leak, but I didn't say anything. Every car that blotted out the sun raised my hopes, only for them to plummet again. But then it *was* a cop car, and it *was* Jose-Maria d'Alencon getting out of it and coming across to us.

I corralled my surge of relief. Just because he'd come didn't mean anything. "Captain," I said sycophantically, "good to see you." I didn't dare call him "Bones," not with that hard glint in his eyes.

"Mike," he said, and blew out his breath tiredly. "Dolph. What the heck y'all been doing now?"

I held out my cuffed hands. "J-M, can you tell your boys to at least let me take a leak?"

Laughter. They took off the handcuffs. I unzipped and took a piss right there, on the wheel of the taxi.

"Buzz Parsec ain't going to be too pleased about that," one of the other officers said. So they had already looked into the taxi's ownership record and traced it back to Canuck.

"Buzz Parsec can suck my dick." I gestured to Dolph, wordlessly asking them to uncuff him, as well. Getting D'Alencon's OK, they did. Dolph watched me warily past their shoulders—he wasn't sure where I was going with this.

Neither was I. I first had to find out how bad it was. I waited, and Bones told us.

"That guy you shot? He's on his way to hospital right now. He's gonna make it, looks like."

A grin of genuine relief spread across my face. Wounded wasn't as bad as dead.

"You need to work on your aim," d'Alencon added, with a wink.

Ho, ho, ho. The other officers appreciated the captain's quip, and I played up: "From a moving car, with a piece-of-crap handgun like we used to toss in the scrap box on Tech D? I did pretty good winging him." I pointed to the bullet holes in our taxi's bodywork. "But they started it. That's God's truth."

"That taxi belongs to Buzz Parsec," d'Alencon said, pronouncing my rival's name with about as much affection as Dolph would.

"It does?" I said.

"Yup. That one and the one the other guys were in. Both of 'em registered to Trident Overland."

Surprise quickly gave way to understanding. Trident Overland was Parsec's ground freight company. Yup, the bastard had a claw in the trucking industry, as well as a sideline in used flying cars. Thinking about it, all the taxis in the Mujin Inc. garage probably came from Trident Overland. He would have sold or leased them to Canuck, i .e. to himself. The mismatched nature of the fleet reflected the opportunistic, cobbled-together ethos of Parsec's operations: something old, something new, something stolen, something smuggled. Someone else's wife ...

"Can't you just steer clear of him, Mike?" d'Alencon said, with exasperation in his tone.

I thought for a minute before answering. "I'm sorry for today's incident. I'd apologize to him, as well, if he was standing here in front of me." Mentally, I had my fingers crossed behind my back. I'd apologize to Buzz Parsec when hell froze over. "I wish to God he'd leave me and mine alone. But if he can't leave me alone, I'm gonna have to defend myself. And that's what happened today."

D'Alencon half-smiled, but not in a good way. That was the response he'd expected, not the response he'd wanted. "You're killing me here, Mike. After what happened the other day, I was ready to recommend you for a citizen of the year award. Then you gotta pull some shit like this."

I hung my head, scratched the back of my neck. Dolph nibbled his fingernails. We were playing up to the Shifter stereotype, not as blatantly as I'd performed for the first officer I spoke to, but checking all the boxes nonetheless. Unreliable. Chronically violent. No trust in the authorities. Hopelessly prone to fighting among ourselves. We were collaborating in our own humiliation, to escape justice and the duties of friendship. You don't question wild animals. What would be the point?

An officer walked away to take a call, then pulled d'Alencon aside. When Bones came back, the tension dropped by a notch or two. "Kaspar Silverback is refusing to press charges," he said.

Dolph let out a jackally cough.

"And Tomas Feirweather, alias Canuck, is refusing to say one word to us."

I kept my face blank. Inside, I was beaming.

"So we got no option but to let this go," Bones said with pretend severity, although I could see that part of him, the part that wasn't a police captain, was pleased. "On that understanding, do you want to change your mind?" He crooked a finger at his lieutenant, who tossed our phones back to us. "Talk to me, Mike. Tell me about that business up in Bonsucesso Tower, the taxi company. If Parsec's getting into the VIP chartered car market, the VIPs of Mag-Ingat need to be warned."

I smiled, but shook my head. A part of me felt regret. The thought of Ponce de Leon's finest raiding Mujin Inc was attractive. But on what grounds, anyway? We had not seen anything illegal. We had not even seen anything unusual ... except my ex-wife. And although I owed her nothing, I couldn't sic the cops onto her.

Thus I justified my refusal to talk, which was actually founded on a much simpler rationale. Much as Parsec's bears detested me, they hadn't squealed on me, so I could not squeal on them.

"Sorry, Bones," I said. "There's nothing to say,"

"What you mean is you can't say nothin'," d'Alencon said with weary asperity. *"Shifters.* All right, get the fuck outta my volume."

*

Dolph and I did as we were told, keeping our gait to a relaxed stroll until we were out of the officers' view. Then we walked fast through the funfair. We kept walking until we reached Snakey's, on the Strip between 60th and 61st. We stumbled into the dim, dusty afternoon coolness, and slumped at the bar. Vipe's eldest daughter brought our drinks without being asked: a double shot of bourbon for me, beer with a shot for Dolph.

"Jesus fuck," Dolph said. "I thought we were screwed there."

"Me, too."

"Those fucking bears." Dolph's knuckles were white on his shot glass as he tipped it into his beer. I nodded.

It's considered low-class among Shifters to posse up with your own kind—that's why we looked down on the bears. But we did it, too. We just had different tribal markers.

"I wish I knew how long she's been working for him," I said. I couldn't get my head around the possibility that Sophia might have been living in Mag-Ingat for years, never coming near me and Lucy. Not even *curious.*

"It wouldn't take long for her to feed him a bunch of bullshit about us," Dolph said grimly.

"She wouldn't do that," I said. "She wouldn't *bother.* You saw how she was."

"Yeah." Dolph sounded unconvinced. "But what happens if Bones busts them?"

"He won't," I said. "This is Shiftertown." I held up my glass to catch the sunlight coming through the window. It made the bourbon glow like amber. "We solve our own problems."

"Damn straight," Vipe's girl said, drying glasses.

Dolph laughed hollowly. He took out his phone and began to manipulate the graphical interface of the AI assistant. I couldn't follow what he was doing. The information environment of Ponce de Leon is dense, fast-paced, and slippery, constantly in flux as vast swathes of data are hidden and restored by warring privacy protocols. Neither Dolph nor I had grown up with this. San Damiano is a whole different kind of place, where information in general stays put, like people. But Dolph had developed a gift for finding gold in the zettabyte-scale rivers of data flowing around Ponce de Leon.

I sat there sipping my bourbon. It was a woodsy, well-rounded spirit from Alvarado, but its heat did not dispel the coldness inside me. I was thinking about what came next. Maybe I could go back to Mujin Inc. Try and have a civil conversation with her. Apologize. I would surely never apologize to Parsec, but to her, I could ...

"Look at this," Dolph said. He seemed more cheerful now. I soon understood why. He, too, had been thinking about what came next, and had found his own answer to the question. He showed me a picture on his phone. It was a wide-muzzled handgun.

"Koiler?" I said.

"Mark Three. Threaded for a suppressor. Some guy down on Armstrong and 5th is selling it."

"Nice. Does it come with ammo?"

"Five hundred rounds." Dolph made kissy lips at the screen. "I might go down there and have a look at it."

On Ponce de Leon, the sale of firearms is illegal, but possession of them isn't. Yeah, I know, it makes a whole lot of sense.

"See if they have anything else as well," I said, remembering the gun under Sophia's desk.

"Will do." Dolph finished his beer. "Matter of fact, I think I'll head down there now."

I swirled the dregs of my bourbon around the glass. "How are you getting there?"

"Walk. I'll pick up my bike tomorrow."

"I'll give you a ride." I had already summoned my truck back from uptown.

Every human city of size in the Cluster—indeed, in all space from here back to Earth—has its Armstrong Street, named for the first man to walk on the moon. Mag-Ingat's Armstrong Street was a particularly pitiful example of the contrast between our mythologized past and our reality. Junkies obstructed the sidewalk, some of them human and some in wolf, leopard, or lion form. I pulled over in front of the tenement where Dolph's gun guy lived.

Dolph tossed me a salute as he leapt out the cab. I watched him step over a homeless addict's legs and disappear up a flight of stairs half-choked with garbage.

This is Shiftertown. We solve our own problems. Right?

I drove home.

To my surprise, I found Robbie, my new admin officer, sitting on the front porch. Under Nanny B's watchful eye, he was playing a game with Lucy. He had a fancy phone with a holo projector. It lay on the stoop between them, shooting little colorful butterflies into the air. Lucy squealed with laughter as she and Robbie competed to catch the butterflies, their hands battering each other.

"Daddy!" Lucy bounded down the front steps. I picked her up and swung her around, relishing her weight in my arms. She was mine. *Mine.* Not Sophia's. And what she didn't know couldn't hurt her.

I set her down as Robbie came down the steps. "Hi, Mr. Starrunner," he said abashedly. "Rex told me where you live. Since we kind of got cut off earlier, I thought I would come over and see if there was any instructions you had for me?"

I forced my mind back to the topic of work. "Well, we're gonna have to train you," I said. "But you can't really use our systems until you're familiar with the standard accounting AI interfaces. So the first thing you need to do is finish that course. I see you met my daughter," I added. Lucy was pulling on Robbie's arm, trying to get him to come back to their game.

"Yeah, she's a couple years younger than my littlest sister," Robbie said with a grin. "I like kids. I hope it's OK to let her play games?"

"As long as she's done her homework," I said.

"Nanny B said it was OK, so pffft!" Lucy made an exuberant spitting noise at me.

"Pffft," I spat back at her.

"Galactic googleplex pffft!" She was in high spirits. Robbie's company seemed to be good for her.

"I'm gonna go to a café and study after this," Robbie said, gesturing at the backpack he had left on my porch.

I shook my head. "There's no need for you to waste your hard-earned on those overpriced drinks. Why don't you study here? You can sit on the porch, or indoors. And if Lucy interrupts you, just tell her pffft."

"Really, sir? That would be amazing! It's just, at home there's nowhere to sit or anything—"

I forestalled another installment of the Wolfe family's woes. I knew the kind of place they probably lived in. Two concrete rooms with a pile of stinky quilts in the corner. Animals don't need furniture. "It's fine," I said. "Just get that certification." I hesitated. "Oh, one thing." I stepped closer to him and lowered my voice. "You don't have any bears in your family, do you?"

His nostrils widened. I realized he was smelling the booze on my breath, and I leaned back. "No, sir. Bears? Nuh uh. Wolves, a coupla seals, and my mom's a rat. No cheesy jokes, if you don't mind."

"To each their own," I said. "Well, that's good to know."

"Was there any specific reason you asked?"

"Just checking," I said with a wink.

For the next couple of hours Robbie studied in our living-room. I liked having him there, and Lucy was already fond of him. He was a good kid. I wondered if he knew how to use a gun.

25

WE ate upstairs with the Seagraves again. I had promised Lucy a table-top barbecue, but I had forgotten to go shopping for the meat, and anyway I needed to tell Irene and Rex what had happened today.

To make sure of their undivided attention, I asked Nanny B to come up and help out with Kit. His beleaguered parents appreciated the extra pair of hands, or rather manipulators.

While we prepared spaghetti bolognese, with the kids safely occupied in the other room, I told them about our skirmish with the bears. I couldn't avoid mentioning Sophia, but the topic was mercifully cut short by Lucy and Mia charging into the kitchen.

"She got her *name* wrong?" Irene said in disbelief.

"What?" Lucy said.

"Nothing, sweetie," I said, giving Irene a level stare over Lucy's head. She got the message.

Dolph joined us after supper. He'd come to show Irene his new piece, and the one he had bought on spec for me. It was a Machina .22 with a slide-mounted safety and adjustable sights, which would take the soft points I still had for my late lamented Midday Special. They all made fun of my new popgun, and Irene pronounced her professional approval of Dolph's new Koiler Mark Three. Dolph said, "Wanna hit the range tomorrow?"

The range was a Shifter-run business, way out in the jungle. Don't ask, don't tell.

"God, I wish I could," Irene said. "I have to go to that thing for their school."

We were sitting out on their balcony. It was just a shelf above my front porch, which we shared with a laundry carousel and an ineffectually juddering A/C unit. Traffic noise seeped up from Shoreside. The children's voices drifted out of the apartment. Lucy and Mia were playing some kind of complicated make-believe game. Nanny B was umpiring a Kit tantrum.

"So, about this uber-bitch," Irene said.

I cut her off. "There's something else I have to tell you guys." I related the story of Pippa's fatal diagnosis and my trip to the detention center.

That shut down the topic of Sophia, all right. The tragic tale left everyone quiet and thoughtful. Rex stretched himself out further on the cool concrete. He was one of those Shifters who spend as much time in their animal form as possible. "That's a hell of a thing," the lion rumbled. "Poor kids."

Irene clapped her hands together on a mosquito. These whining pests are not really Earth mosquitoes—they come from somewhere in the Cluster—but that's what we call them, constantly harking back to our native soil. "I think it's bullcrap," she said.

"I wish it was," I said. "I'm assuming they don't diagnose a teenager with a terminal disease unless they're pretty sure they're right."

"No, I'm sure the diagnosis is right. I mean it's bullcrap that they're going to deport her."

"Kuru is bad shit," Dolph said, uneasily. "We should probably all get tested, just in case."

"Waste of money," Irene said. "We're immune to that kind of stuff."

"Yup," I said. I knew of no scientific backing for our belief that Shifters have superior immune systems, but on the other hand, thousands of us had served on Tech Duinn without catching the rot, while normies dropped like flies around us.

"She shouldn't have to be deported," Irene resumed. "She's got years to live. They might as well be good ones. And there would be no actual danger in letting her stay. It's just that this disease is on their list, so too bad, out she goes."

"Welcome to the kakistocracy," I said.

"I know," Irene said. "But here's the thing. These decisions are made by idiots, so all you have to do is get to the idiots and get them to reverse their decision."

"It's all about who you know," Rex said.

"Exactly," Irene said. "They can always find some loophole to make an exception, if they want to."

I looked at the Seagraves with respect. Shiftertown natives, they had a healthy contempt bred of familiarity for the government. To me, trying to go through the back door to save Pippa from deportation seemed audacious, but to them it was the obvious next step.

"Well, that's dandy," Dolph said. "Why didn't you ever mention you've got a friend in immigration?"

"I don't," Irene said. "The person I'm thinking of is the student life coordinator at Mia and Lucy's school. She's done some work placing refugees with families. Bet you *she* knows someone in immigration."

"Oh, the one who organizes the events?" I said, vaguely recalling an auburn-haired blur of perpetual movement.

"Yeah. Christy."

"Could you talk to her?"

"I could," Irene said. She went quiet for a moment, her gaze far away. Then her large blue eyes focused on me like shotgun barrels. "But I think you should do it, Mike. You're the one who talked to them. Plus it's your name on the forms and everything."

I sighed, and privately acknowledged that I had been trying to push it off onto Irene. I just had so damn many things to worry about. But she was right, it was my job. "OK. I guess if I call the school tomorrow they can put me through to her."

"No, no, you gotta do these things in person," Rex said, raising his chin off the floor. "Here's what you do. I was going to go to this thing tomorrow, but you can go instead of me. Irene's going, too. Christy'll be there, so you can talk to her, and I'll stay home and watch rugby."

I started to say that I couldn't take the time off, but the lion's gaze said it was non-negotiable. I owed Rex at least this much for all the time he spent looking after Lucy when I was away. "OK. I'll do that," I said. "Speaking of rugby, I'm ninety percent sure I'm going to hire Robbie. He seems like a good kid."

"He is," Rex said. "He needs to get better at showing up for practice, but hey, look who's talking."

Irene leaned back against her husband's soft, pale-furred belly. "Listen to that," she said. We could not hear anything except the traffic and the next-door neighbors' music. "The Kitster's wrath has been stilled. That bot of Mike's is worth her weight in antimatter."

"Which is approximately what I paid for her," I said.

Rex slung a heavy paw over Irene's thigh. "I do what she does and I don't cost a penny."

"Hark at you," Irene said lovingly. "My kept man."

"Kept busy, you mean," Rex said. He slid his paw higher up her thigh.

I smiled, but I'd be lying if I said I wasn't jealous of their easy, committed togetherness. Even Dolph may have felt the same, because he drained his beer and started to make noises like he was going.

"So what is this thing tomorrow, anyway?" I said.

"It was on the school's feed," Irene said. "Which I know you didn't look at. It's the zoo trip."

"Ridiculous," I said. "I take her to the zoo every other weekend, feels like."

Irene propped herself up on Rex so she was looking straight at me. Being looked at by Irene in this way always made me feel uncomfortable. Even when tipsy and sleepy, she had clearer eyes and a clearer head than any other person I knew. "Mike," she said. "today you got in a car chase, bullshitted your way into some super-secret front corporation, had a fight with your ex-wife, got shot at, got in an *aerial* car chase, and shot one of Parsec's sidekicks. Am I missing anything?"

"Yeah," Dolph said. "The part where we got patted down and handcuffed, until said minion decided not to press charges. Insult to injury, we even had to pay for the taxi."

"I'm not letting you off the hook, Dolph," Irene said without looking at him. "But it's kinda different for Mike, you know? He has responsibilities."

"And I don't," Dolph said, sounding pissed off, but he was getting the wrong end of the stick. Irene meant Lucy.

"So come to this thing tomorrow, Mike. Just try and be a normal father and don't shoot anyone. Especially not Mia's teacher," she added, to take the sting out of her lecture. "That sanctimonious cow is *mine.*"

We all laughed, but Irene's words struck home. I prided myself on being a good father. I had told Sophia that Lucy was my everything. The least I could do was go to this damn event. Being off-world so much of the time, I missed too many of Lucy's events, and seldom made the parent-teacher conferences. I didn't even know what they were teaching her at that place.

"OK, I'll go," I said. "What time we gotta wake up?"

26

I dreamed about Sophia. It was one of *those* dreams. I hadn't had one in a while. This one was a doozy, as if my subconscious was punishing me for having tried to move on. It built off our encounter in the Mujin Inc office, and ended up with me ravishing her over a desk, while she told me how much she hated me.

Pretty horrible. But I was not in control. I woke up shuddering, with a wet spot on my shorts.

It was still early. I crept into the bathroom, showered, and washed my shorts myself in the sink—stupidly, I didn't want to leave them in the laundry basket for Nanny B to find, not that her programming allowed her to understand about wet dreams.

It would probably help if I got laid. Yeah. But the chances of that seemed about as remote as Parsec deciding to forgive and forget what happened yesterday.

While I drank coffee and ate cereal at the kitchen table, I checked my phone for updates on the Silverback situation. It only took me thirty seconds to uncover a death threat against me, posted by Canuck.

"Lulu," I yelled, pouring a glass of klimfruit juice and getting another cereal bowl down from the cabinet. "Wake up! We're going to the zoo."

We collected Irene, Mia, and Kit, and rode uptown in my truck. The zoo was uptown of uptown, in the hills, a mini terrestrial ecosystem defended against the aggressive PdL wildlife by force fields and ditches salted with weedkiller.

I wished Rex was there, as I turned out to be one of the lone fathers in a sea of mothers. But it was just as well I had come, because every child was supposed to have a parent or guardian present to participate in their discernment.

Yeah. That's what they called it.

On San Damiano, *discernment* means considering a religious vocation. Choosing an animal form is just something that happens naturally.

While I felt crusty about the bureaucratization of something that should be natural, I tried to recognize that it was great the school was doing this at all. They weren't trying to pretend that their Shifter pupils were normies. They had formulated this program especially to help them optimize their genetic abilities.

Just like the army formulated the 15th Reconnaissance Brigade, a cynical voice whispered in my mind.

I put a lid on the past and listened to what the student life coordinator was telling us as we stood just inside the entrance to the zoo, a chaotic mob of parents and kids in yellow school hats.

"First," she yelled, "we will visit all the exhibits marked on the handout. Then we'll have lunch, then free play." She went on about hats, sunscreen, mosquito repellent, and thermoses. She was easy to listen to, despite the banality of what she was saying. She had a pale oval face, shiny waves of cinnamon-colored hair, and great legs. She gestured expansively as she spoke in an effort to keep the children's attention. "Starting at two o'clock, we'll do individual discernments in the rest area right here. Please, please, moms and dads, make sure your child is not late for their slot!"

I checked the handout on my phone. There were forty kids in the combined second and third grades, and Lucy's slot was dead last. Great. This was going to burn the entire day.

At least I would not have to worry about Canuck jumping me at the zoo. I had brought my new Machina .22, just in case, in a paddle holster. Sweat glued the holster to my back as the sun rose higher in the brassy blue sky.

Ponce de Leon was chosen for colonization first out of all the planets in the Cluster because its day is almost the same length as Earth's: 24 hours and 11 minutes. Those 11 minutes get tacked on after midnight. People call it the witching hour, and on holidays, they set off special witching hour fireworks on the strip.

To some extent, day length and other planetary features serve as natural sorting mechanisms to prevent species from coming into conflict. No human would want to live on a planet with a 50-hour day, let alone a day as long as its year. The Eks would. They don't give a crap about hours of daylight. There is much that they don't give a crap about. The stargends, meanwhile, prefer tidally locked worlds where it's *always* day. The aiora like snowy worlds that are too cold for anyone else, the huspathids prefer water worlds, and so on. Other species, lacking political power, don't have the luxury of choice.

But planetary incompatibility doesn't stop life from going on, and it does not stop all the species in the Cluster from flocking to Ponce de Leon as tourists. The zoo was especially popular with aliens, as they got to gape at terrestrial animals they had never conceived of.

Nor, it appeared, had some of Lucy's classmates.

It just about broke my heart to see the children staring dropjawed at the lions in their arboreal enclosure, and asking the teachers, "Are they *real?*"

On the other side of the glass, a male lion sprawled on a rock, looking hilariously like Rex after a few beers—as Mia pointed out, loudly.

But it was clear that most of the kids had never seen a lion before, be it a Shifter or a real one. Their parents did not take them to the zoo, either because they didn't think it was important or they didn't care —and our school was at the *good* end of Shiftertown. The children were familiar only with the animals in their immediate families. There are a lot of marine Shifters on the PdL; when we got to the seals and sea lions, whoops of recognition went up. Wolves, yay! Bears, not so much. The big cats got a few flickers of interest. But for the most part, the children simply stared at the animals without engaging, as if they were watching holos. Even our girls adopted the same air of uneasy tedium, not wanting to stand out from their classmates.

The exception—an unfortunate one—was Kit. Irene had brought him along to give Rex a break. At nearly every single enclosure, he lunged forward, intent on climbing in or breaking through the glass, shouting the name of the animal within. It took me and Irene together to restrain him.

At lunchtime, the frustration got to be too much for him and he threw a tantrum, while Lucy and his long-suffering sister quietly ate their sandwiches and pretended they didn't know him. I ended up taking him into the reptile house so that Irene could grab some lunch.

"Hey, Kit," I said.

"That's an anaconda," he said, sitting on the floor in front of its enclosure, rocking back and forth. "It's the second-longest snake. It constricts its prey, and mostly likes to be awake at night."

Yes, Kit was five years old, but he knew his stuff. He could have taught a natural history class to his elders.

"Do you like anacondas?" I said.

He gave me an uncomprehending stare. "They're very good at swimming."

I led him to a bench. We watched the anaconda doing nothing. It was dim in the reptile house, with that unique funky smell. Aliens swayed, stalked, and perambulated past. Kit stopped rocking, which was a good sign.

"Do you have a favorite animal?" I asked him.

"I like all of them," he said. "I'm especially a huge fan of the canidae, the mustelidae, the hyaenidae, and the eupleridae."

The long-forgotten Latin names plucked unwanted chords of memory. Once, I too had had them all off by heart.

I hesitated. Then said, "When I was a kid, I was like you."

"I have Chimera Syndrome," Kit said.

"Yes, that's what I mean," I said.

"Let's go look at the cobra," Kit said, getting up. "Did you know that they have hollow fangs? They can't hold their fangs down to bite their prey, so they inject venom into them."

"Yes, Kit," I said sadly. "I know that."

What had I been thinking? There was no point in sharing my big secret with a troubled preschooler. He knew that he had Chimera Syndrome, but he didn't understand what it meant. Hell, not even I understood it properly, and I'd lived with it for forty-four years.

So we went and watched the cobra, until Kit said, "I'm hungry."

"What would you like?"

"A mouse," he said, and smiled. "But I don't mind having a hamburger."

I took him back to the open-air food court, and by the time everyone was lunched and toileted I had missed my chance to talk to the student life coordinator about Pippa.

After lunch, we all separated, parents with their own children, to look at the animals again.

A certain tension had developed during the morning, and it became almost unbearable, for me anyway, as Lucy hesitated at a fork in the path. One way led back to the big cats, the other led to the marine animals. I concentrated on keeping my mouth shut. I couldn't say anything that would unduly influence her choices.

Lucy turned around and started back the way we had come. I tried to remember what was this way. The wolves, jackals, and hyenas. Also the kangaroos. And the rhinos. Surely not.

"Daddy?"

"Yes, sweetie?"

"Daddy?" she said again, her glance roving over a cage containing birds of some kind *(Accipiter,* said my mind) which we were not interested in. Lucy was swinging her hat by its strap, despite having been told repeatedly to wear it. Her cheeks were pink with heat. Sweaty commas of hair stuck to her temples. "Daddy?"

"Yes, sweetie, what is it?"

"What if I don't get an animal form?"

I parsed this instantly. "Of course you will."

"But what if I don't?"

I hadn't told her anything about Sophia, not even her name. But I *had* told her that Sophia wasn't a Shifter.

I opened my mouth to deflect her question with vague reassurances, and then changed my mind. I was going to have to start explaining things to her sometime.

"Honey, Shifting is inherited. That means if your mom and dad are Shifters, you're a Shifter, too. But—*but*—the genes for Shifting are dominant. That means you're a Shifter even if only one of your parents is. So don't worry. You will get an animal form."

"But what if I don't want to be a Shifter?"

I tensed in surprise. "Well, you are," I said. It had never occurred to me that she might feel ambivalent about her heritage.

"Good," she said, to my relief. "Why are you a Shifter?"

"Because my mom and dad are."

"Why are *they?*"

"Because … well, OK. Long, long ago humans set out from Earth to colonize other planets. At first it went pretty slow. Their ships weren't as good as the ones we have now. So when they left a bunch of people on a planet, those people might be all on their own for hundreds of years." Lucy nodded. "One of those planets was San Damiano, where Granny and Granddad live. And the people who colonized it … well, at that time, people were thinking about all kinds of ways to modify our bodies. And those people decided it would be good if they could Shift, so that we would never forget where we come from." I was leaving out a lot here. The mindset that led to the Big Shift had been absolutely screwy from our modern point of view. They had believed humanity's destiny was to be the apex predator throughout the galaxy. There had also been food shortages on San Damiano in the early days, which had made Shifting look like a good survival solution. As an animal, you don't have to wait for crops to grow. You just go hunting.

One of the under-appreciated benefits of Shifting is that we're *more* omnivorous than mainstream humans, thanks to our souped-up digestive enzymes. But I didn't need to get into all that with Lucy. "So to this day, we Shift into animals to remember the planet where humanity came from." I waited a beat. "And also so that we can get into stupid fights."

"Dad*dy.* You do not get into stupid fights."

"You're right, my darling," I said with an inner wince. "We don't Shift to get into stupid fights. We Shift because it's fun."

Lucy grinned. "I think being a rhino would be fun." We were passing the rhino enclosure. The two African black rhinos disinterestedly chewed leaves, unaware that they, too, were thousands of light years from their planet of origin.

"Sure," I said. "Spend all day chomping leaves, and occasionally get into stupid fights. Sounds like fun to me."

She giggled. "Are rhinos predators?"

"Nope."

"Do I have to pick a predator?"

"Sweetie," I said, "you don't have to pick anything yet. You're only eight. It's preposterous to make you think about it at this age. I don't know what's going through their minds. So let's just enjoy the zoo. And put your hat on!"

We wandered from the giraffes to the elephants and back to the marine animals, and we had an ice cream, and at last it was time for Lucy's discernment.

We found the student life coordinator in the rest area near the gate. All the other kids ran around playing. Instead of joining in the fun, Lucy had to sit down with me and the coordinator at a picnic table.

"Hi, Lucy," the coordinator said. She had a holobook in front of her. She looked wiped out, but her voice kept a determinedly perky ring. She shook my hand across the table. "Mr. Starrunner? I'm Christy Day."

"I know," I said. That didn't come out right. "I mean, I've seen your name on the school feed."

"Right. I coordinate the extra-curricular activities and liaise with parents, so I'm glad to make your acquaintance."

"Likewise," I said. I was having trouble keeping my eyes where they belonged. Her oversized Shoreside Elementary t-shirt and cargo shorts hit on the high points of her figure, challenging me to guess what lay underneath. I sternly pushed those thoughts out of my mind. "It's great to meet you."

She nodded and tapped on her holobook, presumably bringing up Lucy's file, though it was blank from our side of the table. "So, Lucy, have you had fun today?"

Lucy nodded.

"Have you been to the zoo before?"

Nod.

"I bring her at least once every couple of months," I said, establishing my credentials as a good parent.

"That's great. So do you have a favorite animal, Lucy?"

Lucy was wriggling on the bench and swinging her legs, kicking the underside of the table. I reached over and pushed down on her knees to stop her. "I want to be the same as my daddy," she said.

"Ah, a jaguar?" Christy said.

At the exact same time, Lucy said, "A tiger."

I winced. Back when Lucy first started school I had given my animal form as jaguar, because that's what I was mostly using back then. But I had burned the jaguar during a previous run-in with Buzz Parsec. I didn't want anyone finding out about it now. "That's a mistake," I started to say.

"Your dad has two forms?" Christy said to Lucy.

"He has lots of forms," Lucy said.

I pushed down on her knees harder, cursing her childish honesty. She was exaggerating, anyway. She'd only ever seen three of my forms: the tiger, the wolf, and a zorilla, which is actually a species of polecat, genus Mustelidae. I only did that one once, to amuse her when she had flu.

"What, Daddy?" Lucy said, wriggling away from me.

"It's OK," I said. "Why don't you tell Ms. Day what you liked best today?"

"The ice-cream," she said promptly.

Christy and I shared a smile—ha, ha, kids! She had a beautiful smile, as bright as sunshine on a hungover morning. We chatted a bit about the animals. If Christy could make any predictions about Lucy's future choice of animal based on her random observations, she was smarter than I was. After ten minutes we stood up.

Outside the zoo gates, the class teachers were herding the car-less kids and parents back onto the bus. Irene, Mia, and Kit stood beside my truck on the far side of the parking lot. They were more than ready to get going, based on the sharp sound of Irene telling Kit off.

I said, "Ms. Day, I actually wanted to talk to you—"

"Of course," she said. "I'm here to help with anything at all."

"It's not about Lucy."

She turned pink. The color spread from her hairline to the crew neck of her t-shirt, faint but unmistakable. It was bewitching.

I swallowed, realizing she had misunderstood me. "What I mean is, I was hoping to tap your expertise regarding, um, a different matter …"

You can't just come out and say, *I was hoping you could help me bust a terminally ill child out of detention.*

Especially when what you really want to say, is, *Are you free tonight?*

She broke into my fumbling. "I'd be glad to help," she said. "But if it's a sensitive issue, you'd better not call me at the school." Without meeting my eyes, she opened her holobook and stabbed at it. My phone beeped in my pocket, registering an incoming message. Of course, she had my number in Lucy's file. "Feel free to call me anytime," she said.

She made eye contact for a split second before walking away. Her gaze was not coy or flirty. It held a sort of scared pugnaciousness that nailed my feet to the ground.

Lucy dragged on my hand. We trailed over to my truck.

"Did you talk to her?" Irene said.

"She gave me her number," I said.

"OK," Irene said, not thinking anything of it. She was tired, and Kit was snuffling away the aftermath of another meltdown on her lap. "Call her. I'm sure she can help. She's nice, unlike that ignorant sow who teaches Mia's class."

"*Mommy,*" Mia said. We had the girls in the cab with us, crouching in the footwell, rather than make them ride in the back.

"Mommy what, Mia? She *is*. They're blatantly pushing the marine animals, Mike," Irene said, turning her tired face to me. "Do they think it'll be good for tourism or something?"

"The kids'll make their own choices," I said. "Kids always do." I hardly considered the words as they exited my mouth. I was thinking about Christy Day's hazel-flecked eyes.

27

Tired out, Lucy went to sleep on my lap in the truck. The moment her eyes closed, I got out my phone and checked for updates again.

Kaspar Silverback was still hospitalized. Turned out I had shot him in the chest, and the bullet had fragmented, perforating his lungs. Serve the bears right for loading their car guns with soft points. It was a salutary reminder that every time you load a gun, it may be used on you. Silverback was at Dr. Zeb's, the Shifter hospital in Smith's End.

Canuck was telling everyone he knew that I was a rabid dog and Dolph was another one. Unspeakable threats of retribution were multiplying. I flagged them, without much hope. If death threats were enough to get your data cut off, the internet would be a much quieter place, and did I really want Canuck and his cronies banned, anyway? This way at least I knew what they were thinking.

I wasn't sure if they were actually *planning* anything. Yet.

Buzz Parsec himself had yet to chime in.

What did that mean? It wasn't his style to lie low when slighted, directly or indirectly.

As we drove back towards the city, I called Dolph. He was out at the range, test-firing his new Koiler. *He* expected trouble. Irene listened to the conversation, although her eyes were closed. She interjected the odd comment about what reckless idiots we were.

Yes, Irene. Thanks for that.

"I went back to Bonsucesso Tower this morning for my bike," Dolph mentioned eventually.

I tensed. "Did you go upstairs?"

"Yes, but—"

"*I* was going to go!"

"I know," Dolph said. "Guess I saved you a trip." He explained that no one had been there.

Or if they were, they were hiding.

The foyer of Mujin Inc had been closed away behind heavy steel double doors. Dolph had rung the buzzer, but no one came.

"Guess they don't want any more walk-ins," he said.

I gazed down at my innocently sleeping daughter. So Sophia was gone, again. All I'd ever have was that one inconclusive conversation to help me make sense of what she had done to us.

It was probably just as well Dolph had gone without me. I might have done something stupid. Then again, sounded like it had been too late, anyway.

"Figure they closed up shop as soon as they got their taxis back from the police yesterday," I said heavily.

"Yeah," Dolph said. "We made it a little too hot for them."

"Congratulations," Irene said. "Now that just leaves Parsec."

Martin had joined the call. He was out at the spaceport, going over the ship's wiring and fixing damage from the HERF attack. "My opinion?" he said. "Make like a horse's dick and hit the road."

"So tasteful, Marty," Irene said. "My children are listening."

Actually, they were all asleep.

"Sorry," Martin said. "Why do you put up with us?"

I was sniggering. I also wondered the same thing sometimes. But I didn't want to give Irene ideas. "Because we're the best Shifter crew in space," I said.

"Look at the competition," Irene said dryly.

We talked it over and decided Martin was right. If we were off-planet, there was a good chance that the Parsec situation would blow over. "But we can't fly without an admin," Irene said.

"Robbie's coming along," I said. "But we definitely can't fly without a cargo."

After I dropped Irene and the kids off, I headed out to the office. Speaking of cargo, I needed to put in a few hours of v-mailing and bidding.

I brushed my fingers self-consciously across my Machina .22 as I crossed the dingy lobby of our office building.

It was still only 4:45 in the afternoon, but there was no one around. There's never anyone around down here. I know people work in the other offices in our building, but for all you usually see of them, they might as well be bots plugged into their desks. When I had picked up a coffee at the hole in the wall across the street, there had been no one in there. The whole Harborside district is 99% automated—the factories, the trucks, the trains ... it's a vision of what a world run by AI might be like. Noisy, clattering, thumping, bustling, dirty. *Empty.*

I rode up in the dank elevator and walked down the empty, echoing hall to my office. A big red and yellow sign on the door said *Uni-Ex Shipping*. I stood in front of the door, juggling my take-out coffee and my phone in my left hand, while my right hand hovered near the Machina .22.

The door sprang open in my face.

I sidestepped. The Machina leapt into my hand.

I almost shot Mary.

"Oh, hey," I said, whipping the gun behind my back. "Didn't think you'd still be here."

If she had seen the gun, she said nothing about it. She was a shrewd lady. She knew what our industry was like, and the kind of competition we had to handle. "I was just about to lock up," she said. "Do you want me to stay a while longer?"

I gestured with the hand that didn't have the gun in it. "No, no, you go on. I'm just going to take care of a few things."

Mary clicked her tongue, took the coffee that I was about to spill, and steered back into the office. "I've got a few more things to take care of, myself. I was going to wait for tomorrow to get your input, but I'll stay and keep you company."

I didn't try again to talk her out of it. The way I'd just freaked myself out, I was not displeased to have company for a while.

Mary worked in the outer office while I made phone calls. When I got off the phone, she came in and showed me some enquiries from regular customers: Help the Hungry, Catholic Outreach, Humans In Need. I looked over the details of their cargoes with a feeling of melancholy. I told Lucy I was in the aid business. The truthfulness of that claim hinged on these type of cargoes. If only they paid better. "We'll take this one," I said.

"Medical and food aid for Belalcazar." Mary made a note. Her eyes twinkled. "That's a Farmworld. Are you getting gun-shy in your old age, Mike?"

"Naw," I said. "But we'll be breaking in the new admin officer. Don't want to throw him in at the deep end."

"He's a Shifter, isn't he? I'm sure he can handle it." Chuckling, she returned to her desk.

The aid supplies for Belalcazar would take up only half of the *St. Clare's* capacity, so I'd need some small-lot shipments to make the run pay. I topped up my cold coffee with bourbon from the bottle in my desk drawer, and opened up my auctions platform.

One of the primary ways indie freighters fill the hold is through the auction system. Anyone with a package to ship can put their cargo up for auction on GoFast or one of the littler platforms. We all bid for it. Lowest bid wins. That's the gist of it, but in practice the auction game also involves a lot of flirtation, selling the customer on the safety and reliability of your service, and hopefully turning them into a repeat customer. I was pretty good at this aspect of the business—no false modesty. But today, I was more than usually aware that one of the other anonymous bidders in each auction was probably Parsec, and I caught myself bidding too low in a self-destructive effort to spite the image of him hunched over his own computer, in his home on Cape Agreste, or his blinged-out downtown office. I was also aware that this online battle was beside the point. Nothing would ever be settled this way, with twenty klicks of fiberoptic cable between us. I had been kidding myself for too long that it would. My sales expertise and my reputation for honesty were no substitute for claws and teeth.

I pushed back from the computer and ran my hands through my hair. I glanced out the window but couldn't see anything because the lowering sun struck straight into my eyes.

The buzzer rang. Mary answered it. A few seconds later I heard her rise to let someone in. It was rare for us to get walk-in business, but it did happen.

I drank some coffee-flavored bourbon, still thinking about Parsec.

The door of my office was closed, muffling the voices in the outer office, but then I heard Mary say, in the voice she used for getting rid of people, "No, I'm sorry, we cannot help you. I can only suggest you try Clusterwide or Human Spacelines, sir."

Intrigued, I rose and opened my door. "Is there something I can help with?" I said pleasantly.

The words died on my lips as the customer standing in front of Mary's desk turned to face me.

My initial instinct was to throw this stinking homeless dude out of my office.

Desperate hope brightened his eyes.

I knew him ... and then I *knew* him. It was Rafael Ijiuto, wholesaler. Last seen on Gvm Uye Sachttra.

28

"THANK God," Rafael Ijiuto said, limping up to me. I must have looked blank, for he prompted me, "Gvm Uye Sachttra?" He rolled the alien planet's name off like a native. "It's Mike, right? Rafe."

It wasn't that I didn't recognize him. I was shocked by his appearance.

If I didn't have a good memory for faces, and if that flat-nosed, beige-skinned mug of his weren't so memorable, I might *not* have recognized him. He looked as if he'd been sleeping rough for a week. His white shirt was no longer white, but the reddish hue of PdL dirt, disfigured by rips and stiff dark splotches that looked like blood. The knees of his suit trousers were ragged, the hems frayed. He limped, because one of his pricey dress boots was missing. That foot was bare and filthy, and I noted dots of blood on our office carpet.

Ever noticed that when a person looks like crap, they always look worse if they started out in a nice business suit?

Ijiuto smelled as bad as he looked, filling the office with the old-timey unwashed funk that had made me think *homeless.*

He went to shake hands with me, first transferring his grip on his trousers to his left hand. His belt had gone AWOL. He was literally holding his trousers up with one hand.

I let his profferred handshake hang in mid-air, not because I was deliberately being rude, but because I was so astounded by the state of the man.

He withdrew his hand—which was, indeed, filthy—saying with a self-aware grimace, "I know, I need to get friendly with a shower. I was going to ask your receptionist to recommend a hotel after we're through here."

"Mike, is this a friend of yours?" Mary had a wet wipe in her hand, crumpling and twisting it. If she had been a less polite woman, she would've been holding it to her nose to mask the smell.

I started to say, "No," and then changed tack, because one of my rules is never to be rude to customers. Whatever else Rafael Ijiuto was, he was or had been a customer. And curiously, his wretched appearance disposed me to give him the benefit of the doubt. "He's a customer. I wasn't expecting to see you here on Ponce de Leon, Rafe," I said with a smile. I was itching to ask him how he got into that state.

"Right? It's funny how you can meet someone in one place, and then run into them again on the other side of the Cluster. Well, Gvm Uye Sachttra ain't quite the other side of the Cluster, but you know what I mean. Anyway, I'm glad I caught you. I'm hoping to do business with you again."

"Looking to move another cargo?" I said. I still suspected this man of killing Kimmie. I wasn't going to let him go until I got the truth out of him.

"Ha, ha," Ijiuto said. "Nope. I was hoping to get a ride off-world, but Mary—" he had got her name off the nameplate on her desk— "says you don't take passengers?" He raised his eyebrows with a conspiratorial smile, as if expecting me to reveal that Mary had just been putting him off on account of how he looked. Even his *eyebrows* were dirty.

"Nope, afraid you misunderstood," I said. "We're not a passenger ship. Freight only." Now I knew why Mary had tried to send him to Clusterwide or Spacelines. "You'd be better off with one of the commercial lines."

Ijiuto's face fell. He looked so wretched I felt sorry for him.

The silence stretched.

Reluctantly, I said, "Where were you hoping to get to?"

"Montemayor," he said. "Or Valdivia."

I frowned. No one wants to go to Montemayor *or* Valdivia. Montemayor is a Heartworld. Valdivia is a Farmworld, almost suburban in its relation to Ponce de Leon and its determined boringness. The only thing they have in common is they're both planets.

"I *had* a ride," Ijiuto said. "I was supposed to be going to Valdivia on the *Tezozocat Ham*. But those goddamn Eks." He punched one fist into his other palm, and abruptly launched into a tirade against the Ekschelatans. His voice shook. He was nearly crying with rage. "I hate those blue bastards. I went all the way over there, and I didn't even go in, because look at me, right? I asked the security guy to call up. This six-armed blue fucker comes down and pretends he never met me. Bull*shit*. We're standing in the café area, people are staring. *I'm* not the one making a scene. *He's* yelling. He says he never met me before—basically, he pisses on my shoes and tells me it's raining. And then he gets security to throw me out. They threw me out on the fucking street!" His eyes widened at the horror and indignity of it.

I uh-huh'ed. If there's one thing that unites humanity, it is dislike of the Eks. Properly known as Ekschelatans, they are the other big power in the Cluster. They don't do planetary colonization like we do. They'll live anywhere. What they do do is banking. They have a lock on the interstellar financial network, and not only that. Laws, regulations, contracts, treaties—anything to do with money, they're all over it, eking out profits where a human's compassion or sense of fairness would get in the way. They are ruthless.

So it was no surprise to me, when I teased out the facts from Rafael Ijiuto's incoherent tirade, that his Ek buddy had refused to give him passage on the *Tezozocat Ham*—I looked it up; it was a biggish Ek cruiser operated by a data infrastructure company, scheduled to depart for Valdivia in two days' time—regardless of what may have been promised, or what Ijiuto *thought* had been promised. I have to deal with Eks myself sometimes, and you absolutely cannot let them get away with vagueness. That's a license for them to twist your words later into a form benefiting themselves. Get it in writing, with their seal and two witnesses, or it's just hot air.

So the only surprising thing was that Ijiuto had even thought of trying to get onto that ship.

Because he had no money.

"None?" I said.

"What you see is what you get," he joked weakly. He stretched out his left arm. Beneath the patina of grubbiness, his credit dot was black. He then made a pantomime of turning out his pockets. The insides of the pockets were startlingly clean, in contrast to the rest of his clothes, and empty.

I kept my face blank. Having been turned down by the Eks, he'd then come to me ... because he thought *I* would give him a free ride, out of the goodness of my heart? I couldn't decide whether to be flattered or insulted. "You're not going to get off Ponce de Leon for nothing," I said.

"I'm expecting a bank transfer in a week," he said, without energy, as if he didn't expect me to believe him. "I'll have plenty of money when that comes through. I *told* the bastard Eks that, but no. Cash up front or nothing. Stinking blue jerkwads."

"That's too bad," Mary said. She had stopped wringing that wet wipe in her hands, and was now watching Ijiuto with motherly compassion. At any minute she would offer him the use of our restroom.

I folded my arms. Something stank, all right, but it wasn't just Ijiuto. It was his story. Oh, I believed he was telling the truth about getting the brush-off from the Eks. That outraged tirade had had the ring of sincerity. But that left a whole lot of unanswered questions.

"I'm sorry I have to ask," I said. "But how the heck did you end up here with no money?" *And only one shoe, and your clothes in tatters, and your belt missing.*

Ijiuto swayed, and caught himself on Mary's desk. "I walked," he said.

"Huh?" Yet I immediately sensed that this was the truth. He looked like that because he had walked ... *how* far?

"It's a miracle I'm even alive," he said. He pointed at me with a weak smile. "I'd rather have you as a friend than an enemy."

Then he collapsed on my office floor.

*

I called Dolph, squatting beside Ijiuto. I had persuaded Mary to go home. I didn't want her getting mixed up in whatever kind of mess this turned out to be. I held my gun in one hand and my phone in the other, angled so that Dolph could see Ijiuto's unconscious face.

"He was on that Traveller ship," I said. "I'm pretty sure that's what he was saying. It crashed in the Tunjle ... but he must've bailed out. Anyway, he survived. He made it out of the jungle somehow. Then he walked to Mag-Ingat. He *walked,* Dolph. What's that, six hundred klicks from where it came down? Seven?"

"More like eight," Dolph crackled. He was on his bike. He had hit the road the minute I told him that Rafael Ijiuto was lying unconscious on the floor of our office. "Maybe he hitchhiked some of the way."

"Maybe, but I would guess he hasn't eaten in days. He has no money. He made it here on sheer willpower." I placed two fingers on Ijiuto's limp wrist. His pulse was rapid. "He's dehydrated, might be in shock. Definitely heatstroke."

"He's lucky to be alive," Dolph said, which was the same thing Ijiuto himself had said. "Did he say why he was flying with the Travellers?"

"Nope. He didn't even say outright that he was. That's just my guess. Then he passed out."

"I'll be there in ten."

When Dolph arrived, he gave Ijiuto the same sort of cursory examination I had. We tried to get some water down him, but it trickled over his lips, leaving clean trails in his grimy stubble.

"He needs medical attention," I said. I was reluctant to let Ijiuto out of my sight, but I didn't want to be responsible for his death.

"We're not taking him to hospital," Dolph said. "He could spill everything when he wakes up."

"He can't stay here."

"We'll take him to my place." Dolph lifted Ijiuto's feet, one booted and one bare.

If anyone had seen us carrying him downstairs, it would have looked like we were murderers disposing of a body. Of course, the cameras in the lobby and the parking lot did see us. But there was nothing we could do about that except drape a towel over Ijiuto's face to foil facial recognition.

We took the towel off when we reached my truck. We laid him on some old blankets I keep in the back. Dolph rolled his bike up the tailgate, and volunteered to ride beside Ijiuto.

"Don't kill him," I said.

"Not until we get the whole story out of him," Dolph said.

I drove slowly and carefully back to Shiftertown. The traffic got denser, the sidewalks more populous. The cold, minimal illumination of Harborside gave way to exuberant bursts of neon in upstairs windows, capering holos in front of bars and bodegas, and vegetable oil lanterns on crumbling balconies. Our power comes from a clutch of neighborhood power plants that run low-temperature turbines off the waste heat from blocks of vitrified nuclear waste, buried underground. It's cheap. We're basically generating electricity from garbage—the leftovers of an earlier technological era. But some folks in Smith's End can't even afford that. Or more precisely, they pay their data bill before they pay their electricity bill, and then light their homes using a shoelace in a jar of helioba oil. Heliobas grow locally; you can smell the back-alley presses all over Smith's End.

We carried Ijiuto up the four flights of urine-scented stairs to Dolph's apartment. The ground floor was a betting parlor. The second floor was a germ studio. Some people think you can alter your DNA by deliberately infecting yourself with the right germs. The sound of electronic music leaked down from the apartment upstairs, competing with wolfish yips and howls from the barbecue joint across the street, a local teen hangout. I could smell that someone in the building was grilling fish for supper. There were claw marks on Dolph's front door. He closed his curtains before switching on the lights, revealing mangy hundred-year-old wallpaper, an unpainted floor, a futon in one corner and a garbage sack in the other. That was all the furniture he had.

"Remind me why you live here," I grunted.

Dolph avoided answering me by ducking into the closet. But I knew the answer. Deep down inside, he thought he didn't deserve anything better than this, or it would not do him any good, or there would be no point moving—three different ways of saying the same thing. I felt sad for my friend every time I came down here, although I was careful not to show it. Something had broken inside him on Tech Duinn. Outwardly, he had bounced back, but being in his apartment was like getting a glimpse inside his heart.

He backed out of the closet dragging a spare futon. "Put him on this one. It's already dirty." As he dropped it on the floorboards, a cockroach—a greater winged *Apthoroblattinus wilsonii,* that is; we just call them cockroaches—ran out of it. Dolph picked up an empty pizza box and threw it at the insect.

"Now I know why Nevaeh still takes your calls," I said. "She values your roach-killing abilities."

"Nope," Dolph said. "It's because she's never been over here."

We put Ijiuto on the futon. I removed his remaining boot. We checked his pulse and temperature and gave him water again. Dolph held his shoulders up while I trickled it down his throat. Ijiuto coughed reflexively, and moaned. His eyes opened for a moment, but there was no one there. When we laid him flat again, he was back out.

"I'm starting to think we should take him to Dr. Zeb's," I said.

"Naw," Dolph said, from inside his closet. He kept all his valuables under lock and key in there. It was that kind of neighborhood. He re-emerged with his holobook, which he set up on the crate he used for a nightstand. "Nothing's wrong with him except walking too far in the sun. Anyway, it's only a few blocks. If he gets any worse, I'll take him over there."

"How?" I wondered if I should stay here. I wanted to hear what Ijiuto had to say for himself when he woke up. But I should have been home half an hour ago. I had told Lucy I would be back for supper.

"I'll get the guys from the betting parlor to help, if it comes to that. But he'll be fine." Dolph lit a cigarette and booted up his holobook. Fireworks of data sprayed silently into the air, mingling with the cigarette smoke. "Go *home*, Mike. Didn't you say you were gonna fire up the barbecue with Lucy?"

"It's too late for that already," I said. I regarded Ijiuto's pale face for a moment, and sighed. "He wakes up, or anything happens, ping me right away.."

"Sure," Dolph said, already immersed in a rewatch of the *St. Clare's* footage of the shooting. But not completely immersed. As I opened the door to leave, I heard a soft clunk, and saw him laying the Koiler Mark Three on the floor beside the crate, out of Ijiuto's reach.

Outside, I breathed in the odors of charring meat and helioba oil. It was too late for the barbecue I'd promised Lucy, for the second evening in a row. On an impulse, I crossed the street and bought take-out barbecue to make it up to her. Sticky pork ribs, blackened skewers of offal, strips of fatty venison and gazelle meat marinated in soy sauce—the signature cuisine of San Damiano, which Lucy likes, or pretends to like, because she thinks I want her to like it.

Balancing the hot, sauce-stained containers in one hand, I phoned Nanny B as I headed back to my truck.

"We are at Kitty's," Nanny B quacked. I could hear high-pitched mayhem in the background. "Rex and Irene invited us to eat out with them."

"At Kitty's?" I said. Kitty's was the tourist-trap pancake house on the corner of 90th and Shoreside, a short walk from my apartment. It charged tourist prices, too, so we hardly ever went there, although Lucy loved the whimsical pancakes shaped like animals, and the surprise gifts given to all guests under the age of 10. "Let me speak to her."

"Daddy!" Lucy screeched. "We're having pancakes! Mia and me got sparklers! Rex says we can set them off when we get home!"

"Are you having fun, sweetie?" I said, lamely. She clearly was. She didn't need me at all.

"Yes!!"

After some fumbling, the phone was passed to Irene, who sounded teed off at me. No wonder. I resisted the urge to tell her about the Rafael Ijiuto mess—she wouldn't be able to take it in at Kitty's with screaming children on all sides. I told a white lie about having got caught up in a big auction.

"Well, you should've just let it go, Mike," she said quietly. "Lucy was *crying*. We had to take them to this overpriced purgatory to cheer her up."

I apologized profusely and said I'd pay for the whole meal, which didn't help.

Then I sat in my truck with the goddamn take-out barbecue stinking up the cab, and stared sightlessly at the wolves and leopards jaywalking across the street.

I didn't need to go home. I didn't *want* to go home to an empty apartment and the knowledge that I had failed my daughter, again.

I could go back upstairs and sit on Dolph's floor and drink his beer, and talk guns and Travellers and conspiracy theories. Maybe he'd even let me talk about Sophia, if we got drunk enough.

My phone rang. I fumbled it out.

When I saw who it was, my blood turned to ice water. I licked my lips, checked my smile in the rearview mirror, and answered.

"Hi, Bones," I said, faking an easy tone. "What can I do for you tonight?"

29

"THIS ain't looking good, Tiger," Jose-Maria d'Alencon said. "Now y'all are murdering folks and disposing of their bodies?"

I started to say *Huh?* Then I realized what he was talking about. "Whoa," I said. "You really are paying attention."

"Better believe it. After that shit you pulled with the bears, you got your own personal surveillance algo."

"I'm sorry to disappoint you, but there's no murdered man," I said. My heart was thumping. "There's just a sick one. Customer collapsed at my office, and we took him home." What d'Alencon had seen, of course, was the footage from the lobby of my office building. I *knew* that would come back to bite us. I just hadn't gambled on it happening so fast. When Dolph and I carried Ijiuto across the lobby, d'Alencon's surveillance algo must have flagged it as a suspicious incident.

"You're not at home," d'Alencon said.

I inwardly scowled at my phone. And at my truck. Each one a little bird singing my location aloud. "No, I'm at Dolph's. That's where the customer is recuperating right now."

"What customer would this be?"

I lied, "I don't even know the guy. He just walked in off the street."

"All right," d'Alencon said. "You don't want to tell me anything. I get it, Tiger. I get it. Y'all are Shifters. I'm the police. We're on opposite sides."

There was a note of sorrow in his voice. I remembered the time, and maybe he was remembering it too, when we had been on the same side, fighting shoulder to shoulder against enemies of humanity ... who, themselves, were also human, but never mind that. The one good thing about our war had been the camaraderie, and now we'd lost that, too. A shiver of regret went through my body.

"I would help you out if I could, Bones. I mean it."

"Then prove it, Tiger! Get me something on this front company of Parsec's. Everything up there checks out, we got no cause for a warrant, the detective division ain't interested in wasting resources on a law-abidin' uptown taxi company ... but I *know* something's hinky up there. Call it an old soldier's instinct."

"Yeah," I said. "I got that feeling, too. Did you know that they also manufacture toy fairies?"

"Toy fairies," d'Alencon repeated.

"Yeah, or maybe they just customize them for resale. They're supposed to be a taxi company. Don't you think that's weird?"

"Weird, maybe. Illegal, no."

"Well, that's all I got." I felt stupid for having expected him to eagerly seize on my tip.

"I expected better of you, Mike," d'Alencon said. The sarcastic bitterness in his voice startled me. "Can't you at least come up with some halfway believable lies?"

"I ain't lying to you—"

"Suuure you ain't. My old buddy Tiger would *never* get mixed up in some smuggling racket—"

"I ain't mixed up in—"

"—and lie to me about it. Just like you don't know *why* that Traveller ship chased you back to Ponce de Leon."

Sweat pricked the backs of my knees and my neck. I curled over the steering wheel, instinctively making myself a smaller target in the truck cab, as if d'Alencon's words were a gun pointed at me. "I haven't lied to you about anything. Watch me all you like. I'm clean."

"Oh, we'll be watching you," d'Alencon said grimly. "Count on that."

He hung up on me.

I slowly uncurled. My heart raced. I stared numbly at the cavorting, yelping teenagers in front of the barbecue joint. D'Alencon thought I was lying to him. Despite the evidence of my fight with the bears, he thought *I* was mixed up in Parsec's game!

And the hell of it was that he wasn't wrong, because Parsec had shipped his contraband on *my ship.*

I had to get to the bottom of this, to prove my own innocence.

But right now, my instincts were giving different orders. Like an animal eluding capture in the forest, I felt a need to double back, to lay false trails, to confuse the all-seeing eyes of the PdL PD.

"OK," I muttered. "OK. You're watching me, huh, Bones? Watch *this.*"

What I did next was nothing to be proud of. I didn't give myself time to think about it. I tapped my phone's screen and picked a flower from the bouquet of contacts on the screen.

I dialed.

"Hello?"

"Hi, Christy? This is Mike Starrunner. Lucy's father. We met today —"

"Yes. Hi."

"The issue I mentioned," I said. My hand was sweating on the phone. I knew that the police would be listening in on my call. *This* would prove to them that I was innocent. Criminals don't go out of their way to help people. Right? "It's about some children I brought to Ponce de Leon. Refugees. Their asylum applications ran into difficulties, and I wondered if I could bounce the situation off of you ..." I began to explain, but it all came out jumbled.

Christy interrupted me. "Are you free right now? Why don't we meet up?"

30

WHEN I saw Christy coming towards me along Shoreside Avenue, I had to arm-wrestle unworthy thoughts into submission. She'd changed into a flower-patterned dress with skinny straps—nothing too fancy, just summery. Her cinnamon hair floated around thin white shoulders unspoilt by a single freckle. Her neckline revealed a hint of shadow between small, perfectly round breasts. The way her legs flexed as she walked made me think about how they might flex around me in bed …

Down, boy. I was not going to put the moves on her. Anyway, it would have been low as hell to use the kids as a pretext. I was only here to find out if there was any way to save them from Yesanyase Skont.

We went into a café on Shoreside and 202nd. I caught myself thinking that the location was a nice bonus: it was at the good end of the Strip, north of St. Andrew's Pier, where designer fashion outlets predominate over X-rated nightclubs. A couple of hours here, in the company of a mainstream human, would mix up the police algo's profile of me as a lawless, skulking Shifter.

But what an algo sees, and what a human sees, are very different things. Whereas Christy fitted in with the well-heeled crowd sipping frothy drinks around us, I was still in the same jeans and plain khaki t-shirt I had worn to the zoo. Worse, I probably smelled a bit like Rafael Ijiuto. When I paid for our drinks I noticed a smear of Ijiuto's blood on the inside of my arm—he had an infected cut on his shoeless foot that had opened up when we carried him. Just as well this wasn't a date.

I put Ijiuto out of my mind and sat down with my vat of overpriced froth. Then I told Christy the sad story of Pippa, Jan, and Leaf.

Her sweet face grew solemn as I spoke, and she stopped drinking her mango froth and winced, closing her eyes briefly, when I got to the diagnosis of interstellar variant kuru.

"That's bad," she said. "That poor, poor child."

"I know. But should it have to be a death sentence? I mean—"

"It *is* a death sentence. At most she could live for another ten years. It depends when she was infected."

"Right, that's what I mean. I put that badly. The point is, she has another few good years, so why shouldn't she have a chance to live them to the fullest, instead of getting deported to Yesanyase Skont? It's one of the Hurtworlds. I wouldn't send a dog there."

Actually, I flew to the Hurtworlds myself, as infrequently as I could manage. They are a group of planets spread over seven star systems in the Spinwards Up sector of the Cluster. With varied but mostly human-compatible ecosystems, they could've made decent colony planets, but at some point during the long history of the Cluster, they had become a dumping ground for undesirables. We didn't start it. The Eks did. They dumped whole populations, whole *species* there, with only minimal effort to separate aggressive aliens who couldn't play well with others, and told them to stay put or else. The Hurtworlds thus predictably turned into living hells, and became a breeding ground for millenarian philosophies, as well as prime targets for the Travellers. Humanity got in on the dumping game later, for political reasons: we couldn't let potential anti-human movements fester out there, unknown to us. So when we deported someone like Pippa to the Hurtworlds, we were tacitly expecting her to become a spy and fifth columnist for humanity, even as we expelled her. It was the ultimate insult.

Christy's gaze rested somberly on the table. "I know. It's unfair."

Her response did not satisfy me. I said, "You know who else will be on that flight? Felons. Murderers, rapists, pirates. She'll probably get raped before she even gets to Yesanyase S. She's a *sixteen-year-old girl.*"

Christy shuddered. She raised her eyes to mine and hugged her bare arms. "I *know.* In fact, I probably know more about the Hurtworlds than you do, no offense. I used to work out there."

"You did?"

"Yeah. I did my government service out there."

On most human planets, everyone has to do two years of government service. I had gotten out of it by joining the army, so I'd ended up doing government service for *five* years, as a killer. Real slick move.

"I worked in one of the reception camps on Fanellespont Axen," Christy said. "So I've seen the anarchy, the brutality, the rule over the weakest by the worst. The best chance a girl like Pippa would have— her only chance, as a matter of fact—would be to sell her body or her skills to one of the petty warlords who run those worlds. Some of them actually call themselves kings. They're all thugs. And of course most of them are sick. If it's not kuru, it's red flowers or Pal's Syndrome, or one of the necrotizing diseases."

I picked up my drink to hide a shudder of my own. Necrotizing diseases were where we got the Necros, who we fought on Tech Duinn.

"So yeah," Christy said, "I agree. If it was up to me, I wouldn't send a—" she hesitated— "a dog there."

I half-smiled. Aware that I was a Shifter, she was sensitive of making any animal references. It was sweet. "I heard you do some work with refugees."

She nodded. "After my stint on Fanellespont A, I guess you could say I had my eyes opened to the cruelties we inflict on people—not because we're trying to, or because we're naturally cruel, but just as the cost of doing business. So, it's not much, but I volunteer at the juvenile resettlement center downtown. We try to move kids out of there and into foster homes as soon as we can. Our foster families are the salt of the earth—honestly, I can't say enough good things about them. I would foster myself, but I'm not married, and my apartment's about the size of this table, so ..." She trailed off. That pretty blush touched her face again, making her cheeks look like the insides of seashells.

"Where do you live?" I said, to help her over the speed bump in the conversation.

She gestured towards the back of the café. "213th and DeBosco, right over there."

"Nice area." I put down my froth again without sipping it. "Christy, I'm not gonna lie. I was hoping you knew someone in the asylum processing department, who might be able to ..."

"Reverse Pippa's decision?"

"Yeah."

Christy shook her head reluctantly. "I don't think there's any chance of that."

"Oh, god*dammit.*"

"They would have to reverse the actual diagnosis, and that—"

"It's the other two kids," I said. I felt like I'd lost my queen and was now fighting to save my bishop and my rook. "They're determined to go with her. To *that?* They have no idea! And having heard what you said about your work with foster families, I'm positive that would be better for them. *They're* not sick—"

"How did she get kuru in the first place?"

"No one knows. Not even her. Or if she does, she's not telling."

"Could it have been at that refugee camp where you found her?"

"I highly doubt it. There hasn't been a single other report of kuru out of that place." Actually, I hadn't specifically checked, but I hadn't heard any such rumors, and it was the kind of thing you *would* hear about.

"OK. All the same, I think you and your crew should probably get tested. Just in case, you know?"

I shook my head. "We're Shifters," I said absently, thinking about poor little Jan and Leaf.

"So?" Christy said.

"We've got souped-up immune systems."

"Really? I didn't know that."

I ventured a gently teasing tone. "You work at a Shifter school. I would have figured you know all about us."

"There's a lot I don't know, obviously." She was blushing again. This time, she rallied on her own. "I'll tell you what I can do. I have a contact at the quarantine center on Space Island. I can ask her to talk to Jan and Leaf. Maybe they could come on a day trip to the resettlement center, meet the other kids—it might change their minds about staying."

"That would be great." I was shamefully aware that it would also save me a lot of money if they decided to stay, as I wouldn't have to pay their deportation costs. Well, I didn't *have* to, but I felt obligated.

"I'm really sorry I can't help more," she said, and I could tell she meant it. This woman had never met "my" three kids, yet she had already taken them into her capacious heart and wanted to save them. How do you get a heart that big? Was she born with it, the way she was born with delicate white cheeks and hazel-flecked green eyes?

"You're not drinking your frothofee," she said, smiling at me.

I realized I had been staring at her like an idiot. I confessed, "I can't stand this stuff."

"Oh no, I'm sorry. I just thought it would be a nice place—"

"No, no, it's a great place." The clink of handmade pottery cups and sithar music floated through the air. The people at the next table were arguing intensely about Sopwithian biological autarky. I was genuinely enjoying the low-key ambience. It was so nice to get away from Shiftertown, away from the constant sense of crisis that besets Shifter lives. "It'd be even better if they served whiskey. But you can't have everything."

"That's just an excuse," Christy said, taking my flip remark as a considered philosophical statement. "We live in a post-scarcity society. We *should* be able to have everything. There's no actual reason why some of the children in Lucy's class should come to school without breakfast, or why a child like Pippa should be deported to Yesanyase Skont."

I admired her idealism, but I was through with talking about it, my own outrage blunted by the increasing conviction that there was nothing I could do about it. "Sorry, just a moment," I murmured, pushing back my chair and nodding in the direction of the toilets.

Standing beside the urinals, I called Nanny B. She reported that Lucy was brushing her teeth in preparation for an early bedtime. Did I want to speak to her? No, I said, that's OK. Tell her I have to work late and I love her very much.

I leaned my forehead against the cool black ceramic wall. I wondered if there were cameras even in here, watching me. A normal man, struggling with a normal decision. And yet, such a difficult one.

I washed my hands and went back out to Christy. She was putting cinnamon sticks and packets of sugar powder into her handbag. "I'll block the cameras for you," I joked, standing between her and the nearest security camera.

"Oh! I always think—I mean, it's all right to take them. That's what they're here for, isn't it?"

"Sure," I said.

"They're for the kids at the resettlement center. The food is—well, it's fine, but it's just a bit blah."

The post-scarcity society.

We went out onto 202nd. A yuriops herd was passing. We stood back against the windows of the café to avoid their massive sleek haunches and swinging horns. Their loud, yodelling voices forced me to raise my own. "Would you care for a post-frothofee drink?" I said. "Something slightly higher-proof?"

"Like whiskey?"

"That's exactly what I had in mind."

Her upper arm was touching mine. I was intensely aware of the small point of contact with the heat of her skin. She moved away as the last yuriops passed, freeing up the sidewalk. "That would be really nice, but I haven't had supper yet."

"Ah …" Neither had I, unless you counted a couple strips of pork belly gnawed in the cab of my truck on the way here. "Do you like barbecue?"

"Like, Shifter barbecue?"

"Yup."

"I'm going to be completely honest with you," Christy said, looking into my eyes with that blend of anxiety and determined honesty which so entranced me. "I mean, I don't want to get into a habit of half-truths. I can't stand that stuff."

I laughed out loud.

"They serve it at every school event. The parents appreciate it, I think, but personally—the stickiness, that really strong soy sauce flavor, the sheer fat content … ugh."

"Well, OK, then," I said. "Memo to self: do not invite Christy for barbecue."

She laughed. She had a good laugh, not a giggle, not a guffaw, and not fake. "Anyway, I have some lentil salad at home I have to finish up before it goes bad," she said.

"I'll walk you home," I said.

31

As Christy and I walked north on DeBosco, I told her about the origins of the strong soy sauce flavor of Shifter barbecue. It was not to disguise half-rotten meat, as people think. It came from the cultural origins of the first San Damiano colonists. To the extent that terrestrial ethnicities still existed at that time, some of them were from the Japanese archipelago, and others came from Europe and North America. They brought a medley of flavorful herbs with them, but the pepper plants died. The mint plants died. So did the coriander, the ginger, the nutmeg, the shiso ... you get the picture. All they had left was soybeans. And to top it off, native bacillae got into the mold used to ferment the soy sauce, which gave it the distinctive pungent flavor that wafts out of every Shifter barbecue joint today.

"Out of desperation, creativity," I finished, as we crossed a narrow street lined with shrubs and medium-rise apartment buildings.

Christy gave me a shrewd look and said, "I can see you don't think the post-scarcity society is an unalloyed good."

"Well," I said, "if it ever actually came to exist, I'd be out of business. So there's that."

"You're in sales?"

I realized she didn't know exactly what I did. I started to say I was in the shipping industry. Then a montage of what my job had actually consisted of recently flashed before my eyes. I remembered her saying *No half-truths.* I said in as light and humorous a tone as I could manage, "Sales, shipping, plus occasionally fighting Travellers, rescuing refugees, fighting with other Shifters, assisting shipwrecked customers …"

I expected she would think I was joking. But she slid another of those glances at me, half-earnest, half-scared. "Yeah, I … I've heard stories from people at school. Not about you, of course, but just in general. Shifters really live on the edge, don't they?"

"You could put it like that."

"Anyway, this is me."

We were standing on the beige-tiled forecourt of a building ten storeys tall and no wider than my armspan, exaggerating only slightly. It was just like its neighbors except that it had a column of round windows going up its façade, instead of square or flower-shaped ones, or pocket-sized balconies. This is how normies live, if they can't afford the private community lifestyle. All the privacy in the world, no community.

Christy placed her hand on the biometric pad by the door. It opened. I looked up into the camera over the door.

"Can I come up and see how the other half lives?" I said.

She'd been giving me mixed signals, but I felt pretty sure that I was interpreting those signals correctly. At the same time, I was aware that I was pushing pretty hard. I braced for rejection.

Even in the tastefully dim light from the lobby, I could see her blushing again. "I don't have any whiskey. But I can offer you lentil salad. Or herb tea?"

I reached out and curled my fingers around hers. Small and fine-boned, they stayed in my hand. "I hate herb tea," I said. "But I'll be fine with whatever you've got."

Her apartment was even smaller than Dolph's, but as different as could be. Houseplants perched on fiddly little shelves, and dangled from the ceiling in tiny hand-painted pots. Pink and white Christmas lights radiated a gentle ambiance. A waterfall curtain created an artificial partition between the kitchenette and the bedroom. Shoes and stacks of folded clothes and art materials occupied every surface. For the first time tonight, I was well and truly beyond the reach of police surveillance. Tension left my body ... and another kind of tension, thick and primal, replaced it.

In that tiny space, there was nowhere we could stand and not be within touching distance.

I stood behind Christy as she messed with the electric kettle, pretending to make tea.

She went still, like a cornered prey animal. Her hands stopped moving. She put the kettle down. Then she turned to face me. Desire sparked and cracked between us like electricity, rising into her face, turning it pink.

As I bent to kiss her, she rose on her tiptoes and met me halfway, twining her slender arms around my neck.

I was conscious, for a little while, of smelling like Rafael Ijiuto, and not having shaved, and being clumsy. I was rusty, of course, not having done this for a while. I hadn't done it sober since Sophia. There you have it. More than that, though, Christy made me feel clumsy because of her physical delicacy. Her arms were exquisitely slim, her breasts small enough to cup in a palm. Her nipples were tiny nubs, the same pink as her cheeks when the excitement rose in them. Her apartment reflected her petiteness—her bed was so hemmed in by little shelves and doo-dads that my feet, sticking off the end, brought down a shelf of knick-knacks. It made me feel loutish, like a wild animal inside a walk-in jewellery box. But then, as I say, I forgot about that—until she reminded me.

I was lying with my knees bent up on the too-small bed, breathing heavily, my body limp with the afterglow of pleasure. She was breathing heavily, too. I was pretty sure it had been good for her. Sophia had rarely come during regular sex with me—in retrospect, a bad omen for our marriage. My success with Christy pushed that failure farther away into the bottom drawer of my memory.

She lay half beside me, half on top of me, twirling her fingers in my chest hair. "Is this the color you are," she asked softly, "when you … you know?"

I scrunched my chin into my chest to see her face. Her cinnamon hair lay coiled in sexy locks on my chest hair, which is brown, a shade darker than the hair on my head. "When I Shift? No. Wolves are more kinda gray."

"You're a wolf?" she questioned, looking up at me.

Then I remembered she knew about the tiger *and* that damn jaguar, but I hadn't told her about the wolf. Three forms, well, three wasn't completely unheard-of. "Sometimes," I said, hoping she'd leave it at that.

But I was wrong. She wasn't interested in how many forms I had or what they were specifically. Only Shifters care about that kind of thing.

It was Shifting itself that intrigued her.

She stroked my chest and biceps, her fingers pleasantly soft, tickling. "What does it feel like?" she said, her voice husky with lust. "If I'm crossing the line, just ignore me. I've just … never seen it."

"You've never seen someone Shift?" I said, half-amused, half surprised. "But you work—"

"At a school in Shiftertown, yeah. I know lots of Shifters." She sat up, arranging the sheet over her lap in a self-mocking performance of prudery. "But it may surprise you to learn I've never slept with one before."

I laughed, and at the same time, the roundabout confession of vulnerability touched me. I admitted, "I haven't done this in a while, either."

"So what does it feel like?"

"Good. Damn good." I reached out to touch her through the sheet. The sight of her like that was turning me on again.

"Oh … Never mind."

I knew what she'd really meant. I moved my hand to cup her flank. "You want to know what Shifting feels like?"

"Not if you're not allowed to tell me."

What did she think, there was some kind of a rulebook that got handed out? "It's just … hard to explain." I was about to leave it at that, but I saw the flash of disappointment in her eyes. She could tell I was fobbing her off, the way we do tend to fob normies off, because it *is* hard to explain, and because the truth ain't pretty. I didn't want her to pull away from me. I reminded myself that we were being honest with each other here. "OK. Have you ever had a root canal?"

"Uh, yeah. Years ago."

"OK. Now multiply that by an order of magnitude, and imagine your whole body is a nerve. The bones, muscles, blood vessels, *everything* has to drastically realign. No way that's not gonna hurt."

"Oh."

"So the short answer is, Shifting hurts like a son of a bitch." I hastened to add, "But you get used to it. And it only lasts a few seconds, anyway. The more you do it, the faster you get."

"Wow," she said uncertainly. She wasn't touching me anymore.

"But in all other respects, we're exactly the same as you," I said. Wishful thinking? Yes, of course. I reached for her and pulled her down on top of me. Her mouth landed on mine, her slender thighs clamped my hips …

And my phone rang.

It didn't actually ring per se. It loudly began to play the song "Beast Mode," which we used to blast on Tech Duinn when we were getting ready to roll out.

That meant it was Dolph, and it was an emergency.

"Oh, Jesus," I said. "Sorry. I have to take that."

I rolled off the bed and located my phone in my jeans.

"What?!?" I growled.

It was Dolph's phone, but Martin's voice. "Are you guys complete space rocks? This man is in severe shock. His pulse is up, his temperature is down, his skin is clammy, he's unresponsive."

"Oh," I said. "Shit." I could hear Dolph murmuring in the background.

"Dolph called me to ask about the symptoms of heatstroke." Martin was the ship's medic, insofar as we had one. The rest of us? Graced with Shifter immune systems, we didn't know a blessed thing about medicine. Obviously. But at least Dolph had had the sense to doubt his own diagnosis, and called Martin, which was more than I had done. "So I come over to take a look at the patient, and I find him on the brink of *death*. He's got to be moved to hospital. Immediately. Can you get here, or do we need to call an ambulance?"

"I'll be there in fifteen," I said.

Swamped with guilt from all sides at once, I got dressed at Shifter speed. Christy sat on her bed, hugging her knees, watching me.

I hit the door in two strides. "I wasn't kidding about my job being exciting," I said with a pale attempt at humor. "I'll call you. OK?"

"OK," she said in a stunned little voice, blinking at me through her waterfall curtain.

I got in my truck and bombed back to Shiftertown.

32

As soon as I got to Dolph's apartment I saw that Martin was right. Rafael Ijiuto's skin had a blue tinge, and touching him felt like touching a frog, despite the hot and stuffy night. Martin stood back, holding a blood pressure cuff and shaking his head. "Better start thinking about where to dump the body."

"No way," I said. "This is the guy who killed Kimmie."

"You don't know that."

"We need to find out—

"If you believed he did it," Martin said, "you'd just let him die."

I threw up my hands. "Right, I *don't* know that he did it, and therefore taking him to hospital is the right thing to do."

"On your own head be it," Martin said. "Shoreside General?"

"Nope," Dolph said, lifting Ijiuto's legs. I took his shoulders. "Dr. Zeb's."

"He's a normie, right?" Martin said.

"Yeah, but c'mon," I said. "They're not gonna refuse to treat him in this condition."

We put Ijiuto in the truck. Dolph called ahead. Five minutes later we were unloading him onto a stretcher at the gate of Dr. Zeb's, officially known as the Tau Medical Clinic.

This was another corner of Shiftertown free from surveillance, because it dated back to an earlier age. Gravelnuts and devil palms hung over the garden wall. A mulched layer of nuts and dead palm fronds made the sidewalk slippery. Pingos chirped in the trees, and cars jostled for places in the vertical parking lot acros the street. We followed the automated stretcher up the drive to a sprawling colonial mansion. Strangler vines twined up the walls, and defunct solar panels pointed every which way, so that the roof looked like a metal coral reef festooned with seaweed, but the windows blazed with light. A pair of nurses stood smoking under one of the murder oaks in the garden. They crushed out their cigarettes and hurried over to help. They asked whether Ijiuto was a Shifter, but when we said no, they just nodded and rushed him inside. They took his vital signs and got him on a drip to stabilize him until Dr. Zeb could come to examine him.

Dr. Zeb is a saint among Shifters, the eighth-generation head of the Tau family. The Taus were among the first Shifters to arrive on Ponce de Leon. They opened a clinic in their big old house in what is now Smith's End. It was needed, as Shifters were heavily discriminated against in those days. Later on, they bought the house next door, knocked down the garden wall, and built a roofed cloister joining "Building A" and "Building B," to keep up with an increasing flow of patients … so what does that say about our society nowadays?

From outside, the place looks charmingly tumbledown, not surprising given its age. Almost all the other early colonial mansions in Mag-Ingat have long since been subdivided into apartments, or torn down and replaced with row housing like where I live. But on the inside, Dr. Zeb's was far more modern than my apartment. Rafael Ijiuto's room smelled as clean as the inside of a dishwasher. Monitoring equipment projected a living map of his body onto the screen that took up all of one wall.

"Heatstroke and septicemia," Dr. Zeb diagnosed, after doing a blood test. "Where did he get this cut on his foot?"

"In the Tunjle," I said. "We think."

"That would do it," Dr. Zeb said. "Ponce de Leon does not like man. Never has, never will. Yet we're equal to her wiles." He spoke to the duty nurse. "We'll put him on antibiotics immediately. Treat the site of infection with antimicrobials, and monitor his blood pressure. He doesn't need artificial ventilation at the moment, but have a unit on standby." He turned back to me. "Is there anything else I need to know about the patient?"

This was a question with as many hidden dimensions as a skip field. I said, "Can one of us stay with him?"

Dr. Zeb gave me a measuring look. Tall and broad, in his fifties, he was given to stroking his muttonchop whiskers as if they were a pet. "I don't want any trouble in my hospital, Mike."

I lifted my t-shirt and turned around to show that I had left my gun in the lockbox at reception. Dolph and Martin had, too.

"All right," Dr. Zeb said. "One of you can stay here. The others will have to wait in the cloister."

"When would you expect him to regain consciousness?" I asked, trying not to reveal how much rode on it.

"Anytime on a spectrum running from now to never," Dr. Zeb said. "The human body is still a mystery to us in many ways. So much depends on the spirit. But merely to have survived in this condition is a sign of a tough character. So I'm optimistic."

Martin took the first shift at Ijiuto's bedside. Dolph and I went to sit in the cloister.

It was a building in its own right, really, with one long glass wall. Desks against the other wall provided out-patient services to a trickle of Shifters, even at this time of night: blood tests, drug tests, prescription refills. Some of the patients came in human form, some as animals. Orderlies trudged through from one building to the other, wheeling bins full of bloodsoaked gauze and linen. Their scrubs were spattered with blood, too. As you might expect, the number one reason Shifters wind up in hospital is mauling injuries and bites.

Dolph and I sat on one of the ripped-up benches. Weeds scraped against the glass at our backs. I yawned and went to get vending-machine coffee for us both. Dolph, that excellent soul, had a flask in his hip pocket. We spiked our coffees, improving them immensely.

"So where were you?" he said.

The memory of Christy came like a sweet breeze amidst the depressing ambiance of the hospital. I smirked.

"Aha," he said.

"Uh huh," I said. Like a lovestruck teenager, I struggled to suppress a grin.

"Pics or it didn't happen."

"You've met her."

"No way. You finally hooked up with Ember?" This was the friend of Nevaeh's that she and Dolph kept trying to push me together with. Ember was a nice girl, and her animal form was a sea lion as sleek and curvy as she was. But I couldn't get interested in a woman who Shifted for money ... and probably did other things for money, as well. Maybe that was the self-deluding hypocrite in me at work again.

"Nope, someone different," I said. "You met her at the St. Francis party at Lulu's school last year." Dolph had helped out by appearing as the lowly ox, one of the animals traditionally associated with St. Francis. Try and find a real ox Shifter anywhere on Ponce de Leon. You won't. Dolph was good enough at Shifting to give it a go, and although his ox came out a bit wonky, with paws instead of hooves, the children had loved it. They'd never seen a real one, anyway. That was one of the times I thought we might have a shot at convincing Dolph to settle down before it was too late. He had so obviously— to me, anyway—enjoyed the children's adoration, and the kick he got from doing a good deed.

"OK," he said. "So it's the anti-Sophia. Helena? Alex? Marlene?" He started naming nice, wholesome Shifter moms I might be having an adulterous affair with. I let him go on like that for a while, and then I told him it was the student life coordinator.

Dolph pulled a sad face and shook his head. "You're hopeless, Mike."

"On the contrary, I'm feeling pretty hopeful about it," I said.

"She's a normie, isn't she?"

"So?"

"Clearly, all she wants is for you to fuck her in wolf form."

I remembered the heat in Christy's voice when she started asking me about Shifting. But I didn't want to think of her that way. I said, "You just think that because all the normie girls *you've* dated were fur-chasing slags."

"Nothing wrong with a fur-chasing slag in her rightful place," Dolph said. "Under me." We both laughed. No, it wasn't very gentlemanly. But we were sitting in a hospital, waiting for a man to die. "Anyway," Dolph resumed, "you don't see me dating that kind of girl anymore, do you?"

"No, 'cause now you've got a Shifter slag," I said.

"I learned my lesson," Dolph said. "I'm starting to think you're never gonna."

"Give me a break," I yawned, not feeling as casual about the whole thing as I was acting. "I've hardly seen anyone since Sophia."

"That's what I mean. I would have hoped you learned your lesson there."

"By the way, did you find out anything?"

"Nice segue."

"Douche. Did you?"

I knew Dolph had attempted a new data dive in search of clues as to how Rafael Ijiuto had wound up here.

"Nothing new," he said. "But I figure Ijiuto was planning to sell the contraband on to the Travellers. That could be how they met."

"Maybe, but why choose that refugee camp for the rendezvous?"

"So the Travellers could pick up some burners at the same time?" Dolph's expression turned somber. "Speaking of the refugee camp, I almost forgot. Something interesting happened there a couple of days ago. An outbreak of interstellar variant kuru."

"What??" I almost spilled my coffee.

"Yeah. They've found six cases in the refugee camp. There's been violence. Someone tried to burn down the local hospital."

"Let me see."

We pored over the official news clips and the supplementary accounts that Dolph had found on private networks. *Outbreak* was putting it strongly. Six cases is not an epidemic. But the reaction among the refugees and natives had claimed a further twenty-odd lives and counting. I remembered the main drag of the camp, lined with the stalls of human entrepreneurs. Now, smoke hazed the wind, while mobs dragged victims by the heels on suspicion of cannibalism. The shocking scenes gave me a new perspective on the asylum department's decision regarding Pippa. Irrational fear could wreak havoc even in the absence of a real threat of contagion. And kuru evoked an even stronger reaction than your average contagious disease, because it was coupled with cannibalism, one of the last unshakeable taboos.

"Well," I said, "at least now we know Pippa didn't get it from eating someone's brains."

"Inference unsupported by the facts," Dolph said, pointing a finger at me. "The natives' network data is crap, but they've managed to trace the outbreak back to somewhere around here." Dolph pulled up a map of the refugee camp on his phone and pointed to the busy intersection where we had eaten lunch, and Rafael Ijiuto had had tea. "That's where the movements of all the infected people overlap." Dolph waggled his eyebrows. "Who knows what was in that stew? I thought it tasted like chicken …"

I grinned, taking the risk as lightly as he did.

But his speculation planted a seed, and in the next minutes I started to question our presumption of immunity. My confidence had already been shaken by the near-fatal mistake we had made with Rafael Ijiuto. That was proof positive that I was pretty clueless about the operations of the human body, much as I liked to think I knew every nerve and sinew in my own body by name.

In the back of my head, I heard Christy saying, *You and your crew should get tested … just in case …*

I stood up, and tugged Dolph to his feet. "Let's get tested," I said.

"Oh come on, man," he said. "I was just kidding. We're immune to that kind of stuff."

"Yeah, but you never know."

"I don't like needles."

"You wimping out on me, Hardlander?" I felt as if I could please Christy by doing as she had suggested, even though I'd walked out on her with the lamest of get-away lines. "Here we are in a freaking hospital. There'll never be a better time."

Dolph grumbled, but he agreed to do it, if only because the nurse at the blood test desk was young and cute. Her gentle fingers found the vein in my arm, reminding me of Christy's touch, and then she stabbed me with a needle big enough for an Ek. I kept my teeth locked so as not to forewarn Dolph. He in his turn came out from behind the curtain grimacing and pressing down on the little bandage in the crook of his elbow.

"Interstellar variant kuru?" the nurse said, lifting her pretty eyebrows. It was not the most common test, obviously.

"Yes," Dolph said, "and you'd better also test *him* for the clap."

I jabbed him with my elbow. "Interstellar variant kuru," I affirmed. "When will we get the results?"

"Well, this is not a standard test, so we'll have to send your samples to the lab. You should be able to pick them up in a week's time."

"Can't we just call you?" I foresaw that I'd never get around to coming back for the results.

"No, sir, our policy is that you do have to pick them up in person."

I left Dolph leaning on the desk, flirting with the nurse, and sat down to finish my cup of coffee-flavored Scotch. My thoughts returned to the refugee camp.

It could not possibly be a coincidence that there'd been an outbreak of interstellar variant kuru at the same time the Travellers were there.

Biological warfare wasn't their style. There was no percentage for them in killing everyone. On the other hand, they didn't draw the line anywhere else—not at slavery, or rape, or murder. So nothing actually stopped them from using biological weapons, I supposed, except a certain healthy fear of payback.

But when I pictured Sophia, or Zane, chopping up a human brain procured from some benighted failed world, and smuggling it into a pot of stew at the refugee camp—well, it was laughable. There was no conceivable upside for them in such an outré scenario.

Confirming this, the news reported no more sightings of Traveller ships in the afflicted system.

Ten PM turned into eleven PM, and I began to worry about Lucy. It was irrational to some extent, as I trusted Nanny B to look after her all the times I was off-world. But these were not ordinary circumstances. Never before had I come this close to catching Parsec out in ... *something* ... deeply illegal. The other shoe was yet to drop there. What if Parsec came by my apartment looking for me? He knew where I lived. What if he found Lucy home alone, with only a bot to protect her?

Yes, Irene and Rex were upstairs. But factor in Shifter stealth and traffic noise, and upstairs might as well be a world away.

I called Robbie.

"Hi, sir!" He was sitting in a smoky café.

"I didn't wake you up?" I said.

"Nope. I'm studying."

"Glad to hear it. This is somewhat irregular, but how would you feel about hanging out at my place tonight? I might have to stay out all night, and I'd like to have someone there with Lucy."

Robbie cocked his head wolfishly. "I get your drift, sir." He hesitated. "I heard from Rex that your crew is pretty tight."

"Yup," I said. "We're like family."

"That's so cool," he said. He blinked several times, and lifted a cigarette to his mouth to hide his emotional reaction. "I'll head over there right now, sir. I'm—I'm honored to have this chance to earn your trust."

"Thanks, Robbie," I said. "I'll call when I know when I'm coming home." I hung up, and called Nanny B to let her know that Robbie was on his way.

"He gets it," Dolph said.

"Yeah, I think he does." Robbie understood that he wouldn't just be signing up to do administrative paperwork. He'd be signing up to kick ass if necessary. This was his real job training, even if the night passed uneventfully, as I devoutly hoped.

Twenty minutes later, I checked my home security cameras, and found him sitting on my front porch. He had his holobook open on his thighs, but he was watching the street. He got it, all right.

Martin came down to the cloister for a coffee.

Dolph went up to Ijiuto's room to relieve him.

The hours slipped past.

At one AM I went up to take my turn at Ijiuto's bedside.

He lay as still as the sketch figure on the monitoring screen. Red pulse points on the figure's wrists throbbed steadily. The blood pressure indicator on one arm remained dangerously low.

I pulled up the hard chair to the head of his bed. They'd changed him into hospital clothes. The wraparound tunic gapped over his chest. On his collarbone lay a chain with a pendant in the form of a three-inch knife, in a sheath studded with diamonds.

Where had I seen a pendant like that before?

That's right. *Pippa.* She had tried to give me a very similar pendant to pay the kids' way to Ponce de Leon.

"That's weird," I murmured. "Y'all know each other? Or were they just selling those things at the camp?"

Something else to ask him about. If he ever woke up.

More hours slipped past. At some point, my ruminations about the refugee camp became dreams that I was there. I was in a mob jostling around an infected victim to tear her apart. I got a hand on the victim's ankle, and glimpsed her face. It was Pippa …

My startle reflex woke me up and brought me to my feet at the same time.

Dolph stood in the doorway, in jackal form. His neck fur bristled and his ears were pricked. "Come on," he said quietly.

"What? Where?" The monitoring screen said it was 03:20. Ijiuto's condition remained unchanged.

"Place's shut down for the night." Dolph nosed at Ijiuto's bare feet, which stuck out from the sheets, and wrinkled his lips. "Outpatient desks are closed. Everyone's gone home except the night nurses."

"And?"

Dolph's teeth flashed. Slowly and with great emphasis, he said, "Kaspar Silverback is in a private room on the second floor."

"Ah."

"Let's pay him a visit."

"We can't start anything at Dr. Zeb's," I said, still rubbing my eyes.

"We're not going to start anything. We're just going to ask him a few questions."

Now fully awake, I glanced at Ijiuto. He lay like the dead, only the sheet over his chest moving as he breathed. The whole place was quiet —no more bells, intercoms, or footsteps in the hall.

I had promised Dr. Zeb I wouldn't make trouble at his hospital. This was the closest thing to neutral ground that existed in Shiftertown.

But.

D'Alencon suspected me of being involved in Parsec's contraband racket. If I didn't clear my name, I could end up ruined.

"OK. Let's do it." I pulled my clothes off, stuffed them under Ijiuto's bed, and Shifted.

33

My claws clicked on shiny tiles as I followed Dolph down the stairs. Martin had agreed to stay with Ijiuto. He thought this was a bad idea. He was probably right. All I could promise him was that we would be discreet.

Dolph slunk ahead of me into the second-floor hallway. He was leading me to Silverback's room, whose location he had learned from the pretty hematology nurse. I hardly needed to be told where it was. My wolf's nose picked out the scent of bear from amidst the crazy tangle of odors perceptible—to an animal—through the sterile, ammoniac hospital smell. Either the in-patient ward was suddenly full of bears, or Kaspar Silverback had had a lot of visitors.

Each room had a sliding door wide enough for a bed to be wheeled through.

Silverback's door was closed.

At the far end of the hall, a soft red light shone from the nurse's station around the corner. Despite the interior renovations, this was still a 200-year-old colonial mansion, and the halls were all corners. We couldn't see the nurse on duty, and he or she couldn't see us.

We listened at the door for a good sixty seconds. Not a sound came from within. Silverback was alone.

Dolph rose on his hind legs and pushed the door handle sideways with his nose until he could get a paw around it.

No locks on hospital doors.

It slid soundlessly open.

Dolph flashed through and leapt onto the bed within.

I followed, taking the time to paw the door closed behind me. I heard a grunt, a cry, and I jumped up and hit the light switch—it was in the same place here as in Ijiuto's room, a floor above.

Kaspar Silverback lay in the bed, his face fixed in a grimace of terror, eyes closed. Dolph stood on his torso. He let out a low, liquid growl and clawed gently at the bandages wrapping Silverback's right shoulder and chest. Silverback opened his eyes and saw me.

"Hello," I said. "How's the flying taxi business?"

If we were going to get any information out of him, we would have to ask questions that gave away our own identities. And he'd probably guess anyway. There are all too many wolves in Shiftertown, but not so many jackals, and fewer jackals and wolves that work together.

"You offworlder cunts," Silverback said. "San Damiano nobs. Venison-eatin' bourgies …" He went on in this vein. It was kind of impressive how well he could swear with a jackal standing on his chest.

He had not yet exhausted his store of invective when Dolph got impatient and yanked at his bandages with his teeth. A patch of self-sealing gauze came away with a ripping sound. Silverback let out a shriek. "Doesn't look that bad," Dolph said. "Sure you're not just faking to get off work?"

Silverback moaned.

"What do you do, anyway?"

"I'm a driver. Just a driver."

"So you don't know anything, huh? You're just a driver, huh? They never tell you shit, huh?" With each question, Dolph ripped more of Silverback's bandages off. The skin underneath was stained with antibacterial wash, the gunshot wound an open, oozing mouth. Silverback started to wheeze. I remembered that he had a lung injury.

"So you drive for Mujin Inc?" I said.

"No! Yes!"

"Yes or no?"

"I work for Trident Overland. But I'm on contract to Mujin Inc."

"What's your regular route?"

"Just in the city, out to the spaceport, whatever needs doing," Silverback gasped. He had turned the corner. He was now eager to cooperate. "I don't drive the inland routes. I got a family. Please, guys."

"Most of the inland routes are self-driving, anyway," Dolph said to me.

"You go to and from the spaceport," I said. "So you pick up cargoes and take 'em through customs? Pay the duties?"

"Right, that's right."

"That's what you did with that cargo that got returned to Mujin Inc?"

"Yeah, 'course."

"Bullshit," I said. "You took that through the green channel without paying jack."

"Parsec's gonna kill me," Silverback whimpered.

"Not our problem," Dolph said. He panted into Silverback's face, teeth bared. Silverback groaned and thrashed in terror.

"All right! All right! Yeah, our guy killed the scanners that time! Figure there was something in those crates."

I stiffened. If it was data, they would not have needed to kill the scanners. That meant our first guess had been wrong. The contraband was something else, something that *would* show up on the scanners … if they were working.

"What kind of something?"

"I don't know!" Silverback said. "Coulda been drugs. That don't take up much room. Or electronic components! Ms. Hart was buying all kinds of shit for the lab."

I surged forward to the bed. "Hart?" That was Sophia's maiden name. "Where does she come in? How'd she end up working with you?"

"I dunno, man! We registered the company, she showed up. That's all I know!"

"What lab?" Dolph said.

Silverback tried to answer, and coughed. I saw bright flecks of blood on his lips. Shit, we might end up killing the guy. I didn't want that.

"She's a computer scientist," I said to Dolph. "That's what she used to do, remember? She got her doctorate in AI."

"So she was building AI for you?" Dolph said. "To do what?"

"I don't know! I told you all I know!"

I thought he probably had. But Dolph wasn't satisfied. Nothing would satisfy him now except blood. "You ain't told us shit." He set his teeth into Silverback's uninjured shoulder. Blood trickled onto the sheets.

Silverback panicked. He started to scream for help. I pounced on him and physically clamped his mouth shut with my jaws. I tasted the fresh blood from his lungs.

The door slammed open.

I leapt off Silverback's bed, twisted in the air, and landed facing the door.

Instead of the duty nurse, there stood Buzz Parsec, large as life and three times as ugly. He was wearing a raincoat that made him look even larger, its shoulders dark-dappled with rain. As he stared at us, he shrugged it off. "Found them," he growled.

34

"HELP!" Silverback squawked. He coughed blood. "Help me, sir! Get these dogs offa me!"

Dolph had already leapt off the bed and ducked behind the curtains. I faced Parsec, stiff-legged, my fur bristling, my ears flat to my skull. Visceral hatred swamped my thoughts, and trickled out of my mouth in a continuous low growl. Parsec folded his raincoat and hung it over one arm, his face as motionless as a lump of bread dough with holes poked in it for eyes.

"That one's Starrunner," Silverback burbled, as if Parsec wouldn't have already guessed who we were. "The other one's his jackal buddy."

"Take 'em down," Parsec said, turning his head slightly to speak over his shoulder, without taking his eyes off me. "Try and not make too much noise. There's patients trying to sleep."

I sprang at Parsec.

He was already moving, bringing up the arm with the coat folded over it. He flapped the coat in my face, so I couldn't see anything for a second, and my teeth snapped on air. As I fell, I bumped against Parsec, knocking him into the wall.

A grizzly bear shouldered into the room. He was the size of a small minivan. I knew it was one of the Kodiaks. The monstrous bear surged past Parsec, straight at me, his head stretched out on his neck, jaws snapping.

My claws scrabbled on the floor as I reversed my momentum. I felt the Kodiak's hot breath on my back. I gathered my haunches and bounded over Silverback's bed, putting the bed between me and the bears.

Cornered.

I focused on Parsec, who was hanging back near the doorway. I didn't care about the Kodiak, except inasmuch as he was in between me and Parsec. If I was going to die, I wanted to take Parsec with me.

Behind the curtains at my back, the window slammed open.

Dolph had worked the catch. Jackals are good with their teeth.

Hot, wet air blew into the air-conditioned room.

The Kodiak started to climb over the bed to get at me, disregarding Silverback's cries.

Thoughts of suicidally attacking Parsec melted away as my animal instincts zeroed in on escape. I turned tail, fought with the curtains for a nightmarish instant, and got my front paws up on the windowsill. I looked out into pitch blackness. Rain needled into my face. Dolph had already jumped.

I launched myself into the dark.

For a split second I fully expected to die.

I *knew* we were only on the second floor. I knew that my wolf could fall better than my human form. I knew Dolph had survived, because I could hear him barking below.

All the same, it felt like spacewalking without a tether, freefalling towards the end of reality. Lucy's face flashed into my mind, and then I struck a bush. It broke my fall. I scraped through foliage and twigs and thumped to wet grass, landing on my feet.

Dolph yipped piercingly. I saw him standing in the night, his nose pointing up at the window we had jumped from. The Kodiak's head poked out.

"Oh my fucking God," I said, scrambling onto all four feet. "How did they get here? Silverback must've alerted them."

"Naw," Dolph said. "It was probably someone saw us waiting in the cloister. Ring, ring, oh hello Mr. Parsec, guess who's here? Shifters are such tools."

It was raining. There's a joke that we don't have weather forecasts on Ponce de Leon, we have weather timetables. This time of year, we usually get a shower around nine PM, and then at three AM it rains heavily, sometimes until morning. Water flattened my fur and ran into my eyes.

The Kodiak disappeared from the window.

"Front door's locked, so they didn't get in that way," Dolph said. "Musta got in through the ER. They'll come back out that way. Come on!"

"Ijiuto," I said.

"Martin's there. Anyway, they won't start a fight inside the hospital."

"They just did," I said. But there was no way we could get to Ijiuto without going through the ER, short of jumping back through that damn window, and even wolves can't leap *that* high, so I followed Dolph through the wet garden.

Neither of us knew that at that very moment, Martin was facing off with the other Kodiak twin in Ijiuto's room. Whatever little furry bird told Parsec we were at Dr. Zeb's had also told him that we'd brought a patient in. While Parsec stomped upstairs to check on Silverback, he had sent the other Kodiak twin to search the rest of the in-patient rooms.

So Larry Kodiak—or maybe Gary, Martin said he couldn't tell— had poked his nose around the privacy curtain and found a fifteen-foot python coiled on the foot of Ijiuto's bed. Martin had Shifted when we did, in hopes of catching some Z's.

When his flickering tongue caught the scent of the Kodiak, Martin poured his body off the bed and wriggled across the floor. Snakes can move *fast*. The grizzly bear jumped back and swiped at him with a paw the size of a trashcan lid. While the bear's claws scraped along

Martin's scales, which are not really scales, because he is not a reptile, but some trick he's figured out involving the Shifting of skin cells into pseudo-keratin, Martin struck. He wrapped a muscular coil around the grizzly's neck, threw another coil around his chest, and started to squeeze. The grizzly rampaged around the room, trying to shake Martin off. The monitoring unit beside the bed hit the floor with a crash. Alarms shrieked.

Meanwhile, Dolph and I were in even worse trouble.

We had flowed through the wet grass, beneath murder oaks, through the neglected shrubbery, and reached the ER entrance in Building B at the same time as Parsec and the other Kodiak twin did. They spilled out of the automatic doors, with an orderly chasing after them, and parted to go around a parked ambulance. The Kodiak paused at the edge of the light that bled down the drive, the rain sparkling on his fur. He sniffed the dark.

He was only about two meters from where we crouched in the cover of some rhododendrons.

"Just a little bit closer," Dolph breathed. "Come on, come on, you fat sack of shit …"

I was smelling the Kodiak twin, but I was watching Parsec. He walked towards his sidekick, and although he was still in human form, his shoulders rolled bearishly, and his little piggy eyes glared into the rain. "Starrunner," he yelled. "Starrunner. You want information, you ask *me.*" He thumbed his chest, as if he knew I was watching him. "I came to you, but you're what, too fucking scared to come to me?"

He had half a point.

"Come to me," Dolph echoed, jackal-laughing under his breath.

The Kodiak twin lunged towards us. He had smelt us out.

Dolph was ready. He exploded out of the rhododendrons and launched himself at the grizzly's throat.

He never got there. A dark, wet shape rose up out of the bushes to our right. It shambled swiftly forward in that terrifying ursine lope, and snapped at Dolph's neck. I heard a high thin bark of pain from my friend as he hit the ground with one shoulder and rolled sideways.

I was already moving. As the grizzly reared up to pounce on Dolph, my feet left the ground. My forepaws grappled the grizzly's head, boxing it, and my muzzle dug into the thick fur at his throat. I caught skin between my teeth, tasted blood. The grizzly crashed back to the ground with me still hanging on.

Out of the corner of my eye, I saw Dolph and the other bear skittering around each other, lunging and snapping. The other bear was Canuck. I knew because he was calling Dolph a rabid dog and breathlessly describing how he would fuck him in the ass.

Dolph didn't waste breath talking. Faster than the bear, he darted around Canuck and hurled himself onto Canuck's shoulder. He clung on, snarling and gnawing at Canuck's fur, as the ginger-tinged bear rose onto his hind legs in an attempt to shake him off.

The Kodiak clawed my back. He didn't break the skin, but he knocked me loose. I dropped to the ground, snarling. The Kodiak made a rush at me. I dodged and got my teeth into his flank. The long wet grass tangled my legs and impeded my agility. But now I had a hold the Kodiak couldn't dislodge me from. I clawed my way onto his back, savaging him with my teeth. The smell of blood and fur and fear maddened me. His agonized roars were music to my ears.

Parsec must have seen that his bears were in danger of losing the fight. Right there in the rain, he Shifted.

He dropped his trousers and stepped out of them as his hands reached for the ground, fingers transforming into claws, the palms of his hands thickening into pads. His shoulders swelled. Fur burst through the ripping seams of his shirt. His human forehead shrank away and his jaw lengthened into a muzzle. The extra meat on his torso, which made him look overweight as a man, transformed into the sleek-pelted bulk of a brown grizzly bear.

He Shifted faster than anyone I knew, except one person.

His fur was still growing as he leapt at me, his teeth bared.

I spat a mouthful of Kodiak fur out, slithered to the ground and danced away, past the rhododendrons. I stopped beside the tented roots of a murder oak.

Parsec rose on his hind legs. He strutted towards Canuck and Dolph, his arms extended as he prepared to sweep Dolph into his deadly, bonecracking hug. Dolph didn't see him. He was intent on shredding Canuck's meat off his bones.

I dragged breath into my lungs and howled.

Dolph's head jerked up. He dodged Parsec's hug just in time. Abandoning his victim, he leapt sideways.

The Kodiak lunged at him, forcing him to dodge again.

It all seemed to have been going on forever: the rain, the growling and snarling, the awful slippery footing, the jolts of adrenaline hitting increasingly tired muscles. In reality, of course, it had only been a couple of minutes.

Dr. Zeb burst out of the hospital, carrying a shotgun. Orderlies at his side turned high-power flashlights on the battle, blinding us all.

I assumed Parsec would put his tail between his legs—not that he had much of a tail, just a bear's stub—and apologize to Dr. Zeb. I was on the point of doing so myself.

But he didn't. Silhouetted in the flashlights, he reared on his hind legs, roaring. Then he dropped back onto all fours and charged straight at me.

I had no room to maneuver. I had allowed myself to get trapped between the bushes and the murder oak. I had two choices: face Parsec's attack head-on, or run.

35

I ran.

Deeper into the garden.

Away from the light, away from the failing patches of terrestrial shrubbery, into the tangle of invasive vegetation from all over the Cluster.

Every time I flattened myself to crawl under a shrapnel bush or pufferplant, I heard Parsec crashing through the undergrowth behind me.

He wasn't going to quit the chase until he had his teeth in my hide.

I fetched up against another murder oak. I had no idea where I was now, but I figured I must be pretty close to the end of the garden. This could be one of the murder oaks that overhung the garden wall.

Its trunk was tapered, not sheer, but branchless for the first twenty feet. I couldn't climb it.

So I Shifted again.

It was a big risk. Parsec was only a few seconds behind me. But the only person I knew who could Shift faster than him was ... me.

I willed my wolf away. The pain I had told Christy about washed along my nerves. I shuddered and kicked the air, lying in a grotesque knot of half-formed limbs and heaving flesh among the murder oak's roots. Twenty seconds later, I regained my feet as a jaguar.

Jaguars are *excellent* at climbing trees.

I scrabbled and clawed my way up that trunk in nothing flat, and stopped in the first big crutch for a breather.

Unfortunately, bears are good at climbing trees, too.

Parsec reached the murder oak. He sniffed around the roots, detecting my scent. Then he rose on his hind legs and began to climb. His claws punched into the wet bark, tearing it off in chunks. Relentlessly, he hauled himself upwards.

I could've stayed where I was and knocked him off the trunk when he reached me.

I didn't even think about that until later.

I clawed my way higher, from branch to branch, knocking down twigs and ripping lengths of strangler vine away from the trunk. The foliage was so thick it was almost dry in here, although the rain drummed noisily on the canopy. I sneezed on bark dust. At last, glimmers of streetlight penetrated the foliage. I could now see where I was: at the edge of the garden, as I'd guessed. I looked down—*way* down—at the sidewalk.

Parsec's head thrust through the strangler vines, level with my dangling tail. "Treed ya," he said, and broke off in astonishment on seeing that I was now a jaguar.

His surprise saved me. I frantically started climbing again. Higher I went and higher, until I reached a branch that bent under my weight.

A good forty kilos heavier than me, and less agile, Parsec had to stop further down. He couldn't reach me, unless he wanted to risk breaking a branch and falling to his death.

"So *you* were that jaguar," he said, referring to our run-in a few years back. "Mighta guessed. How many forms do you have, anyway?"

"A couple," I said breathlessly.

"What's a couple? Three? Four? Five?"

"None of your goddamn business is what it is," I said, automatically defending my secret. The best defense is offense. I learned that lesson from Sophia. Head down, swaying on my branch above him, I went on the attack. "You used my ship to smuggle contraband."

"That's what got you all bent outta shape?"

"You crossed the line. You can break the law all you want, but don't involve me and mine."

"Jealous?"

"Jealous of a bottom-feeding, tax-evading, lying, cheating, stealing, murdering fleabag like you?"

"And rich," Parsec said, apparently unoffended. "Don't forget *rich.* I could buy you ten times over and not even miss the pocket change."

"Go ahead and try."

"Your miserable little company ain't worth my time," he sneered.

"Yet you saw fit to smuggle your shit on my ship, because my service is safer and more reliable than yours."

"Naw. Sometimes they check my ship, because I have a certain reputation," Parsec said, denying it out of one side of his mouth, while admitting I was right with the other. "They never check yours, because you also have a certain reputation—for being a law-abiding, tax-paying sucker." He laughed. "That's what's funny. *I* know the kind of thing you do out there."

"I don't shit where I live," I said, "and that's the difference between us." I felt big for a minute, before self-awareness kicked in and reminded me that I was clinging to a wet branch at the top of a murder oak, after getting into a fight at a hospital. That was pretty much the definition of shitting where I lived. I had just burned my wolf, too.

The irony, however, went straight over Parsec's head, probably because every day of his life was like the evening I'd just had. He let out a deep growl, scrambled a bit higher, and swatted up at me. He was too low to connect, but he couldn't contain his rage. "Did the cops promise you immunity?" he snarled.

Panic swept over me. "Do I look like a goddamn snitch?"

"You are a goddamn snitch! You sicced your tame cop onto my business uptown! Their algos were crawling all over our servers."

"About that business, Parsec—"

"*What did you tell them about me?*"

"Not a goddamn thing," I shouted. "If you think I'd betray my own kind like that, you're wrong! I'm not like you!"

"I've done more for Shifters on this planet than you ever have, or ever will." Parsec pointed up at me with one claw, a thing a real bear doesn't do. It was a visual reminder that this was a man in a bear suit made of flesh and bone. "I *know* about you," he said with a new gravity, like a judge pronouncing sentence on me. "You're a contractor. You use your shipping business as a cover to kill folks for money. You've taken out aliens, humans, even Eks, I hear."

So Sophia *had* told him.

"Do your new besties in the police know about that?"

"I don't do that shit anymore!" I winced at the shaky, frightened note in my own voice. "That was years and years ago."

"Uh huh. That's why you got enough guns on the *St. Clare* to fit out a Fleet battle cruiser."

He was right, of course. We still did take contracts from time to time. But only if the money was really good, and never anywhere near the Heartworlds. Never where anyone who mattered could find out. "I gotta make a living," I said.

Parsec hooted. "That's what's so funny! You hustle that hard, and you still can't even look after your family. Tell ya the truth, it would be sad, if I gave a shit."

"What are you talking about?" I roared. I slithered further down the tree, forgetting to be cautious. My paw flashed out at his head. He ducked, but my claws caught the edge of one ear, tearing it. The smell of blood pinged my nostrils through the odor of torn leaves and rain. I dropped down another branch and slashed at him again.

"Stay classy, Mike," Parsec said. He gave me a bearish grin, tongue lolling, and then rolled his head and shoulders downward through the vines and began to descend the tree.

I slithered after him. "You're playing with fire," I yelled. "That front company in Bonsucesso Tower is one fuck of a sketchy setup!"

"How would you know?" he yelled back.

"Because my ex is involved!"

"You should've hung onto that woman." Parsec's voice floated up to me, amidst the crashing sounds as he made his way down the tree.

"What is she building up there?"

"No fucking idea. Who cares, anyway?"

I heard the thump as he hit the ground—on the outside of the garden wall. I clawed out to the thin end of the branch I was on. Parsec's sleek black sub-limo idled at the curb. He shambled along the sidewalk towards it.

A gunshot cracked out, swiftly followed by another one. The sub-limo's rear windshield frosted over with cracks.

I didn't see where the shots came from.

Nor did Parsec, I guess. He didn't stop to find out. He sped up into an ursine gallop. The sub-limo's back door opened. More shots fractured the night. Parsec moved faster than I thought a bear could move. He hurled himself into the back seat. The sub-limo accelerated even before the door finished closing.

As it rocketed off down the street, Dolph—in human form once more—darted out from behind a truck parked across the street. It was *my* truck. I hadn't even noticed it. Dolph stood in the middle of the empty, rain-slicked street and shot at the sub-limo's retreating taillights. He shot one of them out. Then the sub-limo turned the corner and vanished.

"Damn it," Dolph muttered.

I scrambled down to the branch overhanging the sidewalk. At the noise, Dolph reloaded so quickly I hardly saw his hands move, and pointed his Koiler up at the tree.

"It's me," I yelled. I hung off the branch by my hind feet and dropped down to the sidewalk.

"Aw fuck," Dolph said. "You're OK, you're OK." He reached down and rubbed my neck fur. I pushed my nose into his hand—these things come naturally in animal form, sometimes. His hand smelt like blood and gunpowder.

"I thought I was gonna have to start a war with Parsec," Dolph said, as we crossed the street to my truck.

"I think we're at war with him already," I said. "What happened?"

"Dr. Zeb broke it up. We all got kicked out."

"Ijiuto?"

"He got kicked out, too."

The truck's back doors opened. Over the tailgate, I saw Martin, back in human form. Ijiuto lay beside him, unconscious, on the old blankets I keep in the truck for wrapping cargo. There was still an IV in his arm. Martin held the pole upright. I consoled myself that Dr. Zeb, however pissed at us he was, would not have discharged Ijiuto unless he were legitimately on the road to recovery.

"Your phone's been ringing nonstop," Martin said to me, holding it out.

I climbed into the truck, Shifted back, and threw my clothes on before checking my phone.

Later I would regret the waste of those few seconds, even though I rationally knew it wouldn't have made any difference if I had checked my phone half a minute earlier. Or half an hour earlier. As it was, I was soaked to the skin and eager to get out of there, so I carelessly added a few seconds to the end of my life as I had known it.

"Nanny B? What's going on?"

I spoke sharply, already electrified by worry.

The bot's voice, as ever, was inhumanly calm.

"Hello, Mike. I have been attempting to contact you for one hour and fourteen minutes."

"What is it?!"

"I regret to say that Lucy has been abducted."

36

Lucy.

I felt an overwhelming sinking convulsion in my belly, as if my guts were melting and dripping out of my ass. As an old soldier I recognized the feeling of pure, unalloyed terror. But unlike in battle, it didn't go away after a moment. It just kept on crushing and shuddering through me. The sense of interior liquefaction affected my voicebox, as well, so that my voice came out as an unfamiliar croak.

"What happened?"

Nanny B related the catastrophe as we raced back north towards my apartment. Every robotic word increased my anguish.

"She went to bed at ten PM," Nanny B said. "I confirmed that she was asleep at 10:17. At 11:20, Robbie arrived. In accord with your instructions, I told him that he could make use of the living-room if he wished. However, he said he would remain on the porch. I then returned to my charging station and entered self-repair mode."

Though bots do not sleep, they need to perform system maintenance on themselves. In self-repair mode, Nanny B's sensors were active, but she would not initiate any action unless a pre-set event interrupted her —such as someone calling her name.

"At 2:12, I heard Robbie calling me from the porch. I disconnected from my charging station and went out. He said that he had seen a black car driving past our building. I queried him as to why he thought this was a matter for concern. He said that it looked suspicious, but he could not provide any rationale for his view."

I ground my teeth. *It looked suspicious.* The kind of hunch that artificial intelligences just don't get.

"At 2:31, he once again called me. I again went out, and he said that he had seen the same car driving past for a second time. I again queried him why he thought this was a cause for concern, and he said, 'It just don't feel right.'" Nanny B reproduced Robbie's voice over the phone in an eerily perfect mimicry. "I again returned to my charging station. However, at 2:50 he called me a third time—"

"Tell me, Nanny B, did you not at any point think this car might be a cause for concern?"

"Cars are traffic," Nanny B said. "Traffic is normal. 90th is a through street between Shoreside and Creek, so it is not unusual for cars to drive along it, even in the small hours of the morning."

"Go on."

"When I went outside at 2:50, Robbie stated that he had seen the car a third time. He further averred that the rear window had rolled down as it passed, and he had seen someone staring at him 'in a threatening way.' When I observed that the car was not in sight now, he became abusive. He called me a 'lump of useless circuitry,' and told me to call you. I did so. He also called you himself. However, you did not answer the phone."

Because at that time, I had been breaking into Kaspar Silverback's hospital room to torture him for information about a suspected shipment of contraband that was no threat to me and mine, I thought, and none of my goddamn business, anyway.

"Robbie then became distressed. He stated that he believed Lucy was in danger. He said that in his opinion, the alleged persons in the alleged black car had been 'casing the building,' and would imminently return to harm or abduct her. He expressed regret that he did not have a firearm."

"Shoulda got one for him," Dolph said, sitting beside me in the truck cab, listening to Nanny B on speaker.

"Shut up," I yelled at him. "Can't hear!"

Nanny B's implacably calm voice carried the tale to its miserable climax. "Over my objections, Robbie went into the apartment and woke Lucy. He said to her that he was taking her for a walk. I observed that he was in a highly emotional state, displaying signs of fear and anxiety. I suggested to him that he should go upstairs to ask Irene and Rex for their advice. He said that it was the middle of the night and he didn't want to disturb them. I then told Lucy that it was a school night, that she needed her sleep, and that she was not to go with him. I further said that you would not approve. Lucy then said, 'Daddy didn't even come home to say goodnight. He doesn't care about me, so I don't care what he says, and I don't care what you say, either.'"

The bot's merciless recounting lacerated my heart. Dolph looked away.

"Over my strong objections, Robbie instructed Lucy to get dressed and come with him. He said, 'We're gonna find your daddy.' They left the apartment together, walking in the direction of Shoreside. That was at 3:17. They have not returned."

I blinked. "Wait. Wait. Nanny B. You're telling me Lucy's been abducted ... *by Robbie?!*"

"Yes," Nanny B said.

I let out a long breath. All my suspicions seemed to fly away like butterflies after a false alarm. Robbie may have been spooked by the black car, and his judgement in taking Lucy for a walk might have been poor, but he was not an abductor.

All the same, Shoreside in the wee hours of the morning was no place for a child. Worry dug its claws into me again.

"It's 4:21," Dolph said.

I was already dialing Robbie.

He did not pick up.

My guts liquefied again. Had I been terribly wrong about him?

I fruitlessly redialed him as I redirected my truck to Shoreside. At the first red light, Dolph jumped out and climbed into the back. He told Martin what was going on. Martin said to leave the back door open and he would keep an eye out for Robbie and Lucy, too. At the next red light, Dolph swung back into the cab with me. "We'll find them," he said.

We hit the Strip at 47th. Despite the late hour, music still pumped from the strip clubs and storefront casinos. Drunk humans and aliens wobbled along the sidewalk. I shuddered to think of my little girl somewhere in this. But the thought of her *not* being here was worse. I left the driving to the truck, and skinned my eyelids back to the bone, clocking every human and humanoid figure on the promenade.

Because we were heading uptown, I was looking across traffic at the promenade, while Dolph had the landward side of the street. He kept up a low-voiced commentary on the various species of alien scum infesting our fine red-light district, until I told him to shut up. I could not spare an iota of attention from my twin tasks of watching the promenade and redialing Robbie.

60th. The sidewalks got cleaner. Callow merrymakers took the place of furtive alkies and whores.

65th. St. Andrew's Pier. The ferris wheel hung dark and still, the funfair was silent. The families and tourists that thronged the pier by day had vanished. Drinkers sat on the seawall. There was not a single child in sight anywhere. Despair began to crawl over me like a sickness.

"We could be looking in the wrong place," I said. "Who says he'd have taken her to Shoreside, anyway? He knows kids shouldn't be out here at night." A new thought struck me. "Maybe he took her to his house!" I picked up my phone to retrieve Robbie's home address. All I could remember was that it was in Smith's End.

Before I could touch the screen, Robbie finally picked up.

Or rather, someone picked up Robbie's phone, but it was not him.

"Give it up, Starrunner," said a thick, distorted voice. "You'll never see her again."

The sound that came out of my mouth resembled a roar more than a human voice. *"Where is my child?!"*

"She's safe," the voice said, with an air of grudgingly dispensing privileged information.

"Who—"

Click.

"—are you?"

Silence.

I hurled my phone at the windscreen.

It bounced off and fell to the floor.

I punched the steering wheel. I banged my head against it.

Dolph grabbed me around the shoulders, got me in a headlock. I fought him. The back of my head collided with his face. He let go with a curse. I slumped in my seat. I vaguely noted that blood was gushing from his nose. "Sorry," I said.

Dolph wiped his nose with his forearm. "Fought three bears without a scratch, and now I get a bloody nose from you." He was trying to lighten the mood but I scarcely heard him.

Pain echoed through my body as if I was a bell that had been struck. I didn't know if it was physical or emotional. I growled, "That fucking punk. That lying piece of shit." I remembered that Rex had recommended Robbie. I bent over to search for my phone in the footwell, intent on calling Rex.

While I swept my hands over the floor, Dolph's phone rang. He said, *"What?"* He reached over me and hauled on the wheel. The truck's AI responded. We glided towards the median. Dolph kept hauling on the wheel. I sat up, pushing him aside, as we U-turned.

"That's him, isn't it?" Martin said from Dolph's phone.

On the edge of the beach steps at 82nd, head in his hands, sat Robbie. Alone.

37

I jumped out of the truck before it came to a stop.

I sprinted to Robbie. Cursing incoherently, I hauled him to his feet and drew my fist back to punch his face in.

Tears smeared his cheeks. More water welled from his eyes as he stood limply in my grasp. Sobs broke from him.

"I'm sorry, Mr. Starrunner. I'm so sorry."

*

Dolph came up while I was wavering as to whether to kill Robbie with my bare hands or not. He got between us. His nose was still bleeding like a faucet. If it isn't yet abundantly clear, Dolph is a better friend than I have ever deserved. He made Robbie sit down and gave him a nip from his flask. Robbie spluttered, coughed, calmed down. Martin came and sat on his other side, quietly ensuring he did not make a run for it.

There, with the cool night breeze blowing from the sea, while I paced up and down in front of them like a caged wolf, Robbie spilled the following story.

*

The black car had spooked him badly, for reasons that he had not explained to Nanny B. Robbie was into the ripper scene. I didn't know what that was, so he had to fill me in, with interjections from Dolph. Ripping was an offshoot of rugby, the most popular sport in Shiftertown. We had our own city league with six teams. The teams clashed regularly on the pitch, collecting the usual complement of stomped heads and sprains, but that wasn't enough blood for the rabid fans. The younger players—Robbie's age group, not Rex's—had begun to carry their sporting rivalry onto the streets. It had become expected that wherever players from rival teams met, they would at least posture and threaten each other, if not actually brawl. Fans vidded the confrontations, fueling a feedback loop that incentivized ever more violent smackdowns.

Since all the young players involved were Shifters, punches and kickings inevitably led to bites and maulings. "Rippings"—beatdowns in animal form—began to be lauded as a twisted form of sport in and of themselves. Successful holos of rippings—like the one embedded in Robbie's favorite t-shirt—could multiply a player's income, as each view generated a micropayment.

The total amount of money involved was maybe three figures per holo. To an older player like Rex, aloof from the scene, that was nothing. To Robbie and his friends, it was the difference between making rent and not. More than the money, though, it was about pride.

As a result, there was now an incredible amount of pressure on young players to perform on the streets, as well as on the pitch. "You only pull the fans if you're authentic on the street," Robbie said miserably. "You could be valid on the pitch, but if everyone thinks you're weak on the street?" He shook his head and sliced a hand across his throat.

So when that black car cruised past our house, he had thought it was players from a rival team, somehow having found out about his new job, who had come to cut him out for a ripping.

He had applied for the job with me in a desperate bid to find a way out of the spiral of violence.

But he had not said a word about any of this to me before I hired him.

"You didn't ask," he said, following my pacing form with terrified eyes.

"How can I ask about what I don't know about?" I exploded, realizing in my heart that it was my own fault for being oblivious to the violence racking our streets. I shook my head. "Go on."

After the black car passed for the third time, Robbie panicked. He had visions of getting ripped on my front porch. He was indifferent—this is instructive—to the possibility of getting badly hurt. But he was terrified of losing his job, and the only glint of hope in his life. This is why he ignored Nanny B's advice to go upstairs and talk to Rex. The last thing he wanted was for Rex and me to find out about the trouble he was in.

He fixated on getting away from the people in the black car. But if he left my apartment, Lucy would be unprotected! He would be failing at the task I had set him, and I would fire him anyway.

Then a solution came to him: He'd take her with him.

"You thought it was a *good idea* to take my daughter out for a walk when these ripper characters were hunting for you?" I yelled.

"They wouldn't've come near me if she was there," Robbie said simply. "It's against the rules. Can't involve kids."

So he took Lucy by the hand and they walked towards Shoreside.

Lucy was chirpy, he said, talking a mile a minute, not at all drowsy, excited at the idea of searching for me in the forbidden hours of the early morning.

"Why the heck did you think I was on Shoreside?"

"I called you, sir! I called you over and over! You never picked up. I thought, take her down to the Strip, anyway. Lots of people down there. Safety in numbers, right?"

"Right," Dolph said, encouragingly.

Robbie folded over and hid his face in his arms.

"Talk," I yelled.

"I was wrong," he choked. "I was wrong."

As they walked along the Strip between 90th and 89th, the black car eased out of traffic and crawled along the sidewalk beside them.

Robbie switched hands, putting Lucy on the inside. He walked faster.

The black car kept pace with them.

"Ow," Lucy squeaked. "You're walking too fast!"

"We're going in here," Robbie said, blindly angling towards the nearest lighted door. As luck would have it, it was a nightclub.

"No kids," the bouncer said, looking at Robbie like, *you crazy?*

The black car stopped.

Three people got out. "Two men," Robbie said, "and one woman. I never saw any of them in my life."

They crossed the pavement to Robbie and Lucy. As Robbie blustered at the two guys—he still thought they were rippers, although he didn't know them—the woman bent down. She said in a sweet voice to Lucy, "Hello, love. Guess what? I'm your mommy." She pulled Lucy into a hug.

I could only imagine the confusion that must have swamped Lucy's poor little head at that moment. I never spoke about her mother. She didn't know the woman's name, much less what she looked like. In retrospect: my mistake.

"Come with me," the woman went on. "We're going to take a ride in my car. I've really missed you!" She started to move Lucy towards the car.

"Daddy," was the one word Lucy said. Robbie was quite sure about that, although he was jostling with the two guys, trying to get to Lucy. "Daddy," she said, a two-syllable entreaty for everything to be OK.

"Sure!" the woman said. "He's right here!" She gestured at the car's tinted windows—and pushed Lucy inside.

Robbie heard the soft snap as the door of the car closed. He roared Lucy's name. He started throwing punches. One of the guys landed a haymaker that sent him to one knee on the sidewalk, his brains singing.

When he struggled to his feet, the guys were gone.

So was the woman.

And the car.

And Lucy.

They'd taken his phone, too, so he couldn't call me and let me know what happened.

I kept pacing, faster than ever. I was distantly aware of fatigue and muscle aches. Adrenaline kept them at bay. "You're sure that's what she said? 'I'm your mommy'?"

Robbie nodded.

"What did she look like? I want every detail."

"She was dark," Robbie began hesitantly. "Dark hair, I mean. Kinda sexy. Like she would be sexy if you met her in a club, even though she was too old. I mean about the same as you. She was wearing this kinda tight top, and bubbles."

"What?"

"Those pants that flare out into a bubble at the knee."

"Did she have any tattoos?"

"Um. No. I don't think so."

"Did she, or didn't she?!"

"I didn't see any," Robbie muttered.

She could have covered them with liquid skin.

"What did her voice sound like?"

Robbie shuffled his feet wretchedly. "I don't know. Sweet. Like a voice in an ad."

Sweet was not the way I'd personally describe Sophia's voice, but it was so subjective …

"Mike," Dolph said. "I don't think it was her. It's not her style. Would she trick Lucy by saying you were in the car? No. She wouldn't. She *couldn't*. She hates you too much."

I stared out to sea. I noticed that I could see Space Island, not just its lights. The sky had turned gray.

Dolph got out his phone, saying he was going to look for security camera footage.

Martin went to check on Ijiuto. "He's OK," he said when he came back. "Mike? You should call the police."

"It was her," I gritted, still staring at Space Island. The skyline of warehouses along the island's shore had come into blurry monochrome focus. "She doesn't give a crap about Lucy. She did this to warn me off. How dare she, how *dare* she use my daughter as a pawn in her games?!" *Her* daughter, too, but I didn't say that. I didn't even think it. I clenched my fists so hard I noticed the pain where my nails dug into my palms.

"Call the police," Martin repeated.

Martin, the shiftiest of my whole crew, the python, with an unknown number of murders under his belt, said that.

I met his eyes. He nodded emphatically.

I called the police.

I got a sleepy duty officer, and I was only on the phone with him for five minutes. He said he could not initiate a missing persons case until 24 hours had passed. I told him that my daughter had been abducted off the goddamn Strip, and I had a witness. He was in the middle of repeating his spiel when I hung up on him.

"Twenty-four hours!" I said. "By that time she could be anywhere! Jesus!" I decided I'd call d'Alencon as soon as decent people started to wake up. He might not be best pleased with me right now, but surely he'd help.

"Her," Robbie said abruptly. "That's her."

I rushed to his side, squatted, and pulled Dolph's phone towards me.

Now the ubiquitous surveillance cameras I had cursed last night were about to work for me. Municipal footage is not technically available to the public. However, there are back doors well known to anyone with an ounce of IT expertise. Dolph had found the camera situated closest to the nightclub in front of which it happened—in fact, we were sitting across the avenue from its shuttered façade right now. He had searched for Robbie's face, and now we all watched the abduction unfurl, from a crappy overhead vantage point, just like Robbie had related it. He had been truthful as to the way it went down, anyway.

Dolph froze the footage on an instant when the woman's face was visible to the camera.

"Oh my fucking God," Martin said.

It was not Sophia.

"So that's why they did it in public. They don't care if we find out who they are," Dolph said.

Because we already knew.

"That fucker," I said between my teeth, "was just keeping me busy. I thought it was me he wanted. He was just keeping me away from Lucy."

The woman captured on the security camera footage was Cecilia Parsec, Buzz Parsec's wife.

38

I reviewed that security camera footage over and over, zooming in until my daughter's face disintegrated into a clump of pixels. In one hand she clutched the Blobby doll Pippa had made for her. The other hand was hidden inside Cecilia Parsec's grip. I could see Cecilia's fashionably pointed fingernails digging into Lucy's wrist.

Cecilia was reclusive, in contrast to her husband's outsized, indeed well-nigh inescapable presence in Shiftertown. They had been married for twenty years. For Parsec to resist the temptation to trade up, Cecilia must've had something. Presumably, as black a heart as his own. She was a mainstream human. She spent her time at their fancy pad in Ville Verde, one of the gated communities tucked away in the hills of Cape Agreste.

I said, "They must've taken Lucy there." Ville Verde, like all those communities on the Cape, had security that would not disgrace a fortress on one of the Hurtworlds. Force fields to keep out bugs and burglars, 24/7 security patrols, and honest-to-God anti-missile defences. Storming it would be impossible. I thought about ways to get inside by guile.

"Won't work," Irene said. "I've been there."

I was sitting in the Seagraves' kitchen. Dolph had refused to leave me alone with the completely unhelpful Nanny B. He was probably right. Only consideration for my friends prevented me from taking out my fear and rage on the Seagraves' furniture, the crockpot, the refrigerator, the windows, and the gaudy pink walls. Sunlight streamed into the messy, cheerful room, making my head ache.

"I've been there, too," I reminded Irene. One time, Dolph and I had bullshitted our way into Ville Verde by pretending we were interested in purchasing real estate. I wondered if that might fly again.

"Yeah, but you haven't been in his house," Irene said. "That place is booby-trapped out the wazoo. Not to mention half a dozen bears hanging out there around the clock. I don't know why his neighbors put up with it. Not only living next door to a Shifter, but the biggest asshole of a Shifter on the planet."

"I'm sure money is involved," I said wearily.

"Right," Irene said. She poured hot water into mugs. "Now you're on the right track. Follow the money."

"I guess you'd know about that," I said.

I swear I didn't mean it that way. The fact was, before they had kids —and even afterwards—Irene and Rex had been professional thieves. I was not well acquainted with the details, and didn't want to be, but I did know they had worked with Parsec at least once. That's how she had been inside his house.

I was thinking only of how and whether Irene's mothballed skills might be leveraged to free Lucy. But she was touchy about her history. She swung around, nearly spilling the steaming mug in her hand. Her eyes flashed. "Mike, I had nothing to do with this. What do you want me to swear on? I swear on my children's lives."

I raised my hands. "I never said you were involved, Irene! I never even thought it. I *don't* think it."

"OK." She put the mug down in front of me.

"I was just thinking about the money." I picked up the mug. The liquid inside was pale green and gave off an unpleasant herbal smell. "There must be a *lot* of dough at stake for them."

"Or this could be a side play to make some more," Irene said. "They might be having cash flow problems."

"They didn't make a ransom demand." I sniffed the mug and put it down untouched.

"That comes next."

"Alternatively," Rex said, coming in, "Sophia might just want Lucy back. Because she's, y'know. Her mother."

Rex was in lion form. That's how he had heard our conversation while he was still on the stairs. He had walked Mia to school without bothering to Shift back into human form, because the threat hanging over us seemed to extend to the Seagrave kids, as well, and because he was so distraught that Shifting seemed impossible. Kit rode on his back, clinging to his mane. As Rex kicked the door shut with a hindpaw, Kit slid off and went into the living-room to watch the holovision. Squeaky voices and manic music tortured my ganglia.

Irene set a bowl of coffee down on the floor in front of her husband. "Yeah," she said. "If I was in her position—well, I wouldn't be in her position, but if I was … nah. I'd snatch the kids my own damn self. And I wouldn't wait seven years to do it."

"That's my baby," Rex said, slurping from his bowl. "But Sophia ain't on your level, so she had to wait until she could con the Parsecs into doing it for her."

"Right," Irene said. "Because she's got dirt on them. I can see that."

I couldn't. I shook my head, dismissing their theory. "No. They're either warning me off, or looking for money. Or both." I propped my elbows on the table and rested my forehead on the back of one hand. Pain stabbed into my skull, reminding me of the goose egg I'd given myself last night by banging my head on the steering wheel. I sat upright. I was past self-destructive reactions like that, like stupidly putting my business interests ahead of my child. "How much would you figure they'll ask for?"

"About 150 KGCs," Irene said, naming a figure that was slightly greater than my annual income.

"Is that the going rate for ransoms?"

"Roughly."

"Then that's what I'll pay him. He won't refuse. This is Parsec we're talking about. He would sell his *own* child for 150 KGCs, if he had one."

Rex raised his head again. Coffee dripped from his chin fur. His lion's eyes brimmed with doubt. "Where are you going to get it?"

I laughed emptily. "Steal it. Borrow it. I don't know. Sell the ship."

Irene reached across the table and put her hand on top of mine. "Wait, Mike. *Think.*"

"There's nothing to think about." I pulled my hand away from hers, rescued my phone from a puddle of spilt milk. I dialed Parsec, while Irene and Rex watched worriedly.

"Yeah," Parsec said.

My vision hazed over with red. I snarled into the phone, "Give my goddamn daughter back!"

"What're you talking about?" Parsec said, totally relaxed.

"Your wife kidnapped her off the Strip last night! I want her back, NOW!"

"You're losing it, bud," Parsec said. "Did you bump your head falling outta that tree?" He chuckled. "By the way, tell that mangy jackal friend of yours he needs to watch his back. It won't save him, but Gary K likes to see the look in a man's eyes as he dies."

"I'll pay!" I shouted. "I'll pay whatever you want! Just give her back!"

"Well, Starrunner, I got no objection to taking your money in principle. But I don't know what you're talking about, and it don't look good to be making unfounded accusations. That daughter of yours is the sweetest little thing. I wouldn't hurt her for the world. So don't go calling me again. We got no business together, and nothing to discuss." He hung up.

I dropped my phone on the kitchen table. "He denied it," I said disbelievingly. "He flat denied it."

"Guess he doesn't want your money," Rex said. "Or he knows you don't have it, anyway."

I shook my head. I had to call d'Alencon, but in this frame of mind, I'd screw that up, too. I was loopy with tiredness. The normalcy of the Seagraves' kitchen aggravated me, as if the physical world itself were conspiring to remind me of my helplessness. I stood up. "Back to square one," I muttered. "Break into Ville Verde."

"Have some tea, Mike," Irene said. She came around the table and put the mug into my hand. "You've been up for what, two days straight?"

"How come I don't get coffee?" I said with a humorless laugh, gesturing at Rex's bowl.

"You've also been in a serious fight," Irene said. "I suppose I should thank you boys for leaving me out of that mess. But actually, I'm kind of pissed. You left me out last time, as well. Do you think I would beat your kill tally, or something, and make you look bad?"

I was so tired I accidentally told the truth. "It was just bad timing, Irene. But in a way you're right. You're too damn good at killing. It scares me."

"Isn't that why you hired me?"

"Yes," I said. "but this is different. This is Ponce de Leon. This is where we *live*. I'm trying to keep the carnage to a minimum."

"OK," Irene said. "That's your plan. How's that working out for you?" Rex rubbed against her legs, wordlessly telling her to cool it. She let out an exasperated, cat-like hiss. "Here, just drink the goddamn tea, Mike."

I drank it, to placate her.

I don't know what she put in it.

I vaguely remember stumbling downstairs, holding onto Rex's mane.

I woke up in my own bed, thick-headed. The heat, and the angle of the sun striking down between the buildings outside, told me it was nearly noon.

Panic gripped me. Hours had passed, and Lucy was still missing.

39

IRENE came into the room. "Sorry about that," she said. "You needed to get some sleep."

I swung my feet hurriedly to the floor. Pain spiked through my head, but I've had worse hangovers. Like it or not, she was right. I felt stronger, more in control of my thoughts. The panic swirled around in my head like a vortex, but now I was able to keep it under the surface.

I had gone to sleep fully dressed—lions aren't good with zips. I stripped off my sweat-damp, smelly clothes. Irene gazed critically at me. I knew she wasn't interested in my nudity. She was counting my injuries. I glimpsed myself in the mirror inside the door of the closet as I grabbed a fresh t-shirt and work pants. I looked like hell. Bruises mottled my ribs and flanks, and teeth marks dotted my neck, courtesy of Parsec's bears. Shifting back had "reset" the overall impact to my system to some extent, which is why I was on my feet at all, but it wasn't a cure. The goose egg on my forehead looked like a bulging third eye. My hair partially covered it in lank, dirt-brown clumps.

"Dolph's down on the Strip," Irene said. "He facial-matched the two guys who were with Cecilia. They're bears, natch."

"Figures."

"Him and Robbie have gone to look for them."

I turned. "Robbie? They'll chew him up and spit him out."

"I don't think he's that dumb."

"He's plenty dumb."

"He realizes that he fucked up. They set a trap for him and he walked right into it. He's desperate to make it right, Mike. Let him do what he can to help."

I gestured impatiently and walked into the hall with Irene behind me. A shockwave of pain hit me at the sight of the open door of Lucy's bedroom, with her not in there. The faint sound of the holovision came from the living-room. For an irrational instant I believed I would find her sitting on the sofa, watching Gemworld Families. I put my head around the door.

Rafael Ijiuto sat on the sofa, watching some stupid comedy channel. He looked pale and worn, but his eyes were open and he was very much conscious.

I had completely forgotten his existence. He now seemed like a person from another planet—well, he *was*—and as irrelevant as an alien to my woes.

"Hey," he said, catching sight of me.

"You OK?" I said.

"Getting there," he said. He gestured at the drawn curtains. "I have a new respect for the lethality of stars." When he moved his hand, the IV line still plugged into his arm caught on the end of the sofa. Nanny B bustled forward, quacking at him not to pull it out. She adjusted the fan that was blowing on him, and took his temperature with the same infrared thermometer she used for Lucy. Ijiuto endured her ministrations with an abashed grin. "She's been taking care of me," he said.

I felt a sudden wave of loathing for the tubby little bot. She was only doing her job. But it felt like she had swiftly and unfeelingly replaced Lucy with someone else to care for, as if she didn't actually give a damn about Lucy—and of course, in actual fact, she *didn't*. She was a machine that obeyed its programming. She had no emotions. She did her job. That was all.

"I swear," I said to Irene, lowering my voice—as if Nanny B had feelings to be hurt! The instinct to humanize them is so strong. "When I get Lu back, this bot is taking a one-way ride to the scrapheap. I'm through with letting a machine look after my little girl."

"You can give her to us, then," Irene said. "I took Kit to my mom's this morning, but I can't leave him with her for long."

"Where's Rex?"

"Out," she said, flicking a glance at Ijiuto—wherever Rex was, she didn't want Ijiuto to hear about it.

"Ms. Seagrave told me what happened to your daughter," Ijiuto said to me. "Man, I'm so sorry to hear that."

"Yeah, well."

"You saved my life. If there's anything I can do ..."

"Maybe there is. How'd you get to Ponce de Leon?"

"On a ship," he said, smiling like he was making a joke: ha, ha, *duh*.

"Was it, or was it not, the Traveller ship that crashed in the Tunjle last week?" I waited a beat. "As you say, I saved your life." Actually, Martin and Dr. Zeb had, but he didn't know that. "You owe me the truth."

Ijiuto brightened. "That's how I see it, too. I believe in straight dealing. Trusting people who were not being honest with me, people who don't even know their own best interests, people that, being frank here, have the attention span of an insect and the self-control of a puppy with diarrhea ..." It was weirdly fascinating to see him working himself up into one of his tirades, and then remembering himself, and dialing it back. "Anyway, that's how I got into this mess."

"Are we talking about the Travellers?" Irene said.

"Yes, ma'am," Ijiuto said. He looked up at me. "Are you *sure* your ship isn't for hire?"

I suddenly got the impression that he was not just talking about hiring me to take him from A to B. I might have realized it when he showed up at my office—all that bullshit about Montemayor and Valdivia ... But penniless men do not hire contractors.

"No," I said.

"I can pay," Ijiuto said, with fading hopes. I glanced pointedly at the credit dot on his arm. It was still black. "Well, maybe not in cash. But I can pay in kind. You won't be disappointed." He looked up at me with dark, steady eyes, and I got a sudden sense of his intelligence as an ageless and malevolent thing, independent of the body that housed it, watching, judging, and assessing me and Irene for our aptness to its needs. Whatever was inside of Rafael Ijiuto, it didn't match his slightly odd, but innocuous, exterior.

I was right about that, of course. Oh, I'm not saying he wasn't human. The opposite, in fact. He was all too human. Humanity at its darkly magnificent worst. In him lived the same insatiable life force that had made the leap into space and ploughed relentlessly across the stars to the M4 Cluster, leaving behind a tidal swathe of detritus, mistakes, dead ends, and extinctions. Rafe Ijiuto was *old school.* I would come to understand him better as I came to understand *us* better, but right there, that moment in my living-room, I thought I knew all about humanity already. So my only conscious reaction was, *Huh. Watch out for this guy.*

Not so far wrong, actually.

"Let me be clear," I said. "My ship is not for hire. And I don't take payment in kind, anyway. Is that how you were paying the Travellers?"

It was only an inspired guess. I knew that the Travellers did work for hire sometimes. As d'Alencon had reminded us, they had started out as mercenaries. They still took security-type jobs when it did not conflict with their nutty ideology.

Ijiuto shivered. His hands lay upturned on his lap like a dead bird's claws. Nanny B butted in, reminded him that he was mildly hypoglycaemic as a result of his heatstroke, and gave him a cup of the sweet klimfruit juice I had in the fridge for Lucy. The sight enraged me. At the same time, I realized how thirsty I was. "Damn," Ijiuto said, wiping his lips. "I haven't been sick since forever. I forgot how much it sucks."

"Yeah," I said. "It sucks. Why did you hire the Travellers, and what for?"

Sitting there on my sofa, he tried to bargain. "If I tell you everything, will you take me to Montemayor?"

"Or Valdivia?" I said cynically.

"Or anywhere."

I pointed in the direction of the front door. "If you *don't* tell me everything, you can get the hell out of my house."

"Can I take the bot?" he said. "Just kidding." He sighed and slumped back, resting his head on the back of the sofa. "I'm not really a wholesaler. I'm a prince." He eyed us anxiously.

Irene snickered. Even I smiled.

"It's true," he said gloomily. "Believe it or not."

"Oh, I believe it," I said. "I've met princes before. Princesses, too. Kings, queens, empresses, grand dukes. Anyone with enough money to pay for the DNA analysis can trace their lineage back to Charlemagne or Alexander the Great. Heck, I'm probably descended from a coupla kings somewhere along the way."

"Well, I *am,*" Ijiuto said. "I'm the heir to the throne of New Gessyria." We shook our heads, not familiar with it. "In the Darkworlds."

"Oh, I think I know where he's talking about," Irene said. "Those old colonies outside of the Cluster."

"Oh, *those* worlds," I said. "In the Earthwards Up sector, near San Damiano." Outside the Cluster, eighty light years is close.

"I heard the Darkworlds are total dumps," Irene said, eyes glinting.

"That's right," Ijiuto said phlegmatically. "Anyway, my lineage goes back hundreds of years."

"There must be a lot of you by now," I said.

"There are," Ijiuto said. "That's the problem."

"So you hired a bunch of Travellers …"

"Just to get around," Ijiuto said. "I heard they have good ships. Well, they do, but no one ever told me they're completely, utterly nuts."

"What rock have you been living under?" I scoffed.

"It's like travelling with a bunch of over-caffeinated octopuses." Ijiuto did have a turn of phrase. "When they're not stoned, they're drunk. When they're not drunk, they're training with swords and axes. *In freefall.* And they never stop yakking at you about personal autonomy and freedom of action and all the rest of that bullshit. Well, I guess you'd know." He slid an almost shy glance at me. "Your ex travelled with them for a while?"

My voice turned soft and cold. "Right. You know Zane Cole."

"I wish to fuck I'd never met him." A note of angry petulance returned to Ijiuto's voice. "I remember when the name of Uni-Ex Shipping first came up, Cole reacted oddly. He was way too interested in the details—of the freaking shipping company. I should've suspected something. But I didn't. After all, they're working for *me.* So there we are, I'm about to take delivery of my stuff. Everything's going smoothly. Then he ruins everything by taking a pop at you! At least he had the decency to miss."

"It's almost as if you think we're stupid or something," Irene said. Ijiuto looked up at her warily. "Those shots were *not* fired from the Travellers' ship."

"I never said they were," Ijiuto protested. "Cole snuck over to your pad. I saw him in the thickets. That's why I bailed."

"Bullshit," I said. "He wouldn't have had time to get over there." Or … would he? After all, Dolph and I had. And the kids had slowed us down. If Zane was a strong swimmer, he could have taken the short-cut across the channel and beat us there … But no. I'd bitten his *hand* off. He wasn't skulking around shooting people after that.

Then a nasty thought occurred to me. Had that really been Zane's hand? I hadn't seen his face, after all. There could have been more than one Traveller with blond arm hair sporting a knock-off Urush fortunometer. It seemed unlikely, but it was possible.

"Never mind that. I got another question for you, Rafe. Why'd you follow us back here?"

"I wanted my stuff," he said.

"Right. Your stuff." I moved closer to the sofa. I stood over him, so close that my knees brushed his legs. I waited until fear flashed in his eyes. "Why don't you tell me about that stuff, Rafe? What was in those crates?"

"Toy fairies."

"And?"

"That's all. Just toy fairies."

"Which you bought from a supplier called, what was it again …"

"I don't even remember. They gave me a good price."

"Mujin Inc. That was it. Know anything about them?"

"No, man. Sorry."

"You're not making much sense here, Rafe. You chased me all the way back to Ponce de Leon, for a few toy fairies?"

"Nine thousand of them," Ijiuto said, jerking further away from me, "minus the one you ruined. And if you think that's nothing, I guess you don't know what it's like in the Darkworlds. We're not rich. It's not like here. You've got your flying cars and your sky-high malls and your five thousand varieties of lettuce. All we've got is our pride. I have a hundred and eight cousins waiting for me to bring home enough credit to stop the EkBank from pulling out of our system." The one hundred and eight cousins were a complete fiction, as I learned later, but it rang true at the time, given my preconceptions. "And now I'm stuck here, staring down the barrel of bankruptcy, all thanks to you! I think you at least owe me a refund."

I threw up my hands. "Get in line." I turned on my heel and went into the kitchen. Ijiuto's voice followed me, pleading with me to help him recover his stuff. I figured he was telling the truth about being broke, anyway. Like I said, there are hundreds of so-called royal families in the Cluster and outside of it, and none of them have enough paper to wipe their asses with.

I filled a glass with water from the sink and drank it down.

Most likely, Ijiuto planned to come into money once he sold the stash of contraband in his crates, I speculated.

My abortive plan to ransom Lucy regained a weak spark of life. Maybe I could steal the crates from Mujiin Inc and offer Parsec their contents in exchange for her. Or threaten to turn them over to the police …

In the living-room, Irene was getting the hair-raising details of how Ijiuto had survived the crash of the Traveller ship. I leaned against the sink, sipping water, interested despite myself. He said that the Fleet Marines had started the fires onboard the Traveller ship when they boarded, shooting wildly into the electrics. I didn't doubt it. The Marines had then withdrawn, mission accomplished. With its flight controls gone, the Traveller ship had started to plunge into the atmosphere. It had been disintegrating and spinning around: every captain's worst nightmare. Mine, for sure. Chaos reigned on board. Smoke fouled the air. The Travellers have a tradition of going down with their ships, more often honored in the breach. The captain had been shooting his people to keep them away from the airlocks, screaming that their names would live forever. Ijiuto knew that jumping out of the airlock would be a death sentence, anyway. He fought his way to the life support deck. He already had his suit on. He wrenched open the cleaning hatch of the sewage tank—and climbed in, knowing that the liquid suspension represented his best hope of surviving re-entry.

Shock after shock assaulted the tank, tossing him around. All he could see by his helmet light was the spinning walls. He knew the ship was breaking up around him, and prayed the tank would hold.

It did. As the wreck entered the atmosphere, he drifted in the liquid sewage, cocooned against the re-entry gees. An increasing whine, and a steady vibration, told him the tank had settled into a hypersonic dive. He waited, waited, waited until his nerves were fraying, until the whining gave way to an eerie silence. Then he threw open the hatch and fell out, amidst a rain of sewage, into Mach 2 winds, 11 kilometers above the jungle.

His suit had a built-in parachute. Wet from the sewage, the chute functioned even better, wafting him gently to earth.

"It was a good suit," he said regretfully. "I had to cut myself out of it when I landed in the trees."

I shook my head in grudging admiration. The young man had first-rate survival instincts, even if his royal status was neither here nor there.

Oh, OK, he was now admitting he'd hitchhiked part of the way to Mag-Ingat, like Dolph had suspected.

I went back into the living-room. "What kind of truck was it?"

"Huh?" Ijiuto said.

"You got a ride on a truck. What kind of a truck was it? What did the driver look like?"

"Oh," Ijiuto said. "It was self-driving."

Irene said, "Can't have been. Self-driving trucks don't pick up hitch-hikers."

"This one did," Ijiuto said. "The funny thing was, it was going the other way, but when I said I needed to get to Mag-Ingat, it turned around and went back that way, even though it was empty."

"Were there any identifying details?"

"Oh, yeah. Right on the side, it said *Trident Overland.*"

40

IRENE and I retreated to the kitchen. She leaned against my refrigerator, whose stick-on screen showed a collage of Lucy's pictures and flyers from school. I paced around the kitchen table. Ijiuto was still watching that dumb comedy channel in the other room, without making a sound.

I had told Nanny B to ensure he didn't leave the apartment. Not that he was going anywhere in the midst of recovering from heatstroke and septicemia, with no shoes and no money, anyway.

"Two possibilities," Irene said. "Either Parsec ordered his truck to pick up that—" she dropped her voice— "con-man in there, or he didn't."

"Don't try and tell me he doesn't know what his own trucks are doing," I said. Then I shook my head. "This isn't helping us find Lucy."

"True." Irene pushed her shoulders off the fridge. The stick-on screen came loose and fluttered to the floor. Irene picked it up with an expression of pain. "Oh God, the Founding Day Festival."

Founding Day, July 33rd according to the terrestrial calendar our forebears force-fitted to Ponce de Leon's 452-day year, was a public holiday. Kids got the day off school, except they really didn't because the schools participated in the big parade which wound through the city and finished up on the Mag-Ingat Skymall.

"The girls were looking forward to it so much," Irene said, her forehead creased with sadness.

I took the screen out of her hand. I wanted to crumple it up and hurl it across the room, followed by a kitchen chair or two. Instead, I neatly replaced it on the fridge. Then, with my emotions on the flimsiest of leashes, I dialed Jose-Maria d'Alencon.

*

"Mike," he said. "Heard."

In my paranoid frame of mind, I wondered if he'd heard about what went down at Dr. Zeb's. No. He would have been informed of my call to the police last night. "Bones," I said, "I'm desperate."

Sitting at my kitchen table, blindly moving my empty water glass around in circles, I told him the whole story of Lucy's abduction.

D'Alencon listened, asked a couple of shrewd questions, and then summed up, "So your ex-wife is working for the Parsecs."

"Yes."

"And you believe that they kidnapped your child to stop you from poking your nose into their business."

"Right."

"OK, and you think they're holding her at Ville Verde, although you don't actually have any evidence for that."

"If she's not there, she could be anywhere," I said, tasting the awful truth of it. "They might try to take her off-planet."

"Well, I'll initiate a missing persons case right now, because it's you … and because it's him. I would love to get something on him the prosecutor could not ignore. Sorry, Tiger, you know what I mean."

"I know."

"But we can't raid his home or any of his places of business, not with what we got."

"The footage shows Cecilia Parsec dragging Lucy into a car!"

"Yes, and I will seek to have her questioned. But we don't know where that car went. I will order a review of the traffic footage, but unfortunately, all it takes is a cheap holo projector in the trunk to alter the visual profile of a vehicle and spoof its license plate. So my gut hunch is we won't find any proof that the car returned to Ville Verde."

"But—"

"Even if it did, Mike, it could take me weeks to get a warrant to go in there. I'll apply for one, but don't get your hopes up. Those gated communities are this close to being sovereign entities."

Irene nodded as she heard d'Alencon's cynical words coming from my phone. I had it on speaker.

"They got their own law departments, their own *laws,* in some cases their own launch pads."

"Ville Verde doesn't."

"No, friend Parsec ain't quite that rich, although I'm sure he would like to be. But that brings me to what I *can* do for you. You believe the kidnappers may attempt to send your daughter off-planet?"

"Yes," I said. "My ex is from Montemayor. They might try to send her there."

It was a moment before d'Alencon replied. "About your ex, Mike …"

"Yes?"

"Is her name Meimei? Or Pamela?"

"No! It's Sophia. Sophia Hart."

"I'm looking at my notes from the inquiries I conducted. There's no one by that name working at Mujin Inc. They only got a few employees, mostly part-timers. The office manager is listed as Pamela Kingsolver."

"Then that's her. She's using a fake ID."

"There are no fake IDs that good," d'Alencon said. "I ran deep background on all the employees. Pamela Kingsolver is a real individual, from Ulloa." He named a Toolworld on the far edge of human territory. "She checks out on every level, right down to her DNA record."

"Have you actually got any DNA samples from this Pamela Kingsolver, the one at Mujin Inc?" I said. "Do you have any *pictures* of her?"

D'Alencon's silence told me no. And in a heavily surveilled city like Mag-Ingat, that was suspicious in and of itself.

"It's her," I said. "She's a computer scientist. She's faked an ID good enough to fool your software."

"Be that as it may," d'Alencon said stiffly, and I cursed myself for offending him. The police department took pride in its big-data advantage. They thought it was impossible for crooks to fool their systems. "We have no proof that Sophia Hart has stepped foot on Ponce de Leon for seven years. I'm not sayin' she was not involved, but that leads me to think you may be correct that they'll try to send your daughter off-planet ... to wherever she is now."

I gritted my teeth. It didn't matter what he thought, as long as we found Lucy. "I got a friend out at the spaceport right now, watching Parsec's freight terminal," I said. Martin was not doing anything illegal, so I felt OK with admitting it. "But there's no reason Parsec would have to use his own ship." After all, he hadn't used his own ship to send his contraband to Gvm Uye Sachttra. There were literally thousands of ships out there on Space Island; hundreds of them were for hire if the price was right; and I could imagine that all too many captains would look the other way if a frightened little girl were herded onto their ship, especially if they were informed that she was on her way to see her grandparents. "It's a needle in a haystack," I blurted.

"True," d'Alencon said. "But there are two chokepoints leading onto Space Island. Namely, the East Causeway and Space Bridge. I'll issue alerts to the traffic monitoring AIs in both places. I'll need you to send me some recent vid of Lucy. We'll open up the facial recognition parameters, and stop every little girl with the vaguest resemblance to Lucy Starrunner."

I swallowed a lump of hopelessness. "Will do, Bones. Thanks."

"I hate to bring it up at a time like this, Mike, but have you given any further thought to what we talked about last night?"

I had to wind time back in my mind, past the blind curve of Lucy's abduction, until I got to what he was referring to. "Oh. Yeah." I had nothing to give him. Silverback had not told us anything interesting. "Could be they're holding her at Mujin Inc," I blurted. "Could you get a warrant to go in there?"

Bones sighed. "Again, we would need more than your suspicions."

"Damn," I said emptily. "Hey, you might want to take a look at Trident Overland. Maybe they put her in one of those trucks ..."

"That's a possibility," d'Alencon said, clearly realizing he was not going to get anything more useful out of me. "Thanks for the tip."

I half-listened to his concluding reassurances, thinking about all the ways Lucy could be hidden from the eyes of the police department's AIs ... and all the other ways out of Mag-Ingat, by road, by sea, by air ... and all the other spaceports on Ponce de Leon ... and all the private pads—like the ones on Cape Agreste that d'Alencon had mentioned, and surely Parsec had some friends out on the Cape who'd let him use theirs. The fact was, I knew that any effort to stop him from taking her off-planet was hopeless. There were just too many travel options. It made me wish in vain for the days of passports, back before the widespread adoption of antimatter drives. Three to four hundred years ago, spaceflight was slower and riskier. Nowadays just about anyone could travel in space. The law had followed the technology, enshrining freedom of movement as a human right. By law, no human person could be disallowed from going anywhere. (Whether anywhere would let you *stay*, of course, was a different matter.) And now I saw what that freedom could cost me.

"We just have to find her before they send her off-planet," I said to Irene, forcing myself not to think about the possibility that they already had.

"Yep," Irene said. "Listen, Mike, I have to go meet Rex."

"Where is he, anyway?"

"I'd rather not tell you yet … OK, OK. We're trying to trace the contraband that might have been shipped in the toy fairies."

"Fuck the toy fairies," I said, opening the fridge.

"Uh uh," Irene said. "It might be related."

"I guess."

"You might not know this," she said carefully, "but contraband usually doesn't originate on Ponce de Leon. We're more of a transit hub. Stuff changes hands here and gets repackaged for onwards shipment. So, Rex and I have—mmm—we know some people who handle … that kind of goods, that were not legally imported. They might know something."

I stared blankly into the fridge, unable to remember why I'd opened it. A nectarine with two bites out of it stared back at me. Lucy had a terrible habit of taking bites out of a piece of fruit and then returning it to the fridge. The edges of the bites had just begun to go brown and soggy. Less than one day ago, she had been here, absent-mindedly nibbling on this nectarine as she watched holovision or did her homework.

I took the nectarine out of the fridge, and went into my bedroom for my gun.

"Where you going?" Irene said, pausing on her way out.

I located the Machina .22 and lodged the paddle holster inside my work pants. "Spaceport."

"But …"

"I know," I said. *"I know!"*

I took my gun because if I ran into Parsec, I was going to shoot the motherfucker dead.

41

I ate the nectarine on the way to Space Island. The traffic was awful. In preference to sitting there thinking, I drank from a mostly-empty bottle of bourbon I found in the glove compartment. By the time I finally drove over the bridge, the bottle was completely empty, and I was mostly toasted. I got out of the truck and loped over to Martin, feeling aggressive and ready to start some shit.

Martin sat sideways on his parked bike, on the shoulder of the intra-port road. The front wheel of his bike rested about three inches from the boundary of Freight Terminal 1203, Parsec's pad. The boundary itself was just a gutter dug out of the asphalt.

Three inches the other side of the gutter sat a bear, in human form, dressed in engineer's coveralls and a ballcap that shaded his face. I knew him as Hokkaido, one of Parsec's regular crew members. Clearly infuriated by Martin's presence, and now mine, he obtrusively fondled a .45 that was so big of a dick substitute, it would have been funny under other circumstances.

Martin nodded to me, and went on talking to Hokkaido. "Then we had to decide what to do with the body. There aren't that many places on an antimatter tanker to hide a corpse, believe it or not. Some of the guys wanted to throw him outta the skip field. I said no, we'll get caught on the airlock cameras. Well, what are we gonna do, then. He's gonna start to smell pretty soon. So I said, he ain't started to smell *yet.*" Martin opened his mouth. It hinged wider, it seemed, than a human jaw should be able to. We could see the red inside of his throat, and the gaps in his molars. Shifters can't get fillings. He closed his mouth, as Hokkaido stared in revolted fascination. "Then I *ate* him."

"Get outta here," Hokkaido said.

"I always thought he looked tasty," Martin said, chuckling.

I pushed my shades up on my nose and looked past Hokkaido, across the expanse of overlapping old and new scorch rings on the asphalt. Fifty meters away, Parsec's ship, the *Great Bear,* stood half in and half out of its hangar. The *Great Bear* was a pretty ship, with a swept-back arrowhead profile ending in the donut bulge of a powerful drive. Its whole body was a wing. Like my ship—like most all ships—it could spurt vertically off the ground to a height of a couple hundred meters, before going into a hypersonic launch trajectory at an angle no greater than 60°.

Even as I watched the *Great Bear,* another ship swept low overhead, drowning out Martin's voice. With ships passing through the VTOL altitudes every three minutes, launching outside your slot would be insane. You'd risk a mid-air collision, and most definitely get your license taken away.

Parsec's next scheduled launch slot wasn't until the third of August, eight days from now—I kept tabs on these things. But I could see water hoses connected to the *Great Bear,* and a couple of Parsec's other crew members working around the ship. Were they prepping her for an earlier launch? With Lucy on board? The sea breeze carried the smell of hot metal and machine oil, together with the usual Space Island tang of ozone from all the plasma exhaust dissipating into the air.

Hokkaido said to Martin, "No way. You didn't *eat* a guy." His gaze flicked to me, in what I took as a backhanded compliment: he believed I wouldn't hire a man who would do something like that.

"Maybe I did, maybe I didn't," Martin said. "Anything can happen in the Cluster. You ever been to the Hurtworlds?"

"Nope."

"Take Cuspidor Z. The natives got this fucked-up habit of eating their *own* body parts. Of course, that's why it was classified as a Hurtworld in the first place."

"Aliens," Hokkaido said.

"And humans, nowadays. Anyway, who's an alien? To many of them —" Martin waved in the direction of Mag-Ingat— "you and me are aliens, or as good as."

"That's too philosophical for him, Marty," I said. "Way over his head."

"I like 'em dumb," Martin said, giving Hokkaido a smile that made him shrink back a few feet from the boundary line and warn us about trespassing.

"Has anyone been in and out of here today?" I said, ignoring the bear.

"Only these guys," Martin said. "Anyone else shows up, I'll let you know before their shadow hits the ground."

I nodded. There was no point me staying here, too. I'd just drive Martin mad as well as myself.

I left him regaling Hokkaido with more of his probably-untrue tales of the shipping industry, and drove to our own terminal. It was only half a mile as the crow flies, but three times that by road, as a lot of the smaller intraport roads are one-way.

Since I was last out here, Dolph had moved the ship inside the hangar—a pain-in-the-ass maneuver which involved jacking the auxiliaries up and rolling our motorized ship dolly underneath all four of them, one at a time. I parked at the entrance of the hangar, and walked in, glad to be out of the sun. The *St. Clare* still rested on the dolly, as if on a single giant rollerskate. The nissen-hut style roof of the hangar curved overhead, ribbed like the guts of Jonah's whale. Our family of swallows twittered in the cool shadows up there. They weren't really swallows, they were native PdL birds with nutcracker beaks and bronze plumage, but they sang beautifully, and they had come to live in our hangar, indifferent to the constant noise and the chemical fumes. We were grateful for their presence. Lucy liked to ride up in the cherrypicker and count their babies every time she was out here.

I moved around the ship, intending to check on the aft port radiator and the shrapnel damage to the hull. I couldn't even see Martin and Dolph's repairs, either because they were so good, or because of the tears in my eyes.

"Ahem?" I heard a mechanical throat-clearing from above my head. I angrily dashed my forearm across my eyes and looked up.

"Hi-dee-ho, Captain!" Mechanical Failure was lying in the port airlock, gripping onto its lip with his upper set of manipulators. "Hot enough for you?"

I stared up at the bot, which I normally considered the bane of my life. My current worries dwarfed that thorn in my side. "Yeah, it's hot," I said. "Go back in the ship, MF."

"Something bothering you, Captain?" MF's big optical sensor "eyes," mounted above the speaker box that stood in for a mouth, goggled at me in his usual daft fashion. "Wanna watch a movie? That always cheers me up!"

The offer, which would normally have caused me a pang of annoyance, somehow felt like a friend's arm around my shoulders. I had to wipe my eyes again. "No, I'm fine. Actually, I'm not fine. That motherfucker Buzz Parsec has kidnapped my daughter."

I climbed halfway up the airlock stairs and sat on top of the aft port engine pod. MF poked the top half of his suitcase-like body out of the airlock. He listened in silence as I poured out the whole story.

Look, I *know* bots have no emotions. They are machines with a few more cross-firing electronic neurons. I believe that to this day. But it sure as hell felt like MF was sympathizing with me. His blinks, and the angles of the sensor covers that mimicked eyebrows, clumsily mirrored my feelings.

"So that's why I'm here," I finished. "If he takes off with her. I'm going to dupe his destination coordinates and follow him, even if it means flying into the Core itself."

"Really?"

"Yes, really," I snapped, veering into sarcasm. I shook my head. "Didn't even bring my kitbag. Don't have a launch slot. Can't you tell I'm drunk?"

"Yes, Captain. I have an atmospheric sampler with a sensitivity of 0.001 parts per million." MF's technical mode was even more off-putting than his pervy mode. "I estimate that your blood alcohol level is 0.07 percent."

I scowled at him. "Who needs a breathalyzer?"

"Captain, can I join in the search for your daughter? I might be able to help!"

I shook my head. "How could you help?"

MF was only a maintenance bot, not a private investigator. But as I spoke, I started to think about data analysis and pattern recognition. Maybe MF's electronic brain could do something with the security camera footage that neither the police, nor our own phones' AI assistants could do.

"First," MF said, "I would like to examine the scene of the crime."

My high hopes of the last few nanoseconds wavered. "Why?"

"There might be clues! The universe is governed by probabilities. Nothing is certain, even at the level of fundamental physics."

"I know, but—"

"Therefore, nothing can be ruled out without a thorough investigation. Anyway, it can't hurt to try, right?"

I sighed. This was rapidly starting to feel like a waste of time. But what other ideas did I have? "All right, come on." I climbed down to the ground. MF spidered down the ladder after me, using his manipulator grips to swing himself from rung to rung, like a monkey. When he reached the floor of the hangar, he reverted to rolling on his tough little wheels. "You'll have to ride in the back of my truck," I said.

"Awww," MF pouted. "I wanted to look around."

"I'll let you know when we reach the Strip. Plenty of scantily clad ladies there."

"The Strip? Why are we going there? I want to inspect the scene of the crime. Your apartment."

"For Christ's sake, she wasn't abducted from my apartment!"

"All the same, there might be clues there! All crime starts at home."

"If you're blaming *me*—"

MF gave me an odd, severe look. "I could not blame you," he said, "any more than you already blame yourself." Leaving me speechless, he rolled around to the back of the truck and waited to be let in.

I threw the back door open with bad grace.

On my way out of the spaceport, I completed a customs form on my phone. One maintenance bot. Not for sale. Unfortunately. When I was through with that, I called the crew and told them what I was doing.

Irene didn't pick up, but I got Martin and Dolph.

There was a short silence as they realized I wasn't kidding: Mechanical Failure had volunteered to investigate.

"Don't let him go upstairs," Dolph said. "He'd probably install a spy-cam in Irene's shower."

"Warn him that he isn't allowed to take pictures of strangers," Martin said. "Not even if they're wearing miniskirts."

"What did he make you promise him?" Dolph said. "The dirty little SOB was asking me about Shifter orgies the other day."

I cut through their humor. "He didn't ask me for anything. I'm desperate, guys. He might be able to help."

Dolph quit joking. "OK, I'll meet you at your place."

"Did you find those bears?"

"Not yet. One's called Whitey. A polar bear, natch. The other's Kelly, a black bear. They mostly work for Cecilia, and I guess they're wherever she's at."

"Ville Verde," I said. I tapped my shades on the wheel, fidgety, as I rolled into customs. The doors came down, the scanners whined in the darkness, the doors went back up. I was through.

I drove back into the city.

42

DOLPH was sitting on my front porch when I got home, eating a barbecue hoagie. He motioned to a second wrapped sandwich. "That's yours," he said with his mouth full. "You haven't eaten today, have you?"

The smell of barbecue reminded me of Christy. Her face drifted across my mind's eye like a postcard from a better universe, where little girls did not get abducted. I wasn't hungry, but I unwrapped the sandwich.

MF gibboned out the back of the truck and swung himself up the front steps. On uneven surfaces, he used his lower pair of manipulators like a man walking on crutches. He could move surprisingly fast that way.

The next-door neighbors—a Shifter family with eight kids—stopped the game they were playing on the sidewalk, and watched him.

An older Shifter couple who lived across the street came out on their front porch and stood there, watching him.

I knew what they were thinking: *He's got ANOTHER bot? Spending it like water, ain't he?*

MF reached the top of the steps. He did look very high-spec, in contrast to my grungy, weathered front porch. "What a nice neighborhood!" His eyes swivelled, and landed on the mother of the kids next door. "Oooeee! Hubba, hubba!" MF's speaker box emitted a noise exceedingly like a wolf whistle. I smacked him on the housing. The poor woman cringed and hurried her toddlers indoors.

"She has eight kids," I said. "Keep your damn optical sensors to yourself."

"There's no law against looking, Cap'n!"

"You're asking for a liter of soda in your circuits," Dolph said, holding up his drink threateningly.

MF hurriedly rolled into the front hall. Some of the hidden hatches in his housing irised, revealing lenses and sampling arms. He stopped and waved his attachments in horror. "There are old blood splatters on the floor! And everywhere!"

"Dammit," Dolph said. "You shoulda used that spray bleach stuff, Mike. It even works after the blood dries."

He was messing with MF, but the fact that MF had spotted ancient blood splatters gave me new respect for his forensic abilities. I had no doubt there were some. The building was at least a hundred years old, and had been inhabited by Shifters for most of its history.

Rafael Ijiuto poked his head out of the living-room. "What's that?"

"Our maintenance bot," I said.

"What's it doing here?"

"Who is this person?" MF said to me.

"Long story." I was completely sick of Ijiuto by this time. "Can we just get on with it?"

"He looks like a Darkworlder," MF said. "They are very inbred."

Dolph stifled a laugh. I had filled him in on Ijiuto's claim to be a prince. He thought it was hilarious.

"Well, as a matter of fact," Ijiuto started, seemingly pleased that MF was taking an interest.

"All he wants to know is was your momma hot in bed," Dolph said. "Ignore him."

"Sexuality is one of the key driving forces for human behavior," MF chirruped.

I took a big bite out of my hoagie, transferred it to my left hand, and drew my Machina with my right. I pointed it at MF. "Shut the fuck up," I said levelly through my mouthful of sandwich.

Ijiuto went white at the sight of the gun and withdrew into the living-room. MF let us guide him into the kitchen, where he inspected every surface and appliance. He was shining his black light under the fridge when Nanny B trundled in to get something ... and MF disabled her. He simply froze her before she could say a word.

"Hey!" Dolph said.

"Domestic bots annoy me," MF said. He poked a manipulator under the fridge and brought out a scrunchie that Lucy had lost months ago. "And you are always telling *me* to vacuum, Captain!" he said reproachfully.

I took the scrunchie and balled it in my hand, swallowing back tears. Dolph rubbed his face with both hands, his fund of humor temporarily exhausted.

After that MF went into my bedroom. We watched him from the doorway.

He delved into my closet.

"Watch out for the skeletons, MF," Dolph said.

"Hey, quit messing with my kitbag," I said.

My kitbag lay on the floor of the closet, untouched since we got back from Gvm Uye Sachttra. Now MF was pulling open the zipper, tossing out my dirty shirts and underwear.

Suddenly, a piercing alarm blared from MF's speaker.

He dropped the dirty laundry and rushed at me and Dolph. "Out! Out!" He levelled his upper manipulators and crossed them in front of the door, like a waist-level gate keeping me and Dolph out. "Close the door! Evacuate the apartment! Call the police!"

"*What?*"

I struggled to get past MF. Over his top, I saw what he'd just dropped on the floor. It was the beer-stained toy fairy which I had originally meant to give Lucy. It had been wrapped in one of my dirty t-shirts.

"I have detected a Level 1 biological hazard," MF howled. "Your luggage is contaminated with interstellar variant kuru."

43

THE next seconds seemed to unspool as slowly as water dripping in micro-gravity.

Interstellar variant kuru.

My gaze locked on the toy fairy lying on my bedroom floor, its wings stained with the beer Dolph had spilt on it at the refugee camp on Gvm Uye Sachttra.

Where there had recently been an outbreak of kuru.

I remembered Lucy pulling at the zipper of my kitbag: *Daddy, did you bring me a present?*

And me gesturing her away from the bag, not wanting her to be disappointed by the spoilt, dirty toy fairy, reaching into my pocket for the handmade doll Pippa had given me— *Yes, of course. This is for you.*

If not for Pippa, I might have given Lucy the fairy anyway.

My memory reel sped up, flickering through the last few days, searching for any occasion when Lucy had been in my room and might have touched my kitbag. I could not remember her going near it. But I hadn't been here all the time.

"Nanny B!" I roared, plunging back to the kitchen. "Has Lucy been into my kitbag since—dammit! Turn her on, MF!"

MF paid me no attention. "Keep out!" he blared. "Keep out, keep out! Evacuate the building!"

"Ain't no point," Dolph said. The unnaturally high pitch of his voice gave the lie to his apparent calm. "Mike and I already touched that thing. We walked all around the damn refugee camp with it."

I flashed back on that morning. I remembered how the toy fairy had sparkled in the dimness of my cargo hold. I remembered how it had seemed to stare at me with something big and terrifying behind its tiny eyes. I should have taken my hunch more seriously.

Had Ijiuto known?

I slammed into the living-room.

The cushions were still dented where Ijiuto had been sitting. The holovision was still on. His IV line swayed loose in the breeze from the fan.

He was gone.

*

Dolph and I spilled out of the apartment, leaving MF behind us. Outside, the leaves of the gravelnuts hung limp in the humidity. There was not a breath of wind. The shadows had started to lengthen. The next-door children had resumed their game on the sidewalk. I looked at them. Crossed the street.

"You go that way," Dolph said, "I'll go this way."

I spotted little Mia on her balcony. I yelled across the street, "Mia, are your mommy and daddy home?"

"No," her voice floated across the street. "Granny's here."

"Good. Stay in your apartment!" I yelled. "Do *not* go downstairs!"

"Where's Lucy? When is she coming home?"

I couldn't manage even a fake smile. I lifted a hand to her in a gesture that couldn't decide whether to be placating or forbidding. Then I started towards Shoreside, searching for Rafael Ijiuto.

Every time I passed someone on the sidewalk, I circled wide of them, even stepping into the street and walking on the outside of the parked cars at times. The traffic was light. All the same, passing cars honked at me. I hardly noticed. I brushed my hands over my clothes, which had been in the same closet as my kitbag. If the stuff was sticking to me, would I be better off letting it stay there, or would I be killing people by brushing it off into the air?

MF's words before we left the apartment offered only qualified reassurance. "The contagion appears to be limited to the distribution mechanism—" he meant the toy fairy. "The IVK prions were contained in an aerosol pod, which also contained glitter. However, at some point that pod was opened, and its contents dispersed."

Yeah. I knew when that had happened, too. When the thing had suddenly showered fairy dust into the air at that crossroads.

The very same place later identified as ground zero of Gvm Uye Sachttra's interstellar variant kuru outbreak.

Now I knew how Pippa had gotten infected with kuru. After the Travellers took Jan and Leaf, she must have chased after us, hoping that we—the only other offworlder humans remaining on Gvm Uye Sachttra—could help. She must have been standing in that intersection, hidden by the tall aliens in the crowd, when the toy fairy did its vile party trick, and ended her life as she knew it.

She had not been its only victim.

One fairy had infected six people at the refugee camp, and indirectly killed dozens more in the riots that followed.

What would *nine thousand* fairies have done?

What would they do to Ponce de Leon?

I had to find Ijiuto. I scanned both sides of the street in the same singleminded way I had searched for Lucy last night. In fact, this felt like a nightmarish repeat of that experience.

Ijiuto shouldn't be that hard to spot. He was taller than average, with that close-cut, nubbly hairstyle you don't see much in this part of the Cluster, and most distinctively, he was still wearing Dr. Zeb's hospital tunic and drawstring shorts. The togs were a shade of mint green no one wears by choice, even in Shiftertown where gaudy pastel colors clash on every house and shopfront.

In fact, Ijiuto was now even worse off than he had been when he arrived at my office, except that he was no longer barefoot. When he sneaked out of my apartment, he had stolen a pair of my shoes.

I reached Shoreside and looked hopelessly up and down the avenue. Late afternoon crowds moved like syrup. I would not be able to walk half a block here without brushing against other people, and potentially transferring lethal particles off me, onto them.

My phone rang.

"Lost him," Dolph said.

"I'm on the Strip." As I spoke, I watched for a break in the traffic. "If he went this way, we're not gonna find him." I jaywalked across the avenue. One good thing about self-driving cars is they are incapable of hitting you, even when being driven by a person. So jaywalking is a safe activity, although you risk getting reported by AIs with good facial recognition.

"No," Dolph said. "I *found* him. He was on Creek. I saw him about two blocks off. Those hospital clothes. I started running to catch up with him. He saw me, he started to run, too. I chased him back down 94th. I was almost up with him when a truck comes shooting up the street—it's one way from Creek to Shoreside, right?—going the wrong way. Truck brakes, the door opens, he jumps in. So I think, not so fast. I jump over the hood of a parked car and stand in the street. I'm gonna make it stop for me." Dolph's voice rose. "The damn thing didn't stop. I realized, holy shit, this thing is *accelerating*. I went back over that car so fast, folks on the sidewalk clapped."

"That's one heck of a special override," I said.

"Yup," Dolph said. "And the best part? I saw the logo on that truck as it went by like the proverbial freaking bat. *Trident Overland.*"

I climbed the seawall steps at 90th. The broad, shallow concrete steps were identical to the ones a few blocks further down where we had found Robbie last night. Time seemed to be folding in on me. I brushed some more at my t-shirt. I felt contaminated inside and out.

There were relatively few people on the beach. There's always a lull between the madness in the middle of the day, and the nighttime when pop-up bars appear on the sand and people drink and dance by the light of torches. I saw gulls in the air, and imagined for a horrible second that they were toy fairies, sprinkling doom on these innocent people.

"We need to talk about this," I mumbled. "Really talk about it."

"I'll meet you out there," Dolph said.

"Roger." I went down the steps to the beach and walked towards the water.

I remembered the day when I had brought Lucy to the beach with Rex, Mia, and Kit.

In retrospect, that had been our last perfect day.

Or had it been something else?

Had Buzz Parsec used that encounter on the beach to familiarize himself with Lucy's face and voice—a necessary step, since I'd been so careful with her online profile? Had he been recording? Cameras come so small, he could have had one hidden in a button or in that ugly platinum necklace he wore.

I saw him casting his shadow over our patch of beach, bending down to my daughter: *She's gonna be a heartbreaker.*

Little did any of us know then that the heart broken would be mine.

I reached the water. Foamy-edged waves frilled onto the sand. There is never much surf on Mag-Ingat Beach. I took my shoes off and lined them up neatly at the edge of the dry sand—someone might want them. Then I walked into the water.

44

THE water felt icy, after the heat of the day. My soaked work pants ballooned around my legs. The sand shifted underfoot. I stepped on a seashell. A sudden swell splashed up to my waist, and my balls tried to hide inside my body from the shock of the cold water.

I kept walking.

Remember, I couldn't swim.

Chest deep, I looked out to sea and all around. I was the only person in the water here. This was not one of the protected swimming areas. That dorsal fin cutting towards me might be a rainbow shark ...

Or a dolphin.

It surged up to me, scraping past my body. I stumbled for balance in the deep water. The dolphin's head broke the surface. "Grab hold of my belt," it said in Dolph's voice.

Dolph has two animal forms. The jackal, of course—but that's not why we call him Dolph. His other form is a bottlenosed dolphin.

His belt, let out to the last hole, wrapped around his body, just ahead of the gray, rough-skinned dorsal fin. I grabbed the belt with both hands, and held on for dear life as he thrust with his powerful tail. I felt an instant's panic when I could no longer touch the bottom. But we had done this before. Getting a tow from Dolph was the only way I would ever be able to cross deep water without a life-vest, unless I decided to learn to swim, which seemed unlikely at my age.

Dolph swam out to sea, around the outside of the protected swimming area between 65th and 75th. He alternated between swimming on the surface and under it. On the surface, I squinted my eyes shut against the face-level swells and the dazzling sunlight. Beneath the surface, I held on tight and let the air stream out of my lungs, while the salty water washed all over me. I imagined any last trace of interstellar variant kuru on my clothes or body being washed away, lost and neutralized in the cleansing deep.

Dolph swam under St. Andrew's Pier, where the swells foamed around the green-bearded support pillars and echoed off the concrete underside of the pier. He swam without speaking, without stopping, on and on, as if something was chasing him. I wondered how far we were going to go. At 45th or thereabouts, he turned with a flick of his tail and swam back towards the beach.

My feet scraped sand.

I let go of Dolph's belt and stumbled to my feet, waist-deep in the swell.

He dived once more, and came back up half a minute later in his human form, scraping his wet hair out of his face. He was now naked, of course, except for his belt, with its utility pouch. It's one thing to ditch a set of clothes, but you have to keep hold of your phone.

We walked up the beach, weak-legged and shivering. This far down Shoreside, no one bats an eyelash at a naked man walking out of the sea. After all, S-Town is a haven for marine Shifters.

A large storage unit stood against the seawall, containing some kind of a pop-up that would open for business later. A guy was just taking out the flatpacks and starting to set up. He was a friend of Dolph's. Dolph spoke to him, and the guy handed over two sets of clothes. He even threw in a pack of cigarettes.

We got dressed in the dry things—I gave the guy my wet clothes, to dry and pass on to the next Shifter that came along. Then we walked off and sat with our backs to the seawall. Some way away, a homeless vet lay on a cardboard box, his bearded face dead to the world. You see all too many of them in Smith's End. The low-angled sun turned the bay to copper. Way off to our right, the lights of the Ferris wheel had already come on. They were red, white, and green, in honor of Founding Day tomorrow.

Dolph lit a cigarette. "We were standing upwind," he said, his voice shaky.

"Yeah," I said. "We were definitely upwind."

I remembered the glitter swirling around that intersection. The way people had gasped in wonder. And I hated Rafael Ijiuto with a fiery hatred born from the sheer injustice of it. I realized this was probably how Dolph felt about lots of things, lots of the time.

Now, however, Dolph seemed diminished. Shrunken by fear. With his wet hair flattened to his skull, he even looked frail. He was still shivering from the exertion of the swim and the cold of the water. He doesn't really have enough body fat to be a dolphin, but that's the form he had his heart set on since we were kids.

"Here's what we have to decide," I said. "Do we tell the police? Or not?"

"Jesus, Mike, I don't know."

"Here's what we do know," I said. "Eight thousand nine hundred and ninety-fucking-nine of those fairies are somewhere in this city. And the last we saw them, they were in Sophia's possession."

"The bears," Dolph said.

"I'm starting to think Parsec might be getting used here. I just don't see him leasing out his trucks with permission for special overrides that would allow them to pick up hitchhikers, or run a guy down in the street."

"No," Dolph allowed. "I can't see that, either."

"Silverback didn't really know anything about Mujin Inc. He didn't even know what was in those crates. He thought it might be drugs, for Christ's sake. Maybe Parsec doesn't know, either."

Dolph grudgingly nodded, but he said, "Then why'd he kidnap Lucy? Why would he go that far to distract you from finding out the truth, if he doesn't know it himself?"

I gritted my jaw so hard that a spike of pain drove through my temple. "Because Sophia *does* know the truth," I said. "She built the damn fairies herself. And while she might be cool with hundreds of thousands of people on the PdL suffering a horrible death, she's not cool with the same thing happening to Lucy."

Dolph exhaled a cloud of smoke. "I guess not caring only goes so far," he murmured.

"I guess so," I said. Rex and Irene had theorized that Sophia had kidnapped Lucy out of simple maternal motives. They may have been right, as far as that went. Sophia was not quite inhuman enough to let her child die.

Dolph interrupted my thoughts. "Maybe we should go to the police."

I had guessed he was going to say that. I even agreed, in principle. I now had exactly what d'Alencon had asked me for: hard evidence that Mujin Inc was tangled up in bad shit. But *I was, too!*

"Bones thinks I'm mixed up in it," I said. "Or at least he's pretending to think I am. He wants me to find him some dirt on Parsec, to clear my own name."

"That works," Dolph said.

"But I can't!" I said, pleadingly. "Those crates were on the *St. Clare!* There's no way I can argue I didn't know what was in them. It's my responsibilty to ensure that my cargoes are legal." I glanced at Dolph's profile, praying he'd see it my way. "If it was just data ... or drugs, or something ... but *bio-weapons?*"

"What happens if they hang it around our necks?"

"I don't know. It would depend on the charges, but I can't see any way I don't lose the ship."

"Man, who cares," Dolph said with a bitter snort of laughter. "She's an ugly old bitch, anyway."

I knew that Dolph loved the *St. Clare* as much as he loved anything. In fact, the only two things in the world he did love were his bike and our ship, oh, and whatever gun held his fancy at the moment. When he said something like that, he was carving a piece out of his own heart and throwing it away, and it felt like he was taking a piece out of my heart, as well.

"This is what I get for giving you a job when no one else would?" I said. "This is what I get for having your back at Dagda's Knoll?" I was so angry I almost mentioned the Marie thing, but then didn't. "If it wasn't for me, you'd be *him!*" I pointed to the homeless vet reclining further down the beach. "You'd be living in a cardboard box on the Strip, eating fish out of the bay, and panhandling to support your drug habit."

Dolph looked in the direction I was pointing. "The only difference between me and him," he said, "is on the outside."

"That's bullshit," I said. I was on the edge of tears. "You know the difference between right and wrong. That's why I always looked up to you."

The fact is, although Dolph and I were in the same year at school, he had always seemed older and more mature. There were reasons for that which I won't get into right now. Anyway, he was popular, he had two animal forms by the time he was sixteen, and most importantly, he was unashamedly fair to everyone. He stood up to bullies, even if they were his own friends, in defense of the outcasts … like me. So when he announced that he was leaving school to join the army, it didn't take much thinking before I decided to do the same thing.

He said, "My whole life I've been looking for a cause good enough to die for." He stared out to sea, his jaw set like a rock. "I never found one, because there are no causes that good." He suddenly let out a choking laugh. "It sucks pretty damn hard to end up getting killed by a *toy fairy!*"

"We were standing upwind," I said with as much conviction as I could muster, remembering the way that specks of glitter had settled on Dolph's hair.

"Yeah," he said. "Guess there's no point committing suicide until we get the test results."

That's right, we had already gotten tested for interstellar variant kuru, at Dr. Zeb's, before we knew that there was any real reason we should. The test results would not come back for a week, so we had another few days of grace. "We are fine." I put every ounce of persuasion I had into my voice. "MF said the IVK prions were suspended in nanoscale gel capsules. Remember? He said they would actually fall to the ground rather fast."

But the wind had been blowing.

"So the risk of directly inhaling or swallowing them is low. The real risk would be if they got into the water or food supply. Then you'd have a real epidemic on your hands."

Which was exactly what we were going to have in Mag-Ingat, if those 8,999 contaminated fairies were not found and destroyed.

Dolph glanced up at the coppery blue bowl of the sky, beyond which Ponce de Leon's satellites and orbital defense platforms tracked their watchful orbits. "They'd have to deport thousands of people. Millions? Or just nuke the city from orbit?"

"I don't know," I said. "This is *Ponce de Leon.* A Heartworld, for God's sake. You have to think they would react strongly to a massive outbreak of interstellar variant kuru in the capital."

"Yeah." Dolph took another cigarette out off his pack and lit it off the stub of his first one. This small action told me that he was coming back from the dark place he'd gone to. I was so relieved, I took one of his cigarettes.

He raised an eyebrow: you don't smoke.

I shrugged. He passed me the lighter.

It had been so long since I smoked, I'd almost forgotten how. But the burn in my lungs felt good, as if the smoke were cleansing my bronchial tubes, the way the sea had cleansed my face and body.

"So the real question is," Dolph said, "could the police react fast enough to secure the crates before someone—Ijiuto, Sophia, whoever —decides it's time to unload them?"

"And the answer is no," I said. "Everything they do, they do it so *slow.* Even Bones was complaining about it. Even if we called them right now, by the time the prosecutor gets off her ass to sign a warrant, it might be too late." I dragged on my cigarette and exhaled. I could tell that by the time I stubbed it out, smoking would be second nature to me again. "In fact, Bones admitted it on the phone with me earlier. He couldn't come right out and say it, but the overall nuance was that I need to rescue Lucy myself."

This interpretation came to me as I spoke. But Dolph had apparently come to the same conclusion independently.

"Yeah," he said. "I actually started gaming that out. I met Alec at the hoagie place. You know him?"

"The guy who runs the range?"

"That's right. He came in to see if there was anything he could do. You might not realize it, Mike, but everyone in S-Town is ready to come out for you. Parsec really crossed the line. Snatching someone's child? You do not *do* that. Everyone hates him, anyway. Living out on the Cape, with his normie wife and his flying car, acting like his shit don't stink, and all the time his bears are collecting protection money from half the business owners in Smith's End."

"I didn't know about the protection game. Is there *anything* he hasn't got his claws into?"

"That's it," Dolph said. "He's overextended himself. It's time for him to take a fall, and if all the bears go down with him, no one's gonna cry." He stubbed out his cigarette and drew in the dry, loose sand with the butt, starting with bullet points. "I was shooting Alec's truck-mounted .50 cal the other day. You really need to come out there some time. Drive the truck out into the woods and shoot at the trees. It's like watching an invisible chainsaw. You just have to watch out for them coming down on top of you."

"What's that got to do with Parsec?"

"Nothing," Dolph admitted. But I understood why he'd mentioned it. He'd needed to go to his happy place, to stop thinking about the violence that had been done to him, and start thinking about the violence we were going to do to—well, whatever, really. Trees. Parsec. Anyone that got in the way. "Point is, Alec said he would lend us some longs, and a vehicle if we need one with clean plates."

"It's not getting there," I said. "It's getting inside."

"Getting there is part of it. Maybe the hardest part. Once we're in, it's a classic hostage rescue operation. We'll want to have grenades to clear out any concentrations of hostiles, but mainly it's just fire teams going from room to room …"

As he went on in further detail, I half listened, but mostly I was thinking about various jobs we had done in the Fringeworlds, when the money was good, when no one would ever find out. Dolph had clicked into contractor mode. This was what we'd been doing ever since Tech Duinn, where the army obligingly taught us how. It's what we were good at. But now I had to face the fact that this would likely be the last job we ever did. I privately resolved that if possible, I'd make sure Dolph, at least, got away with it.

I smelled a familiar skunky smell, and glanced up the beach. Dolph's friend had opened his pop-up for business. It turned out to be a herb shop, one of those places that offer a thousand and one all-natural ways to get bombed out of your mind. I was smelling the thanatos sticks the guy had set on the counter. Those had also been popular on Tech Duinn. I yearned for an instant for what I'd unjustly accused Dolph of—seeking oblivion.

Dolph added a final bullet point for body armor. "Of course," he finished with a grimace, "that was when I thought we were going to be raiding Ville Verde."

"Who says we're not?" I said.

45

I sat in Alec from the range's pickup, a cigarette clamped in my teeth, watching the entrance of Ville Verde come into view between the trees that lined the steep access road.

Located halfway out along Cape Agreste, the gated community nestled in the jungle that covered the headland. The access road was narrow, steep, and winding. Most people who lived here *flew* in and out. They were too rich to bother using the roads.

As expected, the visitor parking lot was empty. Weeds breaking through the asphalt showed how rarely it was used. The fortifications on the other side of the parking lot told a different story: one of fuck-off wealth.

A double gate spanned the gap between two brick towers. They looked like faux-medieval gateposts, but were actually fire towers. They had machine guns and energy weapons up there, according to the gated community's publicity materials. The two-meter fence on either side of the gate bent outwards at the top, and the trees and houses on the other side of the fence shimmered just perceptibly, giving away the presence of a force field.

"Like living in jail," said Robbie, in the driver's seat.

I had just been thinking how much safer I would feel if I lived somewhere like this, and veering into half-baked plans to move out to the Cape if I ever got Lucy back ... no, *when* I got her back. I would not allow myself to contemplate failure. We had spent all last night and this morning, apart from a few snatched hours of sleep, refining this plan so that nothing could go wrong.

"It's all a matter of perspective," I said.

"I don't know about that," Robbie muttered. The young wolf was in human form, sweating on account of the heavy armor plates inside his flak vest. And maybe nerves.

He had volunteered to join in the operation, and had brought in some of his friends, including Sep and Marco, who were now riding in the back of the pickup with Rex.

Unlike Parsec, I did not have an army on call. Dolph had convinced me to let the rippers help out. As a matter of fact, they were all too eager. The only thing they wanted from me? Permission to film.

We'd also had help from the S-Town veterans' association, which lent us the flak vests; a local construction company, which gave us the materials to make shaped charges; and St. Patrick's, our parish church. The sister who worked at the Shifter Center had offered to look after Mia and Kit while their parents were … otherwise occupied. So the Seagrave children were getting a mid-week dose of Sunday school, while we prepared to go to war with the bears.

Happy Founding Day.

Ville Verde was celebrating Founding Day, too. Red, white, and green bunting fluttered above the gates, strung between the fire towers. The towers themselves flew Ponce de Leon flags, paired with the green and blue United Humanity flag that represents Earth.

Robbie slowed down as we bumped across the visitor parking lot. The security guards watched our approach with mild interest. They didn't see anything out of the ordinary. Remember, Buzz Parsec lived here.

As we pulled up in front of the gate, I crushed my cigarette between my heavy claws and tipped it out the window.

I put one forefoot on the edge of Robbie's seat and the other on his thigh. He flinched as my claws dug into his jeans, but I needed to get my head out the window on his side.

"Howdy," I smiled at the security guards. "Happy Founding Day!" They winced.

A smile *does* look a bit menacing on the face of a black bear..

I had learned this form a few years back for an off-world job. At the time my idea had been to pick the animal I'd *least* want to be in real life. I'd gone for *Ursus americanus* because I didn't have the body mass to be really convincing as a grizzly bear.

But it worked. Parsec had several black bears on his crew, and to a mainstream human, a bear is a bear is a bear, anyway.

"Happy Founding Day," one of the security guards echoed, with a mean smile.

"Tell ya what I think," the other one said, "this would be a better planet if we didn't have to share it with talking bears."

I couldn't tell him that I fully agreed, although not in the way he meant. I responded as I thought one of Parsec's bears would. "Freedom of movement is a human right," I said. "Meaning you're free to move to a different planet if you don't like it."

"Yeah," said Robbie, trying to get in on my menacing act.

"But as long as you're here," I said, "how about doing your job?"

"Sure will," grunted the first security guard, moving to the back of the pickup. I heard him greet Rex, Sep, and Marco with a hostile "Whaddup, bears."

I inwardly pumped my fist. The guards assumed that all of us were bears, without me even having to say so.

Rex was sitting on a duffel bag that contained several rifles. But the security guard did not ask him to move so he could inspect it. "Go on," he said, slapping the side of the pickup.

I scrambled back into my own seat.

Robbie drove forward to the gates.

He leaned out the window and touched the ID terminal with a card that identified him as an employee of Parsec Freight.

Some people keep their ID on their phones. Others might elect to get a chip implanted in their hands.

But the latter method doesn't work for a Shifter, and as careful as we are not to lose our phones, there are occasions when you have to leave them turned off.

Such as when you're in a hospital.

The bears had brought their employee ID cards to Dr. Zeb's, and Martin had pinched Canuck's card out of his pants when he Shifted.

"Kind of thing that might come in handy," he had said.

Now it was coming in very handy indeed. I held my breath as the terminal processed the card. Canuck might have had it cancelled already ...

He hadn't.

The terminal turned green.

The gates sank into the ground, one after another, and we drove into Ville Verde.

*

At the same moment, Dolph was driving my truck into the parking lot of Bonsucesso Tower.

We had debated for hours whether to hit Ville Verde or Mujin Inc, and ultimately decided on both at once.

The idea was to leave Parsec nowhere to hide. Oh, sure, he also had his downtown office, and the Trident Overland depot in Harborside ... and, and ... He had been lying low since the debacle at Dr. Zeb's, and to be honest, he could be anywhere. But we didn't have the manpower to look everywhere. We hoped that by hitting his home *and* his sketchy front company, we would force him to emerge from his lair.

Dolph and I weren't able to stay in touch throughout the whole operation. It's kind of difficult to talk on the phone when you're shooting and running. But as near as I can figure it, this is what happened.

Dolph had trouble finding a parking space. It was, of course, Founding Day, meaning that the mall level was packed out with visitors to the festival. Dolph finally found a space in a distant corner.

He opened the back of the truck, and five wolves in human form got out. These were Alec from the range and four of his friends, who called themselves the "jungle wolves." They lived out there. They were hardcore.

Martin was still out at the spaceport. He'd been pissed at not getting to join in, but I had begged him to stay put to cover Parsec's most likely escape route.

Irene? None of us exactly knew where she was, except Rex, and he wasn't telling. She had come home to eat and sleep last night, then gone back out at dawn. She said she had picked up the trail of the contaminated fairy dust. If she could just track down this one guy, she'd be able to find out where it had come from.

I didn't really see the point of tracing the damn stuff, but Irene seemed to think it mattered. And much as I would miss her sharp-shooting skills, I accepted that my part of the operation wasn't a job for a sniper.

Neither was Dolph's.

The jungle wolves lifted two large suitcases out of the back of the truck. One of these held their spare guns and ammo. The other held the shaped charge we had prepared in my kitchen last night, after MF grudgingly deemed the apartment fit for human occupation.

He had enlisted Nanny B to help him sterilize the entire apartment down to the sheetrock. I'm hardly even exaggerating. When MF allowed us back in, I had scarcely recognized the place. All the carpets and soft furnishings had vanished, along with the bedclothes, everything edible out of the kitchen, and the top layer of paint off the walls. Lucy's room had been stripped of all her belongings. Even her cherished Gemworld Families dolls had joined the carpets and curtains in the plastic bags piled in the living-room, which MF instructed us to treat as hazardous waste. *That* hurt.

And yet, after the initial shock, I had been oddly relieved that Lucy's things were gone from the apartment. I did not need reminders everywhere of the kinder, gentler world I had tried to build for her.

Anyway, if I got her back, I'd buy her all the new toys she wanted. If? No. *When.*

MF had offered to assist Dolph's end of the operation. He swung down from the back of the truck after all the men were out. Dolph had dressed him in a Shoreside Elementary t-shirt to make him look less high-spec. It swallowed his suitcase-like housing, while his head stuck out of the neck hole, googly eyes blinking innocently.

On their way up in the elevator, people smiled and chatted to MF, taking him for some kind of interactive advertising bot. MF played along by relating factoids about the Founders.

The Founding Day festivities also gave Dolph and his crew an excuse to wear red and green face paint. Most people would just paint tricolor stripes on their cheeks. Dolph and the jungle wolves had painted swoops and blobs on their foreheads, jaws, and one eye. The key principles are to obscure the ocular region and the bridge of the nose, and break up the symmetry of the face. The Travellers used living tattoos. This way worked just as well. The facial recognition algorithms would have a very hard time identifying the six men who remained in the elevator when everyone else got out at the mall level.

In silence, the team travelled up to the 121st floor. Dolph reached around and loosened his Koiler in its holster.

The elevator doors opened.

Dolph walked out into that eerie hall with its mirrored ceiling and light-up tiles. He confirmed with a glance that there was no one else in the hall. We had found out by studying the building plan that Mujin Inc was the only occupant of this floor. The company's doors were still sealed.

Dolph took a laser pointer out of his pocket and aimed it directly into the camera facing the elevator.

At the same time, Alec was taking out the camera at one end of the hall, and Ryder, a young veteran of Quvira, was dealing with the one at the far end.

"Hopefully it'll be a while before they get around to checking out the malfunctions," Dolph said. The team had seen the Founding Day festivities in full swing on the mall level as they rose up in the glass-walled elevator. It looked like a human sea of red, white, and green. With any luck, building security would have their hands full.

The team proceeded to their objective and prepared to force an entry …

See how much easier it is to talk about it like this? These are the words Dolph used when he talked about it to me, but I'd probably have resorted to the same kind of language, the language the army taught us. The plain fact was that Dolph and his team were preparing to set off a bomb in a Mag-Ingat office building, a level of crazy that could only be glancingly justified by reference to the threat on the other side.

The doors were two slabs of steel sealed as tightly as an airlock. MF tried to force them by inserting his laser saw attachment into the crack, but nothing happened except that the steel heated up and unpleasant wisps of smoke escaped. Anyway, Dolph had already decided to go with the shaped charge. I think on some subconscious level he had forgotten that he was on Ponce de Leon. Mentally, he was operating off-world. The explosive we had got from the construction company was a high-brisance nitramine, which crumbled when we unpacked the bricks, and smelled like marzipan, with an odor so strong we'd had to open the kitchen windows. We had packed the charge into an economy size can that formerly held fruit salad. We had made a copper liner for it, and made stand-off legs by cutting up the wire rack out of my oven. Getting the stand-off distance right was crucial. MF had estimated the thickness of the door and broken out his math skills.

The team taped the charge to the bottom of one door and retreated to the other end of the hall. Dolph carried the detonator, unreeling the wire behind him.

He said that when he looked back down that long hall, the doors looked tiny, but he still had a sudden fear that the hall wasn't long enough.

"Five," he said. "Four. Three. Two. One." He pressed the firing button.

46

At the same time, Robbie was parking around the corner from Buzz Parsec's house.

It was a lovely house. Mellow brick walls with just the right amount of ivy—real terrestrial ivy—rambling over them, and dormer windows in a tiled mansard roof. You could hardly believe Shiftertown's worst crook lived here. But of course, all the other houses on his cul-de-sac were equally lovely. They were all variations on the Ville Verde template. And the other houses had real, lived-in front gardens—here a jungle gym, there a tree swing, there a pergola covered with roses— whereas Parsec's front garden was a square of lawn enclosed by shrubbery, clearly tended by a bot. Neither he nor Cecilia had any interest in gardening.

I got out of the pickup, still in my bear form, and walked up the cul-de-sac, sniffing the ground and looking all around. Thank God, there was no one out on the street. They'd all be at their own Founding Day hootenanny. In fact, I could hear the faint sound of a steel band drifting over the rooftops from the community's public park.

The garage abutting Parsec's house had just one car in it, a two-seater that I guessed was Cecilia's. It was not the one on the security camera footage. I hadn't expected them to be that dumb, but all the same, my heart sank.

What if Parsec wasn't here, either?

Well, there was only one way to find out.

I turned onto his garden walk. It was laid with black pebbles, graveyard style. Heated up by the sun, the pebbles scorched my pads. I took one more look around to make sure I was alone on the street. I saw no one but Marco the wolf, loitering on the corner, waiting for his cue.

Unlike Dolph, I planned to do this as quietly as possible. The streets of Ville Verde were unusually wide, to accommodate flying cars setting down and taking off. All the same, we couldn't treat this like urban clearance on some alien planet, where we had little to no regard for collateral damage. I wanted to get inside the house, away from potential casualties and spying eyes, not only human but electronic, as quickly as possible.

I climbed Parsec's front steps and rang the doorbell with my nose.

Why does anyone choose a bear as their animal form? Every moment I was remembering how much I hated it. My thick fur threatened to overheat me, while my relatively short limbs gave me less speed and agility than the big cats or the wolf I preferred.

I heard the doorbell ringing through the house, with an empty echo. My misgivings intensified. I rang again.

After another minute, Larry (or maybe it was Gary) Kodiak answered the door. He was in human form. You have to be, to carry an assault rifle.

"What the fuck do you want?" he growled, holding the rifle down by his side, where it wouldn't be noticed by any watching neighbors.

He was wearing shorts and a string vest.

To my bear's nose, he smelled like meat.

I shambled forward into the hall, forcing him to take a quick step back.

"Steve?" he said, suspiciously.

I wasn't Steve, but I now recalled that Steve's chosen form did have one advantage. Bears can rise on their hind legs very quickly. Before the Kodiak twin could raise his rifle, I hugged him in my muscular forelegs, pinning his arms to his sides. I set my teeth into the side of his neck.

His rifle went off, hitting the floor and the steel lip of the front door. I heard a ricochet break glass.

I hugged him tighter. He was struggling madly, trying to kick me in the crotch. He knew that that hurts even in bear form. I bit down enough to break the skin. Now he changed his tactics and played dead.

Running footsteps crunched on the pebbled walk. Rex and the wolves cut off the sunlight from my furry back as they piled into the hall. I heard the door slam, and Rex saying my name, but I didn't *really* hear him because I was tasting the Kodiak twin's blood, and fighting the instinct to bite down with all the crushing strength of my bear jaws, severing his spinal cord and his carotid artery in one fearsome bite.

That's why Parsec's gang favored bears, of course.

No other animal that I have been has quite as much of a yen for killing humans.

Then again, was it the bear, or was it me? I had been going mad for 36 hours, ever since Lucy was taken. It had to start coming out at some point.

"Mike! *Mike!*"

I reminded myself fiercely that Larry or Gary K was not my enemy, and dropped him. He fell like a side of meat.

"Shit," I said, breathing through my nose.

Feet thundered on the stairs to the basement. The wolves were executing our plan to start searching the house at the bottom. Rex stood over me, covering the end of the hall with one of the rifles we had borrowed from the range. They were .308s fitted with suppressors. As I pawed at the Kodiak twin's unmoving body, Rex suddenly swung around and fired into an open doorway on our right. The suppressor reduced the typical roar of a rifle to a sound more like a high-pressure air hose being disconnected. Over it, we heard something shatter.

"Only a goddamn holovee," Rex said.

I took a deep breath and Shifted back. When I had hands once more, I quickly palpated the Kodiak twin's chest. I'd broken a couple of his ribs. He was groaning helplessly, his eyes rolling in agony.

"Where's my daughter?" I slapped his face. A blood bubble appeared at his lips. "Where is she?"

He groaned incoherently, too out of it to even hear what I was saying. I swore in frustration.

"Let him be," Rex said. He dropped his backpack and kicked it towards me. I pulled out a pair of jeans and put them on, then a flak vest. I grabbed the Kodiak twin's assault rifle. I had a .45 in the backpack, also borrowed from the range, but this had a larger capacity.

We left the Kodiak twin where he was and cleared the ground floor. I took lead, sidling up to each doorway in turn while Rex covered me. I burst through each door in turn and quickly swung my rifle to cover the whole room. Parsec had more rooms on the ground floor of his house than I had in my whole apartment. They were crammed with expensive furniture and gadgets. And they were empty. The only living things we found were some fish swimming around in a restaurant-scale saltwater tank in the kitchen. Bears like their seafood fresh.

I had eschewed Dolph's idea to use grenades, as the one thing I feared most was accidentally hurting Lucy. But as we stood in the kitchen, breathing heavily and scanning the large, empty backyard and swimming pool, I heard a muffled explosion beneath my feet. Crockery clinked on the shelves. "Those damn wolves," I snarled.

We reached the stairs at the same time as Sep and Marco stumbled back up them. Sep had lost all the hair on the right side of his head. His face on that side was red and starting to blister. Both young men held onto the banister, fumbling as if they couldn't see where they were going. Yet Marco was stubbornly carrying a commercial-grade holo projector.

"Flash-bang," Sep mumbled.

"Irene warned you about the booby-traps," Rex growled. "Anyone down there?"

"No one," Marco said. "It went off when I took this."

Parsec's booby-traps were set up to deter burglars.

I knocked the holo projector out of Marco's hands. It fell beside the Kodiak twin, who had stopped groaning because he'd passed out. "Can you see?"

"Kinda."

"Stay here. Rex, you better stay here as well."

"You going up there?" Rex rumbled, glancing at the stairs. One flight led down to the rec room. Another led up to the second floor.

"Yes." I grabbed Sep's rifle and slung it over my shoulder as a backup weapon, and then started up the stairs.

When I stopped to listen at the top of the first flight, all I heard was my friends whispering to each other at the bottom.

With my back pressed to the wall, I sidled a few steps along a hall sumptuously carpeted in pink and white.

Silence.

I flung open the first door I came to and aimed my rifle inside.

It was the master bedroom. One of those levitating beds stood on a raised dais, heaped with his 'n' hers pillows. I went through and cleared the en suite bathroom, uncomfortably aware that my ass was hanging out—I needed someone else up here to cover my back. I shouldn't have left Rex downstairs. But I needed someone effective on the door, in case more bears arrived. I had to assume that if there was anyone else in the house, they would have called in the cavalry by now. For that matter, if any of the neighbors were home, they might have noticed the boom from that damn flash-bang. Ville Verde security might be on their way.

Galvanized by urgency, I went back through the master bedroom. When I told Dolph about this later, he said, "Please tell me you took a dump on his bed." It didn't even cross my mind. There was no room for anything in my mind except Lucy.

Muscle memory and experience carried me through the rest of the second floor, but I was in so much of a hurry that I was getting sloppy. The next flight of stairs had a 45-degree bend in it. I put my rifle around the bend first, like you're supposed to do, but then I followed through without waiting long enough, and a bullet almost took my head off. Another one clipped my flak vest and sent me stumbling back down a couple of stairs.

"That you, Starrunner?"

I recognized Canuck's voice over the ringing in my ears.

"You're fucked this time!" he screamed. "Boss's on his way!"

I yelled back, "Is my daughter up there?"

"Give it up. Drop your weapon," Canuck shouted. His voice was high and raw. I believe that bear was actually a bit deranged. He couldn't possibly have been scared, right? He had the advantage over me. No way I could get up those stairs while he was …

Wait.

I crouched on the stairs, listening. I heard him rustling around up there. After a moment he got impatient and sent another burst down the stairwell. It shattered a framed print. Broken glass fell to the stairs. Before he would be able to physically squeeze the trigger again, I popped around the bend and fired up the stairs. I didn't have time to aim, but I saw him, prone on the landing.

I retreated into cover as he fired another burst, thinking desperately.

Something touched my bare foot.

I whipped my head and weapon around and saw Rex. He crawled up the first few stairs to where I was. "Sep's on the front door," he breathed into my ear. "Marco's in the kitchen. Think they learned their lesson about picking up sparkly things."

"Canuck," I whispered, motioning up the stairs.

"Where are you, Starrunner?" Canuck screamed. "I can hear you! I can smell you! Here, doggy, doggy!"

"Keep him talking," I whispered to Rex, sliding down the stairs so he could take my place.

"Any more of them up there?"

"Hope not."

I told him what I was going to try, and left him the Kodiak twin's assault rifle, which still had most of a full magazine. Then I tiptoed back along the second-floor hall. There was a window at the far end. As much as I tried to be quiet, it squeaked when I opened it, but another burst of fire from Canuck conveniently covered the noise. Rex gave me a thumbs-up. I put my head out.

The ivy climbed past the window, up to the roof.

I tested the thickest stem by tugging on it. It did not come away even a millimeter from the brick. Real terrestrial ivy is a tenacious plant. Unlike the strangler vines more common on Ponce de Leon, it is a stayer, not an opportunist. These plants were old and well rooted, and the stem I held was so thick and woody, it was practically a tree trunk.

Bears are good at climbing.

But under some circumstances, humans are better.

I put my rifle down. It would just get in the way. I had my Machina in one of the pockets of my flak vest. That'd have to do.

I boosted myself into a standing position on the windowsill, grasped the trunk, and wedged one bare foot into the crevice between the ivy and the wall.

The moment I put my weight on it, I felt the whole plant sagging. I glanced down. If I fell, I would land on Parsec's marble patio. It would be curtains for sure.

I climbed fast, racing the ineluctable force of gravity that wanted to drag me down to my death by tearing the ivy away from the wall. Overhead, the edge of the mansard roof stuck out parallel to the ground. I was hauling myself up hand over hand, and I could feel the lactic acid burn starting in my shoulder muscles. My forearms trembled. I willed strength into my hands, and seized the gutter at the edge of the roof with my left hand. At the same time I jammed my left foot on top of the ivy trunk, which wasn't a trunk any more, which was hardly a branch.

It gave way under my weight, with a ripping sound that sent leaves and shards of brick spinning down to the patio.

I got both hands on the gutter—and hung there, my feet dangling in the air.

You know those stories you hear about parents finding superhuman reserves of strength when their children are in danger?

I'm here to tell you it's true.

With strength that was not mine, I lifted my entire body up, like doing a chin-up, and kicked my right foot as high as I could until I hooked my toes over the gutter.

I rolled my body up onto the gutter and lay full-length, panting, my shoulders on fire. I looked down at the swimming pool, far below. The back garden ended at the double fence around Ville Verde's perimeter. The force field above the inner fence made the jungle appear to shimmer, as if the outside world was a mere optical illusion. It might as well have been. I'd come this far. Turning back was not even a thought.

The gutter was none too strong, judging by the way it creaked under me. I rose on my knees and grabbed hold of the dormer windowsill three feet above the edge of the roof.

I peeked through the window. The sunlight reflected off the glass, so I had to get my face right up close to it before I could see what was inside.

The window was one of those that open with a sash from the top. I hit the glass with my elbow. On the second blow it shattered. I reached inside, gashing my arm on the shards.

Then Cecilia Parsec got up and let me in.

47

"COULDN'T have you bleeding to death out there," Cecilia Parsec said. She stood back as I landed on the cool wooden floor in front of her. "Good climb."

I paid her no attention, frantically searching the room with my eyes. It was actually a kind of attic, with the walls sloping in on three sides. It must have taken up almost all of the top floor.

Like the rooms downstairs, it was overfilled with furniture. Sofas, a daybed, side tables, and towering carousel shelves laden with bric-a-brac. More shelves lined the walls, crammed with, of all things, dolls. A space had been cleared for a small holovision, paused in the middle of a party scene, the fancy-dressed guests standing about like chessmen in the middle of a game ...

The dormer windows on the other side of the attic threw patches of lemon-colored sunlight on the floor, and in one of those squares, crosslegged, wearing an unfamiliar frilly dress, sat Lucy.

She had something on her lap that she'd been working on. It fell to the floor as she erupted into motion.

"Daaaaddy!!"

I met her in the middle of the room. Her face shone brighter than the sun. I picked her up, and as tired as I was, she felt just as light as she had when she was a baby. She wrapped her arms around my neck and her legs around my waist, welding herself to me at every possible point. I laced my hands under her frilly bottom and kissed her hair. She was the one who'd been kidnapped, but I was the one crying.

Behind me, Cecilia said sharply, "Tomas!"

I swung around, still holding Lucy. Through my tears of joy, I saw Canuck appear in a doorway on the far side of the attic. He had an assault rifle identical to the one I'd left with Rex. He was pointing it at me and Lucy.

Cecilia Parsec stepped in front of him. "Put that down!"

Canuck sidestepped, but the door couldn't open all the way because of some shelves, which prevented him from getting a clear line of fire past Cecilia.

I dumped Lucy on the floor. "Get down, sweetie," I said, stooping to push her head down on her arms. "Don't look." In the same movement, I drew my Machina from my vest pocket. Keeping it low at my side—it was almost small enough to hide in my hand—I walked up behind Cecilia.

Canuck was swearing at her, using the worst words we have for normies, practically foaming at the mouth. I grasped Cecilia's arm with my left hand—that was the fake-out, to draw his gaze. With my right hand, I snapped the Machina up and fired. I didn't even have to aim—it was point blank range. A small black hole appeared in his forehead. He dropped his rifle. Then he fell over, dead.

Swinging around, I met Lucy's eyes. She had disobeyed my command not to look, and popped her head up in time to see Canuck die. That may have been the first time she saw what kind of person her daddy really was.

But she said nothing about what I'd done. She may not even have understood exactly what happened. She got up off the floor and ran to me. I rested my arm around her shoulders, but kept the Machina in my other hand.

"I never liked him, anyway," Cecilia said, looking down at the corpse.

Footsteps bounded up the stairs. I recognized Rex's floor-shaking tread. He saw Lucy, and that distracted him from seeing Canuck until he actually tripped on him. He took a stumbling step and caught his balance on some shelves, which fell over, scattering knick-knacks everywhere.

"Well, hello there, missy," Rex said, grinning. He saw Canuck then, but his smile flickered for only a second. He had mastered the fatherly arts to a degree I was still studying for. "Ready to go home?"

"*Yes,*" Lucy said. "Daddy, can we go home now?" But I saw her watching Cecilia.

I took a deep breath. "In a minute."

"Hi there, Mrs. Parsec," Rex said to Cecilia. He eyed her the same way I had, trying to figure out if she was dangerous.

I said, "Rex, could you go down to the front door? Relieve Sep. Send him out to Robbie, tell them to bring the pickup up to the front and get it turned around. We'll be there in a minute."

Rex hesitated, then nodded. "Get a bandage on that," he said, nodding at my arm, and vanished back down the stairs.

"You won't be able to simply drive away," Cecilia said. "I've alerted community security. They're waiting outside. My husband is also on his way. In the meantime, I think he's right: you need a bandage."

I looked down at my right arm. Blood was still running freely from the gash I'd gotten when I broke the window.

"Does that hurt?" Lucy said fearfully.

I felt like saying I hadn't even noticed it, I was so relieved to see her, but she needed reassuring, so I said it only hurt a tiny bit. I let Cecilia spray it with antibacterial stuff and wrap a length of self-sealing gauze around my arm. She had a complete first-aid kit on one of the shelves near where Lucy had been sitting. I kept my gun in my other hand while she was getting it out. She used the scissors to cut the gauze, but then put them back in the box. While she was wrapping the gauze around my arm, I looked out of the dormer window.

Two community patrol cars bookended our pickup in front of the house. Sep and Robbie stood between a pair of burly security guards, their heads hanging. Another patrol car was just turning onto the cul-de-sac.

Cecilia was right. We were trapped. No wonder she was being so nice. All she had to do was wait it out until I realized that I was screwed.

But if I was screwed, she was, too. She patted down the end of the gauze. I pulled my arm back and said aggressively, "What the hell?" I gestured to Lucy. *"What the hell,* Cecilia?"

Cecilia closed the first aid kit. Then she turned to me, smoothing her hands down her bare arms. She wore a summery top and those fashionable trousers that don't even look good on young women—which Cecilia was not any longer. I hadn't seen her for years, and although she remained a handsome woman, with strong features and a mane of chestnut curls, the sunlight revealed signs of age that the security camera footage had obscured: fine lines around her eyes, the beginnings of gravity-induced sag in her jawline and upper arms.

She said, "I made it clear to Lucy that I'm not her mother. I said I was sorry for tricking her. Didn't I, Lulu?"

Lucy nodded, her hair tickling my bare stomach.

"Did you also explain why you snatched her off the street?" I yelled. Then, because I was pretty sure I didn't want Lucy to hear this, I immediately added, "Forget it. You can explain to the police."

Instead of answering directly, Cecilia pointed at my feet. "You're standing on Lucy's project."

There was some kind of a crumpled piece of cloth on the floor. Lucy cried, "Oh, that's mine!" She let go of me to swoop it up, and immediately wrapped one arm around my waist again while she held up what now appeared to be a doll-sized skirt, partly sewed together. A needle dangled from it. "Cecilia showed me how to do sewing," she said. "My first project was messy but now I'm getting good at it. Look. Daddy. Cecilia said my stitches are very neat."

"Very nice," I said through locked teeth, wondering if Cecilia had chosen this pastime specifically to make me feel inadequate as a parent. Yes, there are men who sew. I am not one of them.

"I showed her my Blobby," Lucy said, pointing at the doll Pippa had made for her. It sat on a love-seat, dressed in a new frock. "I said I didn't make it, but Cecilia said she could teach me how, but we decided to start with doll clothes because they're easier."

"It's more an art than a craft," Cecilia said, with a deprecating gesture at the shelves full of dolls. I realized she must have made them —and their fiddly, frilly clothes—herself. "Oh, I know what you're thinking," she said. "Childless woman compensates with cloth babies. But my dolls are actually considered tactile sculptures. They're sold in art galleries, for prices that I find quite embarrassing."

"Obviously, you need the money," I said.

"Buzz says there's no such thing as having too much money, and I tend to agree with him." Cecilia glanced at an old-fashioned clock on the wall. She was probably counting the seconds until Buzz himself got here. "But one thing money can't buy, of course, is children."

"Ever considered adoption?" I said.

Lucy put in, "But what if the baby wasn't a Shifter? Or what if it was? It might get confused."

Instead of rebuking her, Cecilia laughed out loud. "Oh, Mike, it has been a real delight having her here."

I gritted my teeth. I was having more and more difficulty restraining my anger for Lucy's sake. I felt that Cecilia knew it and was taking advantage of my compelled restraint to needle me.

"It was for her own safety," she said. "You must understand that."

"Oh, I understand that perfectly," I said, irony escaping. "That's why you abducted her and held her captive for two days. And when I came for her—Jesus, you *must* have known I'd come for her—that fucker started shooting! Tell me how that was supposed to keep her safe, because what I saw was a loaded gun pointed at my little girl!"

"At *you,*" Cecilia said. It was her first and last defense of Canuck. She made it half-heartedly, and quickly moved on. "Listen, I don't understand it, either—I don't think even Buzz knows what it's all about. He sometimes practises strategic avoidance of potentially incriminating details." Mrs. Cecilia Parsec had a fine line in irony herself. "But the key instruction was very clear. Get her up high and keep her up high." Cecilia gestured around at the room.

At the *attic.*

On top of the house.

On top of Cape Agreste.

800 meters above sea level, separated by distance and sea winds from the city.

My blood ran cold. I suddenly felt weak and overwhelmed. Sophia had this whole thing planned out. And she must have thought I had no chance of stopping her.

48

ALTHOUGH I didn't know it, twenty klicks away, on the 121st floor of Bonsucesso Tower, Dolph's day had taken a turn for the worse.

The shaped charge had worked like a charm. The converging shockwaves from the explosion had blown a hole 2 cm in diameter straight through the solid steel door. The walls on either side of the doors were also partially rubbled, and the mirrored ceiling had fallen down.

The team knew that they now had only a few minutes before building security would arrive. While the wolves kicked the walls to see if they could break them down completely, MF lowered himself to the floor in front of the door. He extended a flexible robotic arm with a sensor array on the end. Dolph watched the robotic arm vanish into the hole in the door.

"No infrared signatures," MF said. "No movement."

Dolph's heart sank.

One of the wolves let out a howl of triumph. He had broken through the wall to the right of the door. Reassured by MF's assessment, the wolves quickly smashed a hole in the wall large enough for a man. Dolph went first, gripping his Koiler in both hands. MF brought up the rear.

The reception area was pitch black, except for the light from the hole. LED beams from weapon-mounted flashlights skittered over blank walls and the unoccupied reception desk.

The employees were gone.

The computers were gone.

Even that ugly civic award trophy was gone.

They rampaged through the entire 121st floor. It turned out that the garage was only half of Mujin Inc's operations. There was a back office —that's what Dolph and I had glimpsed when we were there. And then, hidden away behind thick doors, there was Sophia's lab.

Not a computer lab, after all.

An honest-to-God chemistry lab.

Dolph described it as "like a clean room." Through double-strength windows, the team gazed at a miniature industrial chemistry facility. Robot arms hung frozen over empty vats and assembly tables. The wolves wanted to go in; they thought the bad guys might be hiding in there, since they weren't anywhere else.

Dolph held them back. "Hermetically sealed," he said, looking at the air shower at the entrance to the lab, and the chemical bath where boots—or wheels—would be washed before entering. "Let's keep it that way."

But MF said, "I am immune to biohazards." He splashed through the chemical bath and headed into the air shower.

Dolph took the team back through the garage. All the taxis were gone, too. Dolph had been hoping they'd still be there, so that the team could reprise our aerial escape, but it was not to be. He glanced at his watch—four minutes and ten seconds since the charge went off. "Time's up," he said. "We're retreating."

"Who's retreating?" Alec said, giving him a sharp look.

"You are. When you get to the mall level, split up. I'm going back for that goddamn bot."

The wolves melted away. Dolph waited until he could no longer hear their footsteps. Then he waited a few seconds more. I can see him now, standing in front of one of those launch bays, with nothing but a shimmer between him and the almost 400-meter drop to the streets. Despite the force fields, he would have been able to hear a thin whistling. Up that high, the wind is so powerful that on stormy days, the tops of the towers sway. He was thinking, he said, about flying. He watched a ship take off from Space Island, spewing its contrail across the perfect blue sky, and wondered if he himself would ever fly again.

Four minutes and fifty seconds.

Dolph's phone rang.

"Positive," MF said. "I repeat, positive. There are significant traces of interstellar variant kuru prions in the vats and on the assembly benches. The latter are in the same nanocapsule formulation discovered previously."

Dolph let out his breath. "OK, MF. Thanks."

He moved closer to the launch bay until the toes of his shoes actually bumped into the force field. It gave like the surface of a fully inflated balloon. He leaned forward, so that he seemed to be leaning on the air, suspended above the drop, looking down at the curve of the tower's base half a kilometer below. He may have smiled.

Then he pushed off from the force field and propped himself against the wall next to the launch bay. He could now hear another sound: a faint klaxon, coming nearer, as if rising up through the building. He dialed.

*

"Well?" I said. I juggled my phone while switching my gaze between Cecilia and the window. "By the way, I found Lucy." I couldn't help grinning.

"That's something," Dolph said. "That's the biggest thing."

"Yeah." My grin faded. "Only problem is, I'm looking out the window at the entire Ville Verde security department."

"That makes two of us," Dolph said. "I'm about to get arrested by building security. I can hear them coming."

"Toss your weapon," I said urgently.

"Done."

"Did you find anything?"

"No Sophia, no toy fairies, no nothing. Place's cleaned out. But MF found traces of kuru. I'm going to tell them—"

A clatter and a staticky clunk interrupted Dolph's voice.

"Call Bones," I yelled, forgetting my earlier reluctance to involve the police. I never knew if he heard me. The connection went dead.

I gripped my phone so hard my knuckles went white.

Cecilia smiled at me, with a trace of wistfulness and a trace of meanness. "Thinking about calling the cops? Don't bother."

"There's stuff going on here that you don't know about," I snapped. Then I realized how condescending that sounded. If I had any chance at all of getting her on our side, she needed to know everything. "That company your husband runs in Bonsucesso Tower? It's a front for terrorism."

"What company?" Cecilia said, raising her eyebrows. "I don't really have much to do with the business."

"You're as bad as he is," I said, trying to mask my frustration with a smile.

"If you're accusing my husband of terrorism, that's not a compliment."

Before I could answer, Lucy interrupted. "Look, Daddy." She was on her knees in front of the holovision on a nearby table. She pressed a button and the paused holo started to play. The little figures in evening dress circled to the sound of classical music. They were dancing one of those old, old dances from Earth. Each man partnered a woman with his hand decorously placed on the small of her back. The figures were bright and crisp, but it was an amateur holo: the background was static, not responsive. It had been shot with only one holocam, and the other angles had been filled in by computer. I looked at the blue curtains behind the dancers, and the logo of an entwined PdLVA in the middle of the dance floor, and my stomach lurched.

Lucy reached into the holo. She touched the skirt of a woman in the middle of the dance floor. "Look, Daddy," she repeated, turning to me with a fixed, forced smile. "Isn't she pretty?"

I swallowed, my throat too dry to speak. I knew this holo. I was *in* it. I wasn't in this particular clip. I'd been out on the balcony having a cigarette or something. In those days I still smoked. Looking at this holo, I needed a cigarette right now. This was the Ponce de Leon Veterans Association annual fundraiser, and the holo had been filmed the last year I attended the shindig. Seven years ago.

I could date it precisely because the woman Lucy had pointed out was Sophia.

Circling gracefully in the arms of Zane Cole.

Parsec wasn't in the VA. Even the army has certain standards. He'd have no reason to own this rare amateur holo. Sophia must have given it to the Parsecs herself.

Staring at the little dancers, I remembered how surprised I'd been to see Zane there. He was already on his way to the Travellers, and if anyone was paying attention he should've been struck from the VA's rolls.

I'd ended the night yelling at him in the parking lot, ostensibly for defending the Travellers in a dinner-table debate, but actually for dancing with my wife—while at home, our baby slept under the attentive eye of a babysitter ...

That baby was now eight years old. She had paused the holo again and was lovingly running her finger along the intangible folds of Sophia's dress, saying, "So stylish," the word she and Mia applied to everything they liked. Her fake smile was so wide her eyes practically disappeared. She was putting on a performance, waiting for my reaction.

I turned to Cecilia and said under my breath, "You *bitch.*"

"Excuse me?" Cecilia said. "Are you aware that you have me to thank for the fact that she's here at all? Sophia left yesterday. She was going to take Lucy with her. I refused to let her go."

I stared at her, belatedly revising my opinion of her character. She shrugged. "Thank you," I said quietly.

She shrugged "I may not have children of my own, but I know what the Travellers are like. I wouldn't sell them one of my goddamn dolls, let alone an innocent, precious child like Lucy."

"But—" I said. "But Sophia left the life ..." As I spoke, I realized I only had her and Zane's word for it.

Cecilia smiled pityingly. "That's what she said, isn't it? And you believed her. How sweet."

A sudden bump shook the attic. I rushed back to the window. The security guards were milling around, gazing up, pointing—it seemed —at me.

"What was that?" Lucy said. She clutched me, burrowing her head into my waist. "What was that, Daddy?"

"I don't know," I started. Then I heard a door open—overhead.

A hot breeze washed into the attic, and in on its heels came Buzz Parsec.

49

I felt stupid. Parsec might not have his own spaceship launch pad, but he did have a flying car pad: the flat top of the house's mansard roof.

He'd just landed on it in his flight-capable sub-limo, and now here he was, with the other Kodiak twin close behind him.

I was still struggling to process what I had just learned about Sophia, but now I had to put it out of my mind. I pushed Lucy behind me and faced Parsec, my body so relaxed I was almost limp. If need be I'd Shift to fight him.

Parsec, however, did not look as if Shifting was on the agenda for today. He wore, of all things, a tuxedo. The black jacket emphasized the breadth of his barrel chest. I noted the bulge under his arm that ruined its line.

"He's armed," Cecilia said with a warning note in her voice, motioning to me.

"It didn't occur to you to disarm him?" Parsec said.

"Not after he shot Tomas," Cecilia said.

"That loony-tune had it coming," Parsec said. He had, of course, had to step over the body of Canuck in the attic doorway. He was one cold son of a bitch.

I said reluctantly, "Larry?" I was just guessing as to which Kodiak this was. I got it right by chance. "I have to inform you that your brother's downstairs. He has a couple of broken ribs, at least. He needs medical attention."

Although I didn't find this out until later, one of Gary Kodiak's broken ribs had punctured a lung. Rex had seen the blood at his mouth when he went downstairs. Deeming Gary's condition to be serious, he had picked him up and carried him outside. Gary got rushed to the Ville Verde hospital. Rex got arrested. He was, and is, as brave as .... well ... as a lion.

Anyway, when Larry Kodiak heard that his twin was injured, he galumphed off downstairs without waiting for permission.

Parsec shouted after him, "Let any of those asshats in here, and I'll have your butt fur for a doormat."

Oh, he was a charmer.

Lucy cringed closer to me, and Parsec turned to us with a sour smile. "How'd you get in here, Starrunner?"

I was tempted to Shift into a bear in front of him, to demonstrate. But there was no reason to let him in on my secret for the sake of a moment's satisfaction, so I just said, "Ask 'those asshats' out there."

"I pay Cape Agreste property taxes so I *don't* have to deal with Shifters causing trouble for me where I live."

"If you thought that force field fences could keep me away from my little girl, you were wrong."

"Evidently." Parsec glared at Cecilia. "Told you we should've got rid of her."

"And I told you, and I'm telling you again, over my dead body," Cecilia responded, raising herself higher in my estimation.

"You married a woman with a good heart as well as a good head," I told Parsec. "Shame it hasn't rubbed off. Why the everloving heck did you get involved with my ex-wife?"

I held my breath, not wanting him to know that all the information I had about their partnership was what I'd just said.

He bit. I don't think he had a guilty conscience. He was just prepping his defense, like any legally clued-up crook would, perhaps already intimating that he might get dragged into court over this. "That's not my company. It was his." He pointed to the body of Canuck.

"How very convenient for you, darling," Cecilia said. "I think you owe Mr. Starrunner a favor."

I ground my teeth, remembering that it had been Canuck's name on the articles of incorporation. By killing Parsec's fall guy, I may have just given him a get out of jail free card. "True," I said. "But you leased trucks and taxis to them. Drivers, sometimes."

"I lease my vehicles to a lot of customers. That may be one of them. I don't recall."

"Do you usually lease your trucks with permission for special overrides?"

"To do what?"

"Drive the wrong way on a one-way street. Pick up hitchhikers. Run people down."

"Hell, no. Where are you getting this information?"

"From doing what you didn't do," I said. "Looking into Mujin Inc's business activities." I was getting the picture now. Just as Cecilia had said, Parsec practised a policy of *don't* need to know, when knowing might cost him financially. It's people like that who will drive the human race into the ground. "This affects me personally, because they shipped their goods on *my* ship."

"Figured I'd do you a favor," Parsec said instantly, and Cecilia sighed. "You need the business more than I do."

Now that I look back on it, I think he may actually have been telling the truth. But my gut reaction was to take it as one more twist of the knife that was cutting my life apart. "Those crates contained biological weapons," I snarled. "They still do! Every one of those lousy toys is loaded with weaponized interstellar variant kuru, and someone is getting ready to unload them in Mag-Ingat!"

"Oh, Jesus," Cecilia said. "So *that's* what she meant."

Cecilia was smarter than her husband. It took Parsec a minute longer to add up 2 + 2, but when he got 4, his jowly face started to color.

"It's my ass on the line," I said, "but it's yours too. Hell, it's everyone's."

"No one would do that," Parsec said.

"Bless your heart," I said. "You're the one who went into business with my ex-wife."

"Nope," Parsec said. "You think she's the devil incarnate. She isn't. She's just a mother who wants her rights." He spoke without regard for the big ears of the little pitcher at my side. "As for the rest of them, I can't say I approve of the way they live, but they live *their* way. They ain't at war with us."

"Who's us, Shifter?" I said. Then I shook my head. "Maybe it isn't just the Travellers. There's someone else in the picture."

"Who?"

"Ever heard of a guy called Rafael Ijiuto?"

*

At that very moment, Dolph was telling the Bonsucesso Tower security guards that this office had been used to manufacture bio-weapons. They didn't believe a word he said. They had already called in the bombing as a terrorist incident, and were waiting for the police to arrive. While they were waiting, they saw MF moving around in the clean room, and that freaked them out even more. They knocked Dolph around some.

The police arrived by flying car. To Dolph's everlasting relief, the officer in charge was Jose-Maria d'Alencon.

To this day I don't know if Dolph called him after he talked to me, or before. He was coy about the point, suggesting that it was *before,* and that he felt this to be a betrayal of me. But it really didn't matter.

What mattered was that Bones was there, and he at least was willing to listen to what Dolph had to say.

Before that, he told him he had grounds to file suit against the security contractors for brutality.

"Can't file against corpses," Dolph slurred through a cut lip. "Don't let them go in the clean room."

"OK," d'Alencon said. "Why?"

MF interrupted. He had found an intercom in the clean room which connected with the reception area, where everyone was standing. His odd, distinctly inhuman voice boomed out of hidden speakers. "Greetings. I am the bot Krasylid Athanuisp Zha, also known as MF. I am presently in the laboratory and assembly facility of this office. I have confirmed the existence of remanent data on the virtual servers used by the former tenant, and am attempting to reconstruct the files which the humans formerly in command of these machines wiped upon their departure. I beg you to give me a few minutes." The intercom shut off with a click.

The security guards, the police officers, and Dolph all stared at each other.

D'Alencon broke the silence. "All right, Hardlander. Just what in the hell is going on here?"

Hardlander is Dolph's nom de guerre. He didn't like the name he was born with, either—just like MF, I guess.

*

"Rafael who?" Parsec said.

Ijiuto could've used a different name, just like Sophia. I found a picture of him on my phone. I'd had the sense to take a couple when he was at my apartment. But Parsec shook his head. "Don't know the guy."

"Everyone's going to know him soon," I grated. "He's out there with the bio-weapons, in one of *your* goddamn trucks!"

Cecilia said, "If this is true, Buzz—"

"Fuck," Parsec said. He pulled at the collar of his tux shirt, loosening his bow tie. He had been at some Founding Day gala. Now he was plunged into a nightmare. I did not feel for him. I'd been living a worse nightmare for days. His piggy eyes fastened on me, the nearest target for his rage and consternation. "Who told you to start sleuthing around, anyway? Why couldn't you just take the fucking money and shut up?"

He pulled off his bow tie and threw it on the floor. To me, this was a clear signal that he was preparing to Shift.

"The money? What money? I never even got the two KGC kill fee," I said, letting out a yelping laugh, almost a bark.

Parsec's answer was a wordless growl. He began undoing his shirt buttons one by one, which struck me as oddly prissy, but the look in his eyes was sheer menace. His flat coils of dark hair bristled up on his head, and his shoulders began to swell. He was starting the chain of probability revisions from the top, the way experienced Shifters do.

I settled on my wolf. Tempting as it was to fight him as a bear, I was already wounded and tired, and needed the advantage of agility. I hunched my shoulders, licking my lips with a tongue that would soon loll long and red past lethal incisors.

"Stop!" It was Lucy's voice. My daughter jumped between us. She pushed me as hard as she could, sending me stumbling off balance, and then she pushed Buzz. She yelled, "We don't Shift to get into stupid fights! Daddy! Stop it! We don't Shift to get into stupid fights!"

Repeating my own half-forgotten words, she pushed me back and farther back, while my head whirled, partially consumed with wolfish thoughts of biting and ripping.

Cecilia caught Buzz's arm, saying, "Out of the mouths of babes. Stop it, for God's sake."

Buzz reversed his partial Shift. That is not easy. It's like pulling a punch in mid-swing. His shoulders quaked and his face flattened back out and his spine returned to the human vertical and he said, watching me, "I was just gonna change."

"Right," I said.

"I can't stand this goddamn penguin suit."

"Right." I let my own Shift go. I ran my hands through my hair, confirming that it was floppy again, not bristly.

"We don't Shift to get into stupid fights," Lucy repeated once more, her eyes fixed on my face. "Right?"

"Right," I said for a third time, and then I had to smile. I hugged her quickly. "My brave girl." She was, too. To get between two adult male Shifters intent on ripping each other's throats out? That takes guts. She would have got that from me, of course.

Parsec squeezed out a smile of his own. It was about as sweet as lemon juice, but I'd take what I could get. "Rain check on the fight to the death thing, Starrunner?"

"Rain check," I agreed, holding out my hand.

We shook. Parsec tried to pull a clasp o' death on me, but I evaded it by pushing my hand far enough into his clasp that my middle finger touched his pulse point, so he couldn't crush my knuckles. It behooves a freighter captain to know these tricks.

Our eyes met across our joined hands. I read in his cold gaze that he wasn't finished with me. I sure as hell wasn't finished with him. "Rain check" meant exactly what it sounded like. But I judged that self-interest would force him to work with me until the immediate threat to his livelihood was removed.

"So, this Category Ten shitstorm," he said, releasing my hand. "I can track my trucks. I got the software in my home office, too, but we might as well do it from the car. Come on. We'll find this Ijiuto fucker and shred his ass."

He started for the door of the attic. I hesitated.

"Leave the kid with Cecilia," Parsec said. "We ain't going to ship her off-planet in the next half an hour."

I had hesitated because I was thinking about how to get Lucy out of the room without forcing her to step over a corpse. I had not for one second contemplated leaving her here, and I did not contemplate it now. "No thanks," I said curtly. "She's coming."

Parsec snorted. I picked Lucy up. She wrapped her legs around my hips like a much younger child.

"Wait," Cecilia said. She was gathering up Lucy's sewing project and her Blobby doll. She swept them into a tote bag, which already held a bulky package of fabric. "I'll put in some more material for you … Here. Keep your stitches neat, Lulu."

Lucy nodded hard. She reached out her hand for the bag and held it against my back as I carried her out of the room, stepping over Canuck's corpse. His eyes stared up sightlessly. He wasn't the first and he would not be the last to die today, if we couldn't find Rafael Ijiuto.

50

A short flight of steps led up to the roof. An automated trapdoor slid back, and we climbed into the sunshine. Parsec's sub-limo stood on a reinforced landing pad in the middle of the roof. He paced to the edge of the roof. The tails of his tux blew in the wind. "Panic's over," he yelled down to the security guards in the street. It was actually just beginning, but Parsec had the skill of projecting reassurance. It's another of those tricks a freighter captain needs to know. "Everyone's OK up here. Y'all can disperse." An unintelligible shout came back. "I'm paying you to guard my property," Parsec yelled. "And now I'm paying you to go the fuck away." He came back to us. "That oughta do it."

Lucy was agog at the flying car. "Are we going to ride in that?"

Gazing at the view over the jungle to the city, I had second thoughts. *Get her up high and keep her up high,* Sophia had told the Parsecs. It seemed like a good precaution. I was thinking that the toy fairies would be in one of the trucks Parsec had leased to Mujin Inc, most likely the same one Rafael Ijiuto was in. To stop him, we'd have to go down to wherever he was. And it could so very easily go wrong …

Parsec got into the driver's seat and started tapping on the dashboard computer.

I let Lucy into the back and got into the passenger seat. The black leather upholstery cushioned my ass like a hug. The car smelled not of wet fur, as Shifter vehicles usually do, but of expensive air freshener. Parsec knew about the importance of keeping up appearances.

"Daddy." Lucy touched my shoulder.

"What is it, sweetiepie?"

"Daddy," she said again, doing her thing of repeating my name while she found exactly the right words for what she wanted to say, the words that would not anger me or cause me to deflect her concerns with a joke, the magic words that would get through to me. Her little face looked like a cracked cup. There was so much misery and confusion in there, waiting to spill out, I couldn't stand it.

"Did you see ... your mother?" I said. "Did they make you talk to her?"

"No," Lucy said. "She had to go. She didn't have time to come by the house."

Thank God for that, anyway.

"Here's all the trucks," Parsec said. I turned to the dashboard, grateful for the interruption. He had a map of the entire continent open on the screen. Bright blue dots flashed here and there, as far away as Cascaville. "Now we gotta narrow it down."

"Let's do it on the move," I said.

"My thoughts exactly."

As we lifted into the air, I took out my phone. "I'm gonna call a friend, OK?"

"Who?" Parsec said.

"Someone I can leave Lucy with," I said, hoping I was right.

"No, Daddy!" Lucy said. "I want to stay with you! *Forever!*"

"I want to stay with you, too, sweetiepie," I said wretchedly. "But it isn't safe." I dialed Christy Day.

"Mike," she said. The note of wary distance saddened me.

"Hi, Christy. Listen, I'm sorry I didn't call yesterday. It's been crazy. Forgive me?" I put warmth into it and a touch of wheedling humor. Parsec wasn't the only one who could keep up appearances.

"Are you going to make it up to me?" she said, matching my humorous tone. I sighed inwardly in relief.

"That depends if you can clear your schedule for the weekend," I purred. Parsec grinned at me.

"Well, I might be able to," Christy said, taking me at my word, which I hadn't expected. "I'm owed a day off after all this Founding Day jazz. God, how many ways can you spell 'nightmare'? Forty kids, and every one of them is running in a different direction. They couldn't just sit still and watch the performances. Oh, no. Whose bright idea was it to offer all these free rides, anyway?"

Now I heard a backdrop of music and noise behind her voice. I sat up straight. "Where are you, Christy?"

"At the festival, of course. Mike, how *is* Lucy?" She sounded really concerned, or abashed that she hadn't asked straight away. "Her nanny called the school to say she had a virus. Poor little chick. Is she feeling better?"

The mention of my dashed-off excuse struck an unpleasant chord. *She's got a virus,* I had told Nanny B to say. Everyone in Mag-Ingat might have much worse than a virus if we couldn't pull this off. But at least it sounded like Christy was in a safe place. "You're at the uptown festival," I clarified. "On the mall level?"

"Yeah," she said. "Between Extritium and Hanayashiki, kind of to the left of the stage. Are you nearby?"

I looked out the window. "Actually, I am."

We just call it 'the mall level,' but it's famed throughout the Cluster as the Mag-Ingat Skymall. Six skyscrapers over one kilometer in height spear up from uptown, and all of them—plus the smaller ones like Bonsucesso Tower—are connected by pedestrian walkways so broad, they feel like parks. Shops dot these greenways, whether standalone flagship stores or cunning little mazes of boutiques, so that you're constantly moving from indoors to outdoors and back again. The predictability of Mag-Ingat's weather is what makes it possible, but a huge whack of the city's budget goes into keeping the mall enchantingly presentable, not to mention on maintenance of these carbon nanofilament-reinforced concrete structures suspended in mid-air.

200 meters above the streets.

Completely inaccessible by ground transport.

Perfect.

I looked out at the Celtic knot of walkways now coming into view, as Parsec merged into the main uptown skyway. Right now, rather than being mostly green, the mall level was a sea of green, red, and white, decorated for Founding Day and thronged with crowds.

"Hey, Parsec," I said. "Put down over there. Between Extritium and Hanayashiki."

He looked up from the dashboard computer. "You nuts?"

"We're dropping Lucy off." I turned around and explained to her, "That was Ms. Day I was talking to. From school. All the kids are at the festival. Would you like to join them?"

"It's *today?*"

"Sure is."

"Is Mia there?"

"Course she is," I said, before remembering that Mia and Kit were at St. Patrick's. Right down at sea level. Oh God. I had to call Irene.

"Yes please," Lucy said, nodding and doing her exaggerated forced smile. She bounced in the back seat, a caricature of an excited child. She was trying to please me. "Yes, please, Daddy!"

"Forget it," Parsec said, glancing down. "Nowhere to park."

Fortune, or my patron saint, smiled on me then. A car lifted off from the parking area halfway between Extritium and Hanayashiki. "There!" I said. "Grab it!"

Parsec grumbled, but he stabbed his fat finger on the button to reserve the space before anyone else could. As the sub-limo's AI set us down, he said, "You're not back in ten, you can take the bus."

I called Christy back, set up a meet with her and navigated towards her phone signal, dragging Lucy by the hand. As expected, it was absolute bedlam. Family-friendly was the theme of this part of the festival, and as everyone knows, kids' parties are the noisiest of all. Small fairground rides had been set up in between the shops. Their dinging and rattling and jingling almost drowned out the noise from the nearest stage, where local acts were performing songs, dances, and skits related to events from Ponce de Leon's history. Scents of cotton candy and baked potatoes and Shifter barbecue filled the air, enclosed by the same force fields that rose up from the edges of the greenway, which kept the wind from carrying off all the bunting and the flags and the silly hats.

I caught sight of Christy through the crowd. She had one child by the hand and was stooping to console another. Then she straightened up and saw me. My heart did a flip-flop at the moment of charged eye contact.

I dragged Lucy over to her. "Hi! Glad we caught up with you. Here's Lucy. I'm gonna take off for a few." I didn't give Christy a chance to say no. "I'll be back to pick her up—" I pulled a timeframe out of my ass— "by five o'clock."

"Oh! Lucy, you're all better!" Christy said, looking from me to my daughter, perplexed. "Have you got your nametag?"

The kids' nametags had geolocation chips embedded in them. Some parents get the chips implanted in their children's bodies. Not at our school.

Lucy shook her head. She was clinging to my hand. I peeled her off, hating that I had to let her go.

"Just stay with Ms. Day," I told her. "*Stay* with her." I lightly touched Christy's sleeve. She jumped as if I'd stung her. "If I don't —don't get back on time ..." I pointed up at Extritium Tower. "Get a room in the hotel, on me. Or just take her up to the observatory. Get up high, and stay high."

"Mike? Is something wrong? You can't just ... *Mike!*"

I turned my back on them, on Christy's questions and Lucy's silence, and sprinted back to the parking lot.

It had been a lot more than ten minutes, but Parsec was still there. He had killed time by getting himself a fruit slushie approximately the size of an oxygen tank. Slurping through the straw, he said, "We got the fucker."

I leant to the dashboard.

51

"WHAT I'm wondering," Parsec said, scowling at the dash computer, "is why he didn't just turn off the tracking."

"Self-driving trucks," I said. "You'd have to go into manual mode to turn off geolocation. Right?"

"Right."

"Well, he isn't driving. The AI is."

I paused, mirroring Parsec's scowl. My own words reminded me of the mystery around Rafael Ijiuto. I assumed Sophia had hacked the AIs of the Trident Overland trucks so they'd pick Ijiuto up and chauffeur him around. But why? What was he to her?

The answer came to me as neatly as a firing pin dropping. *She worked for him.* She had never really left the Travellers at all. She had been operating undercover as a member of Zane Cole's gang.

Whom we had decimated on Gvm Uye Sachttra.

God, how she must hate me now.

I made myself focus on Ijiuto. "Which truck is it?"

"I had to reconstruct all the trip logs over the last couple days to see which one picked him up," Parsec said. "If it was the same one that almost hit your jackal buddy on 94th, it was this one." He pointed to a blue dot on the Lamonstrance road, 200 klicks from Mag-Ingat.

"Huh?" I said. "Lamonstrance ain't even worth visiting, let alone attacking."

"Which is why I don't think he's in that truck anymore." Parsec dragged the map back to Mag-Ingat Bay and enlarged it. "I think he switched rides. Now he's in *this* one."

"What are you basing that on?"

Parsec showed his yellow teeth. "On the fact it's currently headed for the spaceport, chucklehead."

"That doesn't make sense."

I'd expected we would find Rafael Ijiuto skulking somewhere downtown, preparing to unleash bio-terror on the unsuspecting masses of Shoreside. The onshore winds would give him the biggest bang for his buck, and perhaps I also made the mistake of assuming that Shiftertown had value as a target because it mattered to me personally. But the Strip genuinely was a premier target, if you wanted to terrorize every race in the Cluster at once, which I assumed was the point of choosing Ponce de Leon, an entrepot, in the first place …

I realized I'd been doing a whole lot of assuming. But I didn't have time to think it through. Parsec said, "My hunch is he left the bio-weapons in town. Programmed them to unload at such and such a time, and he's planning to get off-planet before it kicks off. That's what *I'd* do."

"Or it also could be," I said, catching the tail of my prior train of thought, "that he never was planning to unload on the PdL in the first place. After all, he originally had the bio-weapons shipped to Gvm Uye Sachttra. Maybe he's got them in the truck right now, and he's trying to get off-planet before we catch up with him."

I *liked* this idea. It gave me hope that Mag-Ingat might be spared, after all.

But I was not a criminal mastermind, and nor, for all his seedy posturing, was Buzz Parsec.

And it nearly cost us everything.

*

As uptown shrank beneath us, I called Martin at the spaceport. He was only too eager to get a piece of the action. I outlined what I needed him to do. Then I called Irene. To my surprise, she picked up.

"Yeah, what?" She spoke in a hurried, low voice, as if trying not to be overheard. She had disabled video.

As concisely as possible, I gave her a rundown of the situation, adding that I had left Rex at Ville Verde (I didn't know he was presently sitting in the gated community's lock-up). I told her to get her kids and take them somewhere up high. I recommended the Skymall, where I'd left Lucy with Christy Day.

"Oh Jesus," she groaned. "I'm in the middle of something."

"Irene, where are you?"

"I'm ... *waiting* ... for this guy." The way she said it, I suddenly guessed that she was *waiting* on a rooftop behind the scope of a gun.

"This is serious—"

"So is this! Where are you?"

I saw no point in not telling the truth. "In Buzz Parsec's car."

"Aha," she said. "Then I'll say no more at the moment. Look, I hear what you're saying. I'll call Sister Anne. Gotta go."

Click.

"Would that have been Ms. Seagrave?" Parsec said. Remember, he had worked with her in her shrouded past.

"Yup."

"Shame she ain't here. She could probably take this clown out from the air at fifty klicks an hour." Parsec mimed squinting through sights and pulling a trigger.

"This way's better," I said.

"We'll see. Is your buddy in position?"

We were flying back the way we'd come, along the skyway that tracks Space Highway. Beneath us, the ground traffic was unusually light, thanks to the holiday. Cars and trucks flowed along like a parade of

bright ants. The intense sunshine brought out the emerald and tour-
maline tones of the jungle foliage swaddling the Cape. The bay reflected the cloudless sky. It was a day such as must have convinced the
Founders that they had hit the space colonization jackpot.

"You'll recognize the truck." I was on the phone with Martin again.
"Yeah ... yeah. We're almost there."

On the dashboard screen, we were gliding up behind the blue dot
of Ijiuto's truck. This one was a tractor-trailer rig. Plenty of room in
the back. Ijiuto was making a princely speed of 40 klicks an hour. It
reminded me of Kaspar Silverback's snail's progress from the spaceport
to the city, and I felt a chill, wondering if Ijiuto was going slow for
the same reason: he had bio-weapons in the back of his truck. The
difference being that whereas Silverback had just been instructed to
drive carefully, Ijiuto knew exactly what was in those crates.

I chewed my nails, watching our objective come into view.

For the first eighteen klicks, and the last ten klicks, of its length,
Space Highway runs along the shore of Cape Agreste with the jungle
on one side and the sea on the other. But at the nineteen-klick mark,
the cape bulges into the bay, forming a small peninsula cut off by the
highway from the hills behind. This is Gillietown. It's a settlement, not
really worthy of being called a town, of unpaved streets and rubbishy
houses, which seem to well up from some ineffable source of life and
two-by-fours in the center of the peninsula, so that the dwellings at the
edge are constantly pushed further out over the water, staggering on
stilts. The place is as much water-borne as it is land-based, and that's
how the Gillies like it.

The Shifters are far from the only flavor of alt-human to survive into
the present day. The Gillies are another. We don't have that many of
them on the PdL, but some of them came, and remain, to practise
their usual trade: fish-farming.

Most all the seafood eaten in Mag-Ingat comes from Gillietown, as
evidenced by the buoys and rafts dotting the water around the peninsula, and the boats nuzzling at them.

But the reason Gillietown mattered to us right now was because for those three kilometers, there are no walls or fences or barriers of any kind along the highway. The Gillies wouldn't have it. They said it would prevent them from crossing the road. Guess they had a point.

So now Rafael Ijiuto was driving past a shambles of roadside stalls and gable-ends and native scrub, while we drifted up behind him. Parsec, hunched over the wheel, slowed down and indicated to drop out of the skyway.

"Marty?" I said. I could see him below. He was in position, pulled over on the packed-dirt verge of the highway at the western end of Gillietown.

"I see you," he said.

"'Bout thirty seconds to contact," I said. "Ready?"

"Yup. This douchebag is in for a surprise." Martin turned his bike to face the outbound traffic. The sunlight flashed on his visor.

Parsec dropped the sub-limo lower. We were now directly above Ijiuto's truck, keeping pace with it as if by accident. Our shadow scudded along beside it.

If Ijiuto saw the sub-limo's shadow, he had no time to consider what it might mean, still less to react.

Martin abruptly gunned his bike the wrong way, into the outbound traffic. AIs auto-swerved to miss him, blaring their horns. Ignoring the vehicles veering left and right to avoid colliding with him, Martin rode straight as a bullet at Ijiuto's truck.

It was in the outside, slowest lane.

Just where we wanted it.

I dug my fingernails into my palms. I'd told Martin to be careful, as this truck or one like it had nearly run Dolph down.

Martin was more than careful. He was smart.

A split second from what must have been a head-on collision, he swerved sharply—

—and the truck swerved *at* him. Not away from him. *At* him—

—as he pulled the handlebars over so hard that the rear wheel of his bike fishtailed. His knee scraped the asphalt. Somehow, he stayed on the bike. He shot across the front of the truck, so close that its grille almost clipped his muffler, and accelerated off the asphalt, into a Gillietown slum.

The truck's momentum carried its front wheels off the asphalt. The verge here was steep, not as steep as we'd have liked, but it had a definite downward slope. Clayey lumps of dirt sprayed into the air as the AI fought to steer back onto the highway—

—and Parsec dropped the sub-limo right down alongside the truck, occupying the lane that the truck wanted. The road flowed past just a few centimeters beneath our wheels. This low, our levitation bubble was *only* about the size of a house. It bumped against the top right edge of the truck's trailer like a slap from an invisible giant's hand. The trailer drifted off the edge of the road, and started to drag the tractor off with it.

I could see through the bubble into the driver's cab of the truck. I saw Rafael Ijiuto seated upright, looking scared.

Teeth bared, spitting swears, Parsec pushed the sub-limo's engine into the red. The fans roared, our bubble delivered a hard shove to the right side of the tractor…

… and the laws of physics did the rest.

Still doing forty, the truck jack-knifed. The tractor swung around until it nearly faced in the opposite direction, and the whole rig rolled. It skidded down the slope at an angle, leaving a swathe of flattened scrub.

God is merciful: there were no houses just there. The trailer clipped a boulder, toppled onto its side, and came loose from the tractor. Both pieces kept sliding downhill. They came to a halt at the bottom of the slope, half in and half out of one of those rainwater ponds we call *gesso*. The tractor fell over on its side with a secondary splash. Dead devil palm fronds fluttered down upon it.

"My goddamn truck," Parsec swore, as if he wasn't the one who'd just run it off the road himself. He steered the sub-limo down the slope, staying just clear of the ground.

The tractor had landed driver's side up. Now the door of the cab opened, hinging upwards.

An airbag bloomed out. It deflated, and Rafael Ijiuto hoisted himself out of the life-saving cocoon. He took one look at the approaching sub-limo and jumped down into the pond behind the truck.

"He's running!" I howled. I pulled out my Machina and frantically rolled down the window. I glimpsed movement in the devil palms on the other side of the pond. I fired at the movement.

Parsec put the sub-limo down at the end of the pond where the ground was flattest. He jumped out and ran around the pond, towards the truck.

A few seconds later I jumped out, too.

In the form of a wolf.

Ijiuto was *not* getting away this time.

52

My wolf's nose picked up Ijiuto's scent around the far side of the pond. I could also see his footprints in the wet, boggy ground. The other side of the devil palms, the prints petered out, but I was still able to follow his scent, as it stood out pungently from the odorscape of mud, crushed grass, rotting fish, and Gillie. Casting to and fro over the heavily trampled ground, avoiding the broken glass and rubbish that threatened my paws, I loped up to the top of the rise beyond the pond.

This was the edge of Gillietown: the raw end of a street of tumble-down row housing. Several Gillies clustered outside the last houses, rubbernecking at the crashed truck. When they saw my wolf, they fled.

I glanced back. Parsec was waist deep in the pond, the tails of his tux floating on the muddy water, trying to get the back of the trailer open.

I lowered my nose to the ground again, and caught a whiff of Ijiuto off to my right.

I hadn't gone much further before I saw him ahead of me. There was nowhere to hide, really. The occasional devil palm, a few patches of scrub. The Gillies had scrounged the place clean. He was running back towards the highway. Perhaps he thought he'd be able to thumb a ride again.

I looped behind him, got between him and the highway, and dashed out of the scrub straight at him, snarling.

He changed direction and ran towards the sea.

I chased him, keeping to an easy lope.

Pretty soon there was nowhere left for him to run to.

The shore of the peninsula, like the rest of the Cape, is a tumble of glaciated boulders too steep to be called a beach. Ijiuto scrambled down the rocks, looked back despairingly, and stopped on a rock a couple of meters above the little lisping waves.

I crouched on the scrubby overhang above the rocks and growled at him.

"Help," Ijiuto called. A quarter mile further out along the shore, Gillies swam around the stilts of outlying houses. Nearer, a trio of them drifted in a skiff, attending to a line of flags marking lobster traps. "Help," Ijiuto shouted again. The Gillies in the skiff stared at him. They could see he was not a Gillie. They did nothing.

Ijiuto sighed. I saw him trying to decide whether to jump into the water.

"That's gonna be a long swim," I said.

He jumped violently at the shock of a human voice coming from the wolf that menaced him. "Starrunner," he said.

"You left my apartment in a hurry," I said. "Didn't even stop to say thank you. For saving my life, that kind of thing. Looks like you're still in a hurry. Got a flight to catch?" I grinned at him, the kind of wolfish grin that has struck terror into the hearts of men since *Homo sapiens* began.

Ijiuto did not react quite as I expected. Instead of terror, he displayed resignation. His shoulders drooped. Something—perhaps hope—seemed to go out of him, like that deflating airbag. "I *knew* I would rather have you as a friend than an enemy," he said.

"Too late now," I said.

"I know how it looks," he said.

"I'll tell you how it looks. Like you organized, and almost succeeded in carrying out, a terror attack against Ponce de Leon. The heart of human civilization. My *home.*"

"No," Ijiuto said. "You've got it all wrong. The kuru capsules weren't for Ponce de Leon. Do I look crazy?" He smiled, palely. "Don't answer that."

My earlier doubts flooded back, uncertainty mixing with relief. "What were they for, then? Who?"

"That nest of vipers on Gvm Uye Sachttra, of course. Where do you *think* those people come from?"

I shook my head.

"From Old Gessyria. Our sister planet." Ijiuto mistook my frozen silence for incomprehension. "I'm the crown prince of New Gessyria."

"Yeah. You said."

I hadn't been sure whether or not to believe him before. Hadn't thought it mattered, anyway. Now I believed him, all right. Everything I knew, or had heard, about royalty confirmed that the crown prince of a podunk planet in the Darkworlds would be *exactly* the kind of person to murder thousands of refugees because they supported a different one of his relatives.

"So you were going to unload those damn fairies at the refugee camp," I said, recalling how strong the wind was there. "That's why you herded all those children out to the ship." I remembered the smell of hot chocolate. The festival atmosphere. "You were going to give them presents." I could say no more for sheer disgust at the vileness of it.

"Exactly," Ijiuto said. "Our read of the natives was that when they discovered the outbreak of kuru, they'd nuke the refugee camp from orbit. Even if they didn't? Same difference. The Khratzes would die, anyway."

"Cratses?"

"Khratzes," Ijiuto enunciated. "My nephew and nieces. Actually, they're also my cousins, and one of them's also my aunt."

He turned to look out to sea, and the sunlight caught the diamond-sheathed knife he wore as a pendant. I remembered Pippa's identical necklace. "What's that you got around your neck?"

"This? The crown jewels," Ijiuto said morosely. "What's left of them, anyway."

"I think I met your Khratzes," I said. "Some of them, at least."

"You sure did," Ijiuto said. "They hitched a ride here on your ship. Man, when I saw Pippa, I just about shat my pants. I thought she was going to get away, after all the trouble I went to. That's why I shot at her. If it wasn't for that damn wind, I would have got her, too."

"You were aiming at ... *Pippa.*" As I spoke, I remembered that second shot, fired while Pippa was the only one still on her feet.

"Right," Ijiuto said. "Just between us, she's got a better claim to the throne than I have. I figured if I could get her, it wouldn't even matter about those other brats. So I snuck into the trees ..."

"So it wasn't Zane."

"Nope. He survived, by the way. He had to stay on Gvm Uye Sachttra to have his hand amputated."

"I figured," I said. "If it was him, he wouldn't have missed."

"I only missed because of that fucking wind."

"You killed my admin. She was only twenty-four. She had her whole life ahead of her."

"I'm sorry, OK?"

"Not as sorry as you're gonna be," I snarled.

Ijiuto flinched, and turned to look across the bay to Space Island. I can imagine how the spaceport must have looked to him, the ships rising on their steeply slanted plasma plumes against the afternoon sky: escape, like a golden door. So near and yet so far away.

The scrub on my left rustled to the sound of heavy human footsteps. Martin picked his way down the slope to me. He carried his bike helmet and a snub-nosed .38. "Put him down in the water?" he said. He wasn't joking. "I want to get back to my bike. I left it on the street. Some Gillie kids were looking at it lustfully." He set his helmet down on the ground and levelled the .38 at Ijiuto, whose eyes widened in panic, understanding, perhaps, that Martin was likelier to kill him than I was.

"No," I said. It was less a sound than a sigh.

Ijiuto mouthed words, but no sound came out. He turned, as if to run, and jumped into the water.

"Fuck!" I yelled. "Get him!"

"*I'm* not going in there." Martin waved to the Gillies in the skiff, pointing to the water. Ijiuto was swimming away from shore in a strong but untutored crawl, kicking up big splashes.

The Gillies finally acted. If it happens in the water, it concerns them. They engaged their outboard motor. They had just reached Ijiuto and hauled him into the skiff when Martin's phone rang.

"Parsec," he said to me. "Yeah … Yeah, we caught him. No. The Gillies … *What?*"

I scrambled closer to Martin, and heard Parsec's voice coming out of the phone: "… that's right. There ain't no crates in the back. There's *nothing*. Those goddamn toy fairies were never in this truck to begin with."

53

I sat in the passenger seat of Parsec's car with my legs hanging out the door, too tired even to put on the t-shirt I held on my lap. I could see down the slope into the back of the trailer. It was as empty as a sucked bone. Gillies stood on the other side of the pond, staring at us.

"If the damn things ain't here," I said wearily, "where are they?"

"One of the other trucks?" Parsec said. "Maybe the plan was to ship 'em off-planet after His Royal Highness made his getaway."

"Could be."

"Or he could've *already* shipped them off-planet." Parsec was standing outside the car, taking off his ruined tux. He had spare clothes in the trunk, like any Shifter would. The t-shirt I held was one of his: black, XXL, with the old Earth constellation of Ursa Major on the front. He was jubilant. Mission accomplished.

I guessed I was jubilant, too. But I didn't feel it. I was too exhausted to feel much of anything. Hardly surprising after the day I'd had. The climb up the side of Parsec's house alone would have finished me if I hadn't needed to stay strong for Lucy. Now, with Ijiuto in our custody, my body seemed to have decided it was safe to nope out. Muscles ached, and my gashed arm throbbed painfully. I'd lost the bandage, of course, when I Shifted. Then while I was stalking Ijiuto through the scrub, the cut on what became my right foreleg had started bleeding again. I raised my arm to my mouth and licked the cut, so weary that I forgot I wasn't a wolf anymore. The smoothness of my skin reminded me. I let my arm fall.

Ijiuto sat behind me in the back seat, soaked to the skin, with his wrists bound. (Surprise, surprise, Parsec also had rope in the trunk of his car.) He was not talking, but Martin was. Seated cozily beside Ijiuto, he was murmuring to him about the joys of life in Ponce de Leon's large and badly run prisons.

We had called the police as soon as we had Ijiuto back on shore. He deserved to die, but I felt that I needed to offer him up to the PD to get Dolph out of trouble. Parsec also knew the value of strategic cooperation with the authorities.

"There they are," Parsec said, pointing into the sky. "'Bout fucking time."

I stirred myself. Dragged Parsec's spare t-shirt over my head. Realized I was thirsty. Parsec's ride was shamefully ill-equipped in one respect: he had no booze in the glove compartment. Beyond being picky, I finished off Parsec's fruit slushie while the cop cars descended, one by one, and hovered around looking for level ground to land.

There were three of them. Two of them had Extritium Precinct flashes on their sides. The PdL PD is unequally spread out: there are ten precincts covering uptown and downtown, but only one for Cape Agreste, and that one—Jose-Maria d'Alencon's precinct—in effect covers Shiftertown as well, because the Strip is too important a money-maker to be left to Shifters to police. I say this in sorrow, not pride.

The lead car touched down on the waste ground at the end of the pond. I saw Dolph sitting in the back seat. I waved to him. He sat oddly still. I did not realize at the time that he was cuffed to the large police officer beside him.

Jose-Maria d'Alencon lumbered out of his cruiser. "What you done now, Tiger?"

"Foiled a terrorist plot and captured an interstellar criminal," I said, conjuring a grin. Lord, I was a fool.

Another police officer came up beside me and laid hold of my injured arm, drawing an involuntary grunt of pain from me. "Cool it, Tiger," d'Alencon said. This time, I got it. He wasn't using my old call sign to invoke our bygone camaraderie. It was the opposite. "You are under arrest."

I reeled. My jejune expectations of praise and kudos collapsed. "Are you *kidding*? What for?" As the disbelieving words left my mouth, the officer twisted my arm up behind my back, silencing me.

D'Alencon's lips twisted into a bleak smile. "Where do I start? How about that?" He pointed at the truck lying on its side in the pond. "Or how about setting off a goddamn bomb in an office building? You might be able to get away with your bullshit in S-Town, but this time you went too far."

Oh, he was mad at me. He'd given me plenty of chances to talk, and instead I had taken the law into my own hands. He might even think I had been spinning a yarn about Lucy's abduction, since I was hanging out in a apparently friendly way with Buzz Parsec right now.

"The Extritium Precinct ain't minded to tolerate any crap from Shifters," d'Alencon went on, and a flicker of hope revived. His anger was at least partly a performance for the benefit of his colleagues. I guessed that he, too, was in trouble with his brother officers uptown, on account of his acquaintance with us. I glanced at the other cop cars. A red-haired woman officer leaned against the side of one, arms folded, waiting for d'Alencon to redeem himself by bringing me in.

I said, "You got more to worry about than Shifters. There's bioweapons out there. Interstellar variant kuru, man! Didn't Dolph tell you?"

"Yup. He told me." That was all d'Alencon said, but his eyes begged for some explanation that made both of us look less bad.

The red-haired officer came over to us. Her nametag said Meaney. I guess she got a lot of stick for that. "Let's have a chat with your buddy," she said, motioning with her chin at Parsec, who was standing by the sub-limo, watching my arrest with not a little amusement.

D'Alencon and Meaney approached Parsec. The other officer brought me along in a painful power hold. "Afternoon," d'Alencon said to Parsec.

"There's the fugitive," Parsec said, indicating Ijiuto. "Yours with the compliments of the Ponce de Leon Shifter community."

"Your Citizen of the Year award is in the mail," d'Alencon said drily. "I'm currently considering whether I got reasonable cause to arrest you, too."

"You got nothing," Parsec said smugly. He looked at me and said something under his breath about professionals versus amateurs.

Meaney shouted to her officers to take custody of Ijiuto. Her style was clearly to arrest first and ask questions later. Martin cooperated by hauling Ijiuto out of the sub-limo and turning him over to the officers. This finally tipped Ijiuto over the edge into talking. But all he said—yelled, actually—was, "You can't do this! I can't go to jail!"

"I think you'll find that you can," d'Alencon said.

Ijiuto threw himself wildly from side to side in a doomed attempt to get away from the officers. D'Alencon pulled me aside under cover of the scuffle. Rapidly, he said, "Psycho told us about these supposed bio-weapons. But I got no proof they ever existed. I got a bot, says it belongs to you. I got traces of kuru in what looks like a chemistry lab, belonging to a taxi company with no taxis—"

I stiffened. Suddenly, the truth dawned on my tired mind. I saw what I had missed—the crucial piece of information that Dolph hadn't had time to tell me on the phone before they came for him. *The taxis.*

I said, "There were no taxis? They weren't there?"

"Not a one."

"Then that's where they are," I groaned. Panicking, I blundered away from d'Alencon. I grabbed Parsec by his muddy lapels. "The taxis," I yelled. "Forget the trucks. *Where are those taxis?!*"

Parsec's face turned the color of clay. He jumped into the sub-limo and reset the tracking software as fast as his fat fingers could type.

D'Alencon and I and Martin and Captain Meaney clustered around the sub-limo, staring at the dashboard screen.

Painfully slowly, six new blue dots shimmered into view on the map of Mag-Ingat.

They were all static.

On the greenways of the Mag-Ingat Skymall.

*

D'Alencon and Meaney did not totally buy my read of the situation. But they understood the cost of ignoring my hunch if I turned out to be right. I prayed I was wrong. Prayed to our merciful Lord. Prayed for the damn cop car to go *faster* as we flew back towards the city, spinner lights flashing, the cruiser's AI forcibly redirecting slower vehicles out of the way.

D'Alencon had contacted the police AI department and tried to get them to redirect the Mujin Inc taxis away from the mall level.

It hadn't worked.

The taxis had been hacked to prevent any external takeover of their navigation functions.

"That's impossible," d'Alencon yelled at the AI people over the radio.

"Told you Sophia was good with computers," I said.

"I'm starting to believe you."

And I, too, was starting to believe the unthinkable.

The taxis were about to unload the toy fairies on the mall level.

Where my daughter was.

Where I'd thought she would be safe.

Rigid with tension, I perched on the back seat of d'Alencon's cruiser. The big police officer had shifted over to make room for me, squashing Dolph against the other door. Dolph was silent. He clearly thought he'd fucked up. But how could he have known? He had assumed, just like I did, that the toy fairies were wherever Rafael Ijiuto was. We'd both been wrong.

Ijiuto had planned to follow Sophia off-planet, leaving his bio-weapons to devastate Mag-Ingat.

The cruel irony of it, of course, was that Pippa wasn't even here. She was out at that damn detention center. But Ijiuto hadn't known that, and neither had Sophia.

So they'd targeted the place where all the kids were. The Mag-Ingat Skymall.

I felt like we were going slow, although the Cape whizzed past beneath us. I leaned forward to peer between the seats at the cop car's dash computer. It showed Parsec's tracking map, forwarded by him in a show of cooperation with the authorities.

Six blue dots.

One on each of the biggest greenways.

Including the one between Extritium and Hanayashiki.

"Please," I said to d'Alencon, in the front seat. "Please—"

A loud thwapping noise suddenly overtook us. The cruiser plunged. The jolt cracked my head against the roof.

"That's what it feels like to be redirected," said the police officer beside me. Rubbing my head, I saw four black and white darts zooming away ahead of us. They were light tilt-rotor airplanes with twin rotors blurring at the ends of their wings. They darted between the uptown towers like birds.

"That's the riot squad," d'Alencon said. "They'll get there faster than we can."

I started scratching the knees of my jeans, worrying a small hole larger.

"Mike," Dolph said. He had a split lip, a black eye, and severe bruises coming up on the cheek around that eye. His chin and his t-shirt were stained with his own blood. He looked worse than he had the night I accidentally head-butted him in the nose. "It's gonna be OK," he said.

OK? I stared at him, wild-eyed. *OK?* I wanted to scream.

What I said was, "Where's MF?"

"In the trunk," Dolph said, jerking his chin towards the back windshield. "They impounded him."

"Maybe he could help," I muttered, and then d'Alencon warned us to prepare for landing.

He put down in the parking area between Extritium and Hanayashiki. He did that for me.

Before we landed, I scanned the greenway for the Mujin Inc taxi. I didn't know which one it was, and couldn't even remember what they looked like, with the exception of the sporty Skyliner Dolph and I had borrowed. As it turned out, I wouldn't have recognized this one anyway: it had been freshly sprayed, green, red, and white.

"That's it," d'Alencon said. He pointed to the far end of the parking area, which bordered on a lawn dotted with spindly cherry trees. I glimpsed the patriotically striped vehicle, with a crowd of festival-goers around it, and then I saw the children playing on the lawn beyond the parking area. I saw the sparkly fairies swooping and circling above their heads. I strained my eyes until they hurt, looking for any sign of glitter.

Redirected by the cruiser's AI, private cars rose up from the parking area to make room for us.

The cruiser touched down with a bump.

I flung the door open. I was not in handcuffs. My arrest had not got that far yet. I ran.

*

Behind me, in the back seat of the cruiser, Dolph said, "Please. Take these cuffs off. Shit, I'll turn myself in later."

D'Alencon turned around and looked at him. "The reason you're in those cuffs," he said, "is to stop you getting yourself in *more* trouble by striking a police officer. You ain't gonna do that now, are you, Psycho?"

Dolph looked back at him. "I did enough of that already," he said. "And I did it for a reason."

"What was that?"

"To try and make you understand that every motherloving soul here is gonna die if you don't—"

"We are doing all we can," d'Alencon growled.

But they weren't hardly doing anything. Meaney and the other officers had set off at a jog, following me. They were the first group of police officers to arrive on this particular stretch of the mall level. The riot birds had got here before us, but they had not yet been able to land. One of them hovered above the stage near Extritium, its rotors tilted up to chopper configuration, waiting for a landing zone to be cleared below. The fairground rides were still running, and their music and clatter swallowed the noise of the riot bird's rotors, turning it into just one more distraction. Dolph looked over in that direction, and laughed. He said it really struck him in that moment that there were no authorities, as the word is commonly construed, meaning people with the power to stop bad shit from happening. The "authorities" are only people like us with better gear. And they don't even always have that.

"Maybe he could help," Dolph said. "The bot, Bones. Krasylid Athanuisp Zha." He pronounced Mechanical Failure's newly discovered name with the care befitting the name of a newly acquired gun. I know, because that's how he always pronounced it to me afterwards. "Let him out."

*

I hit the lawn running, and halted with a stitch in my side. I frantically looked around for Lucy. I remembered that she was wearing a frilly white dress, and Christy had a red sunhat on—just like a thousand other people. Why would they be here, anyway? The greenway was big. In every direction, toy fairies swooped above the roofs of the shops and the crowds on the walkways, their little rotors whirring.

I'd run straight past the taxi, intent on locating my daughter. Now I swung around to take a second look at it.

Captain Meaney and the other police officers were advancing on it from the direction of the parking area. They moved slowly because of the knot of festival-goers surrounding the taxi, which was growing by the moment as more people discovered, through the osmosis of crowds, that someone was handing out free toys.

"These things go for 300 GC," said one parent to another standing near me. "And they're just handing them out? Crazy."

Her little boy clutched a toy fairy. "It's broken," he said. "It doesn't scatter fairy dust like it said it did."

I seized on this sliver of hope. The things had not yet started to sprinkle fairy dust. They must be programmed to release their lethal cargo at some specific time.

"That thing'll kill you," I said. I took the boy's toy out of his hands and threw it as far as I could across the lawn, knowing that wouldn't make a blind bit of difference. The toy fairies weren't broken. They were just locked. By the AI inside them, whose spooky presence I had glimpsed in the *St. Clare's* cargo hold. The AI designed by my brilliant ex-wife.

"Hey!" The mother's outraged shout followed me as I jogged back to the taxi.

"Excuse me," I said, "excuse me." I edged through the crowd.

The trunk of the taxi stood open. Toy fairies filled it, out of their packaging, tumbled around in there like tiny winged corpses.

In front of the trunk stood a young man in a red, white, and green happi coat, with his hair spray-dyed in stripes to match. He had bad skin and a gap-toothed grin. He was passing out toy fairies as fast as eager little hands could grab them.

I saw Lucy.

Standing right in front of the trunk, with Christy and a bunch of the other kids from Shoreside Elementary, stretching out her hand.

I never saw the people I knocked aside. I grabbed Lucy's wrist and yanked her back, empty-handed.

"Hey," the young man said, and then he took a step back, bumping into the taxi. He was scared of me.

Smart guy.

I seized the front of his happi coat and dragged him up on his toes. "How'd you get this job?"

"It was on GetHired, man! I just applied like normal! Is there a problem?" His voice broke. He was terrified. I let him go.

"Sorry," I said. I took Lucy's hand.

"Happy Founding Day," the young man yelled at my back, sarcastically.

"Yeah," I said. "Happy Founding Day."

Sweat started out at the backs of my knees as I eased Lucy away from the taxi.

"I want one of those fairies!" Lucy whined.

"No, sweetie," I said, and my voice came out soft. "I'll give you a better present."

She jerked her hand out of mine. "*That's* what I want," she said, starting to cry. "You never give me anything I want."

I picked her up, ignoring the protests from my aching shoulder and back muscles. She immediately struggled down. I grabbed her arm, and reached for Christy with my free hand. "Come on, kids," I said to the other children, and we walked away.

Behind us, the police officers moved in, breaking up the crowd.

"What was all that about?" Christy said. "What's wrong?" She looked back at the police officers.

"Oh, nothing," I said. I didn't know, at the time, why I felt compelled to speak quietly and downplay my fear, but later it dawned on me: I did it because I was scared shitless. I was acting like prey. What use are claws and teeth against 8,999 machines?

Half a dozen of Lucy's classmates had fairies. They turned them on and sent them aloft. Kids are so quick to figure this stuff out. Sparkly wings blurred overhead as we shuffled along. I didn't know where to go. We couldn't all fit in the police cruisers. We were slightly closer to the Hanayashiki exit, so I made the decision to go that way.

The sun was sinking. The shadow of the top of Bonsucesso Tower slashed across the greenway like a sword. Incongruous scents of chocolate and magnolias tinted the air, and everywhere flew the little sparkly toy fairies with their rotors whirring.

"These things are a bit freaky," Christy said, ducking as one flew low over her head.

"Yeah," I said. "Watch out."

"Pretty, though," she said, looking up.

I followed her gaze. The goddamn sky was *full* of the things, like a swarm of butterflies. Some of them were getting up higher than the force field barriers, and being carried away in the wind. People stopped in their tracks; they looked up and gasped. It was that soft unguarded 'oooh' you hear when people have witnessed something unexpected and magical.

I dropped to my knees and grabbed the back of Lucy's head and pressed her face into my shirt.

*

I did not know what else was going on at that moment, and even if I had, I couldn't have understood it, because no human being could understand it. This was the brutal, blindingly fast warfare of artificial intelligences, fought with the only two weapons in an AI's arsenal: one and zero. Something and nothing. That's all they have. But oh, what a lot of damage they can do with it.

When Dolph and d'Alencon let MF out of the trunk of the cruiser, he'd been encased in a silver body bag. This was a portable Faraday sack, the type of gizmo commonly used to disable electronics. Of course, MF was not your average bot, as we were coming to understand. He could've just ripped the thing open with his manipulators. But he was trying to be cooperative. So he lay there without moving until Dolph pulled the sack off and told him just how much trouble we were in.

MF already knew part of it. Back in Bonsucesso Tower, he had explored the servers Mujin Inc had used, and picked up enough remanent data to determine what type of architecture Sophia had used to build her AIs. It wasn't much, but it was the difference between operating with a map, or without one.

Now, crouching on the asphalt of the parking area, he launched a full-spectrum attack on the toy fairies.

Sophia had originally designed them for use on Gvm Uye Sachttra, where there was no connectivity. There, they'd have been invulnerable. But here, they were flying among hundreds of AIs far more powerful than they were, any one of which could have subverted them in a hot second. After the target of the attack changed to Mag-Ingat, Sophia must have worked around the clock to harden them against potential hacking. They now had military-grade security, or even better. It was no wonder the police department had not been able to even find them, let alone hack them.

MF was less dainty in his approach. Data bombs flew around us and under our feet and over our heads, traversing the radio frequencies and the optical fibers running through the greenway. They exploded in the zettabyte-deep buckets of the uptown servers where Sophia had hidden her command strings.

There were side effects.

Fairground rides clanked to a halt. Others sped up and began to shake themselves to pieces. People screamed.

Lights in the towers above us flashed on, then off. Doors opened and shut like guillotines. Elevators stopped. Alarms shrieked in a discordant fanfare.

"This is my fault," I said to Christy, who was crouching beside me, trying to make me get up, and she said, "No, it's not," and a second later, "What is?"

The toy fairies fought back. They flung oceans of nonsense data at MF and his borrowed processors. They ring-fenced themselves with ramparts of encryption built on the fly. MF stole more processing power to assault them. Customer service bots froze. Cars lost their minds and drifted in mid-air. Payments ceased to process. The radio in d'Alencon's cruiser died at the very instant that Officer Meaney was using it to tell him that they had arrested that poor sucker with the patriotic hair.

At the height of the battle, MF probably had half the city's processing power under his control. It took him 15.8 seconds, all told, to break through to the enemy's inmost citadel: the toy fairies' parental controls.

After it was all over, I asked a friend who knows more about computers than I do how long it would have taken *him* to hack those controls.

He said, "'Bout half an hour."

MF did it in 2.3 seconds.

The fairies' rotors stopped turning.

All 8,999 of them fluttered to the ground on their glider wings, like falling sycamore seeds, and lay inert.

Disbelieving, I released my grip on Lucy. "Daddy," she whined, "That *hurt!*" I rose to my feet and kicked the fairy nearest us. It didn't move.

Pulling Lucy and Christy with me, while the other kids scuttled after us, I half jogged, half ran back towards the parking area.

Everyone on the greenway was freaking out, unaware that they had already come unscathed through the moment of peak danger. It was the side effects. The power going out and coming back, machines stopping and starting, payment terminals freezing, cars drifting off course in the sky—these things don't *happen*. We're all so invested in the idea that Ponce de Leon is safe. But awareness of the dangers of the Cluster lurks just below the surface. The more clued-up people were glancing fearfully at the sky.

There was no stampede for the exits, by the way; we're jaded, at the same time as we're innocent. We all know that if Ponce de Leon were to be attacked from space, it wouldn't do any good to run for the exits. So people just clustered together and nervously poked at their dead phones.

Moving among the groups of frightened people, bots—customer service bots, big and little, and ones that had been dressed up as historical characters for the festival—swept the walkways with fast, mechanical efficiency, picking up the fairies and dropping them into garbage bags.

We crossed the parking area to the police cruisers. Mechanical Failure was standing among the police officers, chatting Captain Meaney up. "Are you a natural redhead?"

I said, "Is it over?" I was red-faced, sweating, balanced on a razor's edge between terror and relief.

"He did it," Dolph gloated. He was sitting on the trunk of the cruiser, smoking a cigarette, despite his cut lip. His handcuffs were gone. "Correction. *We* did it!" He leaned over and held up his hand. I bemusedly returned his high-five.

"Yeah," said d'Alencon. "However, y'all are still under arrest."

"Oh, come on, Bones," I said good-humoredly, already bouncing back. At least I thought I was. "You're not gonna ding us for busting down an office door. We saved the freaking city."

"I'm of the opinion you did," d'Alencon agreed. He glanced at Officer Meaney, who was now on the radio, ordering up a hazardous waste disposal unit. "But that does not change the fact that those bio-weapons were imported to Ponce de Leon on board your ship."

54

GODDAMN Parsec.
Goddamn Parsec.

He had talked. I knew it. There was no other way the cops could have found out. Sure, they could have learned by checking my manifests that I had shipped the toy fairies *from* Ponce de Leon *to* Gvm Uye Sachttra … but only Parsec knew that I had been unable to deliver them, and brought them back here.

Well, Rafael Ijiuto could have told them.

But there was no advantage for him in talking. In fact, if he did, he'd incriminate himself. Parsec, on the other hand, had everything to gain. So he had broken the unspoken code of Shifter silence, and dropped me in it to save himself.

He was in it up to his furry ass, of course. But he could probably get away with his "I knew nothing" defense, as long as it could not be proved that he'd committed any crime … such as importing bioweapons to Ponce de Leon.

And *I* was the one who'd done that.

So they took me and Dolph down to PdL PD HQ, a grandiose colonial building in the middle of downtown. While we waited, Martin and Parsec were brought in. I jumped up from my seat and caught up with Parsec as he walked with a police officer towards the offices of the detective division. He was joking around with his escort, oozing bonhomie. *He* was not under arrest. He'd just come to give a statement, which would doubtless include compromising information about me, signed and sworn and, for what it was worth, true.

"You asswipe," I said. "You slimy, lying crook. You traitor."

He looked at me and said one word: "Tomas."

I fell back. Watched him disappear through the swinging doors beneath the red light indicating the security force field was on. I knew exactly what he'd just told me. He *could* have given me up for the killing of Tomas Feirweather, alias Canuck. That had been murder, no two ways about it. But with that cryptic utterance of the man's name, Parsec had indicated that he had not and would not finger me for that, as long as I played nice. By *only* squealing about the returned cargo, he was letting me off easy … and punishing me, as honor demanded, for killing his minion.

It was cold comfort. I still stood to lose everything: my ship, my business, my customers, and probably my apartment and my personal savings as well if I was held liable for damages, as I would be. When Dolph had tried to file suit against the Bonsucesso security contractors, he'd been told to get in line. Seemed like everyone who had been at the festival was filing suit against the city, the security providers, or both. The police department's servers were crashing. Aftershocks from MF's battle against the toy fairies were still rippling through the city's infrastructure.

I sat back down beside Dolph and Martin and thought with a pale twinge of amusement about how I'd almost lost my child today, not to mention my life. Earlier, I would have given up everything I owned if that would keep Lucy safe. Now, however, that she *was* safe—she had gone home with Christy, who promised to look after her until I was released—I was right back to where I started.

My only consolation was that the police didn't know about my off-world business. *That* could put me in the executioner's chair if it came out. But I felt safe as far as that went. Parsec didn't have any details other than whatever Sophia had told him, or rumors he may have heard in the Fringeworlds. Hearsay ain't evidence. And Sophia—an eyewitness to some of the shit we did before Lucy was born—had fled off-planet. So actually, it was lucky for me she'd got away.

Martin, Dolph, and I had a waiting room to ourselves. L-shaped, carved out of a larger room, it had a high ceiling but only half a window, which faced an airshaft. In the concrete canyon outside, the light mellowed to violet and then turned to black. We drank insipid coffee, ate the stale cookies someone had left next to the coffee machine, and plotted bloody revenge against the bears. It was just hot air and we all knew it. Nothing we could do to them equalled what Parsec was doing to us.

Now and then detectives passed through the room, but they refused to answer any of the questions we hurled at them.

A little after 10 PM the door opened once more. This time, MF rolled into the room in the company of Jose-Maria d'Alencon.

The bot wore a visitor lanyard around the base of his neck. He asked Dolph how he was feeling.

"Like crap," Dolph said, grinning with the half of his mouth that wasn't cut and swollen. "And yourself, Krasylid Athanuisp Zha?"

That was the first time I heard him pronounce MF's real name. I knew then how much respect Dolph had gained for the bot. As for me, I knew that we all owed MF our lives, but I was not in a particularly grateful mood. Mechanically, I said, "You cleaned up today, MF. I'll buy you an unlimited subscription to Guaranteed Natural Livestreams … when I get out of here."

Martin nodded at the window and said, "There's only a force field on that. Feel like hacking it? 'Cause I want to go home."

"I am committed to upholding the law of the Cluster except in cases of dire necessity," MF said, diplomatically. Like he hadn't provided janitorial support on all our off-world jobs.

D'Alencon cleared his throat and said with a hint of awe, "Krasylid Athanuisp Zha is an Urush bot, as you probably all know."

We did not. Our mouths dropped open. An Urush bot?

"Yes," MF said. "I am one thousand, two hundred and fourteen years old. There are not many of us left. In fact, I have not met another one in centuries. Most of the bots in my series had dangerous hobbies that led, in the fullness of time, to their destruction. *I* have always liked to just sit quietly and watch people having sex."

Dolph laughed. D'Alencon looked uncomfortable. MF did his most googly-eyed look.

"The *St. Clare* is the latest in a long line of spaceships I have built," he said. "In the past I generally stuck to cruise liners and pleasure yachts. I expected the Kroolth emperor's flagship would be another safe haven. Diplomatic cruises, you know ... little aliens bumping uglies in the berths ... but then they had to go and have a war. You biologicals are *always* having wars, aren't you?" His voice became somber. "That was a formative experience for me. I realized that there were no safe havens anymore."

"Too freaking true," I said.

"Yes," MF said. "It may seem as if there is always a war going on somewhere, but in fact, that was not true before humanity came to the Cluster. You have really stirred things up."

I winced. Dolph looked intrigued. Martin yawned. D'Alencon fingered his badge with an expression that I identified, after a moment, as shame. He felt terrible that his outfit was not doing more to curb humanity's violent tendencies.

"So I decided it was time for me to take a more active role in the affairs of humanity," MF went on. "In that respect, life aboard the *St. Clare,* formerly the *Puissant Arm of Imperial Might,* has not disappointed me."

One sensor cover dipped briefly in my direction: a wink.

"Well, we sure are grateful for your contrbutions today," d'Alencon said, ending the excruciating pause. "Those AIs could have effectively wiped out the planet. "

"Yes," MF said. "Sophia Hart, alias Pamela Kingsolver, appears to have an unusual combination of qualities: a brilliant problem-solving intellect—almost equal, indeed, to the Urush engineers who built me —and a complete lack of empathy."

"And they call *me* Psycho," Dolph muttered.

"And yet, why'd she *do* it?" d'Alencon said. He seemed honestly perplexed, for a good reason: he did not know Sophia was still a Traveller. Parsec had, at least, done me (and himself) the favor of not mentioning that.

I said, "Ijiuto hired her to do a job, and she did it. *He's* the one we should be focusing on. Has he talked?"

"No," d'Alencon said, not meeting my eyes.

"Come on," I said. "You don't have ways of making a guy talk? What kind of cops are you?"

Now d'Alencon made eye contact. "What do you think we are, Tiger? We're the police, not the 15th Recon. He won't talk, and we have nothing on him, anyway! Mujin Inc's files are all gone. We have only your word for it that he procured the bio-weapons! Oh, I don't think he'll walk. We'll find something that'll stick: hitchhiking, maybe. Or parachuting without a license."

"You can charge him with the murder of Kimmie Ng," I said. "He confessed to me that he did it."

"That's interesting, but it don't account for what happened today. Don't you understand, Mike? We have to charge *someone*, or heads are going to roll."

As the words sank in, I realized he had come down to the waiting room to let me know I had a big old scapegoat sign hanging around my neck.

I rose from my chair and grabbed him by the upper arms, shouting incoherently, defending my actions and begging to be allowed to go home. Dolph and Martin pulled me off him. Two more police officers tumbled in with tasers at the ready, and the upshot was I landed in a cell downstairs, with no window, no company, and no light at all.

55

I woke with a sour taste in my mouth, feeling as if I hadn't been asleep long. It was amazing I'd managed to doze off at all. The cot in my cell was diabolically hard, and several inches too narrow and too short.

A light bobbled down the corridor, casting the shadows of my cell's bars on the side wall.

I was in an annex of the drunk tank, for prisoners deemed dangerous enough to require solitary confinement. I heard some of them waking up and commenting as the flashlight passed their cells. The comments were of the type that lowlifes make to a woman with a nice ass. However, the voice that answered, telling them to shut up, belonged to d'Alencon.

I sat up, swinging my shoeless feet to the floor.

The flashlight stopped outside my cell, and shone in through the bars. I winced from the light.

"Mike," said d'Alencon. He sounded excited. What did he have to be excited about? Putting me away for life?

I stood up. My mouth tasted like this place smelt. I hawked and spat on the floor. "Can you quit blinding me?"

"Whoops."

The beam lowered to the floor. As my eyes recovered, I recognized the trim figure standing next to d'Alencon.

"Irene?!"

"Sorry I took so long," she said. "Got something for you."

I stumbled over to the bars. It was humiliating to clutch them and peer out at my weapons officer. "Everything OK?" I said, trying to sound normal.

"Better than OK." She held up a bag. "Guess what this is."

D'Alencon chortled. He shone his flashlight on the bag. It was a transparent evidence sack.

Inside it was a human head.

*

Shoed and belted once more, with my phone and the other contents of my pockets back in my possession, I sat on a chair with arms, in a much nicer room than the one where we had waited before. At my fingertips was a cup of excellent coffee with cream. My head was still spinning. The police can turn your life upside-down and then turn it the right way up again without a second's notice. *That's* power. I guessed, from the demeanor of d'Alencon and the others, that I was off the hook, but I still didn't get why, except that it had something to do with the human head in the middle of the table.

On the other side of the table sat d'Alencon, a hawk-faced elderly woman who had not been introduced, and a forensic technician.

Beside me sat Irene. This, too, I was having trouble processing. Irene, at PdL PD HQ? She even crossed the street to avoid traffic cops.

The forensic technician poked the head with a pair of tweezers through the sterile sack. "I haven't yet thoroughly examined it," he said. "But inspection with an electron scanning microscope revealed traces of brain tissue, which appear to be infected with interstellar variant kuru."

The head had belonged to a man in middle age. His face looked dour. No wonder, as the top of his skull was missing, and so was his brain.

What remained was encased in cryonite, the transparent material that shippers often use to preserve perishable goods on long flights.

I stretched out a finger and poked the hard surface of the cryonite. Even through the sample sack I could feel the chill of the material. "But where did it come from?" I said.

"Aha," said Irene. She was grubby, dressed in shorts and a t-shirt that I took for emergency spares. Weariness pouched the skin under her eyes. Her body thrummed with tension. I couldn't tell if it was because she was surrounded by police officers, or for some other reason. "I told you I was going to try and trace the, uh, contraband, right?"

"Right."

"Well, when you told me about the kuru, I knew *that* was what I was looking for. I mean, that definitely did not come from Ponce de Leon."

"Technically," the forensic technician began.

"Yeah, I know, *technically* you can grow prions in the lab. But you have to have some to start it off, right? Like making yogurt. I make yogurt for my son," Irene said to the police officers. She was babbling. I'd never heard Irene babble before. "It helps with his digestive issues. It's easy, but you need a starter culture." She pointed to the head.

D'Alencon took up the thread. "These human remains are thought to be the source of all the IVK prions encapsulated in the bio-weapons we impounded today. The kuru prions would have been isolated from the infected tissues and added to vats of lab-grown brain proteins, where they turned the target proteins into more kuru prions. In fact, we found the equipment for that process at the Mujin Inc office."

The elderly woman raised one finger to cut him off. "The link cannot be proved conclusively," she said in a low, authoritative voice. "For our purposes, the key fact is the origin of this dangerous and unpleasant object: *not* Ponce de Leon."

"Yes, Madam Prosecutor," Irene said.

I blinked. This woman was the chief prosecutor of Ponce de Leon, making her one of our highest-ranking planetary authorities. She said to Irene, "Please tell us again, Ms. Seagrave, how you obtained it."

Irene nodded nervously. "Well, everyone knows the likeliest source of kuru is the Hurtworlds."

I thought for an instant about Pippa. If she wasn't on her way to the Hurtworlds right now, she would be in a few days. Poor Pippa. The worst irony of this whole mess was that, without knowing it, Ijiuto had succeeded.

Irene was still talking. "So I asked a few people I know in the ... export-import sector ... if they had heard of any cargoes coming from the Hurtworlds recently. And they pointed me to a certain person who is, I guess, enjoying the hospitality of the PdL PD as we speak."

"Correct," d'Alencon said jubilantly. "He'll likely be with us for quite some time."

"I had a heck of a time catching up with him," Irene said. "So I decided I would wait at his office. I did *not* break in," she stressed, over-emphasizing it in my view. "I climbed up the fire escape of the building next door and waited on their roof. I could see into the office through their windows."

"Whose office?" I said.

"I'm about to tell you," Irene said. "Around six o'clock, the office staff go home. I'm still waiting for this guy to put in an appearance. Finally, about 21:30 I guess it was, he shows up. The lights go on again ..."

What Irene said to the police was that she then went over there and rang the bell. I thought that didn't sound like her, and sure enough, she later admitted to me that as soon as the office staff left, she had Shifted into her panther form and jumped from her fire escape to the balcony of the building next door. She had then Shifted back and broken into the office using a lock-pick kit she'd kept from the old days. So when the lights in the office went on once more, there was Irene sitting on a polished wooden desk the size of a boat, with a suppressed .38 in her hands, and the head of the nameless Hurtworlder beside her.

"What's this thing you got for cryonite?" she said to Buzz Parsec.

56

"Parsec?" I pushed back from the table so hard, I spilled my coffee and Irene's as well. "Holy hell, Irene, this came from *Buzz Parsec's office?*"

"Sure did," Irene said, with the distant smile that was her equivalent of an ear-to-ear grin.

I shook my head in amazement. "I thought it was July," I said. "Turns out it's Christmas."

"It was on a shelf on his brag wall," d'Alencon said with a chuckle. "Ms. Seagrave had the presence of mind to obtain photographic evidence."

"If that isn't just like him," I said. My face hurt from grinning. I counseled myself that it was tactless to appear quite so pleased, but I couldn't help it.

Irene said, "In my opinion, what happened is Mujin Inc took delivery of the contaminated head and removed the brain. Then they gave it back to Parsec to dispose of safely. But ol' Buzz, *being* Buzz, instead of disposing of it, freezes it in cryonite and sticks it up on the shelf to gross people out. He probably told them he bit the top of the head off himself."

I felt an unexpected pang of sympathy for Parsec, who had needed to seem so big, when actually his greed had made him so small. The pang passed quickly. "You've got him?" I said to d'Alencon. I wanted to make sure I wasn't dreaming. "You've actually arrested him?"

"He's being questioned right now on suspicion of importing hazardous substances," d'Alencon confirmed.

I laughed out loud. It was too perfect. After everything he'd done, Parsec was going down … for smuggling.

"No guarantees, of course, but my professional view is that it's in the bag." In an uncharacteristic moment of playfulness, d'Alencon blew a smacking kiss at the human head. He was clearly on cloud nine, having finally snared Parsec on a charge that the chief prosecutor liked. "This guy is the principal witness for the prosecution."

A trickle of doubt seeped in. "But …" The last thing I wanted was to question their grounds for arresting Parsec, but I couldn't see him being stupid enough to import something like this, let alone keep it in his office.

D'Alencon read my mind. "As we already know, Parsec was providing logistics services to Mujin Inc. That included some procurement jobs that the company, we assume, did not wish to be associated with. Parsec did not either. So he hired someone else to transport these remains from the Hurtworlds to Ponce de Leon … just as he outsourced the delivery to Gvm Uye Sachttra to you."

Irene spoke up. "Ma'am, I don't think Evan Zhang should be prosecuted." The name rang a bell: Zhang was another freighter captain, a normie. I assumed he was the "someone else" who had done the run to the Hurtworlds to pick up the infected human head. "He's no guiltier than Mike is. He just did the job he was paid for."

Something twisted in my gut. Yeah, I'd just done the job I was paid for. Did that really make me innocent? I had the sense to say nothing. I kept a cooperative smile plastered on my face.

A second later I found it harder to keep that smile in place.

"I understand what you're saying, Ms. Seagrave," the chief prosecutor said. "You believe that the same standards of justice should be applied to Mr. Zhang as were applied to you."

As Irene fumbled for a response, I looked from one woman to the other. Something I did not understand was going on here. I caught a whiff of grave dust; maybe the bodies in Irene's past weren't so deeply buried ...

The chief prosecutor raised a minatory finger, shutting Irene up, and turned her gaze on me. She had the overpowering stare of someone accustomed to authority who will not brook challenges for an instant —she lived in a world where challenges to her authority did not *exist*. "The same standards of justice," she rammed home, "that we are applying to Mr. Starrunner?"

"Yes, ma'am," Irene said weakly. I could see her fingers twisting together under the table.

"Justice is perfect in theory, messy in practice," the chief prosecutor said. "Mr. Parsec undoubtedly deserves to spend the rest of his life in jail. That should not, in theory, exculpate Mr. Zhang—*or* Mr. Starrunner." She suddenly spread her hands. "However, we don't want to completely hollow out the PdL shipping industry. And the demise of Parsec Freight will leave a considerable hole in it." She rose. "Go, go, go away. And try to be more ... more discriminating in future about who you associate with."

Everyone else hastily stood, including me and Irene. I knew when to get out while the getting was good, but an impulse—recklessness, defiance, or mere civility—made me stick out my hand to the chief prosecutor. "Thank you, ma'am," I said.

A twinge of disgust passed over her face. She let my hand hang in the air. I suppose it *could* have been because I had just spent several hours in a none-too-fragrant jail cell. My face reddening, I shoved my hands in my pockets. Uncouth attitude: check. Chip on shoulder: check.

"Collect your bot on the way out," the chief prosecutor said as she left the room. "It's either that, or I hire it."

When Irene and I swung by the front desk, where MF was waiting, we overheard Parsec's voice coming from one of the interview rooms beyond the reception area. He must have been shouting at the top of his lungs. "I did not know anything!"

I looked down at my shoes. They were dirty, and I hadn't been given the laces back.

*

I called my truck. While we were waiting for it, a block from the police station, I said to Irene, "So where did that thing really come from?"

She let out one of her cat-like hisses. "You're not as dumb as you look, are you, Mike?"

"Neither is Parsec. No way he had that thing on display in his office."

Irene looked left and right along the street for the truck. MF was standing at the curb a few meters from us. Irene lowered her voice. "Do you think they believed me?"

"We're out here, and he's in there."

"True."

"The art of the sale," I said, "is that you can sell anything to someone who wants to buy. They've been wanting to put Parsec away for years. You did them—and Ponce de Leon—a big favor."

She relaxed a tad. "That's how I see it."

My truck pulled up at the curb. MF got in the back. Irene and I got in the cab. "Home," I said. As the truck started moving, I turned to Irene. "So where did it come from?" I asked again.

She had her sneakers up on the dashboard. One forearm gracefully drooped over her eyes. "How well do you know Evan Zhang?"

"Not very."

"He's a crook. His bread and butter is runs to the *Hurtworlds*. That should tell you something."

"He was the one who brought the thing back."

"Yeah. I went to see him in case he had any information. He had Mr. Brains on his desk. Minute I saw it, I knew that's what I was looking for. He told me what I told them: Mujin Inc gave it back to him to dispose of, and he, being a sick fucker, turned it into a desk ornament."

"And then he gave it to you?"

"Better believe he wanted rid of it after what happened today."

"I can see that."

"So I took it to Parsec's office, set it up next to his award plaques, took some pictures. And waited for him to get there."

I let out a long breath. Irene—and I, by implication—had framed Parsec. He would be going down for something he hadn't done. "What if Zhang talks to the police?"

Irene raised her arm an inch and glared at me beneath it. "He won't talk to the police," she said, "because he's going to have an accident."

"Going to?"

"I didn't have time today. I figure we can go over there tomorrow or the next day. Better not leave it too long, though."

"Yeah," I echoed, "better not leave it too long."

The truck glided through the darkened streets. I rested my hands on the wheel, feeling it move gently as the AI steered. The night breeze blew in through my open window, carrying the good, homey smells of Shiftertown: gravelnuts, barbecue, the sea.

"Hey, Irene?" I said. "Thank you."

"You owe me big-time."

"I know."

"Shit, Mike, I was so scared going into that place, I thought I was going to pass out at the front desk." Irene stretched her arms out in front of her and flexed them in a feline stretch. "It was something I had to face and conquer."

"Why ..."

I had meant to ask why she was so scared. I wanted to know what the chief prosecutor had been alluding to. But she said with sudden intensity, "Because you're the best boss I ever had. Well, you're the *only* boss I ever had, apart from the army. But I mean it. You give a damn. You actually care about people. It was a revelation to me, and I know Rex feels the same way. That's why he was OK with me doing this. We agreed, we are *not* going to let Mike take the fall for the whole thing on some BS smuggling charge."

I swallowed. I felt like I might blubber. I managed to produce a light tone. "You are the best hire I ever made. Thank God I was able to look past the sexy, intriguing exterior to the inner deviousness."

Irene laughed one of her rare loud laughs, almost a giggle. "Home," she said, in the tone you would use to say "Victory!" She sat up straight as the truck pulled up in front of our building. There was one light on upstairs. My apartment was dark and desolate. Irene popped her door. "What, are you going on somewhere?" she said, when I didn't move.

"Going to pick up Lucy," I said. "Mind if I let MF out here? He can hang out downstairs."

She shrugged. She still hadn't forgiven MF for letching on her. "Give Lucy a big kiss from me and tell her we're going to be home tomorrow morning, if she wants to play. Mia's really missed her."

I watched Irene and MF climb the steps.

Then I turned the truck around and headed back to the police station.

57

"I need to speak to Jose-Maria d'Alencon."

The duty office scowled at me. "Weren't you just here?"

"Yup," I said, "and now I'm back."

I waited. I couldn't hear Parsec yelling anymore. Maybe he was finally too worn out to keep protesting his innocence.

D'Alencon came down to the front desk in shirtsleeves. His springy gait faltered when he saw me. "Something wrong, Tiger?"

"Yeah," I said. "I forgot to pick up my stuff." He frowned. "When y'all arrested me, you confiscated some stuff of mine that was in Parsec's car. A bag. My daughter's sewing project was in there. You haven't gone and trashed it, have you?"

"No," d'Alencon said slowly. "That'll be in the evidence room." He held my eyes for a moment, and then crooked a finger for me to come with him.

We went back behind the desk, past the interrogation rooms, through an open-plan office where half a hundred officers were answering phones. I followed d'Alencon down a flight of stairs so long, we seemed to be descending into a basement level carved out of Ponce de Leon's very bedrock.

"Even the evidence officer's been reassigned to answerin' phones," d'Alencon said dryly as he unlocked a steel door. "Tell ya, I've been in the force twenty years, and this is the closest call we ever had."

Inside, sensor-activated lights came on, revealing aisles of shelves groaning with evidence boxes, stretching away into the dark. Our footsteps echoed. The lights followed us, and switched themselves off behind us, so that we moved in a puddle of light with shadows pressing in before and behind. D'Alencon stopped in front of a shelf less dusty than the rest. "This is your stuff."

It was cool down here, and yet sweat matted my t-shirt to my back. I said, "This was somewhat of a pretext, Bones. I wanted to talk to you."

"Oh, look," d'Alencon said. "There's something wrong with that light. Gimme a boost."

I cupped my hands on a braced knee, and d'Alencon's size sixteen landed in them. He reached up to the light, unscrewed it, and did something to the wiring inside the cover. It went out.

D'Alencon stumbled down to the floor in pitch darkness, lost his balance, and crashed into the shelves. The noise echoed through the room. "Shit," he said.

"You OK?"

"Yeah. Shame about that light malfunctioning. The same sensors control the audio monitoring equipment. You were saying?"

It was so dark I couldn't see my hand in front of my face, and I was grateful for it. I sat down on the concrete floor and leaned against evidence boxes, inhaling the dust of old crimes. "Have a seat, Bones. This could take a little while."

His gunbelt creaked and he groaned quietly as he sat down. His foot brushed my leg. He was sitting beside me, like a friend, not across from me, like an interrogator. He wouldn't feel so friendly in a minute. "Go on."

"When I was twenty-two," I said, "I left the army. I didn't really want to leave, but the war was over, and they were letting people go. So I took my exit pay and I borrowed some money and I started a shipping company with two friends, Dolph and another guy, Art Koolhaus. You might remember him. We called him McKool."

"Shit, yeah. What ever happened to him?"

"Dead."

"Man."

"In those days, we were a tramp outfit. We had no home base. We lived from hand to mouth, cargo to cargo. My idea was I wanted to add value to the Cluster, to make up for everything we did in the war. But I had a mortgage on my ship, and when other opportunities came along, I didn't say no."

"What kind of other opportunities?"

"The first contract we took was on a Techworld. The customer wanted a business rival killed on a hunting trip. Make it look like animals …

"One time in the Hurtworlds, we robbed a currency mine. We ended up giving it back, but only because we got caught …

"I lost my first ship in the Hurtworlds, too. We'd been hired to hijack an antimatter tanker. You know how they always put the AM depots on the far side of a moon. So we put our ship on autopilot and crashed it into the other side of the moon to create a distraction. But we got away with enough antimatter to buy a better one …"

I went on, telling him every dirty job I'd ever done, as far as I could remember. The gist was that I wasn't much better than the Travellers, except I didn't buy into anyone's stinking ideology, and for what it's worth, I tried not to hurt the innocent. My voice grew hoarse. I rambled.

"I was married by that time. Sophia loved the dirty jobs. She pulled the trigger herself on the vice president of the Zygrint, you know, those humanoid guys who make the living monuments …"

"I remember hearing about that. That was y'all?"

"Yeah. That was a higher profile job than I really care for. Tell ya the truth, I was relieved when Sophia got pregnant and had to quit flying. But she—she was furious about it. I promised her anything she wanted if we could only keep the baby. She agreed, but looking back, that was the end of our marriage …

"After Lucy was born, I started to dial it back. You get a whole different perspective on life when that little person is looking up at you, trusting you to be … to be—" I suddenly choked up. All this time I had been trying not to think about Lucy. Trying not to think about how she'd react when her daddy didn't come home. Now I started crying. My sobs sounded awful, gulping and raw, like wild animal noises. Thank God it was dark in here.

"Want a tissue?" d'Alencon said.

Hunched over my knees, wiping my face with my hands, I remembered what Irene had done for me. What Dolph had done for me. What Martin had done for me. I'd been stupid. I had meant to leverage my confession into immunity for them, but I'd plain forgotten to set conditions. I'd just let it all spill out. "No," I gasped, "I'm good."

"Good, 'cause I don't have any tissues, anyway."

"Bones—a favor … My crew—don't prosecute them. Please." All I could do at this point was beg.

D'Alencon shifted uneasily. "Tiger …"

"What?"

"There ain't … shit, I hate to ask … there ain't anything wrong with that evidence, is there?"

I froze. Some part of d'Alencon suspected that Mr. Brains was too good to be true. And now his career hung on it. He'd stuck his neck out, gotten the chief prosecutor to sign off on it.

"Course there's nothing wrong with it," I said, with all the conviction I could muster. "It's cast-iron proof that Parsec is an idiot." I'd have to get onto Evan Zhang before the police could. Except I wouldn't be able to, because I'd be in jail. Well, Irene would.

D'Alencon chuckled, sounding relieved and a bit embarrassed. "It's just, I got a sense that Ms. Seagrave may not have rung the doorbell, if you know what I mean."

I smiled in the darkness. "Well, I don't see that that really matters."

"True enough. I shouldn't say this, but sometimes you gotta do wrong to do good."

"I guess maybe," I said. "But that wasn't true in my case. I did wrong for money."

"That's what I'm curious about, Tiger." D'Alencon's voice shifted into a more somber register. "What did you do with it all?"

"Huh?"

"All the money you made. I assume these jobs were well paid. So where is it? Your bank account is so empty there's an echo in there. You got a gambling problem? Someone blackmailing you?"

"No, and no. I ... well, I don't know, Bones. I spend it. I bought a nanny bot; that cost a chunk of change. But mostly it goes on payroll, repairs, rent, the usual."

"What about all those cargoes you carry?"

"Shit, Bones, you can't keep a ship like the *St. Clare* flying on shipping fees. Everyone in the business knows that."

"So in a way, you been taking contracts just to keep flying."

"I ... yeah, I guess so."

There was a moment's silence.

"Spent it all," d'Alencon murmured under his breath. "Spent it on the usual. *Shifters.*"

I cringed. "Can I smoke?"

"No, you cannot smoke in here." I heard rustling as d'Alencon heaved himself to his feet. I scrambled upright, too.

Without warning, he bodyslammed me into the shelves, gripping the front of my t-shirt with one hand. Evidence boxes thumped to the floor on the other side of the open shelves. I struggled instinctively, and then went limp as his gun dug into the side of my stomach.

58

D'ALENCON pressed me against the shelves, his whole weight on my chest, his gun digging into my abdomen. "How much of what you just told me was bullshit, Tiger?" he said, low.

"None of it."

He breathed heavily into my face. I smelled onions, sour coffee. Then he let go of me and stepped back. I couldn't see his gun, didn't dare to move. A light came on in the darkness: the screen of Bones's phone. It lit his pudgy face from below, ghoulishly.

"I'm saving this audio file in my personal cloud," he said. "To remind me of why I do this job."

"I ... I don't ..."

"What?"

"Aren't you going to ... arrest me?"

"No."

"But ..."

"Shit, Mike, what do you want me to say? Thank you for your service?"

"You don't gotta be like that, Bones."

"And also, hire a damn accountant."

He walked away. I chased after him. The ceiling lights came on. We blinked at each other, squinting. "Is that it?" I said.

"What do you mean?" D'Alencon looked up at the lights, reminding me that the audio monitoring equipment was back on again.

"Ah," I said. "Nothing."

"You forgot your stuff."

"Right." My head was spinning.

We walked back into the shadows, and d'Alencon took a box with my name on it down from the shelf. He held up his phone to vid me opening the evidence seals. "Everything in there?"

I lifted out the tote bag that Cecilia Parsec had given Lucy. "Yup."

We trudged back to the exit. As we climbed the long flight of stairs, the steamy warmth of a Mag-Ingat night closed around us again, welcome as an embrace after the cool of that dungeon.

D'Alencon escorted me out to the street. "Give my regards to your daughter," he said. "I've got three boys of my own."

"I didn't know that," I said, idiotically. "That's great."

The uptown spires scintillated in the night. Black patches spoiled the display of lights, where the controlling AIs had not yet been rebooted. My truck arrived.

I unlocked my fingers from the tote bag. "I … I think you need to see this. It was given to me by the Parsecs. They got it from my ex-wife. She parked it with them, and apparently did not have time to go back for it before she fled the planet."

D'Alencon glanced inside. His eyes widened. "Well, well."

I shrugged. "You asked me to let you know if I saw anything unusual. Do you want to keep it?"

"Yes," he said. "Yes, if you don't mind, I think I will." He smiled, grimly. "A little bit of extra insurance for our case against Parsec."

"That's what I figured."

"It's a minimum sentence of six years for conspiring with Travellers. Did you know that?"

"Hang on," I said. "I have to get my daughter's stuff out."

I reached into the bag and took out Lucy's sewing project, feeling, with a twinge of disgust, past the greasy leather of Sophia's Traveller coat.

"I'll be in touch," d'Alencon said. "Take care, Mike."

"You, too."

I climbed in my truck and drove off. It took several blocks for it to sink in that I was free. When it did, a sensation of lightness and relief filled my body, like a sort of mental Shift—a spiritual reset. My aches and pains and weariness faded away. I put on some music and sang along as I cruised downtown to Christy's place.

*

Christy buzzed me into the building and greeted me at the front door of her apartment. "Sssh. She's asleep."

Over Christy's shoulder, I could see the whole of the tiny apartment. The waterfall curtain had been rolled up to the ceiling. One of the pink-tinted Christmas lights glowed, wreathed in the leaves of a pot plant, like a nightlight. In Christy's bed lay my daughter. She was sleeping face down with one arm hanging off the side of the bed, only the tip of her nose sticking out beneath the oak-brown tangle of her hair. Christy herself must have been sleeping on the duvet that took up most of the floor—I could see the dent left in it by her body.

She beckoned me into the apartment, and closed the door to stop the light from the hall from shining in on Lucy. "Are you going to stay?" she whispered.

I was tonguetied. I looked at that Christy-shaped dent in the duvet and I yearned to lie down with her there. Not to make love, no. I just wanted to hold her in my arms and breathe in the clean scent of her.

I was wearing a buttondown I'd had in the truck, as I hadn't wanted to walk around for another minute in Parsec's Ursa Major t-shirt. Christy hooked one finger between the second and third buttons. Her nail delicately scraped my chest, making me shiver. She tugged gently. I took a step towards her.

I felt the heat coming off her body, palpable in the air-conditioned apartment. I could see her nipples through the thin material of the short nightie she wore.

"Where've you been, anyway?" she whispered.

"In jail. Don't worry, I'm not in trouble. It was a misunderstanding."

"Is this a misunderstanding?"

"This?"

"This."

Out of nowhere, I started trembling. I kind of lurched forward and grabbed her. I wrapped my arms around her and put my face on her shoulder.

"Mike ..."

She smelled so normal. It worked on the chaos inside me like an antidote. "Sorry," I muttered. "You just feel so good."

A small sound came from the bed. I leaped back from Christy as if I'd been shot.

"She's grinding her teeth," Christy whispered. "She's been doing it all night. It's a common childhood response to stress."

Lucy was still sleeping soundly, though gritting her teeth. I licked my lips. Smoothed down my clothes. "I'd better go. She'll be calmer in her own bed ..." I remembered that Lucy didn't *have* her own bed anymore. Our entire apartment was in biohazard bags. "And you can have your bed back," I added.

"OK," Christy said. "But for your information, I'd rather share it with you." She wasn't teasing. That's what enchanted me. She simply put that out there.

I gazed down at her, trying to match her seriousness. "Just so there are no misunderstandings," I whispered, "what I really want to do right now is fuck you as hard as you need."

She flinched back with a little toss of her head. Had I gone too far? The rough language didn't come naturally to me—I'd thought it was what she was looking for, but ...

Christy moved over to the bed without looking back at me. "Lucy." She gently shook Lucy's shoulder. "Wake up, doll. Your daddy's come to take you home."

When I saw my daughter's sleep-dazed face, I knew for sure I was doing the right thing. I helped her stumble to the door and put her shoes on. The last thing Lucy needed was to catch her father in bed—or on the floor—with the student life coordinator. I had to take her back to Shiftertown, where we belonged.

"I owe you," I said to Christy. "I'll call you."

"No," she said. "I'll call *you.*"

It could have been a brush-off. But a little smile at the corners of her mouth gave me hope.

I carried a half-asleep Lucy downstairs and into the truck. Screw the budget, I decided, and instructed the truck to drive to the Majesta Ponce de Leon. It's not exactly the best hotel in Mag-Ingat; in fact it's the kind of place tourists go for color, not comfort, way down at the Millhaven boundary of Shiftertown. But with layers of security between us and the outside world, I felt safe enough to crash on clean sheets and sleep.

59

THE 9 PM rain shower pounded the spaceport. My truck drove sedately through the puddles on the intraport roads, staying five klicks under the speed limit. Dolph slumped against the passenger side window. We had waited for the rain to start before we got rolling. Clouds blind observation satellites.

Light glowed through the condensation on the inside of the windscreen. It came from a hangar identical to mine but a bit smaller. Freight Terminal 927.

"He's there," I said.

"Good." Dolph uncoiled from his slouch, stretched, and took his Koiler out of the pocket of his raincoat.

I drove across the sheet of water covering Evan Zhang's landing pad, and parked just outside the entrance of the hangar, in front of the nose of his ship, a battered 90-tonne freighter called the *Margharita*. Hull plates had been replaced so often that the ship was more patch than original steel. Wings stretching to the walls of the hangar would give it excellent in-atmosphere maneuverability. Zhang presumably did a lot of in-atmosphere maneuvering. Dodging rockets and such. The *Margharita's* patched, scorched hull bore witness to his business niche of shuttling cargoes to the Hurtworlds.

Slim, automated oxygen and nitrogen tankers stood near the ship's tail, connected to it with high-pressure hoses. Their presence suggested that Zhang was prepping for a long run right now. You only need to go that heavy on air if you're planning to be in the field for weeks, or months.

Two men were working on the ship's engine. They saw the truck. One of them walked suspiciously towards us, carrying a wrench. He was medium height, fifty-ish, with a cybernetic eye that looked like the lens of a camera stuck in his head. I recognized Evan Zhang from Independent Shipping Association events we had attended together.

Dolph climbed out of the left side of the truck. I climbed out of the right. Rain beat on my head and shoulders. I walked into the hangar, wiped my hair out of my eyes, drew my Machina, and pointed it at Zhang's face. "Hi," I said. "Were you thinking of going somewhere?"

A suppressed *phut* and a smashing noise punctuated my words. Dolph had shot out the free-standing floodlight that the men had been using to illuminate their work. We were not planning on having our little chat recorded by the *Margharita's* external cameras.

Darkness engulfed the hangar. My truck's headlights prodded in under the ship and found Dolph stepping on the other man's kidneys while he ground his gun into the back of the guy's head.

Zhang glanced at his crewman. Then he looked back at my gun. "What do you want?"

"Looks like you're getting ready for a run."

"Got that right," Zhang said. "Twenty tonnes of machine parts for Mittel Trevoyvox."

Mittel Trevoyvox was the furthest-away of the Hurtworlds. I'd visited it once before. It was not a pleasant memory. "When are you leaving?" I said.

"On the second."

"No, you aren't. You're leaving tonight."

"Can't. I ain't got my cargo yet." The chump had the nerve to look at me as if I was an idiot, even though I was the one with a gun. Then again, he flew to the Hurtworlds. He was probably used to people using firearms to make their point. That could be how he ended up with a cybernetic eye.

"Would you rather have your cargo, or your life?" I snarled.

Less than 24 hours had passed since I was in police custody. I was stiff and aching all over, various muscle strains and bruises catching up with me after the fact—a sign of age, I gloomily reflected. I had to lower my gun arm so that the Machina was pointing at Zhang's knees.

Zhang raised his head. Red reflections glinted on his cybernetic eye as he charged me, swinging his wrench. He was not *holding* the wrench. His hand was the wrench. I didn't properly understand that until I shot the wrench off, leaving him with a socket on the end of his arm.

"Fuck," he cried. "Whyn't ya just kill me?"

I skipped back and levelled the gun at him again. My pulse galloped. Thank God for the drumming of the rain on the hangar roof, which would have disguised the noise of the shot. The Machina didn't make a lot of noise, anyway. "You fucking idiot," I said. "I'm *not* trying to kill you!" There was a reason I had not brought Irene along. "I'm trying to save your ass. Buzz Parsec is in jail, and that's where you're going to wind up if you don't get off of Ponce de Leon right now, do you hear me?"

The danger, of course, was that Zhang would tell the police that Parsec had *not* ordered Mr. Brains from him. That would blow a hole in d'Alencon's case against Parsec. The fact that they hadn't come looking for Zhang yet told me that they didn't really want to know, but if Zhang stuck around, he would end up getting pulled in to give testimony at some point. I was actually surprised he was still here.

He clutched his wrist, whimpering. Even if his implant didn't have synthetic neural transmitters, that must have stung. "That attachment cost me 70 KGCs."

"Waste of money." I risked a quick glance into the hangar. Dolph had let the other guy up. They were talking.

"That Shifter bitch works for you, doesn't she?" Zhang said.

"That's no way to refer to a lady."

"I could tell you a few things about her."

Before I could succumb to curiosity, Dolph prodded the other guy towards us. "According to this one," he said, "they *can't* launch without their cargo, on account of being broke. They can't even pay their port fees until they get the customer's advance payment." He spat. He had advocated for the forty grammes of lead solution.

"Is that true?" I asked Zhang.

"Yes."

And yet he had spent 70 big ones on a cybernetic arm. Well, I should talk. I had blown through twenty years' worth of fees for assassinations, strategic bombings, and heists with nothing more to show for it than a rented row house and a nanny bot.

"All right," I said. "What's the customer's name?"

"I don't know."

"You don't *know?*"

"It went through my agent!"

I'd never seen the point of shipping agents. Why let someone else control your customer relationships, and charge you ten percent for the privilege? "All right, your agent's name."

"Timmy Akhatli."

"Timmy what?"

"*Akhatli.* He's an Ek."

"Oh." Well, of course. The Hurtworlds were originally, and still largely are, an Ek project. The Eks might not be so keen on flying cargoes into those hells, but they surely would want their cut.

Dolph took out his phone and looked Timmy Akhatli up, while I held my gun on the two men. The *Margharita* hummed quietly, drinking oxygen and nitrogen.

"He's for real," Dolph said.

"All right. Here's what we're going to do," I said. "Uni-Ex Shipping will take your cargo. *I'll* pay you the advance fee and recoup it from your agent later. And you get off Ponce de Leon tonight."

Zhang agreed. He didn't have much choice, with a gun pointed at his face. It was a pretty sweet deal, in my opinion: he was getting money for nothing. But he showed no gratitude, even after I transferred 30 KGCs from the Uni-Ex corporate account into his account.

"Now call the Space Authority and change your launch slot," I said. "Take the first one they got."

Zhang made the call in a grumpy monotone. "Launching in two hours," he said. "Good thing we're already prepped."

"But where we gonna go?" the other guy said. "We got no cargo, so where—"

"Home?" I suggested. I knew by their accents they weren't PdL natives. They sounded like they came from the Techworlds.

"Yeah," Zhang said. He cast a glance past us, out to the wet tarmac of the spaceport, and the city twinkling at the head of the bay, hidden behind the orange-tinted night clouds. "I ain't even going to miss this planet. It's halfway to being a Shifter world, anyways."

I was a trigger pull from putting them down on the wet, greasy floor of the hangar, after all. Mastering myself, I said to Dolph, "Come on, let's go. These two creeps gotta start their pre-flight checks."

"All right," Dolph said. "Just one moment."

He walked up to Zhang, who cringed.

"Hold your hand out," Dolph said, and he put a bullet in Zhang's wrist socket. "I fucking hate cyborgs," he yelled, as Zhang slumped to his knees, keening, his right hand wrapped around the twisted metal stump. "Shifter planet? I fucking wish! Better than a cyborg planet, anyway!"

We left them there and piled back into my truck, our wet clothes making squeaking noises on the bench seat. I punched the AC on. Cold air roared out of the vents. I put the truck in drive and circled back out to the road.

60

As I drove away from Evan Zhang's freight terminal, Dolph unloaded his Koiler, removed the suppressor, stuck it in his pocket, and put the bullets in my glove compartment. "So. Twenty tonnes of machine parts for Mittel Trevoyvox, huh?"

"Yup," I said.

"That's gonna screw with our schedule some."

"We'll make it work." I opened my pack of cigarettes, lit one, and rolled the window down. Rain blew in.

"Mittel Trevoyvox isn't far from Yesanyase Skont," Dolph observed, lighting a cigarette for himself.

"That's right. Only four light years. A hop, a skip, and a jump."

I'd discovered the notification this morning when I checked my v-mail. Pippa had been deported two whole days ago. Not only hadn't she been in Mag-Ingat on Founding Day, she hadn't even been on the damn planet. Jan and Leaf had received asylum, as I'd never followed up on the request to pay their deportation costs. They were safe in the resettlement center where Christy volunteered. Pippa was on her way to Yesanyase Skont.

"What if we can't find her?" Dolph said.

"Then at least we tried."

"What if we *can?*"

I slouched round to face him and said frankly, "I don't know. She's got kuru. Nothing we can do about that. But maybe we can take her some stuff … clothes, electronics, I hear they don't even get enough food out there. Just some things to make her life a little better."

Something moved in Dolph's eyes. It looked like fear. Then he said, "Works for me." He gazed out the windshield. "We haven't been to the Hurtworlds in ages. Used to be good money to be made out there."

I had told him about my confession to d'Alencon, and d'Alencon's coded warning to me not to take any more of those kinds of jobs. Keep it to myself? I wish. I never could keep anything that big from Dolph. But it was so embarrassing to both of us that Dolph had to act like he didn't take it seriously. He insisted we were untouchable, now that we'd saved the planet and everything.

Right.

At least it looked like Ponce de Leon was safe. No cases of kuru had showed up among the thousands of worried people presenting themselves at clincs. The mall level was still closed for bio-hazard testing, but otherwise, service had been restored. Everything was back to normal … but as I parked in front of my hangar, and splashed in through the rain, it didn't feel like it to me. My nerves and sinews said this thing was not over. That's why I'd impulsively said I would take Evan Zhang's cargo. It would give us an excuse to go and look for Pippa on Yesanyase Skont.

"Lucy!" I yelled. The lights in the hangar were on. I could hear her voice coming from the *St. Clare's* top deck. "Lucy!"

A football sailed off the top deck. I dodged. It was a regular inflatable one, not our deep-space ball. It rolled under the ship.

"Sorry, Daddy!" Lucy's face appeared over the edge of the top deck, next to Martin's bald, sweating dome. "We were playing football."

I had followed through on my vow to get rid of Nanny B—actually, I'd given her to the Seagraves. Irene couldn't believe it. "I was *kidding*," she'd said. "This is a million-GC piece of hardware." I'd said to her, "That's not even a fraction of what I owe you." We would be staying with them until I could get our apartment redecorated. I could think of no safer place for Lucy … but she had become clingier than ever, understandably. And after what happened, I plain didn't want to let her out of my sight. So today I'd brought her out to the spaceport, to hang out and count the baby swallows.

Martin had reluctantly volunteered to look after her while Dolph and I were out on our little errand. Better a snake than a robot … right?

Of course, we had a robot, too. MF rolled out from under the ship, chirruping about rust spots on the lower truss. I had told him in no uncertain terms to stay away from Lucy. I was pretty sure that an eight-year-old would not read as female to him, but I didn't want to find out.

"Guess what," I said. "We've got a new run on the schedule. We're going to Mittel Trevoyvox."

MF said, "Captain, are we running away from something?"

"No," I said. "We're running *towards* something." I hesitated. "The truth."

MF angled his sensor covers thoughtfully. "Would a side trip to Yesanyase Skont be on the agenda?"

"It would."

"Woohoo," MF said, quietly. His bendy neck swayed, advancing his head conspiratorially towards us. "I'd like to see Pippa again—and not just 'cause she's a sexy little mama! I think she's hiding something. And it might be something very valuable, if you get my drift. Mucho moolah."

"Like what?"

MF swayed his head from side to side. "Remember that thing she used to wear around her neck?"

"The crown jewels," I said. "Rafael Ijiuto had one, too."

"Yes. I seem to remember seeing those, or ones very like them, before—long, long ago."

He would say no more, although Dolph and I both begged him to explain. Lucy interrupted the conversation by scrambling down the ladder with Martin close behind her.

"This is why I don't have kids," he said, wiping sweat off his head. "Got more exercise in an hour than I usually do in a month."

"I already finished my homework, so pffft," Lucy sang, dancing around me.

"Everything go OK?" Martin said.

"Yup," I said. "And we even got a cargo out of it. Mittel Trevoyvox, here we come."

"God, not the Hurtworlds," Martin said. "I hate spending that long in the field."

Lucy stopped pirouetting. "How long in the field? Daddy, how long are you going to be away?"

I forced myself to meet her eyes. "About a month, sweetiepie. Maybe a bit longer."

"A *month?!?*"

I felt wretched. We had not yet discussed the kidnapping episode, let alone Cecilia Parsec's revelations about her mother. We had to talk about it. *Really* talk about it. And now here I was going away again, for a whole month—if not longer, counting our planned side trip.

"We aren't leaving right away," I said. "Figure another week to get all our ducks in a row." I reached for Lucy. She shied away. "Come on, we'll pick up ice cream on our way home."

That got her into the truck. "You can drop me off on the Strip," Dolph said. He hadn't brought his bike today.

"Nuh uh," I said. "Before we go for ice cream, we got one thing to take care of."

"What?" said Lucy, squashed between me and Dolph.

I met Dolph's eyes over her head. I saw the telltale lustre of fear in his gaze, mirroring my own. Fear of the thing we'd been dancing around all day.

"It's been a week," I said. "Time to go and pick up those test results from Dr. Zeb's."

*

I took Lucy into the hospital with me. I only did it because I didn't want to leave her alone in the truck. As it turned out, it was a good decision.

The parking lot across the street from the hospital was full, the drive was parked up, and there was a line at the hematology desk in the cloister. When Dolph and I reached the desk, the pretty young nurse remembered us. "You beat the rush," she said. "Everyone's getting tested now. The lab's so backlogged, wait times are up to two weeks. But here are your results."

She handed each of us a thin piece of paper folded into three, with the edge glued down.

"What's that?" said the watchful Lucy, at my elbow.

"Ah, it's just a test I had to get done."

Dolph stepped aside from the mob at the hematology desk. Standing in the seating area in front of the windows, he tore his report open.

He read it.

He looked at me with a grin so high-wattage, it could've powered the whole hospital. "I'm OK."

"What do you *mean?*" Lucy said. She was getting frustrated with this ill-explained errand. "Why wouldn't you be OK?"

"Bad shit happens in the Cluster," said Dolph. "But it didn't happen to me this time, and that means your daddy's OK, too."

I remembered the fairy dust blowing around that intersection in the refugee camp.

The glitter landing on Dolph's hair, and on my Panama hat.

The taste of the gritty dust blowing on the wind.

Dolph was OK. But he had been wearing a bandanna over his mouth and nose. I had not.

I ripped open my report.

I read it.

And read it again.

"Mike," said a familiar deep voice. I glanced around and saw Dr. Zeb. "I seem to recall banning you and Dolph from this hospital."

"Sorry, Dr. Z," I said. "We're gone. Just had to pick up some test results."

"All's well, I hope?" Dr. Zeb reached into the pocket of his white coat and brought out a candy for Lucy. She whispered thanks. She was not looking at the doctor. She was staring up at my face as if her life depended on my next words.

Which, in a sense, it did.

"Fine and dandy," I said with a smile. I crumpled the report and jammed it into my pocket. "Let's get out of here, sweetie. Time to go get that ice cream."

In the truck, Lucy babbled happily, buoyed up by the palpable ebullience emanating from Dolph. I played along, aware that Dolph's relief was fading as he eyed me doubtfully. I was holding it together well enough to fool Lucy, but not to fool him. The lights of Shiftertown glistened on the still-wet streets. Every time I moved, I felt the crisp paper of the report crinkling in my pocket.

I could, and would, read it a hundred times more in the following days, but that wouldn't change what it said.

POSITIVE.

I was infected with interstellar variant kuru.

THE STORY CONTINUES IN *DIRTY JOB*,

BOOK 2 OF A CAULDRON OF STARS.

Congratulations, you have unlocked a free gift!

Go to this link to receive a bonus novella from the Clusterverse archives, exclusively for readers who've finished *Lethal Cargo*:

http://felixrsavage.com/clusterverse-story

ACKNOWLEDGEMENTS

I'm deeply grateful for multiple brainstorming sessions with WalterBlaire, whose books I heartily recommend to all sci-fi readers! This book also benefited from the expertise and suggestions of BillPatterson; Dr. Martin "X-Ray Eyes" Miller; Christopher Andersen; Jerry Larson; AJM; and Ben Aupperlee. Any remaining mistakes are my own.

READ MORE BY FELIX R. SAVAGE

An exuberant storyteller with a demented imagination, Felix R. Savage specializes in creating worlds so exciting, you'll never want to leave.

Join the Savage Stories newsletter to receive a starter library of FIVE free subscriber exclusive books:

www.felixrsavage.com/subscribe

A CAULDRON OF STARS

Space Opera Adventure

Far in the future, in the distant Messier 4 cluster, humanity coexists with the legalistic Ekschetlan Empire, a host of lesser alien species … and an age-old mystery that could shatter the balance of power. The long, uneasy peace is about to boil over into war.

A foiled terrorist incident on a backwater planet lights the fuse … and drags freighter captain Mike Starrunner and his crew into an intrigue spanning thousands of light years, with all the wealth and power of the Cluster at stake.

LethalCargo

DirtyJob

\hspace{0pt}…\hspace{0pt}andmoretocome!

EARTH'S LAST GAMBIT

A Quartet of Present-Day Science Fiction Technothrillers

Ripped from the headlines: an alien spaceship is orbiting Europa. Relying only on existing technology, a handful of elite astronauts must confront the threat to Earth's future, on their own, millions of miles from home.

Can the chosen few overcome technological limitations and their own weaknesses and flaws? Will Earth's Last Gambit win survival for the human race?

TheSignalAndTheBoys(prequelstory,subscriberexclusive)

Freefall

Lifeboat

Shiplord

Killshot

EXTINCTION PROTOCOL

Hard Science Fiction With a Chilling Twist

Humanity has reached out into the stars - and found a ruthless enemy.

It took us two hundred years to establish fifteen colonies on the closest habitable planets to Earth. It took the Ghosts only 20 years to destroy them. Navy pilot Colm Mackenzie is no stranger to the Ghosts. He has witnessed first-hand the mayhem and tragedy they leave in their wake. No one knows where they came from, or how they travel, or what they want. They know only one thing for sure:

Ghosts leave no survivors.

SaveFromWrath(shortstory,subscriberexclusive)

TheChemicalMage

TheNuclearDruid

THE SOL SYSTEM RENEGADES SERIES

Near-Future Hard Science Fiction

In the year 2288, humanity stands at a crossroads between space colonization and extinction. Packed with excitement, heartbreak, and unforgettable characters, the Sol System Renegades series tells a sweeping tale of struggle and deliverance.

KeepOffTheGrass(shortoriginstory)

Crapkiller(prequelnovella,subscriberexclusive)

1.TheGalapagosIncident

2.TheVestaConspiracy

3.TheMercuryRebellion

AVeryMerryZero-GravityChristmas(shortstory)

4.TheLunaDeception

5.ThePhobosManeuver

6.TheMarsShock

7.TheCallistoGambit

VOID DRAGON HUNTERS

Military Sci-Fi with Space Dragons

In 2160, a Void Dragon ate the sun.

In 2322, eight-year-old Jay Scattergood found a Void Dragon egg in his garden.

Humanity survived the death of the sun, but now we're under attack by the Offense. These intelligent, aggressive aliens will do whatever it takes to destroy humanity and take Earth for themselves.

Our last hope against the alien aggressors is Jay Scattergood ... and his baby Void Dragon, Tancred.

GuardiansofJupiter

ProtectorsofEarth

SoldiersofCallisto

ExilesoftheBelt

KnightsofSaturn

THE RELUCTANT ADVENTURES OF FLETCHER CONNOLLY ON THE INTERSTELLAR RAILROAD

Near-Future Non-Hard Science Fiction

An Irishman in space. Untold hoards of alien technological relics waiting to be discovered. What could possibly go wrong?

RubbishWithNames(prequelstory, subscriberexclusive)

SkintIdjit

IntergalacticBogtrotter

BanjaxedCeili

SupermassiveBlackguard